HC

The Br...

and Other Stories

The Michael Moorcock Collection

The Michael Moorcock Collection is the definitive library of acclaimed author Michael Moorcock's SF & fantasy, including the entirety of his Eternal Champion work. It is prepared and edited by John Davey, the author's long-time bibliographer and editor, and will be published, over the course of two years, in the following print omnibus editions by Gollancz, and as individual eBooks by the SF Gateway (see http://www.sfgateway.com/authors/m/moorcock-michael/ for a complete list of available eBooks).

A Cornelius Calendar
comprising –
*The Adventures of Una Persson
and Catherine Cornelius in
the Twentieth Century*
The Entropy Tango
The Great Rock 'n' Roll Swindle
The Alchemist's Question
*Firing the Cathedral / Modem
Times 2.0*

Von Bek
comprising –
*The War Hound and the World's
Pain*
The City in the Autumn Stars

The Eternal Champion
comprising –
The Eternal Champion
Phoenix in Obsidian
The Dragon in the Sword

The Dancers at the
End of Time
comprising –
An Alien Heat
The Hollow Lands
The End of all Songs

Kane of Old Mars
comprising –
Warriors of Mars
Blades of Mars
Barbarians of Mars

Moorcock's Multiverse
comprising –
The Sundered Worlds
The Winds of Limbo
The Shores of Death

The Nomad of Time
comprising –
The Warlord of the Air
The Land Leviathan
The Steel Tsar

Travelling to Utopia
comprising –
The Wrecks of Time
The Ice Schooner
The Black Corridor

The War Amongst the Angels
comprising –
Blood: A Southern Fantasy
Fabulous Harbours
The War Amongst the Angels

Tales from the End of Time
comprising –
Legends from the End of Time
Constant Fire
Elric at the End of Time

Behold the Man

Gloriana; or, The Unfulfill'd Queen

SHORT FICTION
My Experiences in the Third World
War and Other Stories: The Best
Short Fiction of Michael Moorcock
Volume 1

The Brothel in Rosenstrasse and
Other Stories: The Best Short Fiction
of Michael Moorcock Volume 2

Breakfast in the Ruins and Other
Stories: The Best Short Fiction of
Michael Moorcock Volume 3

The Brothel in Rosenstrasse and Other Stories

The Best Short Fiction of Michael Moorcock

Volume 2

MICHAEL MOORCOCK

Edited by John Davey

This edition published in Great Britain in 2014 by
Gollancz
An imprint of the Orion Publishing Group
Orion House, 5 Upper St Martin's Lane,
London WC2H 9EA
An Hachette UK Company

1 3 5 7 9 10 8 6 4 2

A CIP catalogue record for this book is
available from the British Library

ISBN 978 0 575 11522 4

Typeset by Jouve (UK), Milton Keynes

Printed and bound by CPI Group (UK) Ltd, Croydon, CR0 4YY

The Orion Publishing Group's policy is to use papers
that are natural, renewable and recyclable products and
made from wood grown in sustainable forests. The logging
and manufacturing processes are expected to conform to
the environmental regulations of the country of origin.

www.multiverse.org
www.sfgateway.com
www.gollancz.co.uk
www.orionbooks.co.uk

Introduction to
The Michael Moorcock Collection

John Clute

H E IS NOW over 70, enough time for most careers to start and
end in, enough time to fit in an occasional half-decade or so
of silence to mark off the big years. Silence happens. I don't think
I know an author who doesn't fear silence like the plague; most of
us, if we live long enough, can remember a bad blank year or so,
or more. Not Michael Moorcock. Except for some worrying
surgery on his toes in recent years, he seems not to have taken
time off to breathe the air of peace and panic. There has been no
time to spare. The nearly 60 years of his active career seems to
have been too short to fit everything in: the teenage comics; the
editing jobs; the pulp fiction; the reinvented heroic fantasies;
the Eternal Champion; the deep Jerry Cornelius riffs; NEW WORLDS;
the 1970s/1980s flow of stories and novels, dozens upon dozens
of them in every category of modern fantastika; the tales of the
dying Earth and the possessing of Jesus; the exercises in postmodernism that turned the world inside out before most of us had
begun to guess we were living on the wrong side of things; the
invention (more or less) of steampunk; the alternate histories; the
Mitteleuropean tales of sexual terror; the deep-city London riffs:
the turns and changes and returns and reconfigurations to which
he has subjected his oeuvre over the years (he expects this new
Collected Edition will fix these transformations in place for good);
the late tales where he has been remodelling the intersecting
worlds he created in the 1960s in terms of twenty-first-century
physics: for starters. If you can't take the heat, I guess, stay out of
the multiverse.

His life has been full and complicated, a life he has exposed and hidden (like many other prolific authors) throughout his work. In *Mother London* (1988), though, a non-fantastic novel published at what is now something like the midpoint of his career, it may be possible to find the key to all the other selves who made the 100 books. There are three protagonists in the tale, which is set from about 1940 to about 1988 in the suburbs and inner runnels of the vast metropolis of Charles Dickens and Robert Louis Stevenson. The oldest of these protagonists is Joseph Kiss, a flamboyant self-advertising fin-de-siècle figure of substantial girth and a fantasticating relationship to the world: he is Michael Moorcock, seen with genial bite as a kind of G.K. Chesterton without the wearying punch-line paradoxes. The youngest of the three is David Mummery, a haunted introspective half-insane denizen of a secret London of trials and runes and codes and magic: he too is Michael Moorcock, seen through a glass, darkly. And there is Mary Gasalee, a kind of holy-innocent and survivor, blessed with a luminous clarity of insight, so that in all her apparent ignorance of the onrushing secular world she is more deeply wise than other folk: she is also Michael Moorcock, Moorcock when young as viewed from the wry middle years of 1988. When we read the book, we are reading a book of instructions for the assembly of a London writer. The Moorcock we put together from this choice of portraits is amused and bemused at the vision of himself; he is a phenomenon of flamboyance and introspection, a poseur and a solitary, a dreamer and a doer, a multitude and a singleton. But only the three Moorcocks in this book, working together, could have written all the other books.

It all began – as it does for David Mummery in *Mother London* – in South London, in a subtopian stretch of villas called Mitcham, in 1939. In early childhood, he experienced the Blitz, and never forgot the extraordinariness of being a participant – however minute – in the great drama; all around him, as though the world were being dismantled nightly, darkness and blackout would descend, bombs fall, buildings and streets disappear; and in the morning, as though a new universe had taken over from the old one and the world had become portals, the sun would rise on glinting rubble, abandoned tricycles, men and women going about their daily tasks as though nothing had happened, strange shards of ruin poking into altered air. From a very early age, Michael Moorcock's security reposed in a sense that everything might change, in the blinking of an eye, and be *rejourneyed* the next day (or the next book). Though as a writer he has certainly elucidated the fears and alarums of life in Aftermath Britain, it does seem that his very early years were marked by the epiphanies of war, rather than the inflictions of despair and beclouding amnesia most adults necessarily experienced. After the war ended, his parents separated, and the young Moorcock began to attend a pretty wide variety of schools, several of which he seems to have been expelled from, and as soon as he could legally do so he began to work full time, up north in London's heart, which he only left when he moved to Texas (with intervals in Paris) in the early 1990s, from where (to jump briefly up the decades) he continues to cast a Martian eye: as with most exiles, Moorcock's intensest anatomies of his homeland date from after his cunning departure.

But back again to the beginning (just as though we were rimming a multiverse). Starting in the 1950s there was the comics and pulp work for Fleetway Publications; there was the first book (*Caribbean Crisis*, 1962) as by Desmond Reid, co-written with his early friend the artist James Cawthorn (1929–2008); there was marriage, with the writer Hilary Bailey (they divorced in 1978), three children, a heated existence in the Ladbroke Grove/Notting Hill Gate region of London he was later to populate with Jerry Cornelius and his vast family; there was the editing of NEW WORLDS, which began in 1964 and became the heartbeat of the British New Wave two years later as writers like Brian W. Aldiss and J.G. Ballard, reaching their early prime, made it into a tympanum, as young American writers like Thomas M. Disch, John T. Sladek, Norman Spinrad and Pamela Zoline found a home in London for material they could not publish in America, and new British writers like M. John Harrison and Charles Platt began their careers in its pages; but before that there was Elric. With *The Stealer of Souls* (1963) and

Stormbringer (1965), the multiverse began to flicker into view, and the Eternal Champion (whom Elric parodied and embodied) began properly to ransack the worlds in his fight against a greater Chaos than the great dance could sustain. There was also the first SF novel, *The Sundered Worlds* (1965), but in the 1960s SF was a difficult nut to demolish for Moorcock: he would bide his time.

We come to the heart of the matter. Jerry Cornelius, who first appears in *The Final Programme* (1968) – which assembles and co-ordinates material first published a few years earlier in NEW WORLDS – is a deliberate solarisation of the albino Elric, who was himself a mocking solarisation of Robert E. Howard's Conan, or rather of the mighty-thew-headed Conan created for profit by Howard epigones: Moorcock rarely mocks the true quill. Cornelius, who reaches his first and most telling apotheosis in the four novels comprising *The Cornelius Quartet*, remains his most distinctive and perhaps most original single creation: a wide boy, an agent, a *flaneur*, a bad musician, a shopper, a shapechanger, a trans, a spy in the house of London: a toxic palimpsest on whom and through whom the *zeitgeist* inscribes surreal conjugations of 'message'. Jerry Cornelius gives head to Elric.

The life continued apace. By 1970, with NEW WORLDS on its last legs, multiverse fantasies and experimental novels poured forth; Moorcock and Hilary Bailey began to live separately, though he moved, in fact, only around the corner, where he set up house with Jill Riches, who would become his second wife; there was a second home in Yorkshire, but London remained his central base. *The Condition of Muzak* (1977), which is the fourth Cornelius novel, and *Gloriana; or, The Unfulfill'd Queen* (1978), which transfigures the first Elizabeth into a kinked Astraea, marked perhaps the high point of his career as a writer of fiction whose font lay in genre or its mutations – marked perhaps the furthest bournes he could transgress while remaining within the perimeters of fantasy (though *within* those bournes vast stretches of territory remained and would, continually, be explored). During these years he sometimes wore a leather jacket constructed out of numerous patches of varicoloured material, and it sometimes seemed perfectly fitting that he bore the semblance, as his jacket flickered and fuzzed from across a room or road, of an illustrated man, a map, a thing of shreds and patches, a student fleshed from dreams. Like the stories he told, he seemed to be more than one thing. To use a term frequently applied (by me at least) to twenty-first-century fiction, he seemed equipoisal: which is to say that, through all his genre-hopping and genre-mixing and genre-transcending and genre-loyal returnings to old pitches, *he was never still*, because 'equipoise' is all about *making stories move*. As with his stories, he cannot be pinned down, because he is not in one place. In person and in his work, it has always been sink or swim: like a shark, or a dancer, or an equilibrist…

The marriage with Jill Riches came to an end. He married Linda Steele in 1983; they remain married. The Colonel Pyat books, *Byzantium Endures* (1981), *The Laughter of Carthage* (1984), *Jerusalem Commands* (1992) and *The Vengeance of Rome* (2006), dominated these years, along with *Mother London*. As these books, which are non-fantastic, are not included in the current *Michael Moorcock Collection*, it might be worth noting here that, in their insistence on the irreducible difficulty of gaining anything like true sight, they represent Moorcock's mature modernist take on what one might call the rag-and-bone shop of the world itself; and that the huge ornate postmodern edifice of his multiverse *loosens* us from that world, gives us room to breathe, to juggle our strategies for living – allows us ultimately to escape from prison (to use a phrase from a writer he does not respect, J.R.R. Tolkien, for whom the twentieth century was a prison train bound for hell). What Moorcock may best be remembered for in the end is the (perhaps unique) interplay between modernism and postmodernism in his work. (But a plethora of discordant understandings makes these terms hard to use; so enough of them.) In the end, one might just say that Moorcock's work as a whole represents an extraordinarily multifarious execution of the fantasist's main task: which is to *get us out of here*.

Recent decades saw a continuation of the multifarious, but with a more intensely applied methodology. The late volumes of the long Elric saga, and the Second Ether sequence of meta-fantasies – *Blood: A Southern Fantasy* (1995), *Fabulous Harbours* (1995) and *The War Amongst the Angels: An Autobiographical Story* (1996) – brood on the real world and the multiverse through the lens of Chaos Theory: the closer you get to the world, the less you describe it. *The Metatemporal Detective* (2007) – a narrative in the Steampunk mode Moorcock had previewed as long ago as *The Warlord of the Air* (1971) and *The Land Leviathan* (1974) – continues the process, sometimes dizzyingly: as though the reader inhabited the eye of a camera increasing its focus on a closely observed reality while its bogey simultaneously wheels it backwards from the desired rapport: an old Kurasawa trick here amplified into a tool of conspectus, fantasy eyed and (once again) rejourneyed, this time through the lens of SF.

We reach the second decade of the twenty-first century, time still to make things new, but also time to sort. There are dozens of titles in *The Michael Moorcock Collection* that have not been listed in this short space, much less trawled for tidbits. The various avatars of the Eternal Champion – Elric, Kane of Old Mars, Hawkmoon, Count Brass, Corum, Von Bek – differ vastly from one another. Hawkmoon is a bit of a berk; Corum is a steely solitary at the End of Time: the joys and doleurs of the interplays amongst them can only be experienced through immersion. And the Dancers at the End of Time books, and the Nomad of the Time Stream books, and the Karl Glogauer books, and all the others. They are here now, a 100 books that make up one book. They have been fixed for reading. It is time to enter the multiverse and see the world.

September 2012

Introduction to
The Michael Moorcock Collection
Michael Moorcock

B Y 1964, AFTER I had been editing NEW WORLDS for some
months and had published several science fiction and fantasy
novels, including *Stormbringer*, I realised that my run as a writer
was over. About the only new ideas I'd come up with were miniature computers, the multiverse and black holes, all very crudely
realised, in *The Sundered Worlds*. No doubt I would have to return
to journalism, writing features and editing. 'My career,' I told my
friend J.G. Ballard, 'is finished.' He sympathised and told me he
only had a few SF stories left in him, then he, too, wasn't sure
what he'd do.

In January 1965, living in Colville Terrace, Notting Hill, then an
infamous slum, best known for its race riots, I sat down at the
typewriter in our kitchen-cum-bathroom and began a locally
based book, designed to be accompanied by music and graphics.
The Final Programme featured a character based on a young man
I'd seen around the area and whom I named after a local green-
grocer, Jerry Cornelius, 'Messiah to the Age of Science'. Jerry was
as much a technique as a character. Not the 'spy' some critics
described him as but an urban adventurer as interested in his
psychic environment as the contemporary physical world. My
influences were English and French absurdists, American noir
novels. My inspiration was William Burroughs with whom I'd
recently begun a correspondence. I also borrowed a few SF ideas,
though I was adamant that I was not writing in any established
genre. I felt I had at last found my own authentic voice.

I had already written a short novel, *The Golden Barge*, set in a
nowhere, no-time world very much influenced by Peake and the

surrealists, which I had not attempted to publish. An earlier auto-biographical novel, *The Hungry Dreamers*, set in Soho, was eaten by rats in a Ladbroke Grove basement. I remained unsatisfied with my style and my technique. *The Final Programme* took nine days to complete (by 20 January, 1965) with my baby daughters sometimes cradled with their bottles while I typed on. This, I should say, is my memory of events; my then wife scoffed at this story when I recounted it. Whatever the truth, the fact is I only believed I might be a serious writer after I had finished that novel, with all its flaws. But Jerry Cornelius, probably my most successful sustained attempt at unconventional fiction, was born then and ever since has remained a useful means of telling complex stories. Associated with the 60s and 70s, he has been equally at home in all the following decades. Through novels and novellas I developed a means of carrying several narratives and viewpoints on what appeared to be a very light (but tight) structure which dispensed with some of the earlier methods of fiction. In the sense that it took for granted the understanding that the novel is among other things an internal dialogue and I did not feel the need to repeat by now commonly understood modernist conventions, this fiction was post-modern.

Not all my fiction looked for new forms for the new century. Like many 'revolutionaries' I looked back as well as forward. As George Meredith looked to the eighteenth century for inspiration for his experiments with narrative, I looked to Meredith, popular Edwardian realists like Pett Ridge and Zangwill and the writers of the *fin de siècle* for methods and inspiration. An almost obsessive interest in the Fabians, several of whom believed in the possibility of benign imperialism, ultimately led to my Bastable books which examined our enduring British notion that an empire could be essentially a force for good. The first was *The Warlord of the Air*.

I also wrote my *Dancers at the End of Time* stories and novels under the influence of Edwardian humourists and absurdists like Jerome or Firbank. Together with more conventional generic books like *The Ice Schooner* or *The Black Corridor*, most of that work was done in the 1960s and 70s when I wrote the Eternal Champion supernatural adventure novels which helped support my own and others' experiments via NEW WORLDS, allowing me also to keep a family while writing books in which action and fantastic invention were paramount. Though I did them quickly, I didn't write them cynically. I have always believed, somewhat puritanically, in giving the audience good value for money. I enjoyed writing them, tried to avoid repetition, and through each new one was able to develop a few more ideas. They also continued to teach me how to express myself through image and metaphor. My Everyman became the Eternal Champion, his dreams and ambitions represented by the multiverse. He could be an ordinary person struggling with familiar problems in a contemporary setting or he could be a swordsman fighting monsters on a far-away world.

Long before I wrote *Gloriana* (in four parts reflecting the seasons) I had learned to think in images and symbols through reading John Bunyan's *Pilgrim's Progress*, Milton and others, understanding early on that the visual could be the most important part of a book and was often in itself a story as, for instance, a famous personality could also, through everything associated with their name, function as narrative. I wanted to find ways of carrying as many stories as possible in one. From the cinema I also learned how to use images as connecting themes. Images, colours, music, and even popular magazine headlines can all add coherence to an apparently random story, underpinning it and giving the reader a sense of internal logic and a satisfactory resolution, dispensing with certain familiar literary conventions.

When the story required it, I also began writing neo-realist fiction exploring the interface of character and environment, especially the city, especially London. In some books I condensed, manipulated and randomised time to achieve what I wanted, but in others the sense of 'real time' as we all generally perceive it was more suitable and could best be achieved by traditional nineteenth-century means. For the Pyat books I first looked back to the great German classic, Grimmelshausen's *Simplicissimus* and other early picaresques. I then examined the roots of a certain kind of moral fiction from Defoe through Thackeray and Meredith then to modern times where the picaresque (or rogue tale) can take the form of a road movie, for instance. While it's probably fair to say that Pyat and *Byzantium Endures* precipitated the end of my second marriage (echoed to a degree in *The Brothel in Rosenstrasse*), the late 70s and the 80s were exhilarating times for me, with *Mother London* being perhaps my own favourite novel of that period. I wanted to write something celebratory.

By the 90s I was again attempting to unite several kinds of fiction in one novel with my Second Ether trilogy. With Mandelbrot, Chaos Theory and String Theory I felt, as I said at the time, as if I were being offered a chart of my own brain. That chart made it easier for me to develop the notion of the multiverse as representing both the internal and the external, as a metaphor and as a means of structuring and rationalising an outrageously inventive and quasi-realistic narrative. The worlds of the multiverse move up and down scales or 'planes' explained in terms of mass, allowing entire universes to exist in the 'same' space. The result of developing this idea was the *War Amongst the Angels* sequence which added absurdist elements also functioning as a kind of mythology and folklore for a world beginning to understand itself in terms of new metaphysics and theoretical physics. As the cosmos becomes denser and almost infinite before our eyes, with black holes and dark matter affecting our own reality, we can explore them and observe them as our ancestors explored our planet and observed the heavens.

At the end of the 90s I'd returned to realism, sometimes with a dash of fantasy, with *King of the City* and the stories collected in *London Bone*. I also wrote a new Elric/Eternal Champion sequence, beginning with *Daughter of Dreams*, which brought the fantasy worlds of Hawkmoon, Bastable and Co. in line with my realistic and autobiographical stories, another attempt to unify all my fiction, and also offer a way in which disparate genres could be reunited, through notions developed from the multiverse and the Eternal Champion, as one giant novel. At the time I was finishing the Pyat sequence which attempted to look at the roots of the Nazi Holocaust in our European, Middle Eastern and American cultures and to ground my strange survival guilt while at the same time examining my own cultural roots in the light of an enduring anti-Semitism.

By the 2000s I was exploring various conventional ways of story-telling in the last parts of *The Metatemporal Detective* and through other homages, comics, parodies and games. I also looked back at my earliest influences. I had reached retirement age and felt like a rest. I wrote a 'prequel' to the Elric series as a graphic novel with Walter Simonson, *The Making of a Sorcerer*, and did a little online editing with FANTASTIC METROPOLIS.

By 2010 I had written a novel featuring Doctor Who, *The Coming of the Terraphiles*, with a nod to P.G. Wodehouse (a boyhood favourite), continued to write short stories and novellas and to work on the beginning of a new sequence combining pure fantasy and straight autobiography called *The Whispering Swarm* while still writing more Cornelius stories trying to unite all the various genres and sub-genres into which contemporary fiction has fallen.

Throughout my career critics have announced that I'm 'abandoning' fantasy and concentrating on literary fiction. The truth is, however, that all my life, since I became a professional writer and editor at the age of 16, I've written in whatever mode suits a story best and where necessary created a new form if an old one didn't work for me. Certain ideas are best carried on a Jerry Cornelius story, others work better as realism and others as fantasy or science fiction. Some work best as a combination. I'm sure I'll write whatever I like and will continue to experiment with all the ways there are of telling stories and carrying as many themes as possible. Whether I write about a widow coping with loneliness in her cottage or a massive, universe-size sentient spaceship searching for her children, I'll no doubt die trying to tell them all. I hope you'll find at least some of them to your taste.

One thing a reader can be sure of about these new editions is that they would not have been possible without the tremendous and indispensable help of my old friend and bibliographer John Davey. John has ensured that these Gollancz editions are definitive. I am indebted to John for many things, including his work at

Moorcock's Miscellany, my website, but his work on this edition has been outstanding. As well as being an accomplished novelist in his own right John is an astonishingly good editor who has worked with Gollancz and myself to point out every error and flaw in all previous editions, some of them not corrected since their first publication, and has enabled me to correct or revise them. I couldn't have completed this project without him. Together, I think, Gollancz, John Davey and myself have produced what will be the best editions possible and I am very grateful to him, to Malcolm Edwards, Darren Nash and Marcus Gipps for all the considerable hard work they have done to make this edition what it is.

Michael Moorcock

Contents

For Angela Carter – one of the great, generous hearts of our age – with respect and love

The Brothel in Rosenstrasse

An Extravagant Tale

Romanesque, Gothic and Baroque crowd together: the early basilica of St Vaclar stands between the sixteenth-century Chemnitz fortress and the eighteenth-century Capuchin monastery, all noteable examples of their periods, and are joined just below, in Königsplatz, by the beautiful new Egyptianate concert hall designed by Charles Rennie Mackintosh. It has been fairly said that there are no ugly buildings in Mirenburg, only some which are less beautiful than others. Many travellers stop here on their way to and from the Bohemian spas of Karlsbad, Marienbad and Franzenbad. Mirenburg is joined to Vienna by water, rail and road and it is common to change here from one mode of transport to another, or merely to make the appropriate train connections. The station is by Kammerer: a Temple to Steam in the modern 'Style Liberty'. From it one may progress easily to Prague or Dresden, to St Petersburg or Moscow, to Wroclaw or Krakow, to Buda-Pesht or Vienna, and beyond to Venice and Trieste, which may also be reached by canal.

Mirenburg's wealth comes from the industry and commerce of Wäldenstein, whose capital she is, but it is enhanced by the constant waves of visitors, who arrive at all seasons.

The revenues from tourism are used to maintain the older structures to perfection and it is well-known that Prince Badehoff-Krasny, the hereditary ruler of Wäldenstein, spends a considerable proportion of his own fortune on commissioning new buildings, as well as works by living painters, composers and writers. For this reason he has been fairly called a 'present-day Lorenzo' and he is apparently quite conscious of this comparison to the great Florentine. Mirenburg is the quintessential representation of a Renaissance which is at work everywhere in modern Europe.

– R.P. Downes,
Cities which Fascinate,
Charles Kelly, London, 1896

Chapter One
Mirenburg

I AM NOW at last able to move my right hand for extended periods of time. My left hand, although still subject to sudden weakness and trembling, is satisfactory. Old Papadakis continues to feed me and I have ceased to be filled with the panic of prospective abandonment. The suffering is now no worse than anything I knew as a small boy in the family sickroom. In fact minor discomforts, like an irritated groin, I welcome as wonderful aids to memory, while I continue to be astonished at my difficulty in recalling that overwhelming emotional anguish I experienced in my youth. My present tantrums and fits of despair cannot bear comparison: the impotence of sickness or old age at least reconciles one to the knowledge there is nothing one can do to improve one's own condition. Those old wounds seem thoroughly healed, yet here I am about to tear them open again, so possibly I shall discover if I have learned anything; or shall find out why I should have suffered at all.

Mirenburg is the most beautiful of cities. Great architects and builders have displayed their best talents here since the tenth century. Every tenement or hovel, warehouse or workshop, would elsewhere be envied and admired as art. On a September morning, shortly before dawn, little paddle-steamers begin to sound their horns in the grey mist. Only the twin Gothic spires of the Cathedral of St-Maria-and-St-Maria are visible at this time, rising out of the mist as symmetrical sea-carved rocks might thrust above a sluggish silver tide.

I was completely alive in Mirenburg. Ironically, during the days of the Siege, I feared death far more than I fear it now when death exhibits itself in every limb, in every organ; an unavoidable reality. Life was never to be experienced so fully. For years I yearned for the dark, lifting sensuality, that all-embracing atmosphere of sexual ecstasy I had known in Mirenburg. To have maintained that ambience, even if it had been in my power, would have led to inevitable self-destruction, so I have not entirely regretted living past the Mirenburg days. I have made I think the best of my life. Since I retired to Italy it has been simpler of course and I have been forced to review many habits I had not much questioned. Friends visit; we have memories. We relive our best times and usually joke about the worst. Changing events have not greatly disturbed us. But there is no-one who shared the Mirenburg period and few believe me if I speak of all that happened. There was so much. Alexandra. My Alice. She is still sixteen. She lies surrounded by green velvet and she is naked. I have arranged blossoms upon her skin, pink and pale yellow against her tawny flesh; flowers from a Venetian hothouse to warm her in our early-autumn days, while in the ballroom below we hear the zither, the Café Mozart Waltz, and I smell my sex mingling with her scent, with honey and roses. Her eyes are heated, her smile is languid yet brilliant in the dark curls which surround it. She spreads her little arms. Alexandra. She called herself Alex. Later it will be Alice. I am enchanted; I am captured by Romance. Beyond the window the spires and roofs of Mirenburg glitter like a mirage. I am about to be betrayed by my own imagination. Those huge eyes, the colour of ancient oak, seem to give me all their attention and I am flattered, overwhelmed. My Alexandra. Her head moves to one side, her shoulder goes up, she speaks my name:

'Ricky?'

I am tempted to put down my pen and push myself higher in my pillows to try to peer over the top of the writing-board and look to see if I really did hear her; but I continue to write, glad to touch just a little of that ambience again.

As a child, when I played with my toy soldiers, arranging battalions, positioning cavalry and artillery, I would sometimes receive an unexpected thrill of intense sexual pleasure, to the point of achieving not only an erection but often an orgasm. Even now, when I see a display of toy soldiers in a shop, I may be touched by that same sensation, almost as poignantly as when I was twelve or thirteen. Why I experienced it then and why I continued to experience it I do not know. Perhaps it had something to do with my complete power over those little men which, in turn, released in me all the power of my sex, full and unchecked by convention or upbringing. Certainly I had very little power as a boy. My brothers and sisters being so much older than I, I had a relatively solitary childhood. My mother was never mentioned. I was to discover she was in disgrace, somewhere in Roumania, with a Dutchman.

Shortly before her death, I met her briefly, by accident, in a fashionable restaurant off the Avenue Victor Hugo and recognised her from her photograph. She was small and serene and was very polite to me when I pointed out our relationship. Both she and her Dutchman were dressed in black. My father's interest was in politics. He served the government and was close to Bismarck. At our estates in Bek I had been brought up chiefly by Scottish governesses, doted on by pretty housemaids who, when the time came, had been more than willing to educate me sexually. I have been in the power of women, it seems, all my life.

Dawn comes and Mirenburg begins to rattle like a beggar's cup: the first horses and trams are abroad. The shutters are being raised, windows are being opened. The sun is pale brass upon the mist which thins to reveal a sky of milky blue. White and grey stone shimmers. She speaks the affected 'English'-accented German of fashionable Vienna; she pronounces 'R' as 'W'. She is captivating, artificial, an object to treasure. From some secluded tree-lined square comes the tolling of a Catholic bell. At certain heights it is possible to see most of Mirenburg's antique turrets and gables, her twisting chimneys, her picturesque steeples and balconies, her bridges built by old kings, her walls and canals. The modern apartment houses, hotels and stores, as noble and inspiring as the palaces and churches which surround them, are monumentally designed by Sommaragu and Niermans and Kammerer. She is a symphony of broad paved avenues and cobbled alleys, glinting spires and domes and stained glass. She lies staring up into my face, her small breasts held fast against my slow penis. It is warm in the room. The sun cuts between the heavy curtains and falls, a single slab of light, upon the bed, across my back. Our faces and our legs are in deep shadow; the white sperm strikes at her throat and she cries out in unison with me; my Alice. I roll to my side and I am laughing with pleasure. She lights me a cigarette. I feel like a demigod. I smoke. Every action is heroic. And she is a spirit, an *erdgeist* out of Wedekind become my very own reality. We joke. She smiles. It is dawn in Mirenburg. We shall sleep later and at about noon I will rise to wrap myself in my black-and-white silk robe and stand on the balcony looking out at the exquisite view which, to my mind, cannot be matched, even by Venice. I glance at the table and the dark blue leather notebook in which I shall try to write a poem for her; the book was a present from my middle sister and has my name in gold stamped on the front: Rickhardt von Bek. I am the youngest son; the prodigal of the family, and in this part I am tolerated by almost everyone. The senile trees rustle in a light east wind. I smell mint and garlic. Papadakis brings me fresh materials and a little morphine. I can feel myself trembling again, but not from pain or infirmity; I am trembling as I trembled then, with every sense at almost unbearable intensity. I touch the skin of an unripe peach. Down the wide Mladota Steps, also known as the Tilly Steps, carefully descends a single student, still drunk from a party, still in his light blue uniform except that instead of his cap he wears a homburg hat at least three sizes too large for him. It covers his ears and his eyes. His immature lips are pursed to whistle some misremembered Mozart. He is trying to make his way back to the Old Quarter where he lodges. Two working girls, pink-faced and blonde in shawls and long dark smocks, pass him as they ascend, giggling and trying to flirt with him, but he is oblivious to them, for all the sharp clack of their clogs. He reaches the bottom of the steps and casts himself off across the roadway. The embankment on both sides is planted with firs and cypresses; immediately opposite him are the wrought-iron gates and carved granite pillars of the Botanical Gardens.

These mansions on the very fringe of the Old Quarter were once the residences of the ruling class but are today primarily public buildings and museums. They retain their grounds and their imported trees and shrubs. The largest house which the student, now clinging to the railings, would be able to see if he lifted his hat was the summer place of the Graf Gunther von Baudessin who said he loved the city more than his own Bavarian estates. He was for a while special ambassador for his homeland and did much to help Mirenburg retain her independence during the expansionist wars of the mid-eighteenth century when three enemies (Russia, Saxony and Austria) converged on Wäldenstein's borders, then failed to agree who should own the province.

From the Gardens come a thousand scents: autumn flowers and shrubs; the small, scarlet deeply perfumed rose for which Mirenburg is famous blooms late and sometimes lasts until December. There is still dew on the grass. The student steadies himself and continues, turning back up the broad avenue of Push-kinstrasse. He is alerted momentarily by the cry of some exotic beast awakening in the nearby Zoo. A milkman's cart, decorated in blue, red and green, passes him, its cans jingling, its bony horse rolling her old eyes in the shade of her blinkers as she takes her familiar course. He reaches the Lugnerhoff at last, where the Protestant martyrs were burned in 1497. Here the houses are suddenly close-packed, leaning one upon the other like a crowd of old men around a game of bowls. In the centre of the cobbled court is a baroque fountain: the defiant Hussites about to mount their pyre. The student crosses Lugnerhoff to reach the narrow entrance to Korkziehiergasse and sunlight touches a green copper roof. Only the upper floors on the right-hand side of the alley are so far warmed by the sun; all the rest remain in deep shadow. The student opens a door into a courtyard and disappears. His feet can still be heard climbing the iron staircase to the room over what was once a stable now used by Jewish street-traders to store their goods.

Further up Korkziehiergasse, ascending the steep grey serpentine slope which leads from here to Cutovskiplatz, her knuckles blue as her fingers grasp inch by inch the metal bannister, the old candy-woman is a threadbare silhouette in the morning light. This hunched, exhausted and vulnerable little creature was once the darling of the Schoen Theatre: 'a spark of true life-force surrounded by the putrescent glow of simulated vitality', as Snarewitz described her fifty years ago. Marya Zamarovski lived for love in those days and gave herself up to the moment thoroughly and generously. Her men, while they continued to be attractive to her, had everything they desired. With every lover, she discarded houses, jewels, furniture and money, until almost simultaneously her wealth became exhausted together with her beauty and her public success. She opened a chocolate shop, but was cheated out of it by the last man she loved. Now she sells her sweets from the heavy tray about her neck. She will stand in Cutovskiplatz until evening, not far from the theatre where she used to perform (it continues to put on popular melodramas and farces). I buy candied violets from her for Alexandra who nibbles at one and offers it to me. I bite. The scented sweet mingles its strong perfume with her subtle cologne and I resist the urge to draw her to me. There is a noise from the river. On the quays the coal-heavers carry sacks to the little steamers. The docks of Mirenburg are sometimes as busy as any sea-port. In winter the merchants, wrapped in over-large fur coats which will give them the appearance of so many sober fledglings standing in concourse, will supervise their cargoes. It is now seven o'clock in the morning and the express from Berlin is steaming into the station. The workmen's cafés, bristling with newspapers in German, Czech and Svitavian, fill with smoking red sausages and dark coffee, purple arms and blue overalls, the smell of strong cigarettes, the sound of cutlery and argument. Waiters and waitresses, their big enamel trays held above their heads, move rapidly amongst the crowded marble-topped tables. We hear a bellow from the Berlin train.

On the balconies of the hotels above Cutovskiplatz a few early risers are breakfasting. One can locate a hotel at this hour by the distinctive aura of café au lait and croissants. Soon the English tourists in their Burberrys and ulsters will emerge and make for

Mladota where they will disdain the little funicular car running up beside it and insist on trudging all one hundred and twenty steps, irrespective of the weather; then they will head for the Cathedral of St-Maria-and-St-Maria, or go to the Radota Bridge which spans the Rätt. The balustrades of this bridge are supported on both sides by Romanesque pillars representing the famous line of Svitavian kings whose power was broken in 1370 by the Holy Roman Emperor Charles IV who, by diplomacy and threat, set his own candidate upon the throne and insisted Svitavia be called by its German name of Wäldenstein and Mirov-Cesny become Mirenburg, with the effect that Svitavian is now only spoken fluently in the rural districts.

The Rätt is a fast-flowing river. Upstream is the Oder and downstream the Danube. She is loved by barge-men as a good, safe river, spine of the most sophisticated canal system in the world. The Rätt is the chief contributor to Wäldenstein's prosperity. Several hundred yards from the Radota Bridge, beside older cobbled quays, are cramped coffee houses and restaurants, covered in handwritten advertisements and posters so that it is almost impossible to see through windows where weathered barge-captains and pale shipping clerks drink thick Rättdämpfen soup from Dresden crockery and wipe their lips on Brno linen. The conversation is nothing but lists of goods and prices in a dozen currencies. Steam from tureens behind the counters threatens to peel placards from the glass and on a misty evening one can go outside and scarcely notice any difference in visibility from the interior.

In the tall white-and-brown café on the corner of Kanalstrasse and Kaspergasse, underneath the billboard advertising a brand of Russian tea, sit drinking the Slav nationalists. Many have been up all night and some have just arrived. They argue in fierce but usually inexpert Svitavian or Bohemian. They quote the poetry of Kollar and Celakovsky: *Slavia, Slavia! Thou name of sweet sound but of bitter memory; hundred times divided and destroyed, but yet more honoured than ever.* They refuse to speak German or French. They wear peasant blouses under their frock-coats. They affect boots rather than shoes and rather than cigars they smoke the yellow cigarettes of the peasant. Though most of them have been educated at the universities of Prague and Heidelberg, even Paris, they reject this learning. They speak instead of 'blood' and 'instinct', of lost glories and stolen pride. Alexandra tells me her brother was for a while of their number and it is the chief reason her parents decided to take him to Rome. I tell her I am grateful to her brother for his radicalism. Her little stomach is so soft. I touch it lightly with my fingertips. I move my hand towards her pubis. She jumps and gently takes hold of my wrist. What yesterday had been of peripheral interest to me today becomes central, abiding, almost an obsession. I take as keen a delight in the contents of jewellery-shop windows, the couturiers, the fashion magazines as I once took in watching a horse-race or reading about exotic lands. This change has not been gradual, it seems to have occurred overnight, as if I cannot remember any other life. Alexandra has me. My blood quickens. Now I am remembering the detail of the pleasure. I wave Papadakis away. I cling to the sensation. It becomes more than memory. I experience it again. What have I invented? Is she my creation or is she creating me? Commonplace events are of no consequence. The room darkens. A background of red velvet and roses. Her passivity; her weakness. Her sudden, fierce passion and her sharp, white teeth. She becomes strong, but she remains so soft. The Cathedral bells are chiming. We are playing a game. She understands the rules better than I. I break away from her and stand upright. I go to the window and part the curtains. She is laughing from the twisted sheets. I turn towards her again:

'You are hopeless.'

Papadakis is at my shoulder, asking for instructions. I tell him to light my lamp. She pushes her head under the pillow. Her feet and calves are hidden by the linen; her bottom curves in the brown gloom and her vertebrae are gleaming. She comes to the surface, her dark curls damp with sweat, and I return to her, forcing her down on her face and laying my penis in the cleft of her rear, denying myself the heat of her vagina: I have never known such heat, before or since, in a woman's sex. She bites at my hand. Traffic is noisy in the square today; a political demonstration of some kind, Papadakis says: he is contemptuous. 'Communists.' We hire a carriage and driver to take us east to Staromest, the hilly semi-rural suburb of Mirenburg where proud-eyed little girls watch over goats and chickens and shoo off strangers as if they were foxes. Here, amid the old cottages and windmills, we shall stop at an inn and either lunch there or ask them for a picnic. One or two fashionable 'Resting Houses' have been built in Staromest. They are frequented by invalids and the elderly and are staffed by nuns. Thus the peace of the hills is somewhat artificially preserved from the natural encroachment of the city. The apartment blocks stand below, silent besiegers who must inevitably conquer. We pass a small convoy of vivid gypsy wagons. Alexandra points at a brown-and-white pony as if I could buy it for her. The earth roads are still dry. From the dust the plodding gypsies do not look at us as we pass. We stop to gaze on the rooftops.

I point out, in the curve of the river, the old dock known as Suicide Bay. By some trick of the current most of those who fling themselves off the Radota Bridge are washed into this dock. We can also see the distant racetrack, dark masses of horses and spectators, bright silks and flags against the green turf. Closer to us is the cupola of the great Concert Hall where tonight one can hear Smetana and Dvořák on the same programme as Wagner, Strauss and Debussy. Mirenburg is more liberal in her tastes than Vienna. Not far from the Concert Hall is a gilded sign, by Mucha, for the Cabaret Roberto, which offers popular singers, comedians, dancers and trained animals in a single evening's entertainment. Alexandra wishes to attend Roberto's. I promise her we shall go, even though I know she is as likely as I am to change her mind in the next half-hour. She touches my cheek with warm lips. I am enraptured by the city's beauty. I watch a green-and-gold tramcar, drawn by two chestnut horses, as it moves towards Little Bohemia, the Jewish Quarter, where from Monday to Thursday a market flourishes.

The tramcar reaches its terminus, near the market. The core of the market is in Gansplatz but nowadays it has spread through surrounding streets and each street has come to be identified by its stalls. In Bäverninstrasse is second-hand clothing, linen, lace and tapestries; in Fahnestrasse antiques and sporting-guns; in Hangengasse books, stationery, prints; and in Messingstrasse fruit and vegetables, meat and fish; while the main market has a little of everything, including Italian organ-grinders, gypsy fiddlers, mimes and puppeteers. Stall-holders and their customers haggle beneath bright stripes of the awnings, all in the shadow of the Great Syna-gogue, said to be the largest in Europe. Her rabbis are amongst the world's most famous and influential.

Dignified men, dark and learned, come and go on steps where gingerbread sellers rest their trays, where little boys sell cigarettes out of inverted drums and their sisters, in pretty tinsel, perform simple dances to attract attention to their cakes and sweets.

The stalls are crowded with toys, tools, jams and sausages, musical instruments and domestic wares. Vendors shout their bar-gains, and sardonic hausfraus challenge them above the noise of guitars, accordions, violins and hurdy-gurdies.

At the far end of Hangengasse a large crimson automobile, imported from France, bucks and rumbles on its springs, its driver seated high above his passengers and wearing the cap, goggles and overcoat of his calling so he resembles a comical lemur in his pro-found sobriety. The chauffeur's gloved fingers squeeze a horn: a tin trumpet blown by a mouse announces the progress of Jugger-naut. The crowd divides, from curiosity rather than fear, and the crimson machine is on its way to more fashionable parts, to Falfnersallee, the Champs-Élysées of Mirenburg, and the Restaur-ant Schmidt, all silver, mirrors and pale yellow. Here the nouveaux riches display themselves, to the chagrin of waiters who until a year or two ago served only Mirenburg's aristocracy. The upper classes, they say, have been driven out by the vulgar owners of steamships and mechanical looms, whose wives wear the pearls of ancient impoverished families about red throats and speak a kind of German hitherto only heard in the Moravian district, the industrial suburb on the far side of the river.

This class has come to be known as 'les sauvages' or 'die Unbe-baut', the subject of cartoons in the illustrated papers and mockery in cabarets which these days all but fill Kodály Square, yet its money allows the journals and entertainments to flourish while its trade, especially with Berlin, increases Wäldenstein's prosperity.

At a large round table near the window, looking out upon the trees, the kiosks and the traffic of Falfnersallee, sits in corpulent well-being, in English tweed and French linen, Pasitch the Press King, a loyal supporter of the government of Prince Badehoff-Krasny and believer in stronger ties with Germany. His newspapers persistently emphasise the Austro-Hungarian threat and pillory an opposition favouring the views of Count Holzhammer cur-rently exiled to Vienna, where he is courted by those who believe firmly in a 'union' between Bohemia and Wäldenstein.

Herr Pasitch eats his Kalbsaxe and discusses international pol-itics with his uncritical sons and daughters. They are expecting a guest. My first memories of Mirenburg are of the Restaurant Schmidt. Father had taken me to the city for a season. I had spent some part of the summer at a private academy before being sent on to school in Heidelberg. I recall skiffs and tea-gardens. Miren-burg had seemed a haven of peace and stability in Europe. I am inclined to resent any politics here. Mirenburg is a retreat; I escape to her. I always expected to find an Alexandra in Mirenburg so I scarcely question my fortune. We drive into the early afternoon.

Herr Pasitch's guest has arrived, seating himself with a flourish and drawing the full attention of the Pasitch daughters. He is Her-bert Block, the popular song-writer; selfish, humorous and charming. Without favouritism he has looted the romantic lyrics of antecedents and contemporaries to considerable profit. Few of the victims complain. His charm is such that, although he is now nearing forty, people still regard him as a schoolboy whose pranks do no real harm, and, while he remains witty and vain, he will always have tolerant friends, especially amongst women. His dark eyes are professionally active. His dark hair might now be dyed. He leans back in his chair and flashes an expert smile. Herr Pasitch explains the strategies of Bismarck. Herr Block turns the conversation to the exploits of Count Rudolph Stefanik, the famous Czech balloon adventurer, who was recently forced to leave Zurich under scandalous conditions and narrowly missed having his vessel seized and burned by outraged citizens. They had welcomed him as a hero and he had thoroughly abused their hospitality. 'Caught in the basket!' says Herr Block. 'He is a dear friend of mine. But, O!' This episode, involving a young lady of previously good reputation, was not dissimilar to many others in the Count's history. 'His adventures have spanned five continents.' Getting some wind of the composer's drift, Herr Pasitch firmly steers the topic back to Bismarck. Herr Block smiles at the women as if in defeat. He suggests that they might like to repair later to the Straus Tea Gardens, to the south of Mirenburg, on the river. 'To catch the last of the summer.'

From these gardens, some five miles away, one can watch the trains crossing the long viaduct which spans the valley where the Rätt widens. It has thirty-two arches and was completed in 1874 by engineers from the Rhineland. According to legend a man lost his life for every arch completed and some of the victims are said to lie beneath the plinths, their ghosts occasionally appearing on the track at night, causing drivers to apply their brakes and bring trains to an alarming halt. Usually these ghosts are discovered to be baffled deer or wolves which have strayed onto the bridge and are unable to escape.

Five minutes from the Restaurant Schmidt, in Edelstrasse, a narrow street running parallel to Falfnersallee, is the Restaurant Anglais. Socialists gather here, followers of Kropotkin, Proudhon and Karl Marx, to debate how much support they have in Parliament and how soon the workers in the Moravia will grow tired of their lot and rise against their masters. They wear grey frock-coats and high collars but only a few have the soft felt hats and loose ties of the conventional radical. In the same street, at the Hotel Dresden, are members of the League of St Ignatz, a little older, on average, but otherwise very similar to the clientèle at the Restaurant Anglais. These strong conservatives are almost as suspicious of the socialists as they are of the Jews, the Jesuits and the Freemasons, whom they term the 'super-national powers', deliberate fomenters of war and rebellion. It is early afternoon. Socialists and conservatives begin to return to offices where they will mingle and conduct the business of Mirenburg with exactly the same degree of zeal shown by their non-political colleagues.

A squadron of cavalry, its bright blues and golds softened by the September sun, rides past one end of Edelstrasse, on its way to guard the Kasimirsky Palace, where Parliament meets (today it debates a new Armaments Bill); and in the other direction goes a closed carriage bearing the arms of Hungarian Archduke Otto Budenya-Graetz, exiled from his own country by relatives who pay him to stay abroad. His reputation is so villainous not even the lion-hunting ladies of the Regenstrasse invite him to their salons. It is said he always has a small revolver with him. So many attempts have been made on his life by jealous lovers or their husbands, he carries the weapon for self-defence. The carriage turns down toward the river, passing the neo-classical Customs House, and heading inevitably for Rosenstrasse. Alexandra's teeth touch the pale flesh of chicken and I raise my champagne glass to her. The shadows already begin to lengthen. I recall my second visit to Mirenburg, the lilacs against a bright blue sky which deepened to violet at sunset; then I had spent considerable time and most of my money at the Casino. I had a passion for roulette and the Circus. Both Casino and Circus still exist, but I have so far visited neither.

Our landau takes us back to our hotel. We smell crisp Leckerli gingerbread in the hands of schoolchildren who file out of the bakeshops on their way home. I tell Alexandra of the summer in the cottage when I was a boy, of my father coming to visit us. I had the impression almost everything was white and yellow, and even now when I recall the cornflowers I am astonished at this sudden infusion of brilliant blue into my memory. I can, I tell her, with effort also re-experience the red-orange of the poppies, but I suspect this might be a false recollection, or at least one from a later period.

The smell of those poppies, however, is almost always with me, whenever I think of them. I am under the impression I am losing Alexandra's attention, but we shall soon be back at the hotel and I know how to recapture her quickly enough. I begin the story of the consumptive twins and their dog, even before we have left the carriage, although my mind is still obsessed with that scent of poppies and I wonder why I should associate it so strongly with sexual passion. Perhaps both are capable of absorbing one's total attention. Yet I could not have been more than seven when we paid our last visit to the country. Papadakis wishes to retire. He asks if he can douse my lamp. I shake my head and tell him to go. I remember, as I escort Alexandra through the lobby, the first woman I became infatuated with. She was married and her husband was abroad in some small German colony. 'You are a sympathetic friend,' she had said to me. 'And sometimes that is the last thing one seeks in a lover.' She had laughed. 'That is the job of the husband.' She taught me an excellent lesson. Once again, as I prepare to bathe, I consider the relationship between passion and power, between sexuality and spiritual fulfilment, the realisation of the Self. I complete the story of the twins. Alexandra begins to laugh and becomes helpless.

Her arms grip my back, her legs encircle my thighs; I begin the slow injection. 'Never stop loving me,' she says. 'Promise me.' I promise. 'And I will never stop loving you,' she says. But I am a fiction. My reality could destroy me. She is a dream and I shall never stop loving her. We are silent now. I move further into that tiny flame, the gateway to a universe of pleasure; beyond her vagina is infinity, immortality, marvellous escape. She is yelling. Her nails stab into my buttocks and my cries join hers. She lies with her curls against my neck and shoulder. I stroke her arm in the long twilight. 'Shall we go to Roberto's?'

'I am too tired,' she says, 'for the moment. Let us have an early supper here and then see.'

In Zwergengasse, once the home of a famous eighteenth-century Italian circus troupe, a knife-grinder pushes his cart over the cobbles. The street is barely wide enough for him and not much more than thirty yards long. It runs up to the old wall of the city. Its lower floors are large and vacant, occupied only by a tribe of beggars who will, when winter comes, move on to warmer quarters near the quaysides; they squat amongst the remains of the circus – painted tin and rotting velvet – discussing their adventures in loud voices while Pan Sladek reaches his premises at last, lowers the handles of his cart and unlocks the doors of his workshop, suspicious as always of the beggars (who would be far too timid to rob him). His grey face shines like a hatchet as he sweats to manipulate his grinding equipment into the shop. His nose is blue and pointed. He has had a hard day. He locks up and enters the doorway next to the shed, climbing the stairs slowly, but two at a time on his spidery legs until he reaches a door painted a fresh and startling yellow. He opens it. The smell of frying comes from the kitchen. Today is schnitzel day. When Pan Sladek remembers this he brightens. He goes into the kitchen and kisses Pani Sladek as he always kisses her. She smiles to herself. Below, as Zwergengasse grows dim, more beggars flit back, rooks to a rookery, their hands full of sour wine and loaves of yesterday's bread. Somewhere close by, students of the Academy and the Polytechnic are fighting again, shouting obscure private battle-cries from street to street and lying in ambush for one another in alleys and shop doorways, brandishing stolen colours, caps and scarves, which they nail to the walls and beams of the beerhalls, their headquarters. Willi's in Morgenstrasse and Leopold's in Grunegasse are respectively strongholds of the Academy and the Polytechnic. Near Leopold's is The Amoral Jew, a cabaret populated entirely by proponents of the New Art, young Russians and Germans with bizarre notions of perspective.

Alexandra likes The Amoral Jew and I have acquaintances there. We arrive at about nine o'clock to watch the negro orchestra which delighted her on our last visit. She is overdressed and heavily painted for this cabaret but so beautiful that nobody cares. Kulacharsky, barrel-chested and ferociously bearded, in a peasant blouse and clogs, fondles the ostrich feathers in her diamond aigrette and says something wicked to her in Russian which pleases her, though she does not understand a word. It is dark and noisy in The Amoral Jew and Rosenblum himself presides, his goatee twitching as he strolls amongst the tables and glances secretly here and there from mysterious eyes which could be drugged. There are murals on the walls, in gaudy primaries. Were it not for the strange manner of their execution they would be thought indelicate. They were painted by a Spaniard who passed through. Alexandra accepts a glass of absinthe, still the drink of the bohemian from St Petersburg to Paris. Voorman, sweating in his heavy jacket and tweed shooting breeches, begins to talk about his telescope; he is considering giving up painting for astronomy. 'Science is today the proper province of the artist.' Alexandra laughs, but because she finds him attractive not because she understands him. Bodies press around us like mourners at a wake. Alexandra enjoys the attention of the avant-garde. In the old barracks a few streets away, built into the walls of Mirenburg, privates at an off-duty card game drink surreptitiously from illicit jugs while avuncular sergeants turn blind eyes. In the upper storeys of the garrison captains and lieutenants passionately discuss the Armaments Bill which, if implemented, will mean a stronger Wäldenstein. 'Everyone is arming. If we wish to keep our freedom, so should we. We are the prize of Europe, never forget that. We are coveted by all: three empires flank us and the only security we have is that one empire will not risk warring upon another in order to win us. Remember Bismarck's words: "Wäldenstein is the most beautiful bride the masculine nations have ever courted: a virgin whose dowry opens the gateway to power over the entire continent. Whoever wins her shall win the world." The Prince thinks our neutrality is all the security we need. But we must be prepared to defend ourselves from within. There are those who would sell the virgin to the highest bidder.' So says Captain Thomas Vladoroff, a distant cousin of mine, as his batman clears away the cheese. Vladoroff has the pale and misleadingly vacant good looks of his family. 'We must be alert for the agent provocateur in our midst. There are many, in the Army and out of it, who support Count Holzhammer.' His friends smile at his zeal. He loosens the collar of his dress tunic. Someone tells him that there could never be a civil war in Wäldenstein. 'We are too sensible, too united, too fond of comfort.' Alexandra dislikes my cousin. He is bloodless, she says, and more interested in machines than in his fellow men. He is leaving now, to visit his mistress in Regenstrasse, the widow of an officer killed some twenty years ago as a volunteer on the Prussian side during their last war with the French. Her name is Katerina von Elfenberg and she was seventeen when her husband died. She told my cousin he could be a reincarnation of that dashing Hussar, who was blown to pieces by a huge Krupp gun he was attempting to recapture. Her other lover is a Baron, a chief of the Stock Exchange, and her advice is making my cousin moderately rich, although he becomes concerned about the nature of the speculation, for it seems to him to anticipate strife. There is a small party tonight. I have been invited but I could not take Alexandra for fear of meeting members of her family. As it is, her servants have had to be heavily bribed to tell callers she is out and to bring messages in secret to our hotel so that she can reply and thus preserve the pretence of being in residence. Her parents write regularly from Rome and she dutifully replies with news of friends and relatives, the weather, expeditions with her friends to museums and the more suitable tea-gardens. She is expected, next year, to go to be finished in Switzerland, but she plans instead, she tells me, to meet me in Berlin. From there we shall discuss the possibilities of Paris, Marseilles and Tangiers, for of course she is below the age of consent.

My cousin is introduced to the members of the Mirenburg Royal Ballet Company, some of the finest dancers in the world. The women offer him controlled hands to be kissed. He will tell me later how he feels uncomfortable, as if corralled with a squadron of ceremonial horses, all of which can pick up their feet and none of which can charge. I look toward the little stage, my arm about Alexandra. She loves the comedy, borrowed from Debureau, she says. Pierrot pursues Columbine and is defeated by Harlequin. A large silk moon ripples in the draught from the door and Pierrot plucks his guitar, singing in French. I am told it is Laforgue. Projected against the backdrop are silhouettes of balloons, trains and automobiles, of factories and iron ships. The song is in praise, I gather, of the machine, for Pierrot's accent is so guttural I can scarcely understand one word in three. Then on come the novelty dancers; some little ballet of primitive lust and discordant fiddles. In the morning, as soon as there is sunlight a lark will begin to sing from our roof. We touch glasses and sip the heady wormwood. There is no time. I am adrift. I lean towards my ink. I have no pain now. I am full of delight. In Mirenburg's gaslight I call for a cab. Around us is ancient beauty, delicate lacework-stone silent under the deep sky. I resist the temptation to brave Katerina von Elfenberg's salon and we drive instead to the Yanokovski Promenade to marvel at its electrical lights and to listen to the music from the bandstand. I am an old man now and my white suits have become yellowed by the sun; but there is a bandstand in the town, where Italians play selections from Verdi and Rossini. A pleasure boat goes past in the jewelled water. Excited girls and boys of Alexandra's age play innocent games amongst the deckchairs and the hatch covers. A flotilla of grim barges passes in the darkness on the other side; a steam-whistle hoots. The pleasure boat disappears beneath the Radota. Mirenburg is the merriest of cities at night. Her citizens belong spiritually to more southern regions of the continent. In Bachenstrasse, which winds down to the Promenade, Carl-Maria Saratov, his heart broken and his mind desperate for diversion, wanders into the unlit alleys known as the Indian Quarter, perhaps because there was once a cheap waxwork show here with its main tableaux representing the Wild West. Carl-Maria Saratov has come all the way from Falfnersallee where he saw his sweetheart entering the Café Wilhelm with his oldest friend, another student at the university. He has heard that opium is to be found in the Indian Quarter and so it is. The den would be unlikely to welcome him. It is typical of its kind, but unlike the one Carl-Maria has heard about from a friend. Mirenburg's best opium den is not the sordid hovel one finds in Hamburg or London. Even the Chinese attendants at 'Chow-Li's' are not really

Chinese, but Magyars dressed in elaborate robes. The place is awash with blue silk and golden brocade. The couches are deep and thickly padded and the owner is British, an exile, James Mackenzie, the Scots military engineer, who committed some crime in the Malay Archipelago and dare not enter any country of the British Empire, yet runs his den with all the tact, discretion and lavish decoration of a fashionable restaurateur. Archduke Otto Budenya-Graetz is there tonight, with two young friends from the military school. Mackenzie will not refuse him entrance, but makes sure he is sent to a remote room and that the pipes are paid for before they are smoked.

The Archduke has not enjoyed his visit to Rosenstrasse and swears the place is overrated and he will never return. He complains of his entrapment in 'this provincial town' and speaks to the fascinated students of the glories of Vienna, Buda-Pesht and Paris, of the women of St Petersburg, where he was very briefly an attaché, of the boys of Constantinople, and he hands them their pipes with his eyes on their serge thighs and takes a deep breath to relax himself before inhaling. He lets himself remember his days in the service of the Mexicans; that splendid time of unchecked satisfaction when the air was so full of fear one had merely to wave a sabre to fulfil one's grossest needs. 'I can still smell the blood,' he murmurs. 'There is nothing like it to enliven any sport, say what you will.' He takes his pipe as if it were a crop and his eyes, full of pagan Asia, brighten and then cloud. 'But the Jews have robbed me of my birthright...' Alexandra is growing bored. She asks me to take her to 'some secret place' and so we, too, head for 'Chow-Li's' for I must grant her everything she asks. Here she will cough on the smoke and complain it has no effect, but later she will ask me about my women and will lick her lips while I describe their charms and become terrifyingly passionate so that my dreams will be of some transfigured Mirenburg, some Mirenburg of the soul, where tawny young lionesses purr above the trembling corpses of handsome baboons. Now, just when I have awakened from a thoroughly restful sleep for the first time in weeks, it seems that Mirenburg is all around me. I can see her

austere Gothic spires in the mist of the September morning. She
is completely alive again. On the river a line of rowing boats drifts
gradually to rest against the Hoffmeister Quay. The smell of bak-
ing comes from Nadelgasse, seemingly from every window there
drifts the odour of fresh bread, of cakes and pastries. As a child I
dreamed frequently of a golden-haired young girl, whom I loved.
I had carried her away from harsh parents in an open-boat and we
had been captured by Norse pirates, but again I was able to save
her. She loved me as wholly as I loved her. I used to think of her
more than I thought of any real person, as I lay awake in my room
in daylight, trying to sleep, but knowing that the rest of the world
was still awake, hearing my sisters' voices from below. Must we
always seek in lovers to satisfy the frustrations we have experienced with parents? An 'echo'. Unable to ease the cares of those
who have given birth to us we attempt to improve the lot of a
mistress, a husband or a wife. So many women have tried to make
me into their ideal father and in resisting I have frequently lost
them. Alexandra would rather I were a demon-lover and this rôle
is almost as difficult, but I play it with more relish, for it entails
very different responsibilities. My ideal is fair-skinned and blonde,
so why should I sense this 'echo' in my little Alexandra, this reson-
ance in the soul which entwines me to her as if we were a single
note of music? We speak again of Tangiers. I would take her there
now, for fear of her escaping me when she tires of this game, but
it is impossible. Instead I acquiesce to every adventure.

She requests instruction. I am inventive. I bring to life every
dream. I add all experience to my repertoire, I tell her. I resist
nothing. I forget nothing. Sexually I am a chameleon. 'You have
the disposition of a whore,' she tells me, laughing. I cannot deny
it. We visit my old friend, Professor Eckart, who teaches at the
University now and continues his experiments. He is obsessed
with Count Rudolph Stefanik and the possibilities of heavier-
than-air flight. He shows us his own designs. His room is almost
bare, save for drawings pinned here and there upon the panelling.
The large window looks out onto geometrical gardens, full of
evergreens and Mirenburg's famous roses. He tells us that he has

personally entertained Stefanik. Alexandra, who has been bored, asks what the Count is like. 'The man is a rogue,' I say. 'And you are not?' she asks. I have forgotten my part. 'But a genius,' says Professor Eckart, tugging at his sleeve and casting about for the wine he has offered us. Professor Eckart looks like a countryman. He is round and bucolic; he might be a huntsman on some Bavarian estate. 'Would you care to meet him? I am giving a dinner party next week.' 'We should love to,' says Alexandra. Privately I decide to discover the names of the other guests before I accept. I am suspicious of Alexandra's curiosity; I have some measure of how far she will go to satisfy it. Papadakis brings me my oatmeal gruel. I breakfast on champagne and smoked salmon with my Alexandra. Not long ago even the gruel was painful to my palate and would sometimes seem over-flavoured, but now I disdain its blandness. Papadakis suggests he should have the doctor in today. Angrily I resist the idea. 'I have not felt so well in two years,' I tell him. He leaves to collect the post from the town. I visited my brother Wolfgang at his place in Saxony about a year before I arrived again in Mirenburg. He had just recovered from tuberculosis. 'My cure was sudden and miraculous,' he told me. 'The disease appeared to be killing me. I was its slave. Then, within a matter of weeks, it had released me. I grew steadily stronger, but as I did so I knew enormous regret for the passing of that warm and permanent eroticism which had attended my illness for over forty months. As I returned to normality I experienced the acutest depression and sense of descent into a world whose ordinary pleasures were no longer pleasurable to me.' At the time I had scarcely understood him. Now I know very well what he meant. There is a kind of debilitating insanity which a person will cling to desperately for as long as it possesses them. Only when it has given them up will they begin to describe it as an aberration. 'The world is a dull place now, Ricky,' my brother had said. He had taken to drinking heavily. If it had not been for the threat of dismissal from the diplomatic service he might easily have become a permanent drunkard. But until he died his face held the look of a man who had once known Heaven. Papadakis returns and helps me to the WC. Today the agony of urinating is not so great and I realise that I had grown to look forward to the pain as preferable to any of the other sensations which my disease offers me. But I hurry back to Mirenburg, urging Papadakis on as if he were a coach-horse and I flying for the coast in fear of my life.

At night Mirenburg is both peaceful and mysterious: a perfect mistress. Her shadows do not seem dangerous and her lights do not reveal any ugliness; her desperate aspects are contained; she is tranquil. She is an intelligent city, willing to accept novelty. She is secure and self-possessed. The secret police of three empires conspire in her, observe each other, play peculiar games of intrigue, and she permits it, a tolerant stepmother; the political exiles make their speeches, publish their broadsheets; she does not discourage them so long as her own peace is not disturbed. In the white-and-brown café on the corner of Kanalstrasse and Kaspergasse, The Café Slavia, the young nationalists have a guest. He is Rakanaspya, an anarchist of uncertain origin; a friend of Kropotkin and Bakunin.

Many believe him to be well-connected in aristocratic circles. Tonight he speaks passionately against privilege, against nationalism, and debates with the youths the virtues of internationalism, mutuality and self-reliance, while in other parts of the café two spies, in the employ of Austria-Hungary and Russia respectively, take surreptitious notes. They are commissioned to report on all agitators. Rakanaspya wears a greatcoat with a fur collar, a bearskin cap; one hand rests on a silver cane. The other hand lifts glasses of brandy to his lips. His voice is unusually thick and husky and is not natural; it was obtained in a duel when his palate was shot away. His imperial hides most of the scar on the left side of his face. He chain-smokes papyrosi so that his fingers, moustache and teeth are stained as yellow as the abandoned tubes which litter his surroundings wherever he stops for more than half an hour. They are made for him by an old Russian woman who works for the British Tobacco Company at No. 11 Kanalstrasse. His thin face is pinched and drawn, he has keen, unquiet eyes behind large round glasses and his emaciated, nervous frame speaks of despairing poverty assuaged by fanaticism, perhaps an inheritance from his days in Siberia. Yet when he smiles his face becomes suddenly innocent; it is sympathetic. He speaks several languages fluently and is well read in every European literature. As a go-between for the émigrés and the Wäldenstein authorities he has become almost an official representative. He manages to conciliate both sides (who trust him). He keeps even the fiercest Bohemian or Russian expatriate from expulsion, in spite of constant pressure on the authorities. Austria in particular would welcome any excuse to go to war with Wäldenstein; but she will not risk war with Russia, Germany or both. Wäldenstein lies balanced between the spheres of these empires, as a small planet might be supported by the opposing gravitation of larger ones, and it is thought to be in nobody's interest to disturb that balance. Rakanaspya has momentarily forgotten his politics. Someone has mentioned Odessa, his home. 'I sometimes feel,' he says, 'as if I am the emissary from one magic city to another.' As he becomes drunk Rakanaspya begins to talk of the sea, catching bullheads off the Odessa rocks as a boy, sailing in flat-bottomed boats around the lighthouse, of the foreign vessels lying at anchor on a turquoise ocean, the sailors in the harbour taverns. Many by now know Rakanaspya himself has never been, and probably never will go, to sea; he is fascinated and comforted by the romance of it. His face becomes completely human only when the conversation is turned to salt water. He never claims experience of sailing, yet believes himself an authority on naval matters and the ways of the world's great ports. The spies are puzzled by this turn in the conversation, wondering at the significance of it. Rakanaspya describes Odessa for his listeners, the smell of the spices in the harbours, the little tramp steamers which ply the Black Sea, the great military ships. Alexandra, wrapped in a coat which hides the extravagant gown I bought her this afternoon, whispers that she finds Rakanaspya intriguing and boring at the same time. 'Are all men so full of talk? Such general stuff?' We slip away from The Café Slavia. She seems angry Rakanaspya did not notice her. We walk beside the river. Men in donkey jackets stand and smoke their pipes, talking in small groups, glancing at us as we pass. Two Customs officials stroll by. They wear dark blue uniforms, their coats belted at the waist and supporting swords; both have large, carefully grown moustaches and their caps are at identical angles on their round heads. Papadakis frets over me. He believes I am feverish. He is becoming too insistent. I indicate the paper. 'I am writing again,' I tell him. 'Is that not a sign of my spiritual and physical recovery?' He goes mumbling from the room. He must forever be simplifying experience. He irritates me. I run my thumbnail down the flesh of her back. She gasps and clutches at bedding but insists I do not stop. I suppose men can learn from women that capacity to make a positive virtue of pain and despair. Women frequently through self-deception and lack of power believe that pain and desperation have meaning in themselves. I tell her she should always seek pleasure and optimism; to seek pain as a form of salvation is to destroy oneself. When we suffer the pain of solitude (as I have done in prison, for instance, or in exile) we are fools if we regard this state as preferable to the ordinary vicissitudes of the world, though we can make of solitude a habit of self-reliance which when needed can stand us in good stead. Pain offers us certain kinds of knowledge which enable us to live in greater harmony with our complex world. An animal which seeks out pain, however, is a mad animal, just as a hermit, who will avoid it, is a mad animal. She is asleep. I rise and go to the window and part the curtains. The square is quiet. I regret, as I smoke a cigarette, I shall not be able to attend the reception being given tomorrow at the Palace.

I met the amiable Prince Damian von Badehoff-Krasny only once, three years ago at a concert given in Munich by his cousin Otto, an old friend from my early years at the Academy. The Badehoff-Krasny family are of Slavonic as well as Teutonic ancestry and came originally from the Ukraine. The province of Wäldenstein was an inheritance, achieved through marriage, and in the seventeenth century, when the family had fallen on hard times and everything else was sold or stolen from them by a variety of warring monarchs, the people asked the Prince's ancestor, who was still an Elector of the Holy Roman Empire, to become their ruler. The family maintained its independence of Germany, Russia and the Hapsburg Empire partly by chance and partly through clever diplomacy, by playing one faction against another and by continuing to marry well. Their intellectual and artistic interests had made them at some time patrons to almost every famous painter, composer and writer in Europe. They had in their possession a thousand mementoes of the scholars and actors who had sampled their hospitality. Indeed, my own little Alexandra is a cousin twice removed of the present Prince. I believe her interest in me was aroused when I mentioned at our first meeting, during the dinner party given by Count Freddy Eulenberg just after my arrival in the city, that I had published one or two small volumes of verse and reminiscence. There is a traditional rivalry in her family for the patronage of any academic or artistic lion, however small and provincial, and I think even Alexandra saw me as something of a kitten, but as the only catch of the season not wholly demeaning. This is not, of course, the chief quality which makes me attractive in her eyes. I have been the subject of gossip both in Mirenburg and in Munich and have acquired that sort of exaggerated reputation which so fascinates young women and so greatly facilitates their seduction. Alexandra speaks of her uncle with considerable affection and some impatience (plainly imitated from her elders), telling me that he lives with his head in the clouds, refusing to be alarmed either by Bismarckian ambition or Austro-Hungarian arrogance, convinced that the likes of Holzhammer mean no great harm and are as content as himself merely to play at politics. I know that soon there must be a scandal; our deception can last only a few more days, but I refuse to confront the problem, as does she. Papadakis hovers at my shoulder. Alexandra breathes deeply. I tell Papadakis to leave me alone. The door closes. The inkwell is crystal. It reflects the light from the window. It is quieter today. The political meeting has dissipated everyone's energy.

Is Wäldenstein, I wonder, too complacent as my cousin Thomas suggests? Should she not defend herself better? I think about that mixture of sentimentality, romance and self-deception which sustains a nation in its myths and which enables it to act in its own immediate self-interest. We are most of us a characteristic segment of the nations from which we spring and it can almost be said we measure our individuality by the degree to which we free ourselves from our inherited prejudices. Many of us talk about it; but talk, I think, is not enough. Words and actions must coincide. Wäldenstein's myth is that because she has for so long been free she can never be enslaved. I turn to look at my Alexandra, who has captured me so thoroughly. I have been swayed by lust before. I have taken considerable risks to fulfil it. But now I am not sure that I am any longer moved by simple lust. It is desire which moves me and I do not understand the origin or the nature of that desire, even though I am obsessed by it.

I deny all reality in order to maintain it; I am even prepared, I know, to relinquish lust, to ignore affection, normal companionship. I feel contempt for the ordinary yet I know this state of mind is self-destructive. Such desire is incapable of ever being satisfied. I believe I have aroused the same terrible energies in Alexandra. With it comes a fierce carelessness which considers no-one: be it myself or the object of my desire. There is only the present, here in Mirenburg. I erase the past; I refuse the future. I tear off my robe and stretch my naked body against hers, turning her towards me and kissing her startled, still-sleeping mouth. I remember being sent on a ludicrous errand by my sister who wished her brother-in-law to put an end to an unsuitable courtship. He had received me in his study. He was not defiant, yet his attention had hardly been on me at all. He was a good-looking man of the conventional, military sort. 'I see her three times a week,' he had told me. 'She gives me no more and no less. My life is ruled by this routine. I let nothing interfere with it. I live in terror that it will be broken. I will go to any lengths to sustain it. She has a husband, you see. He is old but she feels affection for him. Her consideration of his sensitivities drives her to elaborate strategies in her deception of him, even though he acquiesces and even encourages her in her affair with me, whom he has never met. This consideration somehow gives dignity to a life which on the surface is sordid enough. He offers her security. In return she allows him to live in the ambience of her wonderful sensuality. It seems enough for both. She will not, naturally, permit me to possess her completely, but she is equally considerate of me. She rarely fails to keep an appointment. When she does I am in agony until she communicates with me. She will never leave him. So long as she acknowledges his feelings and thinks of his well-being he is content. She is a wonderful creature. She would not harm either of us.'

'And you can stand this stasis?' I had asked.

'It is the best I can hope for,' he had said. A bell had rung then. He had risen. 'If you wish to call on Friday, I shall be able to see you again.' He walked sadly with me to the landing and watched as I descended the stairs. 'Please give my warmest regards to your sister and tell her how much I appreciate her thoughtfulness.'

There is an evening service at the Cathedral. I leave a note for Alexandra and walk the long cobbled way, up the hill, to listen to the music. I cannot argue with Alexandra. She robs me of logic. When last in Mirenburg I had described to a young lady, with whom I had been having an affair, my state of mind. How, amongst other things, I had been confused for several years, since my wife had left me for a ship's officer in Friedrikshaven only three months after we were married, about whether or not I should marry again. The young lady had smiled: 'You do not think I wish to marry you?' I said that I had wondered. 'But I assure you…' She had begun to laugh. She had pretended that her laughter was uncontrollable. I had waited until she had finished. 'There is no question,' she had said.

'Excellent.' I had stood up, wondering at that time why she should have denied what had evidently passed through her mind and why I had not the courage to make a direct proposal, for I had been in the mood to do it. That evening, having disappointed myself so thoroughly, I had taken a cab to Frau Schmetterling's and requested a room and a girl – my habit, twice a week, for nearly a year. This, however, had been a third visit in the week and caused Frau Schmetterling some amusement. As I had taken the key from her hand I marvelled at my ability, without intention, to make women laugh. I had seen no reason to suspect that I was held in contempt by them or even that I was unpopular with them, yet I could not fathom how I aroused their humour.

Why do women seem to triumph so often in men's misery, even when they love them? Again I find myself considering the nature of power and of love. Only a few weeks after my failure to propose to the young lady I had occasion to inform another that I no longer wished to see her. 'But I love you,' she had said, 'with all my heart and soul. I will love you for ever. I wish to be yours, whatever you want me to be. I want to help you in any way that I can.' And within a week (I think it was six days) she had fallen in love with an official in the Revenue Service to whom she was, by all accounts, a loyal and faithful companion. The trees thicken as one nears the Cathedral. It is almost rural. There are wild flowers amongst the grass. In the spring and summer cherry- and apple-trees blossom here. I mount the uneven pavements. The spires of the Cathedral are high above my head. The choir is singing from within: *Gospodi pomiluj ny – Lord have mercy upon us*. I turn and go back. There is other music to be heard, from the cafés, from the street performers. I pause on the corner of Falfnersallee. The last No. 15 tram is on its way to the terminus in Radoskya. I have known Mirenburg in all her seasons, but this is the one I have always favoured. I pass by the statues of Wäldenstein's great men and women. I find myself craving the famous borscht to be found in the Mladota district. It is made with beets and ham bones, in the traditional way, but to it is added a dash of a particular Hungarian Tokay which for some reason affects the palate and makes it sing. I remember Alexandra telling me it even makes her ears tingle. It is delicious: a drug. I decide to return to the hotel, to rouse her and ask if she will join me in a plate. As I turn into Mirozhny Square a group of beggars comes by. I give them all the coppers I have. They are returning to the Schlaff estate, to the old fever hospital and desolate graveyards. Only the railway track brings any kind of life to that area. It is a goods line. Not even local trains to the northern suburbs and outlying villages take passengers through. This estate is all that is left of the Schlaff family lands. The family has lived exclusively in Paris and Berlin for three generations but refuses to lease the estate to anyone who would make use of it. Thus houses, mills, churches and workshops are occupied only by the homeless and the lawless. Orphans and old men climb amongst the ruins and the neglected graves and more respectable citizens pay to have their garbage and other embarrassments they wish to discard transported there. Strange fires burn in this contradictory wasteland; the flames are unhealthy in colour and mysterious in shape. It is Mirenburg's shame. 'Only a little shame, compared to most,' an ex-Mayor of Mirenburg will later insist to me. I will be bound to agree with him. In daytime even the Schlaff estate looks picturesque, overgrown as it is with wild flowers, but at night it must be sought to be seen. It is almost dawn. I hurry back to Alexandra, suddenly afraid she will awake and leave because I am not there to help her maintain our dream.

It was during a particularly drunken expedition to the Schlaff that I had met Caroline Vacarescu, the Hungarian adventuress, who also currently stays at the Hotel Liverpool and whom I pass in the lobby as I make my hasty ascent to our suite. If Alexandra wakes, realises her predicament and decides to go I shall be unable to reclaim her. She might, of course, have similar fears, but if so she does not exhibit them. Caroline Vacarescu smiles at me. She is doubtless keeping an appointment with Count Mueller, her lover. A wonderful mixture of Magyar beauty and English delicacy, her furs and silks exotically scented, she is the illegitimate daughter of an English duke and a Hungarian aristocrat, born in Pesth. Her father was attached to the Foreign Office, her mother, until her pregnancy, was a lady-in-waiting to the Princess. She received a superb education in Vienna, England and Switzerland and at the age of eighteen married Christoff Béraud, the financier. When Béraud crashed as a result of the Zimmerman scandal of 1889, he shot himself, leaving his wife penniless and having to seek the protection of the man who was already her lover, Hans von Arnim, the successful pianist. Unable to be seen with von Arnim in public, Madame Vacarescu grew bored and eventually left Berlin for

Danzig with Count Mueller, who describes his occupation as 'freelance diplomat' but who is known as 'the Messenger Boy of Europe', a spy, an arms dealer and a blackmailer. Mueller will die this year and it will be rumoured that Caroline Vacarescu has rid herself of a man who had in a dozen ways compromised and humiliated her. She is a warm-hearted, rather detached woman; a very cold lover with me. Alexandra is awake and my terrors vanish; she complains breakfast is late. Perhaps it is my own lack of resolve I mistakenly bestow upon her. The breakfast comes and goes. As we make love I have an intense vision of that massive stone Cathedral; her flesh contrasts with the carved granite; such opposites and yet so similar in their effect upon the hand and eye. It occurs to me that there may be fewer better pleasures than to make love in the St-Maria-and-St-Maria with the light from the stained glass falling on our bodies as I pass my fingers from youthful flesh to ancient stone while the organ plays some favourite piece of music. And would it be blasphemy? Most would see it as that. But I would thank God for all His gifts and pray more joyfully than anyone had ever prayed before. The violence of Alexandra's passion had almost frightened me at first; now it becomes exhilarating, infectious and I respond in kind. Sometimes, inexplicably, she becomes nervous of me. I ignore her fear, and press ahead until she has again forgotten everything but her lust. But I must be forever controlling, guarding against depressions, against commonalities which threaten our idyll. I do not always reckon with the power of Alexandra's determination. When they decided to go to Rome her parents had left her in the charge of her aunt, who in turn put her in the care of an old housekeeper. She had already begun to dream, to prepare herself for adventures which, inspired by the reading of certain French novels, she had yearned to experience for several years. I still do not know whether she sought me out for her instruction or whether she instructs me. I was unable, in spite of sane reservations, to master my lust. I swiftly gave myself up to her. I do not know how long it has been, but I know that I did not believe for more than a few days that I was fully in control of her as I began that process of subtle debauchery she so deeply desired and which, of course, she also feared, as the laudanum-taker fears the drug which is friend and enemy in one. That she will eventually resist any dependency upon me and break my heart will be a tribute to her determination and a confirmation, finally, of my judgement that I had not only met my match but been beaten at a game I had played half-consciously for years. Alexandra grunts and pants; her eyes are burnished copper. I am familiar, as are most men, with the woman who will translate her own will to power through a male medium, but Alexandra is either more subtle or more naïve in her attempts to affect her world. This is partly what fascinates me. It has been several years since any woman obsessed me; now I am surely caught. Eros usurps Bacchus. I rise on that dark euphoria which appears to bring objectivity but in fact produces nothing save confusion, uncontrollable misery and eventual collapse. Papadakis steps out of the shadows with a rattling tray. I can only admit now that I gave myself up to Eros deliberately, in the belief it does a man or woman good to make such fools of themselves occasionally; there are few risks much wilder and few which make us so much wiser, should we survive them. Papadakis stretches out his emaciated arms. I smell boiled fish. 'It will do you good,' he says in his half-humorous, half-insinuating voice; a voice once calculated during his own, brief, Golden Age to rob the weak of any volition they might possess; but it had been the single weapon in his arsenal; he had used up all his emotional capital by the time he was forty. He speaks of the past as if it were a personal God which came to betray him. 'They ruined me,' he sometimes says. In his more egocentric moments he claims deliberately to have ruined himself. Even as we fall into the abyss, we men must explain how the descent was predicted and calculated. When the world refuses to be handled by us, we turn to women. And women, for purposes of their own, usually temporary, help us pretend to a power permitted, in reality, only to the securest of tyrants. Papadakis has become a wizened satyr, a monument to misspent juices, keeping me alive from motives of dimly perceived self-interest. I tell him to leave the tray, to bring me white wine. He refuses. He tells me it is not good for me. He is scowling. Perhaps he senses he no longer has any power over me. Alexandra begins to ask me lascivious questions about my other women. I tell her romantically there is none but her and she seems disappointed.

The heat of her saliva is on my penis; the soft lips close, the teeth touch the skin; her head moves slowly up and down and the future is once more successfully banished. Death does not exist. Playing with her clitoris and wiping sperm from her cheek she asks me again about other women. I am anxious to keep her curiosity. I begin to invent stories for her. I tell her of adventures involving several ladies at a time. She says unexpectedly: 'Would you like me to do that for you?' I am interrupted. 'What?'

'Sleep with other women,' she says. 'With you?' I hesitate. 'Have you slept with girls before?' She smiles. 'With schoolfriends, certainly. We have all done it. Most of us. I love female bodies. They are so beautiful. Beautiful in a different way.' She touches my penis which is erect again. I laugh. 'Where,' she says, 'can we find another lady?' I have the solution. Papadakis is crooning to himself in the corner near the wardrobe. He is doing something with a screwdriver. He is not in good temper. 'Have you taken your pills?' I ask, mocking him. He becomes furious. 'You should see the doctor,' he tells me. 'I cannot be responsible.'

Caroline Vacarescu boasted to me once that she had slept with five reigning monarchs and thirteen heirs apparent, four of them women. The Age of Kings appears to have ended in an orgy of royal lust. The Dictators, according to established pattern, seem extraordinarily celibate in comparison, perhaps because they are not so casually acquainted with power. But with Caroline it was a question of service, not pleasure. She was adding to Count Mueller's secret fortune. We are looking for some cigars for me. Walking up Koenigstrasse in bright sunlight we see an old woman leaning against a shop window full of soap and popular potions. She has a half-eaten cake in one hand and seems drunk. Her clothing is predominantly dark brown. It does not fit her properly. Her left foot is bandaged to just above the ankle. She tugs up her skirt and pees on the paving stones. Her collection of bundles lies to one side of her and the urine spreads slowly towards it. Nearby a street-sweeper brushes at the gutter with polite patience, as if waiting to clean the pavement as soon as she has finished. People pass her without stopping, without looking, although they do not appear to be disgusted or afraid. 'There is nothing we can do,' says Alexandra, pulling at me. The sun shines on white roofs and is reflected in elegant windows.

There is a great deal of traffic in Koenigstrasse today; carriages and carts of all sorts. The street smells like a farm. Papadakis refuses to tell me when he will return. He closes the door with unusual force. I am content. A procession of swaggering lancers, jangling metal and bobbing gold braid, trots by on the other side. 'There are so many soldiers about,' says Alexandra. 'Do you know why?' I do not. 'It could be something to do with the Armaments Bill,' I tell her. The Bill has passed through Parliament. The Prince is expected to sign it today. Alexandra takes a cab for Nussbaum-hof to see if her parents have written to say when they are returning from Rome. My earlier fears of losing her have disappeared because we are about to embark on another intrigue; she has set her mind on it. How much of her am I destroying, or allowing her to destroy of herself? I relax with a glass of Alsatian beer and some Cambozola at an outside table of the Café Internationale on the corner of Falfnersallee facing the Radota Bridge and the river. The air is unusually warm: everywhere I look I see beauty, reassurance. If Vienna is gay, then Mirenburg is happy; a sane city whose character may be infinitely explored, and yet she has no real secrets; even her vices are admitted and the subject of common knowledge.

Bismarck says Mirenburg is a feminine city and a natural bride for masculine Berlin. He once said that a marriage with Vienna would be a perversion of everything that was natural. My brother knew Bismarck quite well. Apparently the great Chancellor had a habit of describing nations in terms of their sexual characteristics; he loved France, for instance: 'She challenges us expecting to be conquered, then complains she is a victim, that we have robbed her of her honour. What other country would give herself up so completely to a Corsican adventurer, offering him her liberty, her lifeblood, her fortune again and again, and then continue to love him, even when he has so patently abused and ruined her?' Now Bismarck is dying, caustic and sometimes bitter when he considers the actions of his successors or the policies of his Austrian counterpart, the Graf Kazimierz Badeni, who possesses much of Bismarck's ruthlessness and little of his intelligence. The balance of power is threatened. A detachment of flying artillery makes the bridge noisy with its showy hoofs and iron-shod wheels. The sun bursts upon the bouncing metal of the new Škoda field guns: perhaps this is another deliberate display.

I am resentful of their intrusion into my peace of mind. At the next table a German tourist laughs and points towards the artillery as it turns into Kanalstrasse. His wife looks blank. 'See,' he says, 'the Wäldenstein Army!' He glances at me for appreciation. I smile and ask the waiter for a *Mirenburg Zeitung*. He brings me the newspaper and I give him fifty pfennigs, telling him to keep the change. The editorial sings of the greater prosperity the Armaments Bill will bring to the country. There is news of Count Holzhammer. He seems to have made some progress with his Austrian allies. There is a discussion of preparations being made for next year's large Exhibition, which will represent every nation in the civilised world; again, prosperity is the leitmotif. I seek out the stock-market reports and am reassured. There is an article by a military correspondent on the relative merits of buying arms from foreign sources or of setting up factories at home. I am astonished by prices given for the Krupp cannon and its ammunition: a hint of the significance of the new Bill, which could involve a considerable amount of taxation. Wäldenstein's landowners cannot be pleased at the prospect. Yet the only alternative appears to be in treaties, 'closer union' with one of the Great Powers and a consequent loss of independence. The British have uprisings in India. I fold the newspaper and put it under my beer glass. Alexandra joins me. She is flushed. She is smiling. She has changed her clothes again. 'They will not be back for ages. I've written. And no-one suspects anything. I was full of Marya and our punting expeditions!'

I congratulate her on the cleverness of her deception. Papadakis has returned. I hear him pushing furniture about in the next room. With a rustle of that seductive costume she seats herself beside me and whispering asks me if I have made arrangements to visit Rosenstrasse. I have sent a note to Frau Schmetterling. We shall be expected. In his famous *Pamety* – his memoirs – Benes Milovsky recalls a stream running the length of Rosenstrasse. It had its source in the hills beyond the walls and it fed into the Rätt. This stream became subterranean by the middle of the century. It forms the basis for a sophisticated modern sewage system and can still be heard running beneath the Rosenstrasse cobbles.

In the afternoon we visit the Museum of Antiquities, the concrete traces of fifteen hundred years of history. A diorama represents Wäldenstein's primitive settlers, the Svitavian tribesmen who built their camps in the great valley of the Rätt, between four ranges of mountains, fighting off the Teutonic invaders when they swept in during the ninth and tenth centuries. No Roman ever set foot in any settlement along the Upper Rätt. The diorama gives a lie to the sentimental nationalists. The present descendants of those tribes are no more 'true Slavs' than they are 'true Aryans'; the blood has mingled thoroughly to produce the Wäldensteiner. But blood these days has become another word for ambition, a justification of greed, a rationalisation of those frustrated in their political needs, an excuse for terrible murder, a counter-balance to the Christianity we all profess to cherish and which certainly checks us in any honest, pagan rapacity we still possess. Men need myths to set against myths, it seems. They need the precedent of 'blood' or their consciences could tell them they are ineffectual, ruthless, wicked, and thus deny them what they want. A woman rarely seeks such complicated excuses; the means by which she disguises her desires usually take quite a different form. They say women substitute sentimentality for principle, that a woman's logic is entirely based upon her own immediate physical and emotional needs; yet men display similar logic, couched in terms of the highest ideals, and trap themselves quite as thoroughly when their actions diverge significantly from their words. Alexandra speaks softly of the wonderful past. She leans on my arm. Her body seems to wish to become absorbed in mine. Antiquity is a thing of broken statues and rusty iron. I am quickly bored with it. We descend the wide steps of the museum and look across the city at the magnificent Greek church. Although primarily a Protestant city, Mirenburg represents many other religions within her walls; one would not be surprised to see a mosque here. I go with relief to the nearby Municipal Art Gallery. Here are paintings by all the masters, by new painters who take such an optimistic delight in form and light for its own sake. I am soon restored and my spirits lift. Alexandra examines paintings of women, showing me the figures she finds attractive and those which do not please her, and I know she is deliberately setting the scene for this evening. I continue to be astonished by her, by the violence of her determination to experience every fantasy she has imagined. It is almost inconceivable she will not have destroyed herself, or at very least her capacity for sensation and emotion, by the time she is twenty. And yet I still cannot determine which of us exploits the other, though I know of course what the world would decide. As we drive back to the hotel through the haze of twilight I see the notices advertising evening newspapers. Count Holzhammer, apparently, has returned to Wäldenstein. The importance of this news escapes me. Papadakis enters the room. I dismiss him impatiently. In the hotel we begin to prepare ourselves for sophisticated debauchery. My body has never felt more thoroughly alive. I almost gasp as the silk of my shirt touches my skin. Both of us seem to glow with power as we leave the Hotel Liverpool in a cab and drive towards the West Bank. Rosenstrasse is near the river across from the Moravian Precinct, on the very fringe of the respectable Jewish Quarter near the Botanical Gardens, and only a couple of streets up from the Niersteiner Quay with its trees and awnings and little cafés, between two streets which lead down to the quay, Rauchgasse and Papensgasse. In Papensgasse an archway is the only means of reaching

Rosenstrasse, once a private street owned by a religious order. The monastery still occupies a site here. From Rauchgasse one enters through a narrow gap between two tall, seventeenth-century houses. There is a single gas-lamp at either end of Rosenstrasse's cobbled surface. The plane trees and flowering chestnuts give an air of isolation, of seclusion to what is an ideal setting for Frau Schmetterling's brothel. It is in some ways more like a country courtyard, even a garden, than an ordinary city street. The high houses make it seem even narrower than it is. These are primarily eighteenth-century terraces, apparently the residences of moderately well-to-do tradespeople. On the eastern side is the oldest building, single-storeyed, roofed in red slate, with no outward-facing windows at all and to one side massive double doors set in a Gothic arch. The doors are black wood bound in dark iron; they open directly into the cloisters of the disused monastery. Ivy grows over the roof and up the walls of the terraces from the unseen garden. Opposite the monastery is a short row of shops: a bookbinder's, an artists' colourman, a seller of prints and old books. Dominating these is a mansion, No. 10 Rosenstrasse. It is well-kept, impressive; the town house of a wealthy family until the middle years of the century. The windows at the front are always covered from the inside by heavy curtains or from the outside by green wooden shutters. It is a big, square, solid building, as reassuring as the street itself. Opposite there is a terrace, some more small shops and the entrance to a large apartment house occupied mostly by students. As the sun sets Rosenstrasse fills out with soft shadows. The lamplighter comes through the archway from Papensgasse and ignites the gas, then continues on his business down Rauchgasse towards the river. In the warm September night Mirenburg grows drowsy.

At No. 10 Rosenstrasse shutters are being opened and curtains are being closed, as if the house prepares for guests. Gentle voices can be heard and some laughter. To many travellers Mirenburg is a synonym for Europe's most famous brothel, whose customers speak of it with unqualified affection and respect. Gentlemen will make a diversion of hundreds of miles to spend an evening here. There are women too who will do the same and the friendship they feel for Frau Schmetterling is apparently reciprocated by the madam whose discretion and tact are a byword, as is the range and breadth of her services. The brothel has been described as Mirenburg's greatest treasure. It has become an institution. Those who live near it are almost proud to be associated with it and the few complaints Frau Schmetterling receives are dealt with intelligently and with considerable charm. Her place threatens only those who are patently prone to such threats. It is protected by every authority and tolerated by the Church; important political assignations frequently occur here: one can only enter the doors if one is armed with the most impressive bona fides. Papadakis tidies the sheets. 'You are too thin,' he says. 'You are wasting yourself.' I ignore him. Alexandra and I step out of our cab in Rauchgasse and pass between the tall white houses into Rosenstrasse. A soft, sultry wind blows through Mirenburg's baroque façades; she seems singularly quiescent. Alexandra's breast rises and falls and her little hand tightens on my arm. We mount the steps of No. 10. Her eyes have a distant, drowsy look, inturned; at once innocent and secretive. At the end of my bed Papadakis coughs and makes some banal remark. I think he is trying to joke. I shout at him to leave. I lift my arm and ring the bell of Frau Schmetterling's door. It opens. I press Alexandra through and pause, taking a grip on myself. My legs are trembling slightly. The door closes behind us. Trudi, a pretty young woman, perhaps an idiot, with blonde hair and vacant blue eyes, takes our street clothes from us. She curtseys. She is wearing peasant costume. There is distant music. The small lobby is furnished in discreet crystal, with hangings of heavy wine-coloured velvet, some flowering plants on polished wood, a mirror in a modern 'Liberty' frame, and several paintings, chiefly portraits of the last French emperor. The air is heavy with the scent of roses and hyacinths.

Now Alexandra holds back a little, a wary cat. I smile down at her as we wait to be received. She smiles in response, wetting her lips with the tip of her red tongue. Mirenburg has begun to sleep a deeper than usual sleep. Even her bells, when they mark off the hours, seem muffled and distant. A moon rises to touch the purity of her architecture so that it gleams like bone. The waters of the river hardly move. Alexandra makes a small sound in her throat, then looks at me with the adoring expression of a schoolgirl about to have her deepest dreams fulfilled. I steady myself against her violence and find myself, in turn, hesitating. I have a momentary desire to wrench open the door and flee Rosenstrasse, leave Mirenburg behind me, return to the bland formality of Berlin. But then Frau Schmetterling, that dignified matriarch, appears in the lobby and I bow, extending a hand towards her even as a small, swiftly disguised frown crosses her face. Perhaps she has noticed my hand shaking. She looks towards Alexandra.

'Dear Ricky,' she says, and takes a key from her delicate pocket. 'Everything you desire is ready for you. You know the blue door, of course.' She puts the key into my hand. 'Good evening,' she says to Alexandra.

We climb the dark red stairs, our fingers on the bannister's gilded wood. 'She doesn't like me,' whispers Alexandra. 'She doesn't know you,' I reply. We reach the empty landing and walk on soft carpet towards the blue door. The pen is heavy in my hand; suddenly the paper hurts me when I touch it. Papadakis comes back to busy himself with pillows and I do not resist him. He puts a glass to my lips. I swallow. Mirenburg enjoys her last tranquil night; she fades. For the moment I let her leave me. I can now recall her at any time I choose.

Chapter Two
The Brothel

THE BROTHEL IN Rosenstrasse has the ambience of an integrated nation, hermetic, microcosmic. It is easy, once within, to believe the place possessed of an infinity of rooms and passages, all isolated from that other world outside. Doubtless Frau Schmetterling creates this impression deliberately, with detailed thoroughness. Reminded of childhood security and delicious mystery, the explorer discovers his cares disappearing, together with any adult lessons of morality or self-restraint. Here he may not only fulfil his desires, but he need feel no guilt or concern for doing so: the brothel can be departed from and visited again at will. Money is all he needs. Here there are anodynes for any kind of wound, there are no sharp voices, no pointing fingers, no complicated emotional involvements. Here a man (and occasionally a woman) may feel himself to be what he most wishes to be. Nietzsche's socially destructive admonitions can be safely followed in this enclosure. The ego is allowed full rein. Yet publicly everyone is discreetly polite and compliant; bad manners are frowned upon and must never be displayed in the salon. A maternal and firm-minded woman, neat and plump, Frau Schmetterling runs her brothel with the skill of the captain of a luxury ship. Most of her working day is spent in her headquarters, her elaborately equipped kitchen. This is territory generally forbidden to clients but is a haven for her charges. The kitchen is where Frau Schmetterling interviews new girls and where every day she discusses menus with Ulric, her cook. The room is dominated by a massive oak dresser which stretches from floor to ceiling and displays brightly decorated plates of outstanding quality from every country in Europe; her collection. What it represents to her nobody knows but she is unquestionably in love with it. She will allow no-one else to handle it or even polish the carved surfaces of the wooden shelves. Shrewd in all other matters, she is easily flattered through her china and the taste she displays in it. She sits in a peasant rocking chair to one side of the dresser so that she can observe both the long, clean table and her collection. Her servants, such as the simple-minded Trudi (whom Frau Schmetterling personally dresses), make tea, coffee and chocolate for the women as they come and go. Very occasionally Frau Schmetterling will entertain two or three of her special girls here for dinner. Through the barred windows of the kitchen is her garden which she cares for almost as jealously as her china, though she allows 'Mister' to do some of the work. 'Mister' is the enfeebled, grey-haired gentleman with the face of a boy whom she will sometimes describe as her 'protector'. He lives at the top of the house and dotes on her, showing temper only if he feels she has been threatened or insulted. He is in charge of Elvira, the madam's little daughter (who goes to the Lutheran school in nearby Kasernestrasse) when she visits the brothel on Sunday afternoons. Elvira is ten, a demure, dark-eyed creature, and has no idea of the madam's business. If asked, she would say that it had something to do with ladies sewing things, for on Sundays the girls usually gather in the big kitchen after lunch to do their mending. She is, as any child would be, very popular with her mother's charges. 'Mister' must go every day to the house where Elvira is boarded and check that she is properly cared for and has everything she needs. In the brothel he supervises the cleanliness of the rooms; he frequently goes shopping for the girls; he makes sure that fresh flowers are permanently in evidence, that the paint of the shutters and doors is impeccable; that Frau Schmetterling's black chow dogs are walked and fed twice a day. These dogs are not popular with every customer, most of whom have at some time tried to pet and show a friendly interest in them. They seem surly beasts and have been known to nip the odd client. I have always fed them with paté and little pieces of liver and have consequently I believe won their friendship. Frau Schmetterling will often remark to me how much Pouf-Pouf and Mimi love their gentlemen and will add that she judges people very much by how the dogs take to them. This anthropomorphic fiction surrounding pets is a common one of course with many women and it is within their power quite unconsciously to give signals to their animals as to whether they like or dislike a particular person. Therefore I have never really known if I have become popular entirely by means of bribery or whether, for uncertain reasons of her own, Frau Schmetterling finds me attractive. I think I was an early customer of this particular establishment. My father sent me here as a boy to be instructed, so I am often 'her' Ricky and she shows a mother's interest in my career. She possesses signed copies of my little books and seems quite proud of them.

Frau Schmetterling is Jewish. Nobody knows her real name. She is well-educated. She is fastidious in her habits, always wearing simple but beautifully cut old-fashioned dresses trimmed with lace, and she treats 'Mister' with affectionate formality, a queen to her consort. Their mutual respect for each other is touching. Because of her tendency to plumpness, her comfortable homeliness, it is difficult to guess her age, but I believe she must be close to fifty. She speaks several languages very well, and her native tongue seems to be a Russian dialect, suggesting that she was born in Byelorussia or perhaps Poland. 'My girls,' she says, 'are ladies. I expect them to behave accordingly and to be properly treated. In private with a client they may choose to be whatever they and the client wish them to be but at all other times they must behave with tact and discretion.' The girls, whether on duty or off, are perfectly costumed. Clients are expected to wear evening dress. I myself am clothed as carefully as if I were attending a formal dinner at the Embassy. Alexandra has on rose silk and a deep green cape. I open the blue door for her and follow her in. Our first impression is of subtle perfume, dark polished wood, mirrors and rust-coloured drapery. The room is lit by a single ornamental lamp. From another part of the brothel comes the faint sound of barking. Everywhere is luxury. Everything is soft or heavy or dark and the young woman who waits on the coverlet of the four-poster seems small and delicate in contrast. She is apparently relaxed and rather delighted by the adventure. 'M'sieu.' She rises and walks up to Alexandra, kissing her prettily on both cheeks. 'Are you French?' I ask. I go from habit to the sideboard and pour absinthe for all three of us. The lady shrugs as if to say that it is for me to decide her nationality. 'What's your name, mademoiselle?'

'It is Thérèse.' She has a Berlin accent. Her attention is on Alexandra. 'You are very pretty. And young.'

'This is Alexandra.'

Thérèse is about twenty, with straight black hair drawn back from her oval face. She has light blue eyes. Her skin is pink and her hands are long. In her white undergarments, which are trimmed with peach-coloured lace, her figure is fuller than Alexandra's and tends to puppy-fat. She has a large nose, prominent red lips, and a self-contained way of holding herself. She has small pointed breasts. I stipulated the colouring of the girl and the size of her breasts in my note to Frau Schmetterling. In this familiar ambience I become relaxed and my mood seems to be transmitting itself to Alexandra, who remains, however, a trifle ill at ease and begins to move around the room looking at pictures and ornaments. Thérèse hides her amusement. All three shadows are thrown onto the large autumnal flowers of the wallpaper. Alexandra is a little taller than Thérèse. Old Papadakis is scowling at me. 'What is it?' I ask him. 'You should let me fetch the doctor,' he says. 'You are not in your right mind. You are weak. You should rest. You are overtaxing yourself.' Is he trying to persuade me to dependency upon him? He cannot be genuinely concerned. I do not employ him for that. 'Go to the village,' I tell him. 'Get me something with cocaine in it.' He mutters in Greek. 'The doctor will give me morphine,' I say. 'It will dull my brain. I need my wits. Can't you see I'm doing something worthwhile again?' I hold up the pages. 'These are my memoirs. You are mentioned in them. You should be pleased.' He comes forward as if to see what I have written. I close the cover. 'Not yet. They will be published when I am dead. Perhaps when you are dead, too.' Thérèse says to Alexandra: 'Is this the first time you have been here?'

'Yes,' says Alexandra. 'And you? How long have you worked here?'

'Two years this Christmas,' says Thérèse. 'I was an artists' model in Prague, for paintings as well as photographs. Will this be your first time?'

'With a lady?' says Alexandra. The rose silk hisses. 'No. In a brothel, yes.'

'And your first time with both a lady and a gentleman,' I remind her gently.

'Yes.'

An encouraging smile from Thérèse. 'You will like it. It is my favourite thing. You mustn't be afraid.'

'I'm not afraid,' said Alexandra removing her cape. She stares hard at Thérèse. 'I am looking forward to it. The surroundings are new to me, that's all.' She keeps her distance from Thérèse, who makes a kind-hearted effort to be pleasant to her. In the past it was Alexandra who took the initiative with her schoolfriends. 'What are you receiving for your services?' she asks suddenly. Thérèse is surprised, answering mildly. 'M'sieu has confirmed the usual arrangements with Frau Schmetterling, I think.'

'Thérèse is on a fixed weekly income,' I say. 'It is one of the benefits Frau Schmetterling offers to those who want to work here. It is a form of security. Part of the money is paid directly. Part is kept in a savings account.'

'You're looked after well, then,' says Alexandra. 'Safer than marriage, even.'

'Far safer,' says Thérèse. She continues to assume that Alexandra is shy. 'Your dress is lovely. Levantine silk, isn't it?'

'Thank you.' Suddenly Alexandra puts down her glass and crosses to Thérèse, embracing her and kissing her full on the mouth. Thérèse is a little taken aback. Alexandra grins. 'You're lovely, too. You're exactly my type, did you know? Did Ricky ask for you specially?' Thérèse begins to relax, as if she now has a notion of what is expected of her. She makes no further attempts to put Alexandra at her ease. 'I'm glad I appeal to you.' There is a touch of irony, a swift glance towards me, but I refuse a part. 'I've

always longed to meet a real whore,' murmurs Alexandra, stroking Thérèse's hair. She puts an arm around the girl's shoulders
and leads her to the sideboard. 'Pour us another drink, Ricky. I
want you to make love to Thérèse first.' Her tone implores but
her stance commands. 'I'll wait here.' She indicates a gilded chair
padded with brown velvet. She has the manner of a determined
little girl setting out the rules of a dolls' game. Not for the first
time I find this aspect of her character faintly disconcerting. She
seems almost prim. As I finish my drink Thérèse begins to remove
her chemise, her pantaloons, her cherry-coloured stockings. I feel
some trepidation, not for the action I am about to take but for the
spirit in which I shall commit myself to the performance. Alexandra has discovered a closet. I remove my jacket and hand it to her.
I remove my waistcoat, my tie and my shirt. All are neatly stowed
by Alexandra. I lower my trousers and these she folds. I take off
my socks, my underpants. Alexandra steps back from me and I
turn towards the bed. Thérèse is also naked, with her hair loosened and her head propped against the pillows. She has become
professional; her pink body waits for me. Her lips are slightly
parted, her eyes hooded. There is no apparent difference between
her artful desire and Alexandra's blind passion. If I was not aware
that Thérèse was a whore I would believe that she yearned for me
alone. Her youthful skin might never have known a man's touch.
Do all women slide so indiscriminately into lust? How are they
taught such things? I kiss Thérèse's cheeks, her neck. She moans.
I kiss her soft shoulders, her breasts, her stomach. She shudders.
Her calf presses against my penis. I kiss her face again. Her tongue
is hot on my neck, her hand finds my penis and testicles and fondles them. I hear silk behind me, but I do not turn. I press my
fingers into Thérèse's cunt. It is already wet. I push her legs apart
and she draws me into her. Her body is more generous than Alexandra's, but Thérèse cannot reproduce that thrilling urgency, that
desperation of movement which removes us entirely from the
world of ordinary perception. Several years ago, at the Villa
D'Este, or rather in the little ravine which runs below it and where
there is an older garden, some ancient emperor's villa, I came

upon a very respectable young couple walking there under the trees amongst the toppled columns and broken marble and was certain that I recognised the modestly dressed wife as a whore I had once visited regularly. Then she had been an unreal creature. Now she was a perfectly ordinary bourgeoise. The transformation was considerable. I lifted my hat and introduced myself, saying that I thought we were acquainted. I was in no doubt that it was she. The couple had given some ordinary Roman name and she had politely denied knowing me. But I had confirmed her identity for myself. She was the same nameless child I had fucked at least a score of times at the brothel in Rosenstrasse. I had paid, moreover, a great deal of money for the privilege. Then she had never spoken and it was said by some that she was dumb. Frau Schmetterling had prized her above her other girls at that time; she had referred to this wonderful beauty as her 'niece' and had offered her only to customers for whom she had a special affection. Whenever one went to her room it would always be the same. The draperies would be of darker than usual material and the only light would come from a large candle in a glass funnel, creating all kinds of peculiar, agitated shadows. The nymph would lie upon grey velvet, immobile and passive. About her waist, on a chain as a necklace might be worn, would be hung a massive insect, at least four inches long and about two inches thick, with a wingspan of five inches. The insect's body was carved out of morbid green obsidian, and its wings gave the impression of transparency, being made of crystal and silver. Imbedded as markings on its head and carapace were various murky gems: agates, carnelians and discoloured pearls. This splendid, sickly fly would rest upon her swarthy flesh as if about to dine. From her throat would be suspended a chain of heavy gold, a series of linked scarabs, Egyptianate and massive, reaching to a point just short of centre between her small, rouged breasts. One of her soft arms would be bare, but the other would have on it a gold and amethyst bracelet forming two intertwined serpents, and on her left ankle would be a solid bangle of gold, set with a single large ruby, matched by a similar ring on her fourth toe. She had a variety of small rings on her thumbs and fingers, and the hardness of the gold accentuated the delicacy and fragility of her youth.

As an old friend of Frau Schmetterling I had been allowed to enjoy that child on a number of occasions but I believe my chief delight in her came not from her body, which was delicious, but from a particular quality of mind she possessed: she seemed half-mad. Just as with Alexandra, for whom I have of course far more responsibility, the child had been consumed by a subtle urgency, an almost inhuman sexuality, which had in it a peculiar and per-haps unwholesome intelligence. It was as if she had come into the world with her intellect and her appetites fully formed, with a pagan greed for a conscious and specific form of sensual experi-ence which never waned and was yet never completely satisfied; a mind which was unsleepingly aware of itself, its surroundings, of those souls who came into its sphere. She had feasted upon me during the course of a season and I had been powerless for every second I had spent in her company; as drained and as miserable when I departed from her as I was enriched and inspired when with her. She had possessed virtually no reality for me. I had never attempted to converse with her. I had come and gone in silence, almost in secret. The business had taken on the atmosphere of a shameful liaison. By the end of that season I had become exhausted and my morale was in ruins. Yet that same insect-child who had so sapped my vitality was now an ordinary young woman walking with her husband at Tivoli on a Sunday after-noon. Had she been in any way responsible, then, for my condition? Or had I been entirely a victim of my own dreams? So I wonder as I move my body in and out of Thérèse, forcing myself not to become afraid of the girl who sits a few feet away from me drinking her absinthe and watching me with eyes which neither reflect nor absorb the light: blank eyes, lost entirely in a universe of private fantasy. Yet will she always be like this? Was she like it before? Momentarily the terror grows in me. I began as her sedu-cer and now I feel that I am her pawn, performing sexually for her entertainment. How does she see it? The same? She says she wished only to please me. I have beaten her. I have raised bruises and welts on her body, with rods, with shoes, with straps; I have played the cruel master and she the slave; I have practised all kinds of humiliations upon her with her consent. She has been at times wholly in my power. And yet I feel that I am now in hers, willing to renounce all ordinary happiness, ordinary pleasure, spontaneous lust, in order to please her, while she continues to pretend herself my victim. It is a child's game. I know it is a child's game. I tell myself that I should know better, yet the child in me, the child I thought vanished but whom I had merely silenced, is yelling for satisfaction again. Thérèse thrusts back at me with skilled strength; my orgasm when it comes is thin and quickly dissipates. Alexandra kneels beside us on the bed, still fully clothed. She strokes my rump with hesitant fingers. Perhaps it is her inexperience which binds me to her, why I am so willing to help her discover novelty after novelty so that she will forever be encountering something which is fresh to her. Will I continue to love her when all sexual experience is familiar to her? And what are her motives in this? What does she really want from me, save companionship in her adventure? She says that she loves me, but she is too young for the words to have any substance. She is fascinated by my reputation, which like most reputations of the sort is greatly exaggerated: I have probably been rejected by as many women as I have conquered and for every one who has believed me an inspired lover I have had others whom I have failed to satisfy. The needs of the body are actually as subtle as the needs of the personality. She is kissing Thérèse even as she strokes me. The feel of her dress on my skin is delightful. She touches Thérèse's nipples, again with that same sweet hesitation. She lies across my back, slowly moving her groin against me. Thérèse strokes her wrist. Their perfume almost drugs me. I am passive between them as their passion increases. Alexandra lets Thérèse begin to unbutton her dress. Eventually both naked bodies press on mine and gradually grow more confident with each other. A breast brushes my shoulder; a knee leans on my thigh. Lying face down in the bed I find it almost impossible to tell which little body is which. The sensation is wonderful as their ardour grows; the moans and grunts become sighs and gasps; they touch, they stroke, they scratch, wonderfully oblivious of me as anything more than a body. I slip my hand down to my cock and begin to masturbate as their movements grow more urgent. Papadakis says: 'You haven't enough light in here.' He pulls back the curtains. There is a glimpse of distant blue, the sea. I can hear it quite clearly today and it does not irritate me. The sun seems mild and warm. 'What's today?' I ask him. 'The first of May,' he says. 'You might be able to go outside soon.' I become suspicious of him, protective of my manuscript. I put it under the pillow when I sleep. He must not see it, at least until it is finished. 'It reminds me of Nicosia this morning,' he says. Then he scowls. 'That bastard of a father.' He will often sink into these private references. 'And I felt such a fool in the hat.' I become impatient with him again. 'You are disturbing me,' I say. 'I am not interested in your childhood. Bring me some tea in half an hour.' I am making more of an effort to be polite to him. Perhaps I have misjudged him. He seems to be showing some respect for me at the moment. But I cannot afford to allow him too much of my time now or he could go on about his frustrations and his achievements all day. He claims to have academic degrees, but becomes vague when asked where they were obtained. He also boasts, sometimes, of the famous painters and writers he has known and it is true that he once acted as a go-between for some artists I knew in London. That was how he eventually came to work for me. I do not deny his usefulness, but it is a bad idea to let him begin talking. I know he resents it when I silence him. I know that he sees my work as some sort of rival, although he originally claimed that he wished to support me in my efforts. That was before I became ill. He is abstracted today, still staring out of the window, whistling some popular tune under his breath. It sounds like 'I'm Forever Blowing Bubbles'. 'Let me finish this,' I say, 'and I will earn enough money to send you home to Nicosia.' He is surprised. 'Why should I want to go there? I was thinking of Venice.' I tell him to play some Chopin on the phonograph in the next room. 'And don't let the record wind down as you usually do.' I remember when he was more agreeable, when he thought my title meant something and that I had more money.

Deciding to leave Alexandra and Thérèse in each other's company for a while, since this will benefit me, I believe, in the long term, I dress myself and go downstairs into the public salon. There are a few gentlemen here, chatting in quiet voices, and one or two of Frau Schmetterling's girls, looking like any young ladies one might meet at a provincial ball. Frau Schmetterling, as usual, has retired to her kitchen. The whores are acting as hostesses. I ask for a glass of champagne and take a seat near the far window, casually watching a card game between two upright middle-aged gentlemen and two women whom I know as Inez and Clara. Inez claims to be Spanish (though she speaks German without an accent) and dresses accordingly. Clara wears a costume suggesting that she is an English countrywoman. Her speciality is with the crop and the tawse. The men are probably rich professional people. Both have grey beards and one wears a monocle while the other has pince-nez. All four are absorbed in their bridge at present. I make an effort to read the evening newspaper, but in spirit I am still upstairs with Alexandra and Thérèse. I have decided that I will dine here. Frau Schmetterling always provides an excellent light supper for those who require it. My earlier concern has vanished for the time being. I enjoy a cigar. The salon is furnished comfortably, in restrained good taste, reminiscent of the better class of Parisian hotel. Next to it is a billiard room and I am about to rise to go into it when the double doors of the salon open and the Princess Poliakoff comes in on the arm of a nervous young man whom I assume to be her latest gigolo. I get to my feet and bow. She recognises me and seems relieved to see me. I kiss her hand. She is as usual wearing a mannish black costume with a ruffle of lace at her breast. Her thin face is bright with severe paint and by the size of her pupils I would say she is drugged. She draws her young man forward. 'Ricky, this is my eldest son, Dimitri. We are on tour, to finish his education.' I shake hands with Dimitri. He has a pleasant, awkward smile. 'We shall be leaving for Trieste tomorrow,' she says. 'I am so glad you are here. You are just the man Dimitri should talk to.' I am amused. 'Why so, my dear Princess?' I ask. 'It is obvious, surely! You are a man of the world.' She speaks sardonically and yet it is a compliment. 'I am at your service, m'sieu,' I say to her son, and bow again. We are speaking French. The Princess Poliakoff is a notorious Lesbian. She has for some time had the reputation of frequenting the Rat Mort and La Souris in Montmartre where she gathered about her a group of female admirers, chiefly actresses and opera singers, who would vie subtly with one another to be her choice of the evening. I am glad to see her, for she is a familiar face, but I have no great liking for her. Her beauty is of that neurasthenic, slender kind; her skin seems almost transparent and the rouge only heightens its pallor. She has a long, thin nose and large, wide lips, high cheekbones, exceptionally large, languid hands, and she wears nothing but black or, in winter months sometimes, a tawny wolfskin cap, cloak and gloves. She is rumoured to have had affairs with half the famous female stage performers and painters in Paris and I heard that when she appeared in public with Louise Abbéma at L'Opera, embracing and kissing, her father upon receiving the news at his Russian estate shot himself and has never properly recovered from the head wound which left him with only one ear and one eye. She is now about forty. She still retains that look of boredom which to many makes her so fascinating and apparently remote. It was her boredom, she claims, which led her to experiment with almost every vice and it was vice, she says, which led her ineffably back to boredom. To which, she usually adds, she is now completely reconciled. 'You must explain the secret of your success with women, Ricky,' she says. 'There is no secret, Dimitri,' I tell her son. 'All one needs is a relish for sexual pleasure and a certain amount of time to dedicate to its pursuit. After a year or two one becomes known as a rake and women's curiosity does the rest.' Princess Poliakoff laughs. 'You are such a terrible cynic, Ricky. What would your eminent brother think of you?' I shrug. 'The von Beks have one black sheep in every other generation,' I say. 'It is a tradition. My brother is content because he believes that family customs should be firmly maintained. I have an agreeable nature and the assigned rôle happens to suit me very well.' Princess Poliakoff lights a small cheroot for herself. 'And what are you doing here now? I had heard that you have taken up with schoolgirls. Or was it schoolboys?' I am a little alarmed at this. It means that very soon my liaison with Alexandra will be discovered. 'Negroes,' I tell her, hoping to divert her from the truth. 'What?' she says, 'Really?' She can be extremely gullible. 'They are wonderful,' I tell her. 'I should have thought that in Paris...' She sighs. 'It is their size. I am absolutely terrified, dear Ricky, of large organs.' The girl comes with a tray of champagne. I hand them each a glass. Her son is smiling like a puppet at a fair. 'They are not always monstrous,' I say. 'And this schoolboy?' she continues relentlessly. 'He is black, then?' 'As your hat,' I say in English. 'He is the son of a king in Africa. Being educated here.' She chuckles, willingly believing me. 'You must pass him on to me when you are finished with him.' Princess Poliakoff has always characterised me as a hard-hearted roué who uses people as she does. She makes no allowances for my Achilles' heel, my sentimentality, and I see no reason in admitting to her that I am not what she would wish me to be. 'It's a bargain,' I say. I look at the ormolu clock over the fireplace. 'I shall see you later, I hope, at dinner. I must get back to my little negro.' Again her hand is kissed, her son's shaken. He is blushing deeply. I wink at him and return up the stairs, deciding that we shall have to dine in our room. Knowing what a gossip Princess Poliakoff is I hope that her talk of me will create a useful smokescreen. I am somewhat surprised at how cunning I have become since I began my affair with Alexandra. I pass the two bridge-playing gentlemen as they emerge from the toilet. 'This raising of an army hasn't perturbed him much,' one says. 'But I gather he found the desertion of about half the garrison something of a shock. They say he's at his hunting lodge now, with those mechanical models of his. The business will be bloodless if it comes off at all. Holzhammer isn't a bad sort. And he'll keep taxes down.' The significance of the conversation escapes me. I reach the blue door and knock before I enter. Thérèse and

Alexandra lie in each other's arms, smiling and giggling. Both look thoroughly dissolute, with their hair wet and scratch-marks on their bodies. 'And how have you enjoyed yourselves?' I chuckle, glad that they are happy and that Alexandra is no longer in her original mood.

Papadakis brings me a cup of tea. 'And will you eat something now?' he asks. 'Perhaps some Camembert,' I tell him. 'And something blue and soft. Something tasty. What have we?' He strokes at his beard with his finger and thumb. 'There's a little Cambozola. You used to enjoy that.' I nod at him. 'Excellent. And a glass of red wine.' He purses his lips. 'Wine? It will kill you!' I put down my pen. 'I am better now. Can't you see that? Some red wine.' He shakes his head. He is becoming surly again. 'Not according to the doctor. But I will bring it if you want it.' He leaves. Alexandra, Thérèse and I dine off smoked salmon and cold duck in our room. The two girls manufacture secrets and I pretend to be intrigued, to please them. Later we shall make love again, playing games with considerable zest and good humour. Then, at about three in the morning, Alexandra and I will order a cab and leave the brothel, promising to see Thérèse the next evening.

Papadakis takes the limousine to town. He likes, I know, to pretend that it is his because it gives him stature with the local peasants. Papadakis says he understands peasants and how they think. He hates them, he says. But his information about them is useful to me and gives me a greater knowledge of his attitudes. He is supposed to get me some patent medicine containing a stimulant but he will quite likely forget; most of the time he thinks only of himself, living in a dream of an unsatisfactory past and an unattainable future. Sometimes across his face comes the enthusiastic expression of a boy, a memory of his former charm. Pyat, the famous confidence trickster, had a similar appearance when I met him at Cassis with Stavisky in the mid-'20s. I have told him it is his duty to care for me when I am ill. He will sometimes reply it is the doctor's job. He was hired, after all, to be my secretary. The fact was I took pity on him. I offered him his last chance and he accepted it. Now he wriggles to be free, but there is nowhere for him to go. And he brings me my soup and fish and he changes my linen when the old woman is too drunk to do it. The pain has come back in my groin. Is Alexandra a mirror? Is the ugliness I believe I detect in her simply a reflection of my own? Since I was sixteen women have told me that I must change. I have always said to them that I am too old to change. If they do not like me as I am then they have the right to find someone they prefer. But I think I am changing for Alexandra and that is perhaps why I am occasionally frightened. I tell everyone that I am in love with feminine beauty in all its aspects. The fact is I become bored in the company of women who have no sexual presence, no matter how intelligent they may be. I think I dislike such women because their condition indicates their own fear of themselves and consequently of the world around them. I have known many women who express the same impatience with non-sexual men. Sexuality is the key to personality. She undresses. She removes the rose silk frock, the delicate chemise; she rolls down her stockings and puts them carefully on the back of the chair. She has a habit of slipping her garters over her wrist while she removes the rest of her underwear, then, holding them in her right hand, she will go into the bathroom and set them on the ledge in front of the mirror. If they are a pair she particularly cares for she will give them a little parting kiss. I say it is too late to bathe, we should go to sleep at once, but she insists. While she is in the bath I fall asleep. I awake briefly at dawn. My blood has quickened. I begin to anticipate what we shall do together later. I turn, thinking she is still bathing, but she is fast asleep with her back to me, the sheets pulled tightly about her as if she fears something. Can she fear me? Will she come to resent me? Asleep, with her face in repose, she sometimes resembles a baby. At other times, when she is snoring and her mouth is open she reminds me of a dead rodent. I wonder if that is really all she is when she is not responding to me: a tiny unimportant predator. But when she wakes her eyes destroy my prejudice. Did her eyes always possess that strange, heated glaze? I remember how she had seemed so innocent when we first met. The prospect of making love to a virgin had driven all caution away within a few minutes. Then, I think, the expression had been there, but hidden. She had only glanced at me directly once and her eyes had told me of her desire for me. Is she a natural predator? She says she loves me, but that is meaningless. She loves what she thinks I must be, what she thinks I possess, and she lusts after my cock. She is doubtless surprised, also, that she can achieve control over others through her sexuality. Unless she is an unusual female she will continue to use her sex as her only certain means to power. She will have no notion of any other way to get what she will want for herself. Even if other ways are described to her she will not quite understand what is said, for her chief experience will have been of sexual control coupled, perhaps, with certain practical services given to the one who desires her. Her will to power, which she has in common with everyone, if satisfied only through sex could ultimately leave her empty of feeling and therefore could destroy any ordinary capacity to know desire, causing her to pass from lover to lover in a perpetual cycle of lust to dissatisfaction. As I fall back to sleep I wonder if I have created a whore. More likely, I think with grim amusement, a monster which will turn on me and take my soul. I do not believe I possess the character of a natural whoremaster. I am not strong enough to control her. And this is the knowledge which sometimes excites me and brings flagging senses back to peak again. These are the thoughts of my infrequent solitude. When she is awake I scarcely think at all but remain perpetually fascinated, perpetually on guard, like the tamer with his tigress. We breakfast late in the sitting room. She pours coffee for us both. The light is pale, slanting into our windows from misty skies. The air is cooler today. She sits in her maroon dressing gown, wonderfully composed, seeming thoroughly rested. She makes no reference to the previous night's adventure. Indeed, she seems healthier, younger, more cheerful, than she has seemed for some while. I compliment her on her good humour and her freshness as I light a cigarette. 'I have never felt more alive in all my days!' she says. 'My body is waking up. It never stops now. It wakes and wakes and wakes.' Her smile is spontaneous and beautiful. She says: 'Are you looking forward to this evening?' I am surprised. 'Yes.' I expected her to have doubts. She sits back in her chair in a posture of contentment. She looks towards the window. 'Isn't it wonderful outside?' I smoke my cigarette and stare carefully at her. Her courage, I believe, is the courage of ignorance. But whatever its nature it transmits itself to me. 'You enjoyed Thérèse?' I ask.

'Well enough,' she says. 'I have had better. Younger and without any experience. I think I should like a different girl after this evening. There are things Thérèse told me. Girls with special skills, apparently.' I nod: 'Oh, yes.' She takes my hand and kisses it. 'Could any woman possess a finer teacher? I want to experience everything you have experienced. I want us to be together when we discover new things.' I love the softness of her lips on my wrist, the way her slender body curves in the gown. 'There could be experiences you will not enjoy,' I tell her. 'Of course,' she says, 'but then I will know what they are.' I laugh. 'You are too fond of the novels of Huysmans and de Goncourt. The critics are right about them. They have a pernicious influence!' I am, in my fashion, expressing my hesitation. This is the moment when I could call a halt to the adventure. But of course my curiosity overwhelms me. I acquiesce. She becomes suddenly active and begins to clothe herself. We take a drive in the afternoon, she in her cream frock trimmed with broderie anglaise and a hat with a thick veil, I in my tweeds. I shade my face with a wide-brimmed hat. After a little while I begin to notice that the tempo of Mirenburg is subtly different. There are many more soldiers in the streets today. Carriages hurry past us on their way to the station. An unusual number of people are leaving the city. I tell our driver to stop in Falfnersallee and send him to buy a paper from one of the kiosks. He says: 'It is the War, your honour. The Civil War. Hadn't you heard?' Alexandra looks with some impatience at the newspaper as if at a passing rival. Count Holzhammer has half the country on his side, including a good proportion of the Army. He has issued a proclamation demanding the abdication of Prince Badehoff-Krasny and the dissolution of Parliament. He argues that the new Armaments Bill will ruin Wäldenstein. He claims the

Prince has deliberately set himself against the will of the majority of the people and that he is in the power of a handful of alien industrialists. Count Holzhammer is financed with Austrian money, of course, and his ranks are swelled by Bulgarian cavalry and artillery loaned by Austria but calling themselves Volunteers. The newspaper wonders if the Germans will now send aid to the Prince. So far there has been no response from Berlin. Count Holzhammer has his headquarters in an armoured train. His forces have won a battle at Brondstein. The loyalists have regrouped near Mirenburg. Count Holzhammer awaits a response to his demands. His train is some seventy miles down the line, at Slitzcern. The paper believes the Prince will refuse the Count's demands. Mirenburg has never been taken by siege, says the editorial, in all its long history. During the Thirty Years War she successfully withstood five separate attacks. She remains impregnable. Count Holzhammer must know this and is therefore almost certainly bluffing. There is a likelihood that the Prince will order Parliament to scrap the Armaments Bill and make one or two concessions to the great landowners who are giving Holzhammer their backing. I shrug and hand the paper to Alexandra. The whole business has a comic-opera aspect to it and I cannot take it seriously. It is a storm in a teacup, I tell her. A full-scale civil war is in nobody's interest; the matter is bound to be settled by negotiation. I express some admiration for Count Holzhammer's audacity and remark on the cunning of the Austrians, who doubtless hope their support of Holzhammer will increase their influence over Wäldenstein. But Alexandra is concerned about the effects of the business on her own plans. 'It could mean my parents will return,' she says. 'Or will send for me.' I give the problem swift consideration and arrive at a solution. 'Then go home now. Tell your housekeeper you are leaving Mirenburg with friends who fear for your safety. Give her an address in Brussels – anything will do – then send an appropriate telegram to Rome. In that way we can benefit from this situation.' She is impressed by my cunning and agrees to do as I say. The carriage leaves me at my usual corner opposite the Radota Bridge. The water is like silver in the early-afternoon light. I sit at one of the outside tables and order *anis* and a sandwich while I wait for Alexandra to do as I have instructed. Troops come and go across the bridge. They seem in fine form. The officers wave batons and swords, pointing this way and that. They have a decisive,self-important manner which I find amusing. They are so wonderfully pompous, like eunuchs who have overnight been blessed with testicles. Alexandra seems to take no time at all, even though she returns with two or three new trunks. 'I am going with her full approval,' she says with a smile. 'She thinks it is for the best!' We drive to the hotel. The manager, an anxious beaver, approaches me, seeing the new luggage being taken up by the porters. He would be obliged if I could tell him if I intend to leave the hotel in the morning. I shake my head. 'I have every intention of staying for some time.' He is relieved. Apparently most of his residents will have departed by tomorrow. 'They are running special trains to Danzig,' he explains. He has the distracted look of a man who fears ruin. 'Surely they are being over-cautious,' I say. 'Even if the Count takes control it will scarcely affect your guests. They are all foreigners. This squabble will be resolved in a few days and everything will be back to normal.' His estimation, he agrees, is much the same as mine. 'But there is a panic. Half our business people are leaving for Berlin and Paris. The Stock Market is chaotic. Exchange rates are fluctuating. Such things bother them, you know. Many visitors are returning to their firms. And Count Holzhammer is very direct about his hatred of industrialists, particularly the Jews and the Germans. They have a right to be nervous, I think.' I suggest they will all come creeping back within a week. 'What can they do to Mirenburg? Who would threaten her beauty with cannon-shells? It is impossible.' The manager laughs. He seems relieved by my reassurance. I order a pot of tea and some pastries to be sent to our rooms. We take the lift to the third floor.

We dress ourselves carefully. Alexandra wears her flowing red evening gown and has over it a full cape of dark brown velvet. The streets are almost deserted as we make our way in a cab to Rosenstrasse. Here and there are groups of silent soldiers, standing guard over nothing. Groups of urchins run about pretending to shoot at one another. There are unexpected echoes to make the twilight eery. The brothel, when we arrive, seems like a haven of normality. We are received by Trudi but do not see Frau Schmetterling. Thérèse awaits us behind the blue door and we again enjoy, with increasing assurance and relish, our pleasures of the previous night. As we rest, Thérèse is more talkative. She speaks enthusiastically of Frau Schmetterling and the establishment. She expresses her affections, her jealousies, her dislike of certain other girls. Alexandra has assumed the rôle of her confidante, greedy for every bit of information. We smoke a little opium. Thérèse repeats a great deal of what I have already told Alexandra, about the special rooms, the preferences of some clients (who according to the brothel's protocol she cannot name) and the predilections of the girls, the attitudes they have to their work, their clients, themselves. Growing bored with this I take Alexandra almost by force, deliberately humiliating her in front of Thérèse, then I make Thérèse kneel and accept my cock, wet with Alexandra's juices, in her mouth while Alexandra licks my anus. I come in a convulsion of release that has little actual pleasure in it, forcing Thérèse to swallow my semen. Alexandra stops her activities but I order her to continue, telling Thérèse to fetch one of her ivory dildoes from the drawer. Then I hand the dildo to Alexandra. Together they take turns buggering me while I sob in pain and helpless terror until I am so weak they can turn me any way they please, teasing me, making me shudder. Thérèse lies with her vagina rubbing against my face while her lips nip at my cock, bringing it to life again. Alexandra joins her, fondling my balls and then squeezing them hard to inflict greater agony. They are taking their revenge on me. Slowly they bring me to the point of orgasm and then, with deliberate cruelty, they begin to kiss one another, ignoring me completely. I put my hand to my cock. Alexandra sees my movement from the corner of her eye and forces my hand back while she pushes herself against Thérèse's thigh. I do not possess the strength to take either of them and yet my frustration continues to build. Again I am turned over. Again the dildo is rammed into my anus and left there. Thérèse rests her head on my buttocks while Alexandra sits over her, leaning her hands on my back and scratching at my flesh, letting Thérèse lick her clitoris until she achieves an orgasm which makes her scream and rip at my skin. My body begins to vibrate and it is as if the shock of Alexandra's orgasm has transmitted itself to Thérèse and myself. We are all shaking, almost as if we experience petit mal. I turn and tug weakly at Thérèse's hair, drawing her up towards me. Still shaking I enter her and we tremble together, making virtually no movement, letting our bodies shake us to orgasm. This time Thérèse comes first, her vulva contracting and distending rapidly and I am yelling, feeling Alexandra's hand slapping again and again at my bottom, at Thérèse's thighs, as she laughs in high-pitched harmony with our noises. I become suddenly blank. I have passed out for a few seconds. When I awake Thérèse and Alexandra are lying one on each side of me, cuddled in my arms like two tranquil puppies.

'Tell us a story,' says Alexandra. She is by no means the first woman to make this demand of me. I can think of nothing but sexuality so I begin to tell them of the beggar girl I met in Naples three years ago. It remains one of my strangest experiences. I had been walking alone by the sea just before nightfall when one deep shade of blue merges with the other; over the water I had been able to detect the lights of Capri and Ischia and had come to this area of the front in the hope of meeting an attractive whore since my mistress of the moment had elected to spend an evening with her husband. The air was filled with the music of hurdy-gurdies and accordions coming from the little cafés where the working classes enjoyed themselves at supper. The few whores I encountered were not pretty – Neapolitan women of that sort are generally too plump and lewd for my taste – and I began to long for Clichy or Montmartre. Pimps approached me and were waved away with my stick. The air, I remember, was very humid. I was conscious of the sweat on my back, wondering if it would begin to show through the linen of my jacket. The music kept me cheerful enough and I was preparing to go home unsatisfied when a black-haired little thing with ringlets falling over her oval face appeared before me, deliberately blocking my path. She was slender, in ragged pinafore and petticoats and probably no more than fourteen. Her expression was singularly attractive, that mixture of innocence and defiance. Her boyish stance and figure were very much to my preference and although I could scarcely understand a single word of her voluble patois I humoured her, smiling. This seemed to make her lose her temper. She gesticulated, this little Carmen of the waterfront, rubbing her fingers together in that universal sign for money and pointing over her shoulder with her thumb. 'Do you wish me to go home with you?' I enquired in my polite Roman Italian. This question was unexpected and caused her to frown. Realising I was a foreigner she spoke more clearly. 'I need money,' she said. 'You are rich. I want a few lire, that's all. Are you French?' I told her I was German and this seemed to disappoint her. 'You do not have the look of a German.' She began to turn away but I stopped her, putting my hand on her shoulder. The feel of her tensing muscles under my grasp increased my desire for her. She was lovely. 'Why do you want money?' I asked her. 'It is for my father,' she replied. 'Is he ill?' I said, willing to show sympathy. She became angrier. 'Of course he is ill. He has been ill for years. He fought with Garibaldi. He was one of the conquerors of Naples and was wounded by the Austrians. He has lived on the charity of others ever since. He has educated me. He has supported me. And now he is too ill even to beg.' I was not entirely convinced by her story, even if I did not doubt her sincerity. 'So you beg for him now?' She had rounded on me. 'I ask for Christian help, that is all.'

I smiled at this. It was a phrase often heard in Naples. 'I am willing to give it,' I told her. 'But what will you or your father give me? You see I am not a believer in charity. Giving it or receiving it reduces human dignity. Look at you now. You are angry because you are forced to ask a stranger for help. You resent me and would resent me if I gave or if I refused. This in itself, I will admit, makes you an unusual beggar-girl. However, if your father has something to sell, I'll be pleased to consider a bargain.'

She frowned. 'We have nothing.' I shook my head. 'On the contrary. You possess one of the most wonderful treasures in the world.' She pouted, but I had engaged her attention. 'You sound like a priest,' she said. 'I assure you,' I told her, 'that I am no priest. I have no interest at all in your soul. It is yours and should remain yours. The treasure to which I refer has yet to be discovered by you. It has to be brought out into the light and then it has to be polished before you will believe how beautiful and valuable it is.' I caressed her dirty neck and she did not draw away. Her curiosity held her. I believe she guessed my meaning but wished her suspicion to be confirmed. If I confirmed it at once I would probably lose her. It was up to me to maintain her interest a little longer. 'If you take me to your father I will explain what I mean,' I said. Again she was surprised. 'My father? He is a good man. Few are as saintly. He has taught me virtue, signor.' I offered her my arm, bowing to her. 'I am sure that he has. What father would not? You are a lovely young woman. It is easy to see you are of a different class to most. Was your mother a refined woman?' The girl nodded. 'She was. She owned land. She gave up everything to support Garibaldi and my father. She was a Sicilian. From a very old family.'

'Just as I thought,' I said. 'Well, let me escort you to your home.' She consented, of course, because she had little to fear. She took me into a warren of alleys where children, dogs, women and old people seemed in perpetual conflict, and down the steps of a cellar from which came the faint smell of urine. She pushed open the door. Everything was damp and the mould gave off such a pervasive stench that it almost took on the character of perfume; it excited me. She lit a little oil lamp, nothing but a floating wick, which made flickering shadows and revealed the sleeping face of a man who in health must have been a giant. I was surprised by the face. It had far more character than I might have expected. I could see that my attempt to buy his daughter from him would not be as easy as I had thought. He opened clear blue eyes and looked at me as if he had seen an old friend. An expression of irony crossed his face. 'Signor,' he said. 'I am glad to see you.' He spoke with easy familiarity and it was plain this was not his normal tone with strangers, for his daughter looked from one to the other and said: 'Are you acquainted?' Her father lay amongst rags. It was impossible to tell what was his body and what its coverings. He shook his head. 'Not really,' he said. 'But I hoped it would be this way. You are a gentleman, signor?' There was considerable meaning to the question. 'I hope that I am,' I said. 'And you are wealthy?' I inclined my head. 'I am modestly well-to-do. But, of course, I am carrying virtually nothing on my person.' He nodded. 'I can see that you are also no fool.' He knew exactly my reason for being there. 'Well, have you come to offer my Gina the chance to appear on the stage? Or is it to be service in a fine house? Or do you wish to take her away to educate her, signor?' Gina was still too surprised by all this to speak. She went to the far side of the cellar and sat down on a mattress, her elbows on her knees, her face in her hands, watching us. I smiled at him. 'None of those things,' I said. 'I think it would be insulting to you if I pretended to any but the real feelings which brought me here. I have indicated as much to your daughter. You know what I wish to buy. But I will promise you this. If you sell, I will leave you both with something of increased value, and your daughter will still be yours. I will not take her away.' Gina heard this. 'I would not go!' she said. 'She would not,' said her father, 'unless I insisted upon it. I have some power left, do you see?' I acknowledged this. 'You have considerable power, signor.' I felt almost humbled by his dignity. 'And I am willing to negotiate, as I believe, now, you are.'

He sighed. 'I think so. I think so. You seem a man of the world. You have no disease?' I shook my head. 'None.' He sucked in his lower lip then once more offered me that direct, blue stare. 'The price will be high and there will be conditions.' And so we began negotiations for the virginity of his daughter while she listened without resentment, having absolute trust in her father, who proved to be one of the most honest and realistic men it had ever been my pleasure to meet. A price was agreed and it was, as he said, high, but he understood the rarity and value of what he sold and was relieved that Gina was not to give herself away out of infatuation, which could have ruined her and consequently left him without support. His other condition was harder to agree to. She had to be enjoyed here, in the cellar, and he must be present to ensure, as he put it, that no harm came to her. 'Moreover, signor,' he admitted, 'I am denied most pleasures so it would hearten me to be able to live through what you both experience.' My desire for the girl was so positive that I found myself at last giving in to what he asked. It was agreed I should return the next morning with the money and I said I would arrange for fresh bedding. I did not intend to take possession of my purchase in such utter filth. He told me he could make the cellar into a fairy palace if I chose since everything else I brought would add to his comfort and become an asset. And the price was for a twenty-four hour period. If I wished to stay longer, I must renegotiate the bargain. I accepted this, also. We both asked Gina if she was prepared to enter into this contract and she said she owed everything to her father and she would do whatever he thought best. The old man cared for her very deeply, I could tell, and by this means he was able to maintain his protection and ensure that both of them benefitted from his daughter's defloration without unduly disquieting consequences. I returned the next day with some new lamps, furnishings, in fact a whole cartload of comforts, which were efficiently installed by the two carters I had employed.

Her father's body, seen in good light, was swollen and bloated, although his face and hands were not at all fleshy. He allowed rags to be removed and cushions, carpets and mattresses to be brought in. With the aid of the carters he was transferred from the old to the new without difficulty and sat amongst his new luxuries like a Buddha. Both he and his daughter had washed themselves and were wearing clean rags. I had brought her several simple dresses which she thanked me for and hung on a hook in an alcove, making no attempt to wear them. The beggar directed the carters to replace the pile of straw with the mattress in the opposite corner while Gina spread one of the new sheets on it, together with the long bolster I had also brought with me. The smell of mould remained, but since this was pleasant to me I was not disturbed by it. My lust was building with every improvement to the appearance of the cellar and at one point the beggar reached out to pat my leg, murmuring: 'Patience.' A peculiar conspiracy had grown amongst the three of us. The carters sensed it and were disturbed. I was anxious they should leave and paid them off rapidly. They made a bewildered departure, the door was closed, and we were alone. 'You may begin as soon as you like,' said Gina's father. She poured him some of the milk I had brought. He accepted it gracefully. 'And my cheese, I think,' he told her. 'The cheese I could not eat last night.' She fetched it for him and put it in his other hand. She had begun to blush. He recognised her confusion and took her little face in his finger and thumb. 'This gentleman can be trusted,' he said. 'You could not wish for a better initiation, my love. It will be exquisite, I am sure.' He waved her towards me. I now stood beside the mattress, coatless, ready to embrace her. She brought her slight, delicate body up to mine. I kissed her head, stroking her neck, slowly beginning to undress her. I was unusually gentle. There are some women, no matter how physically strong they are in actuality, who one is always convinced will break if handled too roughly. They are often the fiercest lovers, but it can be an effort to forget that sense of their fragility and give oneself up completely to one's passion. And so I took her and she was as delicious as I had expected. She, under my caresses, completely forgot the presence of her father and at times I was hardly aware of it. She had her back to him, but frequently I could observe him. To my great satisfaction I was able to bring her to orgasm by means of my mouth and hands before I had completely entered her. It is not always possible to do this at such an early stage with a virgin. But she had natural generosity and lust and I have always found that the more generous the spirit of the woman, the more easily she can attain the fullest sexual delight. My chief memory of this encounter, however, is of her father. I can still see the tolerant wisdom in the eyes of that unnaturally bloated veteran republican as he sat amongst his cushions, a piece of mouldy cheese in one strong fist, a wooden bowl of milk in the other, almost gracefully regal in his relaxed and unselfconscious posture, drawing my attention away from the blank, ecstatic face of the girl, even as my body performed its functions and satisfied its lust. He watched without curiosity, without pleasure, almost without interest. He was benign. It was as if God Himself blessed our passion.

As I came he raised his head and sniffed, smiling. The scent of our fluids was an ovation. He took a sip of milk and sniffed again, nodding, approving, perhaps recalling a memory of love. I fell to her side, still regarding him. He saluted me with his piece of cheese and spoke a few sultry words in his own dialect. His daughter, as if noticing him for the first time, turned her head towards me and beamed. Our mutual joy was so intense we all three found ourselves laughing aloud, the sound completely drowning the noise of perpetual contention from those Neapolitan alleys. With Gina's father's consent I returned to their cellar every day for something over a week, paying for every visit. My enjoyment of the girl was not at all marred by the presence of the old man; we made love for his benefit as well as our own. When the time came for me to leave Naples I gave him an address through which he might contact me if Gina became pregnant. 'She is our daughter and our mistress,' he said to me as we shook hands. 'She now knows what it is possible to have from a man. And she knows that she need not feel guilty in seeking that out. Thus I ensure myself of her company while quieting my own fears for her future. On the money you have paid us I will be able to support us for at least a year. Thank you, signor. We'll remember you with gratitude and affection. And we shall pray for you.' Gina kissed me gravely, like a wife saying farewell to a husband leaving for work. I have not seen or heard from either of them since. Thérèse says: 'It is good for a young person to be instructed by an older one, whether it be a man or woman. But the parting can be a great tragedy. Your Gina cried for you, I think, when you had gone.' I am not sure. 'She had her father, don't forget,' I say. I leave them to sleep and dress myself to go downstairs as I did yesterday. Rudolph Stefanik, the Czech aviator, is in the salon. He has dark untidy hair and a look of distracted boredom. His evening clothes seem to restrain his massive body which threatens to burst through them. His beard bristles as he speaks. At least half the men and women in the salon have gathered around him to listen to his balloon adventures, but it is plain he is as impatient with them as he is with his own anecdotes. He looks from girl to girl. He has come to Frau Schmetterling's for a purpose and does not really care to be diverted from it. I hear him say: 'So they caught their daughter sucking at my cock in the gondola. I had no choice but to fling her out and cut the tethering lines. Another two seconds and they would have set fire to the canopy.' And I hear an old Mirenburger bore interrupt with what he supposes is wit: 'You have flown the world in the service of Venus. But what now? Will you fly in the service of Mars? Will you help the Prince against Count Holz-hammer?' Rudolph Stefanik looks over his questioner's head. 'One makes love in silk, and makes war in iron. My balloon is silk and hemp and wicker.'

'What a beautiful combination.' Clara, the Englishwoman, puts long nails on the dark cloth of his arm. She is tall and thin. Her figure and her face have those fine brittle bones one associates with red setters. I have decided that she has no character. Few whores have; or rather they assume so many characters it is impossible to tell if one is real and the others false. In this they are like all mediocre actresses. A great whore, like a great stage performer, has the brains and the sense of survival always to present one face to the world when off duty. Clara looks to me for approval. I am prepared to smile. It costs me her attention, for she immediately detaches herself from Stefanik. Her perfume seems acrid. 'Do you know the Count?' she asks. 'I have not had the pleasure.' I am dragged towards him and introduced. It appears to me that we exchange nothing but sympathetic and knowing looks, and bows. 'You arrived recently, I gather,' say I. 'Yesterday, I think,' he says. 'Poor timing,' say I. 'So it would seem,' he says.

'And you will leave in your balloon?'

He shakes his head. The truth is that he cannot afford to fall, as a Czech nationalist, into Austrian hands. 'Not with those trigger-happy Bulgarians all over the place. They'll shoot at me. There isn't a soldier in the world who doesn't automatically shoot at any balloon. I have stored it and shall leave it stored until this stupidity is over. It cannot be more than a week.'

'Less,' say I. 'Nobody has anything to gain.'

'Oh, let us hope so.' It is little demure Renée. 'My father was at Metz. He told me how wretched the citizens had become when at last the army entered the city.'

'Count Holzhammer is not a brute,' says Clara.

'He is a gentleman. He and the Prince must soon come to a civilised agreement,' says the plump banker Schummel, all insouciant confidence and avuncular good humour. 'My dear von Bek. How is your illustrious brother?' We chat about Wolfgang for a few minutes, about Bismarck, but already I become impatient to return to Alex and Thérèse. The salon contains that blend of cigar smoke and rose water I find delicious, a blend of characteristically masculine and feminine scents. The perfection of the candelabra, cold fire and crystal, the depth of the Persian carpet and the elegance of the company have revived in me that euphoria I was losing. Schummel stands with his back to the rose-marble fireplace. His balding white head is reflected in the mirror, together with the large central chandelier. Renée holds her folded fan at her side and listens while he speaks about his recent visit to Algiers where he stayed at the Grand Hotel St George, Mustapha-Superieur. The manager, a Swiss named Oesch-Muller, is such a splendid, helpful fellow. Do I know him? I agree with his opinion of the manager, though I can hardly remember him. I prefer Kirsch's Hotel, near the English Club. Renée seems very attractive tonight. She wears pale blue and gold. Her auburn hair is allowed to fall on one side in three thick ringlets to her naked shoulder. She, too, has memories of Algiers, where her mother worked as a housekeeper for a German trader. Schummel is delighted. 'Aha, admit it! You were a white slave in a harem. But you escaped!'

'True,' says Renée. 'Life in a brothel is so much more comfortable!'

'Well, at least you have the choice of how to spend your later years,' says Schummel. I feel almost jealous as he offers her his

arm and moves away. I decide I will have a word with Frau Schmetterling and perhaps book Renée for another night. 'And you have
so many friends,' he adds, 'you never need get bored as you would
with one master.'

I glance at myself in the mirror. I am handsome. My moustache is perfect, my figure exquisite and my evening clothes are a
wonderful fit. I have deep, dark eyes and glossy hair. My bearing is
elegant without being in any way arrogant. It is no surprise to me
Alex should find me so attractive. I look at my mouth. The lips are
red and have a kind of refined sensuality. I am a catch for any
woman. Does Alex have hopes of marrying me? I wonder. I cannot think how it would be possible, at present. It would be foolish
of me to consider it. She is too young. And I do not believe she
really loves me. As I return to the group around Count Stefanik I
have a sudden frisson of fear. I refuse to admit I love her. Yet there
is already pain, even at the thought of her desertion.

The talk is still of the War and Count Stefanik grows visibly
restless. I have the notion that soon his buttons will begin to pop
off his waistcoat. 'Four of the new Krupp cannon could destroy
Mirenburg in a day,' says Stefanik, almost with vindictive relish
towards those who are keeping him away from his pleasures. We
look about for a military man who will confirm or deny this. There
is none present. Frau Schmetterling discourages even generals
from Rosenstrasse. She says they spoil the atmosphere, that their
talk is coarse and too much about death. But Herr Langenscheidt,
the Deputy, believes he can speak for the Army. After all, his son is
a captain – a loyalist, thank God – and Herr Langenscheidt supplies
the livestock and provisions to the garrison. 'Holzhammer has no
German artillery,' he says. 'He has inferior Austrian and French
guns.'

'Nonetheless,' says Clara, attaching herself again to me and
scratching delicately at my wrist with her thumbnail, 'it should
not stop you ascending, Count.'

Stefanik is dismissive.

'A white flag would do it,' says Langenscheidt, his little body all
a-quiver. 'Wave a white flag!' Schummel argues that for Count

Stefanik to rise above the walls of Mirenburg brandishing a white flag might mislead Holzhammer into believing the entire city had surrendered and that would not be sporting. Indeed, it could be exceptionally embarrassing to everyone.

The aviator sighs. 'My balloon stays where it is.' He signals to Lotte and Hyacinta, both beautiful natural blondes, and with the briefest of acknowledgements to the rest of the company, departs upstairs with them. I take a glass of red Graves from the buffet which tonight has been placed near the window. As always the windows are thickly curtained in red velvet glowing like a fresh rose. I smell patchouli, and wood-smoke from the fire, the cheeses and cold fowl on the table, and I am now completely relaxed, no longer so eager to return to my two girls. Clara comes to eat another peach. 'It's my third. Aren't I greedy? They're all the way from Africa, I believe.' I wonder why she is pursuing me. I have no desire, tonight, to enjoy her special talents. She fixes me with a compulsive eye. Or perhaps it is Alex she desires, having heard about her from Thérèse. 'I so enjoy Count Stefanik,' she says, 'don't you? He is absolutely committed to the idea of powered flight. He calls it "heavier than air"? What does that mean?'

'Such machines are notional, and probably not possible. It means to fly like a bird, which is heavier than air, not like a dirigible, which contains lighter-than-air gas.'

'What?' she exclaims with a laugh designed to please and flatter me. 'Are we all to be angels?'

'Some of us are already so blessed,' I say with reluctant and unconvincing gallantry, looking up eagerly as the doors open and a woman enters. It is Princess Poliakoff, but now she no longer has her son with her. I cannot leave, for she has seen me and will be suspicious if I repeat my ploy of the previous evening. I smile at her and go to greet her.

I do not recognise her thin female companion. 'Sent on,' she says of the boy, 'to Vienna. I couldn't risk an encounter with Holzhammer. He holds such awfully long grudges. Do you know Rickhardt von Bek, Diana? Lady Cromach.' We are introduced. Lady Diana Cromach is a writer, a correspondent for several

English and French journals. A Lesbian, she lives in Paris. 'What brings you to Mirenburg, Lady Cromach?' I enquire in English. 'I am a professional vulture,' she says. 'The whiff of blood and gunpowder, you know. The War.' Everyone seems to be babbling tonight. The salon is fuller than usual. Someone has placed a record on the cabinet phonograph in the corner. It plays a sentimental German song. All at once the place has the atmosphere of a provincial wedding-breakfast. Lady Cromach wears her dark curls close to her head, a circlet of pearls. She has an oval face, a rounded chin, grey-green eyes, a strong nose and a slightly downturned but full mouth, very flexible for an Englishwoman. Her family estates are in Ireland. She is almost as tall as me and has an excellent, if slight, figure in an ivory gown trimmed with very light brown lace. Her voice is soft. Every statement seems full of implicit irony, no matter how banal it sounds on the surface. Has she learned to modify an otherwise mundane personality by cultivating this mannerism or is she really as clever as the Princess now insists? 'Have you read her articles for the *Graphic* or *La Vie Française*? So perceptive! She is a seeress. You are a Cassandra, my dear.' The Princess is plainly intoxicated with her friend. In her black costume she contrasts so emphatically that I smile and tell them I feel I am addressing a pair of chess queens. This pleases the Princess who laughs coarsely. 'But we play a game without kings, dear Ricky.' At this, Lady Cromach smiles and looks down at her fan. I find the Englishwoman, with her boyish shoulders and gestures, extremely attractive and give her more of my attention than I believe she desires. I am at my most charming, but she is not charmed, though she seems pleased to acknowledge the effort I am making and so is, I believe, flattered at least. Princess Poliakoff notices and almost growls at me. 'Where is your little nigger tonight, Ricky?'

'Resting,' I reply. Lady Cromach displays more curiosity than before and it is my turn to smile a little. Doubtless she has heard an elaborate story from the Princess but only now believes it. Such apparently unconscious confirmations give substance to the most outrageous lies. I feel satisfied on a number of levels and my spirits lift considerably. I have excited Lady Cromach's imagination; I have become interesting to her. I offer them both my cigarette case but Lady Cromach does not smoke and Princess Poliakoff prefers her little cheroots. She is quick to introduce her Diana to a safer acquaintance and once again I find I am with Clara, whom I now believe is either a little drunk or has made use of the box of cocaine for which she is well known. She has never shown such interest in me before and I cannot understand why she is attracted to me tonight. She has an eye for vulnerability. Can I seem vulnerable to her, when I am so full of confidence? The phonograph is playing a Strauss waltz. 'It is like a Friday or a Saturday,' remarks Clara. 'Not like a Wednesday at all.' She is pleased, but I am beginning to feel slightly irritated and claustrophobic. All the same Clara's pursuit has its effect. I have no intention, however, of returning to Alexandra with the marks of a birch on my behind; not yet. 'You are looking so beautiful tonight, Ricky,' says Clara. 'You have only to ask Frau Schmetterling and I could join you a little later.' I laugh. 'You are after my –' I hesitate. She makes a movement of triumphant withdrawal and our eyes meet even as she straightens her back. 'We shall have to see,' I say. 'But I think it could be arranged.' We all seem to be playing the same game tonight. And Clara grins, biting her lower lip, and winks. She is off into the press. I am alone. My first impulse is to leave quietly but before I know it I have crossed the carpet to where Princess Poliakoff and Lady Cromach, arm in arm, are amusing themselves at the expense of a red-faced dodderer who has mistaken them for whores. 'I do hope we shall meet again,' I tell them. I kiss their hands. Princess Poliakoff is a little cold, but I am under the impression that Lady Cromach has almost imperceptibly squeezed my fingers. To the strains of the waltz I make a light-hearted departure and spring up the stairs to our room. I find with disappointment that my little girls are asleep. Alexandra has her mouth open and is snoring. She looks, as she often does, like a replete rat, and I turn my attention first to her youthful flesh, then to Thérèse who, in sleep, seems slightly puzzled, just a trifle worried by something, and yet her lips are

innocently curved in a smile. Alexandra opens alarmed, accusatory eyes, then composes her features in a way I have only seen on
a much older woman. 'I wish I could join you down there,' she
says. 'You've enjoyed yourself, haven't you?' Her voice is low and
loving. 'I was missing you.' I lean down to embrace her. Thérèse
grunts and stirs but does not wake up. 'I think we should go,' I say.
'Are you satisfied.'

'With Thérèse?' She frowns. 'Oh, yes. We'll come again tomorrow, shall we? For a different lady?' I am indulgent. 'You don't
think we should rest, be by ourselves, at least until Friday or Saturday?' She is displeased. 'But it is getting so exciting. Are you
bored already?' I shake my head. 'Not bored. Merely patient.'

She puts her feet to the floor and looks at herself in the mirror.
'What's wrong?' I reassure her and, of course, within moments
am promising her that we shall return tomorrow, that I will speak
to Frau Schmetterling before we leave. I would do anything to
preserve this dream and will avoid, if I can, any hint of conflict
between us. 'You are a wonderful, wonderful friend.' Naked, she
raises herself to put her arms around my neck. 'I adore you. I love
you so much, Ricky.' I kiss her violently on the mouth and then
pull away from her, attempting gaiety. 'Get dressed. We must slip
into the night.' Sadness and distress have invaded me so swiftly
that I am angry, as if faced with a physical enemy. Much as I control myself she notices. When she is ready for the street she says
quietly: 'Have I upset you?' I deny it, of course. 'Not at all. I met
an old buffoon downstairs who insisted on boring me about the
War. He all but ruined my evening.' She becomes tactful. 'Perhaps
you're tired of our adventure? Perhaps we should rest tomorrow,
after all.' But I am by now fierce in my insistence that we continue. 'You're certain you want to?' she says. 'Of course,' I reply.
The anger fades. She appears to be mollified. I, in turn, become
astonished at how easily she can be reassured. But she is a child. It
is experience which encourages us to pursue our suspicions, that
and the memory of past pain. She has not known pain. Only boredom. In a woman of my own age I should sense an echo, some
form of sympathy. But with Alexandra there is no sympathy. And

I continue to conspire in her ignorance because it is the child I love. If she were to become a woman I should lose interest in her in a matter of weeks at the most. We persist in a conspiracy in which I alone am guilty, for I know what I am denying her. I refuse my own reason. I refuse to consider any sense of consequence. She is what I want. I will not have her change. And yet I have no real power in the matter. I can only pray the moments will last as long as possible for it will be Alexandra, in the end, who will make the decision either to stop dreaming or, more likely, substitute one dream for another. I look carefully at Papadakis's sallow, bearded face. At the deep hollows under his morbid eyes whose melancholy is emphasised by the spectacles he affects. Even the grey streaks in his beard have an unhealthy look, as if a saprophytic plant invades it. He turns away from my stare to pick at something with a quiet, fussy movement. I have made him self-conscious. I enjoy my moment. 'You should take more exercise,' I say. He grunts and shifts towards the shadows: a need to hide. His shoulders seem to become more stooped than usual. I am driving him into the darkness where he feels safest. 'Have you been looking for the evidence again?' I ask. 'I have told you, the photographs are not in the house.' He pushes back the heavy green curtain which covers the door of my bedroom. He disappears behind it. I pause to refill my pen. Alexandra is petulant. Her full lips turn downward and she pulls a hand through wet hair. Her skin seems to have lost its lustre this afternoon. Her shoulders and her breasts in particular have a lifeless look: a wax statue. 'You are eating too much custard,' I call after Papadakis. 'Too much bread and jam!' Alexandra pulls herself together, evidently displeased with her own mood. I hand her a glass of champagne. She accepts it; she is placatory – 'Could we find some opium? My nerves. Or some cocaine?' I shrug. 'Are you afraid? Do you want to go home?' I am still sluggish and am not properly awake. She shakes her head. 'Of course not. But with all this news, not knowing who is doing what or where my parents are and so on – Well, it's not surprising I'm a little agitated. Could you get some opium?' She begins to dry her hair, staring hard at her face in the mirror of the dressing table. 'I'm sure it's possible,' I tell her. 'But is it wise?'

She pouts, glares at me in that gesture I have come to recognise as her substitute for direct anger. 'Is any of this wise?' And then turns as if to say What have you made of me? I am in no mood for accusations. 'Are you suggesting –?' But of course she has suggested nothing in words. 'You are only what you were before we met. I am merely the instrument of your desire. I have told you that from the beginning. You can return to your parents' home if you wish and we'll say goodbye as friends.' I know that she will not go. I have countered her attempt at manipulation. 'I love you, Alexandra,' I say. She begins to cry. 'You have overtaxed yourself. Lie down for half an hour. Tonight I'll see if there is any opium to be had. When you've rested we'll go shopping. Some new clothes.' She cheers immediately. She has almost no sense of the future. She lives only for immediate, meaningless victories. She chooses not to rest but to get dressed so we shall not find the shops closed. I put on my dark brown suit with the buff waistcoat and kid boots and gloves, the cream cravat, a pearl pin. I am pleased with the effect. Today I think I look younger than she, but her paintbox and her powder soon adjusts the balance. She wears pale green silk with darker green lace ruffles, a matching hat with pheasant feathers. Her boots and gloves are also of the dark green. I pick up my stick, she her reticule, and we are off on our expedition. Carriages are lined up outside the hotel, eager for business. I am uncomfortable with the situation, for we, almost the only guests left, are more conspicuous than usual. I wonder about changing hotels, but once we are in the carriage and she has lowered her veil I dismiss my anxieties. On the way to the fashionable arcades of Falfnersallee we note the increased number of soldiers. Some of the shops have their shutters up. Here and there workers are moving sandbags against walls. I smile. 'They are taking this all very seriously, eh?' She smiles mindlessly at me for she is already thinking of the dress she will buy. The ladies of Falfnersallee are delighted to see us. We have all their attention as we move from shop to shop. She orders dresses, underclothes, a tea-gown, an umbrella, a Japanese kimono, all of which I must approve and pay for. Trade is slow at present, I am told. For my own satisfaction I take her to a jeweller's and there buy a Lalique brooch for her, green and white wisteria which looks perfect on her dress. She kisses it, kisses me and she is my happy schoolgirl again. We return via the quays and stop the carriage to watch two swans bobbing on the choppy waters. The misty light of the evening softens their outlines and they seem to merge with the silver river and vanish. The poplars in the dusk of Falfnersallee are black as Indian ink on a grey wash and rooks are calling from them like bored boys on a Sunday; noisy but unenthusiastic. Otherwise the great avenue is eery, virtually deserted. 'Has everyone abandoned the city?' I say. 'Have we the whole of Mirenburg to ourselves?' We embrace. In our rooms, with the gas lit, we inspect her parcels, her new hats, her brooch, a gold chain, a silver bracelet, her shoes. She spreads them all over the bed. She has the air of a soldier, triumphant from a looting expedition. She bites her lip and grins. She might have stolen all this. Unexpectedly I realise I could be preparing her for someone else, someone for whom she will make every sacrifice she will not make for me. It is not that I frighten her, though she says I do, it is that I do not frighten her enough, for real, committed love must always have a little fear in it or it would hardly be so precious. It is I who am afraid. I hate myself for my mysterious cowardice. I cannot identify its source. I continue to smile like a fool. I am more intelligent, more powerful, more experienced, even more humane than she: yet I am helpless. I grin like a clown as she parades her booty. My cheque-book is almost exhausted. I must go to my bank and get a new one tomorrow. I can always telegraph for more funds if necessary. I have not yet overstepped the mark with my family, I am certain, although of course they would not support me if they received any word of this escapade. I begin to doubt the wisdom of asking for Clara, as I did last night. There is still time to telephone to Frau Schmetterling. Alone, I would enjoy Clara's attentions, would happily give myself up to her, but now I am afraid Alexandra will think less of me. Even as I smile at her I become determined to make a show of strength tonight.

Just before we enter Rosenstrasse I pause in the darkness, certain I can hear distant gunfire. 'They must be fighting quite close,' I say. She shakes her head, impatient with me, eager to reach the house. 'It's just the river. Loading a boat or something.' It is definitely gunfire. We mount the steps. There is a pretty French song coming from the salon. As usual, we go straight to the room to which Trudi directs us. It is a little larger than the other two, with rather less furniture in it: some potted palms and two vases of gladioli which I know Clara favours. 'Beautiful colours,' says Alexandra. Her maroon linen rustles. 'Not one stem is the same.' Although she has accepted my rules for the evening her hand shakes as she reaches for a flower. I take off my jacket and throw myself into the big armchair. I feel exhausted, but I am controlling myself well. She is far too self-involved at present to notice any subtleties of mood in me. 'I prefer this room,' she says. 'The other one was vulgar.' I light a cigarette. 'I enjoy vulgarity. And surely these are the premises for discarding good taste occasionally.' Someone taps on the door. 'Our mistress has arrived. Open it for her.' With a deliberate gesture of submission she obeys. Clara stands there, all in grey, with a silver choker about her throat. To this is pinned a small, blood-red rose. 'Thank you, Alexandra. You are as lovely as I was told.' She kisses my child on the forehead and closes the door herself. 'Well, another crowded evening downstairs. So hot!' She opens her fan and waves it once or twice under her face. There is a suggestion of mockery in the composed smile she offers me. 'Sit down, Alexandra.' She indicates a straight-backed chair. Alexandra hesitates. Clara frowns. Alexandra sits. She is beginning to join in the spirit of this game. 'First we shall have some cocaine,' says Clara. 'Do you know how to take cocaine, Alexandra?' The child shakes her head. 'I will show you how to prepare it for sniffing. For my part, I prefer the syringe.' She touches her own cheek, laughing at herself. 'Like Sherlock Holmes.' From a drawer she takes a square box covered in black velvet. 'Do you know the stories, Alexandra?' She expects no reply and receives none. Alexandra is fascinated. Clara opens the box and takes a bottle of clear liquid from it. Beside this, on the marble of the chest's top, she lays a silver syringe. 'That is for me. But for you two, the crystals.' Out comes a tiny cut-throat razor with a mother-of-pearl handle, a small green-glass jar with a black screw-top, a hand-mirror in a silver frame. Clara works like a surgeon with these instruments. Every placement is precise. Without turning she says: 'I think you can remove your clothes now, Alexandra.' I avoid looking at either of them until Alexandra has actually begun to undress. Clara's rituals are often different and this one, of course, is completely unfamiliar. 'You may keep the necklace and bracelets,' says Clara. 'Fold your clothes neatly. I hate untidiness. Then come over here.' With deep concentration she shows Alexandra how much cocaine to take from the jar on the little spoon, how to chop it this way and that with the razor until it is as fine as it can be, measuring it into four lines of near-identical length and width on the glass of the mirror. 'You will prepare the next one,' she says. She fills her syringe and takes a little piece of cotton-wool which she has saturated in disinfectant, laying the syringe's needle on it. 'Now both of you may undress me,' she says. 'You may behave as you like during this part of the evening.' Thérèse had worn only a chemise and drawers, but Clara is all buckles and pins and combs. We set upon her, Alexandra and I, like hungry peasants at a chicken, picking and pulling, until our mouths can fasten on breasts, stomach, thighs. And all the while Clara is a statue, hardly moving, maintaining dignity and equilibrium at every tug and pressure, as if she challenges us to move her. Then Alex is kneeling and licking at her sex. 'That is enough,' says Clara. 'Get undressed, Ricky.' I do as she commands. Now we are all naked save that Clara keeps her necklet with the rose and Alexandra retains her jewellery. Clara dabs at her upper arm with more cotton-wool, then very slowly applies the syringe. When she has finished she takes two thin silver tubes from her box. 'One measure in each nostril,' she tells us. 'You first, Ricky.' I lean over the mirror and sniff up first one line, then, changing hands, the second. Alexandra imitates me and is surprised, I can tell, that she feels no immediate sensation. Clara gives a little gasp and looks towards her bottle with the affection one normally reserves for a loved one or an especially fine wine. My head is suddenly all delicious tingling sensitivity, a feeling which spreads through every nerve of my body and seems to excite blood and flesh to new, exquisite life. 'Oh!' Alexandra is receiving the same effect. I envy her this first experience, as I am sure does Clara. 'Oh! Oh, Clara!' She looks with gratitude towards the whore who continues to smile that same knowing smile. Then Clara orders me to my chair, Alexandra to the bed. With cold concentration she begins to explore the girl's body, scratching here, stabbing with a nail there, discovering her most sensitive parts. She takes a hatpin from the table and deliberately slides it down Alexandra's left side, drawing spots of blood, so Alexandra moans and gives vent to a strange, thin wail. She tries to move, to embrace Clara, but Clara will not allow it. She repeats the operation on the girl's right side, from shoulder to waist, over the buttock, down the thigh, the calf, to the foot. She leans to lick the blood, rolling it on her tongue like a connoisseur. I now lie beside Alexandra on the bed and receive two fiery lines to match hers. Then Clara begins to scratch, to slap, to whip with a thin cane until we are both writhing for her, moaning for her and I am certain I shall die if all this delicious agony is prolonged another second. Alexandra's voice is hoarse with those thin sounds she has almost continuously made. Clara is grunting. She turns us on our backs and repeats the process until almost every inch of our flesh is tender with bruises and tiny cuts. Then Alexandra lies with her face pressed to my genitals while Clara produces a china dildo shaped like a penis and, using a minimum of cream, thrusts it into Alexandra's small behind. There is now naked pleasure on Clara's face. With cruel delight she rams the dildo in and out while I hold Alex's head against my groin, glorying in the hot gasping breath on my cock. Alex's nails dig deep into my thighs. The movements of the struggling skull excite me and I begin to roll in unison with Clara's relentless thrusts. I find Alex's lips and try to enter them, but Clara pushes the girl aside and, leaving the dildo where it is, squats astride me to move herself to a banshee's orgasm. She yells. Alex is astonished, but I know Clara of old and begin to shout with her, reproducing all but the act of spending before, with hardly any hesitation, I turn Alexandra onto her front, remove the dildo and replace it with my cock, buggering and buggering while Clara slaps at my arse like a jockey on the winning stretch. My orgasm is monumental, horrifying, draining. Clara takes my place and the dildo is used again, this time in Alex's cunt, brutally, until with arms spread wide, with legs spread wide, she begins to shake like an epileptic, her hoarse screams rising to a shuddering crescendo until it seems to me she is going to vomit. Then it is over. A full five minutes later Alexandra begins to weep. Her sobs are deep-throated and, like her orgasm, move her entire body. Clara leans back on her pillows and smokes a cigarette with an expression of complete satisfaction. I am still unable to move. My vision is blurred, perhaps through the effects of cocaine. I can smell nothing but sex. My skin is still flaming; my groin aches. There is no question of visiting the salon tonight. Lulled by Alexandra's sobs, I fall asleep. When I awake my body feels white-hot and my mind is overwhelmed by such appalling desolation I can think only of death. When I eventually turn my head it is to see Alexandra's bruised and bleeding body bending over the chest as she prepares more cocaine. I am ready to weep with hatred and jealously at her ability to recover so rapidly. I retreat into sleep. I am soon awaked by the soft touch of Alexandra's hand; it is a tender gesture, a gesture of love. My mood changes to one of easy happiness almost at once. 'There is more cocaine for us,' she murmurs. 'Come, my darling. See if you can sit up.' Clara wears a white lace négligée. 'You men have no stamina,' she says affectionately. 'The drug will revive you, Ricky. What a beautiful couple you are.' She has the air of a woman proud of her prize-winning dogs. 'I have some ointment for you to put on.' I lift my head to sniff up the cocaine and almost immediately feel improvement. Alexandra begins to rub the ointment into my skin from top to bottom. When she has finished I tend to her. A certain perspective returns. Clara is in no hurry to leave and just now I have no great desire to be alone with Alexandra. We smoke cigarettes and discuss the charms of other lovers we have known. Clara is rather more willing to gossip than Thérèse. We drink some good claret and eat tiny pieces of cheese. Clara wants to know about Lady Cromach, but I can only repeat what I have heard. 'She seems to like you,' she says. 'Who is this?' asks Alexandra, not really jealous. 'They have a room here,' says Clara. 'She and the Princess. But they do not seem interested, as yet, in any of the girls.'

'Oh, I would love so much to go down there,' says Alexandra. 'Wouldn't it be possible, Ricky?'

'Too dangerous. And I doubt if Princess Poliakoff would be deceived, even if we smeared some burnt cork on your face and lent you a pair of my trousers.' I move in the bed. The touch of the soft linen on my body, the effect of the cocaine, are superb. We are all three so happy that my former fears, my caution, my common sense seem banal to me. 'But what can anyone say?' she asks. 'Oh, there are ways of saying things. But I'll put my mind to the problem. Let's get dressed while we can.' Slowly I lower my feet to the carpet and stand on trembling legs. Clara brings my clothes to me. We laugh as the material makes us wince. 'We've overdone it. Tomorrow we must definitely rest. I thought I was going to die tonight.'

'Me, too,' says my Alex. 'But what a beautiful death. You have taught me so much, Clara. Thank you.' She is far more enthusiastic about Clara than she was about Thérèse. I cannot fathom her tastes or her motives. There is a knock. Frau Schmetterling is apologetic. 'I'm glad I haven't interrupted you. I thought you'd be leaving. I wanted to speak to you, Ricky.' Alexandra is alarmed, like a schoolgirl caught smoking. 'Good evening, my dear.' I have never known Frau Schmetterling to visit one of the rooms before. She is stately as ever, in black and white, but seems agitated. 'Would you excuse me while I have a word with your gentleman? Ricky?' We move out into the passage. 'This is not the best time,' she says, 'but I have decided to go to bed early. It has been too busy for a weekday. We were not really prepared. Poor "Mister" can hardly stand up. Ulric has threatened to leave. It is the War. The threat of death is a great encourager of lust. I thought I'd invite you to stay here, in one of the private suites, if you would feel better. I am keeping it aside for you. Until the business with Holzhammer is over. I have heard rumours. Well, as you'd expect. No truce has been reached and Holzhammer... He means to win, I gather, at any price. The city could suffer. You know how fond I am of you. Your hotel is so near the centre. Here, we are more secluded. Well?' Her dark, maternal eyes are earnest.

I am moved by her concern. 'You have always been so kind,' I say, touching her arm. 'I'm comfortable enough at the Liverpool, at least for the moment. There is also the young lady to consider.'

'If you could promise me there would be no scandal I'd willingly extend the invitation. The Prince intends to defend – Oh, Ricky – Simply reassure me.' She seems doubtful, reluctant to have Alexandra as a guest. Her little fat face is full of worry.

'There would be no scandal, I promise.' But I am lying, of course. If Alexandra's parents were to find out where their daughter was it would be the end of Frau Schmetterling's business in Mirenburg. For that reason I am firm in declining her offer. 'What danger can there be to civilians, even if Holzhammer marches in tomorrow? Mirenburg is not Paris. There is no Commune here!'

'The Prince means to resist,' she says again.

'Then Germany will come to help him and Holzhammer will be trounced once and for all.'

'The guns...' she murmurs. 'They say...'

'Holzhammer will not bombard Mirenburg. He would arouse the hatred of the civilised world.'

Frau Schmetterling is unconvinced.

'I'm a little exhausted,' I tell her gently. 'I desire very much, madame, to get to bed.'

'Of course.' She squeezes my hand. 'But you must remember, Ricky, that I am your friend.' She waddles away down the passage, then pauses. 'I care for your well-being, my dear.' She waves her plump arms as if to dismiss her own sentiments. She lets out a matronly chuckle. 'Goodnight, Ricky.'

Our carriage is loud in the expectant streets; Alexandra wants to know the substance of my conversation with the madam. I tell her. 'But it would be so convenient,' she says. 'Why didn't you accept?' My instincts are against it. I can hardly explain my feelings to myself and I am already tiring. My nerves are bad, my body no longer sings. I desperately want the comfort of the Liverpool's sheets. Alexandra is still euphoric. She kisses and hugs me. I am her master, she says, her beautiful man, the most wonderful lover in the world. Horses race by with soldiers on their backs. I see lamps moving, hear the occasional voice and I wonder how much of the tension I sense is external, how much comes from within. I am thinking of Princess Poliakoff. Several years before, in Venice, I attended one of her parties at which, she told me, I was to be the guest of honour. She had brought in some peasants from her country estate: young men and women whom, I believe, worked for her. 'Here,' she had said, 'are your pupils. They know all about you and are willing to be educated by you.' Those strange, fresh faces, so wholesome and natural in tone and colour, yet so fundamentally degenerate, looked towards me eagerly as if I were Satan Himself, a Magister of Corruption to whom they could offer their souls as my apprentices. The responsibility was completely beyond me. I told Princess Poliakoff such games bored me. I fled the house. I am aware of my own limitations and, to some degree at least, my own motives. I live as I do because I have no need to work and no great talent for art; therefore my explorations are usually in the realm of human experience, specifically sexual experience, though I understand the dangers of self-involvement in this as in any other activity. Those peasants had been creatures for whom sexuality had become an escape rather than an adventure. They had made no choice at all; they were dependent upon the Princess for their bread. They had no faith in themselves, no belief in their rights as individuals to strengthen and maintain their own wills and to accept any consequences of their own actions. And in this they are dangerous. In this, I would go so far to say, they were evil. And I believe Princess Poliakoff evil, I think. Yet, surely, I am now doing something which I refused to do then, in Venice. Have I no morality left to me, after all? Alexandra clings to me, kisses me with soft, little girl kisses. It is all I can do at this moment not to shudder.

We tug off our clothes as soon as we are in our bedroom. She laughs and kisses my wounds. She looks at herself in the mirror at her bruises and welts, as if she surveys a new gown. 'Oh, Clara is marvellous. Such presence! Don't you think so, Ricky?'

I am already in bed. 'Would you wish to be like Clara?' I ask.

'A whore? Of course not. But to have such power!'

I shake my head. 'She has no power in reality. She pretends it, to serve her clients. She is paid to act that part. The fact that she enjoys it is probably why she is paid so well. But she –'

Alexandra crawls in beside me. 'Ssh, Ricky. You are too serious. Can you see me as a Clara?'

I take her tenderly to me. She is almost immediately asleep, her face in the pillows. It is as if she lies just below the surface of freedom; head down in an unsecured coffin from which, if she merely turns her body once, she can immediately escape. I dim the lamp but do not extinguish it. The sky outside becomes grey. I intend to sleep at least until the evening. I dream of a dark *femme fatale* whom I cannot identify, mother and priestess, wicked and tender; she laughs at me and pulls thorny roses from her body; her laughter is guttural and there is a thin, overbred dog at her side which whines, cringes and bares its teeth at me, barking whenever I try to approach her. Panting, I awaken. Dawn is yellow ivory barred with dusty gold. My body aches, my muscles are tense. I have no energy; my skull seems clamped. There are noises from outside. Momentarily I mistake them for the sounds of surf and wind. I hear a distinctive whistling, a boom. I hear voices from the open window. Taking up my dressing gown I walk on stiff legs to the balcony and stand there, supporting myself on the iron railing. The light is painful. There is smoke rising everywhere, as if from large fires. I look across the square where figures are running this way and that. Another terrible whistling, and before my eyes I see a Gothic spire crack and fall. My predictions were meaningless, comforting, without foundation; little tunes hummed to keep dark realities at bay, for Holzhammer is bombarding Mirenburg! I turn into the room. Alexandra continues to sleep. She has pushed away the covers. There is a smile on her face. I check the impulse to wake her and stumble back to bed to light a cigarette and lie looking up at the bed curtains, listening to the sounds of destruction. Then I am drawn again to the balcony. For most of the morning I remain there, still incredulous, as the enemy shells smash a Romanesque column or erode the delicate masonry of a modern apartment building. It is probable that I am not yet free of the cocaine because I begin to think the bombardment is bringing a new kind of beauty to the city, for the moment at least, perhaps also a dignity it has not previously possessed. Just as a woman in middle or late years will achieve grace and poise through vicissitude and pain making her more attractive than ever she could have been in the prime of her youth and looks, so Mirenburg seems now. I do not grieve for her. It seems relief must soon come in the form of a truce. It is not possible that, in all humanity, the besiegers could place upon their consciences the responsibility for the annihilation of so much nobility and optimism, those centuries of civilisation. And sure enough, at exactly midday, the guns become silent. Prince Badehoff-Krasny will not let his city be destroyed. The autumn light is washed with grey; clouds rise from the ruins like baffled souls. I return to bed and sleep, my own wounds forgotten. Old Papadakis brings more boiled fish. I am surprised because I can smell alcohol on his breath. 'You were so proud of all your abstinences,' I say. 'You sought them out as if they were positive virtues; as if they gave you merit. You were so full of yourself. But you know what it is, too, don't you, to be ruined by a woman?' He sighs and puts the tray over my knees, below my writing case. 'Eat if you want to. Haven't you finished your story yet?' We are both exiles. We have no other bond. 'Are you afraid of it?' I ask. 'Look how much I've written!' His dark eyes stare into a corner of the room. I remember when, relaxed, he used to seem like an eager boy. 'Self-denial is not the same as self-discipline,' I tell him. 'You remain an infant. But you have lost your charm. She found out what you were, didn't she? Widow-hunter!' I believe I am making him angry. For the first time he looks me full in the eyes, as an equal. 'All those dead painters! Vulture! Bring me a bottle of decent claret. Or have you drunk it all yourself? Why do you feel you should be rewarded? You have spent your life responding to others and you thought it would always pay. And now you have only me and you cannot bear to respond, can you? I am your nemesis.'

'You are mad,' he says, and leaves. I continue to laugh. I disdain his pieces of fish. I continue to write. I am writing now. The ink is the colour of the Mediterranean, flowing from my silver Waterman. What have the Italians become? What does their Duce mean to me? And Germany is destroyed. What dreadful perversity led to this? Was it all prefigured? How could we have known better? Can God be so small-minded that He disapproves of a Lesbian salon? But it is not that which He set out to destroy. Oh, the pain of movement. Alexandra is whispering in my ear. 'Ricky, I'm hungry.' One dream washes into another. I smile at her. 'I love you. I am your brother, your father, your husband.' She kisses my cheek. 'Yes. I'm hungry, Ricky. Do you feel rested? I feel wonderful.'

I begin to sit up. 'Have you looked outside?' It is nearly dark. 'No,' she says. 'Why should I?' I tell her to go to the balcony and tell me what she sees. She thinks it is a game. Frowning and smiling she obeys. 'What's happened? Oh, God! They have pulled down –'

'They have shot down,' I say. 'Holzhammer's siege is beginning in earnest.' First she is frightened, and then she begins to show delight. 'But Ricky, it means I'm completely free. People must have been killed, eh?'

I draw in a deep breath. I have never known any creature so unselfconsciously greedy. 'What a wonderful animal you are. Don't you want to try to get to Vienna? Or Paris?'

'And leave Rosenstrasse? Is there anywhere else like it?'

'Nothing quite like it.'

'Then we'll see what happens.'

That night we visit the brothel and before the new girl (an

unremarkable creature called Claudia who submits to Alexandra's rather clumsy imitations of Clara) arrives, Frau Schmetterling pays us a call. 'Remember my offer,' she says. 'They are not interested in this corner of town.'

On our way home we are stopped by soldiers. I tell them who I am. Alexandra invents a name. The soldiers refuse to laugh at my jokes and insist on escorting us back to the hotel. The next morning I receive a visit from a policeman with orders for me to accompany him to his headquarters. He is perfectly polite. It is an examination to which all foreign nationals must submit. I tell Alexandra to wait for me in our rooms and if I do not return by evening to inform Frau Schmetterling. At Nurnbergplatz, however, I find an apologetic police captain who claims to have met my father and to be an admirer of the new Kaiser. 'We have to be cautious of spies and saboteurs. But, of course, you are German.' I ask if it will be possible to have a safe conduct from the city. He promises to do his best, but is not very helpful. 'My superiors,' he says. 'They cannot risk anyone reporting to the enemy. Have you been told about the curfew?' No private citizens are allowed to be on the streets after nightfall without special permission. This threatens my routine. I hardly know what is happening. While we are talking, more shells begin to land within the city walls and now I am aware that the defenders are firing back. The policeman is despondent. 'We are being attacked with our own guns. Holzhammer seized the train from Berlin. Those are Krupp cannon. Even more powerful than the ones you used against Paris. But I should not tell you this, sir. It is hard to become secretive, eh? We are not very experienced at such things in Mirenburg.' I return, despondent, to the Liverpool. Alexandra is half-dressed, busy with her pots and brushes. 'Oh, thank goodness,' she says, without a great deal of interest. 'I thought they had arrested you.' She returns to her mirror. I find her amusing today, perhaps because I am relieved to be free. 'The guns stopped at twelve,' she says. 'I thought so. Some ultimatum of Holzhammer's. I believe, though the newspapers are vague. They are being censored.' I put them down on the bed and remove my jacket. 'Are you sure you want to go to Rosenstrasse tonight? There's a curfew. We must leave before dusk and return after dawn. We could eat at the hotel and have an early night.'

'But it's Friday,' she says. 'Clara promised to bring that friend. You needn't do anything. Just watch. I know you're tired. Don't you want some more cocaine?'

I am incapable of complaint. 'Then we must be ready to leave by six. Did you have lunch?'

'I wasn't hungry. You could order something now.'

I go into the sitting room and ring the bell. I tell the waiter to bring some cold ham and a selection of cheeses and patés, some bread, a bottle of hock. I retrieve the papers from the bed and return to the sitting room. The idea that I am trapped in this city makes me uneasy. I hope that my bank will not be affected. I have forgotten to get a new book of cheques. The papers say there is every expectation that the food-rationing system will preserve supplies of basic commodities for the duration of the War. A well-informed source has assured a correspondent that Germany is bound to send troops soon. There is no reference to Holzhammer's capture of the Krupp cannon. A sortie by Bulgarians has been successfully driven back at the Cesny Gate, to the south. Various regiments are deployed about the first line of defences beyond the walls. All the loyalist soldiers are in good spirits. Morale amongst Holzhammer's 'rag-tag' of mercenaries, misguided peasants and treacherous rebels, is said to be already very low and the world has received the news of the cannonade with horror. Comparisons are made to the Siege of Paris, to Metz and elsewhere, but in all cases those cities were, we are told, far less well-prepared. 'Her name is Lotte,' says Alexandra, her cosmetics in place. She smiles at me and comes to nibble on a piece of cheese. 'The one Clara says had to leave Paris in a hurry. Why was that?'

I decide to take a bath. As I undress I tell Alexandra what I know of Lotte. She used to specialise in a bizarre tableau known as The Temptation, Crucifixion and Resurrection of the Female Christ, in which she would resist any temptations invented by her customers, be tried, punished and then tied to a large wooden cross, whereupon she would be revived by the attentions of the clients. This tableau had been famous in Berlin and Lotte had been the most sought-after 'specialist' in Germany. She had transferred herself to Paris and continued with her presentation there until pressure from the Church, which owned her house, caused her to seek the protection of Frau Schmetterling who accepted her on condition that the tableau no longer be performed. Frau Schmetterling, although Jewish in origin, is a pious woman. The last time I had talked to Lotte she told me she planned to return to Berlin eventually and start up in business again; but she would not skimp. You had to spend money to earn money. She prided herself on the elaborate details of her show. She was saving every pfennig in order to make a rapid return from 'the wilderness'. She was an actress, she had told me, at heart. Alexandra listens. 'She sounds an interesting woman. You know Clara has invited us to her own room tonight. She seems to like you very much. And me.'

It is perfectly true that Clara is attracted to both of us and this puzzles me; to some extent it alarms me, also. Refreshed, I dress in my evening clothes. Alexandra is wearing a pink dress trimmed with red. She looks unusually beautiful. Our cab takes us through streets full of gun carriages and supply wagons; workmen labour amongst the half-destroyed shells of houses and shops, shifting beams and rubble. Alexandra hardly notices as she chatters to me, until we have turned into Sängerstrasse and she gasps. 'Oh, my God! The Mirov Palace!' The seventeenth-century building has received a direct hit which has caved in part of the roof and left a huge gap in its upper floors, and yet the trees surrounding it remain as tranquil as ever, the ornamental gardens as orderly. I expect her to be frightened, but she is not. I suspect she has still failed to understand the reality of what is happening. She is half-grinning as she stares around, wide-eyed, at the destruction. 'Oh, my God!' And I realise that for her it is merely another dream come to life. Perhaps that explains her peculiar attitudes: she perceives all this experience as merely a more intense form of dreaming. Something in her still expects to wake up and find everything ordinary again. That is why she is so heedless of consequence. Yet surely I am dreaming, too. A scarlet motor car goes past. In it, looking rather self-conscious, are four high-ranking officers in tall helmets and a great deal of gold braid. Alexandra giggles. 'Each one could be Franz-Josef himself! Are they in the right army, do you think?'

I insist that she wear her heavy veil as we pay off the carriage and enter the peace of Rosenstrasse. Starlings are swarming over-head in the hazy October sky and the beeches are beginning to shed their leaves. 'The air smells so good,' she says, hugging my arm. 'I am very happy, Ricky.' She compliments me for her state of mind. At the door, Trudi takes my hat, stick and gloves, my topcoat, but Alex remains dressed until we reach Clara's quarters, two large rooms near the top of the house, overlooking the lawn and fruit-trees of the garden. I have never visited Clara's private rooms before. The hangings, cushions and upholstery are pre-dominantly dark blue, black and gold, and the perfume seems to come chiefly from the large, yellow lilies which fill vases on either side of a mahogany desk. There are books in this room, and a small piano, showing that Clara has, after all, some taste for cul-ture, for the pieces on the music-stand are by Mozart and Schubert and the books are either German translations of Fielding, Scott and Thackeray, or works by Goethe and Schiller. Clara claims to be English, but she has nothing in English on her shelves. There is a modern novel or two by von Roberts, some French novels of the cheaper sort, as well as Zola's *Nana* (which all the whores of my acquaintance read with jeering fascination, more interested in his originals and how they correspond with the fictitious characters than the story or the moral), a number of histories and biogra-phies, some books of travel. Clara comes in from the bedroom. She is wearing a black-and-white riding costume. 'I am so pleased you could come,' she says. She kisses first Alexandra and then me. 'Lotte will be with us in a little while.' I remark on her good taste. 'I'm easily bored,' she says. 'Only substantial music and books seem to please me these days.' I indicate the bookcase. 'Yet you have nothing in English...' She smiles. 'I prefer German and French. After all, it is years since I was in London.' She resists my interest in her story, cocking her head and smiling into my face. She is so pale. I would think her consumptive if I did not know otherwise. As she chats about her favourite novels and composers she begins to undress a passive Alexandra. She leads my girl into the bedroom and I follow, leafing through a volume of Le Sage and remarking on the quality of the engravings. Alexandra is spread on the dark yellow bed, face down. Clara tells me that the book had been a gift from a novelist who had travelled all the way from Brussels to be with her. She applies cream to Alexandra's anus and crosses casually to a chest of drawers to take out her china dildo. 'Do you care for Le Sage?'

'I had the usual enthusiasm for him once,' I say. 'Like Molière, he can seem like a revelation when one is young.' She smiles in accord, parting Alexandra's cheeks and pushing the dildo in hard. Alexandra groans. 'Cocaine,' she says. 'Not yet,' says Clara. 'You can have some later. This is my little pleasure, before Lotte arrives. And I think Ricky needs arousing tonight. You look tired, Ricky.' I let her know I had not planned to join in much. 'To tell you the truth the only use I have for a bed is to sleep in one. But I might feel better later.' Clara removes the dildo, wipes it and replaces it neatly in its drawer. This exercise, then, has been for me. Alexandra does not move but I can tell from the set of her shoulders that she is petulant, though not as yet prepared to demand anything of Clara. 'Stay there, ma cherie,' says Clara. We both go back into the other room. Clara hands me a book. It is by Flaubert, his *Salammbô*. I admit that it has always defeated me. Clara is pleased. 'I am glad to hear it. My friend from Brussels recommended it. I have started it so many times and have perhaps managed a hundred pages at best. I am not much interested in the exotic aspects of history. So many of these modern painters leave me cold. Moreau, for instance.' I cannot agree with her. 'My moods change. Sometimes I like the smell of incense and the feel of heavy gold. It can be soothing to the senses. You are more of an epicurean than I, Clara.' I give her back the Flaubert and she replaces it precisely. 'Are Princess Polia-koff and Lady Diana still in residence?' She nods. 'They have hardly left their rooms, either. I think it must be the beginning of an affair, or one which was interrupted. I don't know. Certainly the Princess is infatuated. As for Lady Cromach, I am not sure. She seems anxious to please the Princess but not from what I would call any driving enthusiasm. She is perhaps too intelligent. Are you attracted to her?' I shake my head. 'Not attracted, but I think she is interesting. She is a type of Lesbian I have not really encountered before. Very self-assured, eh? Yet... Oh, let's say less narcissistic than the general run of those one associates with Princess Poliakoff.' Clara sits down on a Liberty chair and lights a cigarette. 'I know what you mean. That woman goes about her business and takes exactly what she wants from people. Yet she has none of Poliakoff's greediness. Would you like me to send for Lotte yet?' I shake my head. 'I've been ravenous all day. I can't stop eating. Let me leave you here with Alexandra. She loves you and might like to be alone with you for a while. I'll go down to the salon for half an hour or so.' Clara seems concerned. 'If you would like some of the drug now...?' I shake my head. 'Perhaps later. Really, I am quite content. Tell Alexandra some of your stories. Or let her sleep. I'll come back shortly.' As I descend the staircase I realise that I am curious about the progress of the War and am hoping that I shall learn something more than what has been reported. Newspapers are particularly untrustworthy at this time. The salon is half-empty. There are many more women here than men. Some of the girls have not even bothered to give themselves the special 'poise' which Madame demands. They are still relaxed. The casual way in which their legs are positioned hints not at any particular carelessness of temperament; they unconsciously assume the habitual attitudes of their calling, as a soldier will stand at ease even in civilian dress, or an off-duty coal-heaver will rest one side of his body in favour of the other. But they are beginning to become 'ladies'. Caroline Vacarescu is here, agitated, speaking urgently to an old dandy in a French-cut coat who spreads his hands and shakes his head. 'But why arrest him? What has he done?' She sees me and appeals to me. 'Ricky. Tell Herr Schmesser that the Count is a man of honour.' I raise my eyebrows. 'Mueller?' Herr Schmesser shrugs. 'He was caught red-handed with the documents destined for

Holzhammer. My dear lady, if you had been with him, you too would now be under arrest. Think yourself lucky.'

'They will shoot him, Ricky,' she says. I am sympathetic. She is about to lose a powerful protector and is in no position to find another quickly. I cannot pity Mueller. Indeed I feel only satisfaction he has at last been caught. 'Caroline,' I say. 'If I can help you, I shall. I am not entirely certain at present how much money I have. But I shall do everything in my power to save you from embarrassment.' I have always liked her. 'Mueller is to be shot,' she says, as if we have not absorbed the enormity and then, realising we are unmoved, rushes from the room, presumably to seek help elsewhere. Herr Schmesser looks at me. 'If she goes out after curfew, she, too, will be arrested. But not,' he adds with a small smile, 'shot. You know of Mueller's activities?'

'I can assume he was spying.'

'And you can be sure that Fräulein Vacarescu was helping him. Together with Budenya-Graetz, who discovered an opportunity to reinstate himself, of course, and is probably already in Vienna with every detail of our defences. It is a disgusting business. The treachery, my dear sir! I cannot tell you how much there has been. My faith in human nature has been ruined in the space of a few days. And this bombardment! Can Holzhammer justify it? His own countrymen. His own city!' He sighs and lifts a glass of champagne to his lips. 'I am very sad.' I pat him on the arm. 'You will cheer up here. After all, there are no disappointments at Frau Schmetterling's, eh?' He nods seriously: 'I hope you are right.' I make a good meal of the buffet. The evening begins. The salon fills. The girls become elegant and alert to the conversation of their guests. The phonograph plays a waltz and everything is as normal. At length, I return to Clara's. Alexandra has by now had some cocaine. Lotte, a plump dimpled blonde, all thighs and bust, is using the dildo on herself while they watch her. I take off most of my clothes, and, wearing a dressing gown supplied by Clara, sink down into a chair and become part of the audience. Alexandra will later play the part which Clara played earlier, but somehow without Clara's delicate assurance, and I will continue to watch until I am aroused enough to couple naturally and cheerfully with Clara for a few minutes before falling soundly asleep until morning. At about ten o'clock, after a good breakfast in Clara's rooms, we return through the chilly October sunshine to the Liverpool. The shells are directed more towards the east of the city this morning and our journey seems safe enough until the cab turns the corner into the square and we see that the building next to the Liverpool has sustained a good deal of superficial damage. I look towards our apartment. Servants are nailing boards across shattered windows. We hurry upstairs. There is glass everywhere in the room. The manager is there. He is deeply apologetic and tells us that we can move to 'safer' rooms at the back of the hotel. Without a word to him or to Alexandra I go downstairs and telephone Frau Schmetterling. She has one of the few private telephones in Mirenburg. 'I would like to take you up on your offer,' I tell her, 'if it is still possible.'

'Of course,' she says. 'I'll have the rooms prepared at once. When will you arrive.'

'Probably in an hour or two.'

She hesitates. Her voice becomes faint as the line fades. 'You are bringing your friend?'

'I am afraid that I have no choice.'

'I will see you at lunchtime,' she says.

While Alexandra sees to the packing, I make enquiries after Caroline Vacarescu. She has not returned to the hotel, says the manager. I pay my bill with one of his blank cheques. He continues to apologise so much I feel sorry for him and am able to smile cheerfully enough. 'Please don't worry. I will be back here, I am sure, within a couple of weeks.' I do not inform him of my destination. Alexandra and I are about to disappear. If we should be discovered, when the War is over I can always make her father an offer. I can marry her and save the scandal. But for some reason I do not tell Alexandra of my plan as, with boxes and trunks in three cabs, we flee the ruined Liverpool to the sanctuary of Rosenstrasse.

Chapter Three
The Siege

THE ATMOSPHERE AT Rosenstrasse had become increasingly convivial during that first week of bombardment and, even though the shelling has stopped and the Siege proper has begun (the city now has an air of desperate calm) this mood remains with us. It is Friday, 29 October, 1897. Seven of us who are permanent residents have taken to eating together, rather like passengers on a small ship or guests at a provincial boarding house. Frau Schmetterling presides: our landlady, our captain. Alexandra continues to be my secret and grows resentful of her exile from the public rooms. She is beginning to exhaust me. Clara has developed a habit of keeping her company, largely I suspect to relieve me. 'The child is bored. I'll take her for a stroll,' she says, or, 'I've invented a new game for our little girl.' At night Alexandra and I sleep together as usual, reserving our evenings for 'adventures'. We go out rarely. Mirenburg has become depressing. I cannot stand to see the boarded windows and doors, the sandbags, the rubble. We have now enjoyed, singly or in combination, almost all Frau Schmetterling's whores. The only other residents who hardly ever make an appearance at the table together are Princess Poliakoff and Lady Cromach. The Englishwoman is frequently out, presumably gathering material for her articles. I lunch while Alexandra goes with Clara to Falfnersallee 'to look for bargains'. I enjoy a good borscht and a veal cutlet. 'Mister' and Trudi wait on us. Frau Schmetterling is kind to both of them. Occasionally 'Mister' will be asked to join us, but usually he smiles and refuses, preferring the company of Chagani, the brooding ex-acrobat, who sometimes assists him. His gentleness can be disconcerting, even sinister. His drunkard's face, so youthful and open, and at the same time so cruelly ruptured, expresses a peculiar eagerness. The ruined veins, the rough, red flesh, the set of his soft mouth and the watery innocence of his eyes give immediate notice of his despair, his determination to remain in some way unprotected against the terrors of the world and so, surely by an effort of will alone, retain the untroubled perceptions of boyhood. Elvira, Frau Schmetterling's daughter, sometimes dines with us. When she and 'Mister' are together she seems the more mature; a self-possessed, tiny version of her mother. 'Mister's' expression becomes softer, more attractive, in her company. Madame's chow dogs, black and unpredictable, complete the ménage, panting around our feet as if they are waiting for one of us to drop dead. The Dutch banker, Leopold Van Geest, sallow and animated, wearing a sort of invalid's blanket-jacket, cuts enthusiastically at his meat. He has decided that it will be at least a month before Berlin sends help. 'The Prince should have made a Treaty with one or another of the Powers. Then Holzhammer could not have acted at all. Badehoff-Krasny was too confident. He thought he stood on a platform balanced over the torrent. But it was a tightrope, yes? He leaned back to relax and – Pouf!' He gestures dramatically with his fork. 'Now the Germans will let him drown a little before fishing him out. They want the best terms, after all.' He shrugs. He has a wife and thirteen children in the Hague and is in no hurry to return home.

'The whole city could be destroyed within a month,' says Rakanaspya in that husky voice of his. The anarchist has been placed under a sort of house arrest by the police. Frau Schmetterling had agreed to his staying 'so long as he behaves himself,' she said. 'We want no morbid subjects discussed here.' He wipes his lips and beard with his napkin. 'All those poor people dead while kings and princes play at diplomacy!' Frau Schmetterling catches his eye and utters a small cough. He sighs. Caroline Vacarescu, beside him, is sympathetic. She, too, is on sufferance, having been released from custody four days ago. She is dressed magnificently as usual. She has no intention, she assures us, of lowering her standards. Her face is heavily made-up. Mueller was tried by military tribunal last week and executed for espionage. The papers have been emphatic: his fate was an example to others. Some of us are a little uneasy in her defiant, knowing presence. Count Belozerski, the eminent Russian novelist and the most recent arrival, leans his handsome face over the table and murmurs in French, 'I have never seen so many dead soldiers.' He was turned back from the walls while trying to leave Mirenburg. He alone has witnessed the reality outside and is allowed to say more than anyone on the subject. Frau Schmetterling indulges him because she admires, she says, his mind. But she is also impressed by his connections and his beauty. His pale blond hair, together with his slightly Oriental cast of features, give him a striking and dominating appearance. He is tall and slender and his military stance is tempered by a natural grace which serves to soften the first impression of a distant and somewhat menacing figure. Count Belozerski is proud, he says, of his Tartar forebears. He sometimes refers romantically to his 'Siberian blood'. He is in all important respects a gentlemanly European. 'Of the best type,' says Frau Schmetterling. Caroline Vacarescu also dotes on him, but Belozerski has confided to me that he is determined to have nothing to do with her. 'Her selfishness,' he told me last night, 'is mitigated only by her recklessness. Of course both qualities are alarming to a man like myself. One should be in love with such women in one's youth. To take up with the likes of Caroline Vacarescu in middle-life is to risk too much. My cousin was, for a short while, involved with her. She almost ruined him. She is the most extravagant creature I have ever known and I prefer to admire her from a distance.' I, of course, feel friendly towards her, but that could be because I have nothing that she would want. It is my belief Count Belozerski is attracted to her. He is a little inclined to overstate his case. He adds: 'One is dealing, as a novelist, all day with ambiguities, with problems of human character. One does not need any more ambiguities in one's life.' Perhaps he is right. I am not a novelist. I tell him I thrive on ambiguity. For me a woman must always have it or she is not attractive to me. He laughs. 'But then for you life is a novel, eh? Thank God not everyone is the same, or I should have no readers.'

'The hospitals cannot cope with the wounded.' Egon Wilke sits immediately to the left of Frau Schmetterling, across from Belozerski. He is a stocky fellow, with the body and movements of an artisan. His hands are huge and his large head has brown hair, cropped close to the skull. He wears a sort of dark pea-jacket and a white cravat. He is an old friend of Frau Schmetterling's, apparently from the days when she ran a house of an altogether different character in Odessa, where criminals had gathered. These acquaintances from her past are usually discouraged from visiting Rosenstrasse, but Wilke, who has been introduced to the company as a jewel merchant, is the exception. Frau Schmetterling is evidently very fond of him. He saved her, it is rumoured, from ruin (perhaps prison) in the old days and lent her the money to start the Rosenstrasse house. He always stays with her when visiting Mirenburg and, like me, is treated as a favoured client. He behaves impeccably, never bringing his business to her house, though he is almost certainly still a successful thief. He chews his food thoughtfully, takes a sip of wine and continues: 'They are requisitioning convents, private houses, even restaurants, I have heard. These Mirenburger soldiers, poor devils, aren't used to fighting.'

Frau Schmetterling says firmly: 'We know how hellish it is at the defences, and I am sure we sympathise, but this is scarcely appropriate conversation for luncheon.' Wilke looks almost surprised, then smiles to himself and continues to eat. There is not much else to talk about. We have no real information. Holzhammer has made a grandiose declaration in which he has praised his own sense of humanity and love of beauty in stopping the bombardment 'to give Prince Badehoff-Krasny time to reconsider his foolish and unpatriotic decision which is causing misery to so many'. He claims that most of Wäldenstein is now his. The newspapers on the other hand are continuing to report failing morale and shortage of supplies amongst the rebels. The peasants and landowners have all deserted Holzhammer, they say, and he is entirely reliant on his 'Bulgarian butchers', his Austrian cannon. Prince Badehoff-Krasny took his State Carriage into the streets during the bombardment and rode the length of Mirenburg, from the Cesny Gate to the Mirov Gate, waving to cheering crowds. Deputations of citizens have signed oaths of undying loyalty to the Crown and the Mayor has sworn to take a sword, if necessary, and personally drive Holzhammer from the battlements, should he try to enter the city. Holzhammer has probably decided to attempt to starve Mirenburg into submission, saving his troops and his ammunition for a final attack. The blockade is total. The river is guarded on both sides and water-gates have been installed under the bridges on the outskirts so that no citizen can leave by that route or bring supplies in; while a huge barricade has been thrown up around the city, making it impossible for anyone to come or go either by road or rail. Belozerski has reported seeing corpses left to rot in trenches, or half-buried by their comrades as they fell back towards the walls. Field guns, too, have been abandoned. He observed one trench which was 'a single, heaving mass of carrion crows'. Private citizens are no longer allowed on the walls. We are under martial law. Yesterday, at lunch, Belozerski said: 'God knows what appalling treachery led to this situation. It was a massacre out there.' And then he became embarrassed, since Caroline Vacarescu could probably have answered his rhetorical question, at least in part. She had continued to eat as if she had not heard him. We are all as tactful as possible, even Rakanaspya who sometimes fumes like one of his own anarchist bombs but never explodes. It is only in private, in the company of one or another of our fellow guests, that we express strong opinions. Last night I sat with Clara in her sitting room while Alexandra giggled in bed with Aimée, who comes from my native Saxony. Clara is in a better position than many to hear what is actually going on. Her regular clients seem to make up half the Mirenburg Civil Service and she sometimes has a general come to see her. She is discreet, in the main, but she believes that the situation might be worse than most of us imagine. 'A military train is believed to have arrived from Vienna. If the Austrians give Holzhammer direct aid then Germany must either begin another war, which she does not presently want, or turn a blind eye to what is

going on here. I think she will turn a blind eye.' I found this difficult to believe: 'With so many of her citizens still here?' Clara had
looked at me knowingly. 'How many, Ricky? And how many German soldiers would die in a war with Austria-Hungary?' Then
Alexandra had called to me and I had gone in to smile. She had
tied one of Clara's dildoes onto her in some way and was inex-
pertly fucking Aimée who was helpless with laughter. 'Help me,
Ricky, darling!' There is an ache in my back today. Papadakis says
I am not resting enough. He says I should set these memoirs aside.
'You will kill yourself.' I tell him that it does not matter. 'Can't you
see I am living again? Can't you see that?' He wets his red lips.
'You are mad. The doctor told me to expect something like
this. Let me bring him up.' I set my pen on the pages, across the
words. I am patient. 'I am more purely rational,' I tell him, 'than I
have been for two years. And I should point out that there is hardly
any pain. It is quite evident that much of what I was suffering was
psychosomatic. Haven't you noticed how much better my morale
is? You would rather I was ill, eh? You have no power over me now
that I am recovering!' He will not respond to this. He sits beside
the window, staring down towards the sea. His back is to me. I
refuse to let him irritate me. Leopold Van Geest and I stroll in
Frau Schmetterling's garden. Most of the flowers are gone. It is a
mystery where she continues to find fresh ones to fill her house.
Beyond the walls are the roofs and turrets of the deserted monastery. 'In here,' says Van Geest, 'one is permitted the illusion of
power. But we know that Frau Schmetterling is the only one who
really wields power and that she derives it from her ladies. From
the cunt.' He shakes his head and pulls the blanket-jacket more
closely to him. 'Yet we have power in the outside world to create
a society which needs and permits brothels. Why cannot we exploit
that power directly? Why do we feel the need to come here and be
masters when we cannot feel that we are masters in our own
homes, over our own women – at least, not sexually. Not really.
You can sense the difference.'

'I have very little experience of the domestic life.'

Van Geest nods as if I have made a profound observation. He is moody this afternoon. 'Your instincts are good, von Bek. Marriages are based on romantic lies and decent women demand that we maintain those lies at all costs, lest the reality of their situation be brought home to them. Here the whores are paid to lie to us. At home we pay for our domestic security with lies of our own.' He looks up at the sky. 'Do you think it will snow?'

'It's a little early for that.'

He turns to go back inside. 'Well, I shall probably be home for Christmas,' he says.

Clara comes to join me. 'Our Alice has bought herself a thousand new petticoats!' She kisses me on the cheek. Somehow we have taken to calling Alexandra 'Alice', while I use 'Rose' as a nickname for Clara. She, in turn, calls me 'Your Lordship' in English. Alexandra does not know our nicknames. 'She is upstairs, now, trying them on.' Van Geest lifts his cap and enters the house. 'What were you talking about?' She is all rustling velvet in her long winter coat. 'Marriage, I believe,' I say. 'I'm not altogether sure. Van Geest seemed to want to get something off his chest.' Clara is amused by this. 'That's our job. Whores are trained to listen. What was he saying?'

'That domestic bliss is founded on a lie.'

The argument is familiar to her. 'Working here, one begins to disbelieve in any great difference between people. The girls in this house have more varied personalities than most clients, and that's saying very little, I should think. You cannot pursue individuality here. There's more realism and virtue, perhaps, in celebrating commonality. There are certain lies, surely, we would all rather believe.' She links her arm in mine. We are almost like husband and wife.

We go to peer in at Frau Schmetterling's little hothouse, at the orchids and the fleshy lilies, and at her aviary where a pair of pink cockatoos, an African Grey parrot and a macaw fidget. 'Frau Schmetterling has no interest in birds,' says Clara. She puts her lips together and makes kissing sounds at the gloomy creatures. 'These were given to her at the same time, I believe, as the peacocks. The peacocks died. She's sentimental enough to want to keep her parrots properly, but they get no attention from her. "Mister" looks after them. Some of us have asked to keep them in our rooms, but she says it would be vulgar.' I am becoming impatient to see Alexandra, even though I know she will be demanding something of me the moment I walk into our room. 'Shall you be going to the celebration this evening?' asks Clara. I had forgotten. Frau Schmetterling had mentioned it at lunch. 'To honour the end of the bombardment,' she had said. 'It will cheer us all up.'

'I'll look in for half an hour or so,' I say. 'And you?' Clara nods. 'Oh, yes. I think it will be amusing.' Since Alexandra will sulk if I go I have almost made up my mind not to bother. 'They are difficult, these children,' says Clara. 'More trouble than they're worth, sometimes.' I feel a moment's resentment of what I take to be her criticism, but she squeezes my arm and the mood vanishes. I enjoy Clara's company more and more and continue to be impressed by her tolerant intelligence. 'By the way,' she says casually, 'did you hear that they had attempted to burn down the Synagogue. The Jews are being held to blame, as usual.' I laugh at this. 'Where would we be without them?' But Clara is not pleased with my response. 'I came through the Quarter on the way home. It's miserable. No market, of course, to speak of. Such a terrible sense of fear, Ricky.'

'You must guard against getting too sentimental, Rose, my darling, at times like these. It's not like you.' I kiss her cheek. She shakes her head and does her best to dismiss her mood. It occurs to me for a second that perhaps she is worried about her own fate. After all, Frau Schmetterling is Jewish, at least by birth. I return to the rooms. Alexandra is wearing a new négligée of chocolate-brown trimmed with cream lace and her little body, now marked with the fading reminders of a dozen violent nights, is pale in the afternoon light which enters through embroidered nets at the windows. Couch, floor and chairs are piled with new chemises and drawers, with white ostrich feathers, with an ermine-trimmed stole, like froth on a river, and she tugs at her curls, peering with ill temper into an oval mirror which hangs on the wall over a lacquered Chinese sideboard. 'Another raid on Falfnersallee,' I say with a smile. She pulls down an eyelid, looking for blood. 'They're almost giving things away, Ricky.' She has bought a selection of new cosmetics, which she has scattered over the sideboard, and begins to try them out, asking me for my opinion of this lip-rouge and that powder. 'You'll destroy your skin,' I say dispassionately. 'You have youth and health, natural beauty...' She makes a face. 'You are certainly no lover of what is natural, my dear.' I bridle. 'Nonsense. But play at grown-up ladies, if that's what pleases you. Did you buy a paper?' She is distant. 'I forgot.' I am irritated. 'It's not a great deal to ask.' I pick at feathers and linen, becoming even more angry when I think I shall have to ask Frau Schmetterling for more cash. I have given her a blank cheque, to cover our expenses. 'You should have told Clara to remember,' says Alexandra. 'She's always reliable. Anyway, what do you want a paper for? You told me there's nothing in it now but lies.' The négligée has fallen back to reveal her ribs. 'You're not eating properly,' I say. 'You're getting too thin.' She sets down a little pot with a rap. 'Men want everything. A lady has to be thin in society and plump in bed. Yet you complain about the way I lace my stays!'

'I'm concerned for your health. I feel some responsibility.'

'You should not. It is none of your business.'

I want to put an end to this. I embrace her, fondling her shoulders and breasts, but she pulls away. 'You treat me like a child! You spend all your time with other people. Are you fucking the whores while I'm out?'

'You know I'm not. You enjoy Clara's company. You told me so. You're always off on expeditions.'

'In a veil. Like a Turkish concubine! You don't love me. You're bored with me. You refuse to let me be myself. I'm not your daughter. I wanted to get away from that. You sound worse than my father sometimes.'

'Then you should not behave like a little girl.' Such banal exchanges are terrible. I hate listening to the words on my own lips. I have said nothing of this kind since I was eighteen. 'All the interesting people are downstairs,' she says. 'You talk about them. I never see them. Princess Poliakoff, Count Belozerski, Rudolph

Stefanik. You and Clara joke about them. I am left out of every-thing. Why do you want me? You could have a dozen whores and never notice I was missing.'

'I love you,' I say. 'That's the difference.'

She snorts. 'You don't know me.'

'I'm beginning to think there is not very much to know. Per-haps you are entirely my invention.'

'You bastard!' It is the first time she has sworn at me. She repeats the oath, as if to herself. 'You bastard.' She begins to weep. I go to comfort her. She pulls away again. 'What have you made me!'

'Nothing which you were not already, or did not wish to be. I told you at the start I am the instrument of your pleasure. I put myself at your disposal. And when I have warned you of excess you haven't listened to me. Now you're overtired and self-pitying. And you're blaming me.'

Her weeping becomes more intense. 'I don't know any better. How can I know any better? I want so much to go to the party tonight. But you're afraid I'll embarrass you. And when I try to look grown-up you complain. You confuse me. You lie to me.'

'How dare you pretend to be so naïve,' I say. 'You have no right to demand honesty of me and argue with such patent ingenuity when you know full well what you mean and what you want. It is malice and resentment which motivates you and your methods amount to blackmail. I will not be insulted by you in this way. I will not be silent while you insult yourself. What is it that you want?'

But she refuses to be direct. The rhetoric continues between sobs. 'You have destroyed any will I might have had. Any self-respect. You spend your time with Clara. You laugh at me behind my back.'

'Clara is your friend. You told me that you love her.'

'She criticises constantly.'

'Not to me.'

'I know what she's saying. You're a fool if you don't realise what she's up to.'

I light myself a cigarette. 'You are attempting to manufacture a crisis,' I say, 'and I will not be drawn. Tell me what you want.'

'I want respect!'

'Eventually,' I continue, 'it is very likely that you will wear me down sufficiently so that out of weariness or exasperation I will make you an offer and thus save you the responsibility of making your own decision. Or I will become remorseful and give you that which your conscience cannot demand. Well, I will have none of it. When you have made up your mind to speak to me directly I shall be pleased to continue this conversation.' I sound ridiculously pompous in my own ears. She wants me to take her to the party. I am almost ready to do so, even though I know it would be unwise. But I want her to ask. Somehow I am carrying too much of the burden. I am at the door when she wails: 'I want to go to the party!'

'You know it would be too dangerous for us,' I say.

'I don't know. I only know what you tell me. Are you frightened of their opinion?'

I am frightened, of course. I am frightened of the dream ending, of reality intruding. I leave the room. She has wounded me and I am full of self-pity. I am furious with her. I had thought things had reached a decent balance. But she is not content with promises of Paris and I can scarcely blame her, since there is no means of knowing when the Siege will be over. But she has changed. I can sense that she has changed. What alterations have occurred in her strange, fantastic brain. I am as much at a loss for a satisfactory explanation as if I had attempted to analyse the perceptions and motives of a household pet. Like a pet she is able to take on the colour of any master, to respond to whatever desires that master displays. Yet she is not doing that now. Does that mean she is ready to find a new master? I feel I am somehow making a mistake, as if I have failed to understand the rules of the game. Perhaps I should not have been so direct with her. Perhaps I should have disguised my desires and remained more of a mystery to her. Or will I lose her anyway? To someone else who will represent liberty and escape to her? It seems increasingly important that we should leave

Mirenburg. I will go to Police headquarters in the morning and try again to get passports for us. I have miscalculated. I blame the drugs, the atmosphere of the whorehouse. Sensuality has given way to a sort of erotomania. It could destroy everything. I must make an effort to impress her with my own common sense. I must not weaken. Alice! I want what you were. My little girl! Have you no notion of all the emotions you have aroused in me? The tenderness, the willingness to sacrifice everything for you? You cannot know what I have given up already, what I am still prepared to give up. You are myself. And we are Mirenburg. I find that I am outside Clara's room. I knock. She tells me to enter. She has Natalia, her dark friend, with her. They are drinking tea. 'I am so sorry to disturb you.' I make to go, but both wave me in. 'Is the child sleeping?' asks Clara. 'No,' I say, 'she decided to have a tantrum, so I've left her to cool down.' Clara and Natalia both seem to approve of this decision. I fall into Clara's couch, immediately relieved. 'What am I to do with her?'

'You wouldn't welcome my answer,' says Clara.

'True. You think I should have told her to go back to her parents.'

'It isn't my business to say.' Clara offers me her own teacup. I accept it. 'I intend to marry her,' I say, 'when we get to Paris. As a wife, she will have more power, more self-respect. She'll begin to grow up in no time.'

Natalia and Clara exchange a look which is meaningless to me. 'My father wants me to marry again. Her father will be only too happy to let her marry me once he finds out what has happened. I'm worrying about nothing. She wants to come to the celebration tonight. I'll bring her.'

'That should relieve her boredom,' says Clara. 'I've heard Princess Poliakoff and Lady Cromach have decided to attend. And there are other guests. Some politicians. Some intellectuals. It will be a fine night. You might meet Dolly's fiancé, too.' Dolly is the most sweet-natured girl in the house and much in demand with older clients. She is by no means beautiful, with her long nose, large teeth and her frizz of dark hair, but she is good-hearted and genuinely interested in the doings of her gentlemen, spending hours chatting with them. One of these, a pleasant man by all accounts, the owner of a large furrier's business in Ladungsgasse, is determined to marry her as soon as she wishes to retire. It is a standing joke between them. They often discuss the bridal gown she will have, the church they favour, the places they will visit on their honeymoon. Dolly has taken to wearing her gentleman's engagement ring: an emerald. She will accept presents from nobody else and on Wednesdays and Sundays when he calls will always make sure she is available only to him. Natalia and Clara continue with their conversation. They are discussing a woman I have not met. The mother had been supporting her drug-addicted daughter, I gather, for some years, paying for her opium and morphine, but her daughter had become homeless and needed work. Against her normal caution, and because the daughter was known to her, Frau Schmetterling had agreed she could work at Rosenstrasse for a few weeks until she saved the fare to go to relatives in Prague. 'Frau Schmetterling is so innocent in some ways,' says Natalia. 'She was surprised at the demand when it became known that a mother and daughter were working in the same house. She could not believe so many of her customers would insist on having the two women in the same bed at the same time! She was very glad when what's-her-name went on to Prague.' Clara takes her empty teacup from me. 'She's a funny little woman. Quite prudish sometimes, eh? What do you think, Ricky? You've known her longer than any of us really.

'She's the mother I never had,' I say lightly. 'I love her. She worries about me so much!'

'Oh, I think we all do,' says Clara. She seems to be making some sort of joke, so I smile.

'I hear that General von Landoff will be here tonight,' says Natalia. 'Madame has decided to treat with the military for once. She's making a big concession, eh?'

'A prudent one at this time,' I suggest. 'She would rather have one general invading Rosenstrasse than a regiment of privates. War can make politicians of us all.'

'We are expert politicians here,' insists Clara with a smile, 'every one of us. If Frau Schmetterling had been in charge, there would have been no War to begin with!'

Natalia is weighing a piece of her lace collar in her small palm. 'It's pretty material,' she says, 'isn't it? That very fine cotton which sometimes I prefer to silk. Silk is too much like skin. There is no contrast. Shall I go on telling you what the Mayor asked me to do?'

'I'd love to hear,' I say, settling back in Clara's cushions. 'You old eunuch,' says Clara affectionately. 'I sometimes think you'd rather gossip than fuck!' Natalia begins a rather ordinary tale about the Mayor's make-believe, his penchant for imitating farmyard animals. I learn more, too, about Caroline Vacarescu. Clara says she deliberately pursues and conquers the wives of famous men. 'It used to be her speciality. Her seductions became an inextricable mixture of business and pleasure. Her mistresses were often grateful for the opportunities for dalliance without much risk of scandal and they were party to secrets which proved useful to Caroline in her other activities. They say she's probably a million-airess. The truth is she's probably spent everything. Caroline Vacarescu's extravagances have taken on the nature of an art; her raw materials are other people's money (or, at a pinch, credit) and her canvas is the fashionable world. Her clothes are the most expensive, her houses the most richly furnished and her presents to her protectors (who, of course, supplied her with the means to make the purchases in the first place) are generous. But this affair with Mueller was more serious, I think. His death has affected her quite badly. She's desperate to get back to Buda-Pesht. She's asking everybody. If anyone can do it, Caroline can.' I take my leave of the ladies and return to my Alice to announce she can go to the ball tonight. She hugs me and kisses me as if I am a favourite uncle. We fall into bed together and once again the dream comes alive.

Papadakis seems to be ill. Perhaps he weakens as I grow stronger. 'As soon as this is finished I shall be getting up,' I tell him. 'And we'll travel. We'll go to Venice first and then Vienna, or perhaps Paris. What do you think?' He is a mangey old spaniel. He looks at me and wheezes. 'You must be careful,' I say. 'You aren't getting any younger. What was the name of that woman who worked for you in London? The one I slept with?' He frowns. 'Sonia, wasn't it?' I say. 'She was Jewish, I think. She used to sit in that little basement flat of hers in Bloomsbury and curse you. Then we'd go to the British Museum in the twilight, just before it closed. I can smell the leaves around our ankles. She made you seem far more interesting than you turned out to be. She was obsessed by Egypt, I remember. By the Book of the Dead. What's happened to your daughter? You haven't had a letter in a year. Two years. She has forgotten her papa.' Papadakis has brought an uncorked bottle of Niersteiner and a glass. He puts it on the table beside the bed. 'Tell me when you need more,' he says. 'What? Is it poisoned? Or do you hope I'll drink myself into silence? Your daughter. Isn't she divorced yet, from that foolish Frenchman? Or are you a grandfather, do you think? Are you a grandfather? There is still time to accept the responsibilities of a parent. I am not going to be on your hands much longer.' He pours some of the wine into the glass. 'Think what you like,' he says. 'Do what you like. Say what you like. It's good wine. There are a few bottles left. Let me know when you want some more.' I sip the hock. It is perfect. I am in charge of myself again. 'Buy flowers when you're next in town,' I tell him. 'As many as possible. Deep reds and blues. Good, heavy scent. Whatever you can find. Spend what you need to spend. I'll have flowers instead of food. I am celebrating the death of an old friend and my own return to life. Did you ever really visit that doctor I recommended? That follower of Freud's?' He shakes his head: 'I have no time for psychoanalysis or any other fashionable remedies. My faith remains in Science. The rest is just quackery, no matter how it's dressed up.' He amuses me. *'Oh, what we owe to Vienna!'* I sing. I descend with Alexandra on my arm. I am dressed in perfect black and white, she in scarlet and gold, with diamonds, pearls, rubies, with black-rimmed eyes and gaudy cheeks, her age unguessable, her identity engulfed. She walks with back straight, her head lifted with arrogant cocaine.

We reach the foyer and pause. From the salon comes Strauss and a swell of voices, smoke and the scents of fresh-cooked meat. Alice trembles with pleasure and I am my happiest. We have concocted our masquerade: She is to be the Countess Alice of Elsinore tonight, from Denmark, although her home is now in Florence. She is twenty-three and my cousin. The lie is not meant to convince, merely to confuse the curious. 'No-one will recognise me,' she says. 'Friends of my father or my brother know me only as a little girl in sailor-blouses.' I am feeling so euphoric that I believe I might even welcome a scene in which her father, for instance, was present. We are through the doors now and into the plush and velvet, the crystal and marble, of the salon. The place is alive with potential danger: journalists and several of the great scandalmongers of Mirenburg, including Herbert Block the song-writer and Voorman the painter. Voorman is the only real problem, but he has no memory of her as the same creature he pretended to court at The Amoral Jew. He kisses her hand as he is introduced and she listens with some merriment as he suggests, again, that she is the goddess he has always imagined he will one day paint. A young Deputy, Baron Karsovin, her distant cousin, suggests as he wrinkles his pink brow beneath an already balding head that they must have met before, 'perhaps in Venice', but he is anxious to return to his discussion of the Prince of Wales, Mrs Keppel and French foreign policy. And an old gentleman, wearing all his orders on his coat, says he believes he knew Alice's mother. 'Indeed he did,' she whispers. 'He was her lover four or five years ago and used to bribe me with chocolates from Schmidt's. He bribed Father with secrets of the Bourse and paid for our new house as a result!' The General is already here, back to the fireplace and looking so brave he might be facing a firing squad. I almost expect someone to blindfold him. He is very tall and thin, with blue veins in his long neck and white whiskers a little yellow about the lips and chin. His hair is quite long. He wears outdated evening dress, standing with his hands behind him under his frock-coat and talking to Frau Schmetterling (in unusual off-the-shoulder royal blue and silver with a small bustle) and Caroline Vacarescu whose reputation, I suspect, he knows, for he is wary as well as reassuring, though she has succeeded in flattering him. Alice and I are introduced.

'Is there no chance of getting up a group of those who wish to leave?' asks Caroline, all sweet perfume and vulnerable, whispering russet flounces. 'If only we could reach the mountains, say. Under a white flag. There must be some sort of communication between the two sides. Some understanding that the civilised world would be scandalised when it found out how decent people were being treated.'

'But my dear lady, there is absolutely no danger to you here,' says the General. 'Holzhammer has used up all his ammunition. And the bombardment, you must have noticed, was concentrated entirely on the centre of the city. You are far safer in Mirenburg. There are bandits abroad in the country areas. Deserters. Disaffected peasants. You can imagine.'

'Are we to understand that no permits will be issued at all?' I say.

'No chance whatsoever, at present.' The General speaks as if he imparts the best news in the world. 'Holzhammer can scarcely hold out another week with all the desertions. Then – a quick counter-attack, with or without Berlin's support – then it will be over. We are biding our time. It is a question of choosing the moment.'

'So our losses have not been as great as they say?' says Caroline almost waspishly.

'Our losses, dear lady, have been minimal. Austria is going to regret her involvement in what is, after all, little more than a domestic squabble.' Caroline darts me a look, as if she hopes for an ally, but I am helpless. With a little nasal sigh, like a lioness who has made too short a charge and has seen her prey escape, she stalks off in search of other game. Clara greets us. She has discarded her usual tailor-mades and is wearing a gold dress, her hair in a pompadour. She looks at least five years younger and is arm in arm with a rather drunk Rakanaspya who wears a dove-grey suit a little too large for him, evidently borrowed. He speaks so elliptically to the General, in such thick French, that nobody understands him. 'You have nothing to fear,' says von Landoff, and nods, as if to a simpleton. 'Another week or less and you may go home.' Rakanaspya, with one eye on Frau Schmetterling, lapses into the security of Russian, plainly saying all he wishes to say in that language and so releasing his feelings without giving much offence to his hostess. Clara says: 'Good evening to you both. You look stunning. A perfect match,' and she bears against Rakanaspya with her shoulder to steer him off towards the middle of the room where Block enjoys the flattery of the ladies and Stefanik drones moodily on the subject of flight. Princess Poliakoff makes her entrance. She is in black tulle and pearls, true to form, while her lover is a swan in fold upon fold of Doucet lace, approaching as if she has just landed on water and is coasting towards the shore. Her short curly hair has a torque around it bearing two pale mauve ostrich feathers which match her fan. She seems to wear no make-up but is delicately English in her healthy colouring. Alice wants to know who she is and when I tell her she whispers: 'Let's talk to them. They seem far more interesting.' Occasionally, by a less-than-careful movement she betrays her youth. We make our way to the Lesbian couple. Everyone is introduced. 'We have seen nothing of you,' I say. 'You snub us indiscriminately!'

'I haven't been well,' says the Princess. 'And Diana has been a saint. Also, of course, she has to look for material.' Lady Cromach takes a testy interest in her fan, then offers me one of her soft, sardonic stares and says in that insinuating voice: 'And how is your health, Herr von Bek?'

'Excellent, as usual, Lady Cromach. Thank you. Are your articles about the War already entertaining the readers of the *Gaulois* and the *News*?'

'The telegraph is down. And the carrier pigeons are unreliable. I have no idea. For a while I thought I was bribing a little man in the military dispatch office, but he was dismissed a few days ago. I fear my work will be retrospective when it appears, and nobody is overly interested in the fate of Mirenburg. Are they?' She seems to want to know. 'I content myself with doing atmosphere pieces for the monthlies. I keep busy. What a charming brooch, my dear.'

She peers towards Alice's breasts. 'You say that you are a guest here, too?' Princess Poliakoff looks distracted and jealous. She puts one of those elongated fingers to her mouth, then withdraws it carefully to her side. 'How's the minstrel, Ricky?'

'Singing as sweetly as ever,' I say. 'And teaching me to play the banjo.' I'm surprised she still believes me. She pulls her companion away from us. 'You have a lovely cousin,' says Lady Cromach; she winks at me behind the Princess's back. I find her extremely attractive. I believe she is thoroughly intrigued by me. Alice fumes. 'What an awful witch!'

'Lady Diana?'

'Of course not.' She is on my arm again. We move towards the buffet. 'It's much more ordinary than I expected. I'd imagined it – well – Oriental. Decadent. It's almost like one of Mother's Evenings.'

'Except that most of the women are whores and all the men are lechers.' I hand her some cold salmon.

'Then it's exactly like one of Mother's Evenings.' She laughs. I have not for a long time known her so carelessly cheerful. I love her. It is such a relief to feel that things are normal again. 'You look very handsome tonight,' she says. 'As you always used to look. I'm glad you seem happy, Ricky.'

'I'm happy that you're happy. It is so easy, my little one, to make you happy.' I am full of tenderness for her.

'I'm happy because you've taken me seriously and are treating me – I don't know – as an equal. I'm far older than my age. People have often said so.'

You will always be my own sweet little girl, Alice. My lascivious child, my dreaming daughter-wife. I want the soft, sudden flesh, the sweet dunes, the little caves. The music of your shouts and your pleasure. I bite your neck, your throat, your shoulder. I will do whatever you want. I will say and become whatever you want, to keep you as I want you to be. This turn in her conversation begins to depress me. I ask her whom she would like to meet next. 'That's Van Geest, the banker, with Thérèse. And that, of course, is Count Belozerski. Our Lesbians are talking to Wilke, the jewel thief. Would you like to meet him? He's usually very grave and of course doesn't talk much about his work.' The salon is growing noisier, a trifle more boisterous. The General moves away from the fireplace beaming like a baby with Natalia on one arm and Aimée on the other, to sample the buffet. He is here, after all, to forget the War. There is champagne everywhere. The corks are a cannonade which mocks recent events. We banish Holzhammer and the doors are rolled back before we can approach the Russian novelist; the little ballroom is revealed where, on a curtained dais amongst potted palms, sits an all-woman orchestra. 'How terrible,' says the Princess as she sweeps past with her friend, 'that we should look to Vienna for our gaiety when she is presently causing us so much pain.' And she and her lover boldly begin the dancing, to the applause of the others, who gradually begin to join them on the floor: by Clara and a scowling Stefanik, watching his feet and hers, Frau Schmetterling and the courteous Belozerski, by Alice and myself. 'Ta ta ta, ta ta tum,' shouts General von Landoff, spinning with Natalia. It is as if we are suddenly all much drunker. The real world is whirling silk and painted flesh, wine and perfume and flowers. Soon I am standing back and laughing as Clara dances with Poliakoff and Alice with Lady Diana. Skirts are lifted, ties are loosened, petticoats bounce in the warmth of the chandeliers. The orchestra is made up chiefly of middle-aged women, a little shabbily dressed, and respectable, but there are three young girls, all dark-complexioned and possibly sisters. It is the cellist who attracts my attention. She is as plump as the others but considerably prettier and playing with evident passion, her legs spread to accommodate her instrument, and her whole body swaying as she plies her bow, her eyes as rapt as a woman's in the throes of love-making. Belozerski is talking to Natalia. 'I had decided to visit the estate of a favourite old relative in the Ukraine,' he says. 'I'd spent most of my boyhood summers there but this was the first time I'd gone in winter. Earlier that year I received a pardon from St Petersburg so was no longer an exile, but by then had established a home in Paris and felt no great wish to uproot myself. However, this visit was as much to confirm my pardon as to satisfy curiosity about cousins and aunts and uncles, whom I had not seen in fifteen years. Most of the journey from the railway station was by troika, for it was snowing. I had forgotten how wide the steppe was. The snow was like a white ocean and trees stuck out over the horizon like the masts of wrecks. My wife, who is French, chose to remain behind so I was alone save for the old peasant who drove the troika. We were about halfway to the estate when memory suddenly came back. I have never experienced the like. It was a dream: I seemed to drown in recollections which were as vivid as the original events. I relived those summers, even as the sleigh moved rapidly over the snow, so by the time I arrived I was actually shocked to notice it was winter. The poignancy of that experience, my dear Natalia, is indescribable. It left me rather depressed. I mourned for lost opportunities and deeply regretted the ill-considered romanticism which had led me to take up the cause of nationalism. Yet I know my life has been worthwhile and far more interesting in Paris than if I had remained in the Kiev gubernia where I was born.' He smiles wistfully. She smiles back in some astonishment, then turns to pour him another glass of champagne. Captain Mackenzie nods to me, on his way to speak to Count Stefanik. The Scotsman's eye contains a kind of alert sweetness at odds with his battered and drug-ruined features. Alice and I join him. A scar causes his lip to curl in a sort of grin and his soft German, pronounced with a distinctive Scottish accent, is often impossible to understand. When one of us attempts English, however, it becomes plain that he is even less comprehensible in that language. He speaks enthusiastically with Rudolph Stefanik on the subject of balloons. He has seen them used for scouting, he says, and he has heard they had also been employed in the bombardment of Paris thirty years ago, although the Prussians had of course denied they had ever done anything so inhuman. He laughs. 'Is Holzhammer denying the destruction of Mirenburg, I wonder? They are planning to dam up the river, apparently, and set it in a new course, so that we shall have no fresh water. Have you heard anything about that, von Bek?' I have not. 'I receive virtually no real news, Captain. All we get here are fantastic rumours and a little gossip. We are a desert island. But you must be privy to a hundred revelations a night!'

'I make it my business to hear nothing.' He is almost prim. 'It is necessary, I believe, to the rules of my particular trade. Confessors and the proprietors of opium dens.' He laughs. 'We have something in common with lawyers, too.'

'And doctors,' says Alice.

Captain Mackenzie nods slowly. 'And doctors, aye.'

Rudolph Stefanik moves his body in his clothes as if he is about to burst them and reveal a pair of wings. 'It would make good sense,' he says. 'If they were to dam the river. This whole campaign has been unprofessional. It causes needless suffering, both to troops and to civilians. The Austrians, of course, can be hopeless. I understood Holzhammer was trained in Prussia.'

'Most of the Mirenburg officers received their schooling there,' I tell him. 'But they have had no practical experience. And the conditions are unusual, you will admit. Do you believe that Holzhammer has had as many desertions as they say?'

'I was approached to find out. They wanted me to inflate the balloon and take her up on a fixed mooring. I refused. One shot would destroy my vessel – and me, for that matter. They are now talking of manufacturing their own airships. I said I would willingly give them advice.' Stefanik smiles suddenly down on Alice. 'As soon as this affair is settled I shall be only too pleased to take a pretty passenger into the sky and show her the world an angel sees.' Her eyes are bright as they meet his. 'Oh, I am not innocent enough, Count, to be able to see what an angel sees.'

'But you are able to tempt as the Devil tempted,' I tell him, leading her away. He laughs. Voorman and Rakanaspya are deep in drunken conversation. Voorman is entertained by Rakanaspya's seriousness. 'The lure of this putrid sweetness!' he exclaims. 'How can you resist it?'

'It is the lure of disease, of dissolution, of death – the yearning to absolve oneself of all political and moral responsibility,' says the Russian earnestly. 'It is often attractive to those who have had the strictest of upbringings, who display the greatest guilt about themselves and how they should conduct their behaviour in society. They are, indeed, guilty. Guilty of stealing from the poor. Guilty of creating wars and famines. They are responsible for murder and they come here to find a kind of death, a release, a punishment...' He is a little incoherent. 'They are the fathers of corruption!' he concludes unsteadily.

Voorman giggles and turns to one of the floral displays. 'Lilies, lilies, lilies! I shall be a father to the lilies. I shall tend them as my own children. And when they die I shall bury them with proper ceremony and raise a stone to them and put more lilies upon it so that the scent of the living shall mingle with the smell of the dead. I know where my responsibilities lie. It is to the lilies!'

Rakanaspya appeals to us, but we are laughing too heartily at Voorman. The Russian puts his back against a pillar and pretends to listen to the orchestra as it plays a sort of gypsy dance. The General joins us, with Frau Schmetterling on his arm. His face is red; not wishing to show he is in any way exhausted he controls his breathing. Frau Schmetterling is pleased; she seems to have extracted some sort of promise from him. 'I will put young Captain Mencken in charge of the matter.' He hands her a glass of champagne. He bows to Caroline Vacarescu, who continues to court him. Caroline is talking first to Clara and then, as the two women approach closer, to Alice and myself. She is quite drunk. 'It was the chemistry between us,' she says, 'I could not help myself. I cannot explain. And yet it was failing. I know he felt this loss. The intensity was gone and without it one becomes very easily bored.' She seems to be referring to Mueller. Clara listens patiently. 'We tried to recapture passion which overpowers all constraint, all conscience, but it became hollow. Yet we were linked to each other, by virtue of what we had done to one another and to friends and strangers.' Caroline looks at me suddenly, as if to test my response. 'We were partners in crime. All I could do was watch as he seduced the others who would eventually all become linked to us. That was how we worked, how we affirmed the validity of our habits of life, and justified them. Was that so wrong? Is one reality any better than another?'

MICHAEL MOORCOCK

Rakanaspya is the only person with an answer. 'One is sane,' he says, 'the other reality you describe is not. Such powerful Romanticism eventually destroys its proponents. It is always the case. And the process of destruction is neither Romantic nor bearable. It is merely sordid. Save yourself, if you can, while you have the chance. Never link your star to a man such as Mueller again.'

She becomes uncharacteristically sentimental. 'You can never understand what someone like Mueller has. He radiated authority. He snapped his fingers at convention. He made fools of them all.'

'And now he is dead,' says Clara softly, trying to distract Caroline.

Voorman watches cynically as they move back through the salon. 'I heard Fräulein Vacarescu is only at liberty now because Mueller was caught through information she supplied. Perhaps she found her own way of freeing herself from that "chemistry".'

'Somewhat radically.' I do not believe him. Caroline seemed genuinely distressed by Mueller's fate. I catch sight of a man I have often seen here in the evenings and whom I continue to confuse with the current Mayor. He is in fact the ex-Mayor of Mirenburg. He reels about the dance floor in a kind of vulgar parody of the polka. Herr Kralek's tie is lost. He has spilled food down his shirt front. Dolly, alone, will dance with him. Almost every night he comes to visit the girls, to drink plum brandy and eat cream cakes until dawn, when he returns to his wife, to make love to her, we have heard, until he is inevitably sick. His huge red neck ripples. His face is a featureless mass of purple. He usually displays resentment and self-pity in all his tiniest gestures: demands respectful attention and receives instead the amiable kindness of the girls, which he mistakes for fear. He describes himself as an honest burgher – or rather he describes his opinions as those of an honest burgher: 'Your honest burgher believes the Jews should all be expelled from the city proper,' he will say. 'Your honest burgher isn't happy with the idea of increased taxation.' I remember one naïve visitor asking him why, since he was so evidently the voice of the respectable citizens of Mirenburg, they had signed a petition to have him removed from office. He replied seriously that most of the signatures had been forgeries, the petition had been a plot of Zionist elements afraid of his position of power. 'Where I could no longer exercise my ever-watchful eye.' He stumbles now and falls to the floor. Dolly attempts to help him up. Dolly's fiancé is not here. Voorman tells Alice about another guest, a small, middle-aged journalist on the far side of the room. 'He awoke in the hospital, still convinced he was at Frau Schmetterling's, and immediately ordered one of the sisters to remove her underwear. She had obeyed with alacrity. It was four days before it dawned on him he had somehow been transferred from the brothel. The sister had no wish for him to leave. Being responsible to her superior to report his condition, she continued to insist on his poor rate of recovery. She kept him for another week until one of her colleagues demanded a share of the patient and was refused. The sister was reported and dismissed on the spot. She accompanied him back to the brothel where she stayed for a while as medical advisor to the girls.' Alice is disbelieving. Voorman insists he is telling the absolute truth. The General confides to Frau Schmetterling, also on a medical matter: 'My physician had the nerve to suggest mercury treatment, which means he thinks I have syphilis. But until the fool comes out with it directly and tells me I have the disease I shall carry on as I have always carried on. The responsibility is his, not mine.'

'You have put the question to him?' asks Frau Schmetterling.

'In as many words.'

'But not directly?'

'Has he been direct with me, madame?'

The air is growing warm. It is difficult to breath. We move closer to the door. Wilke, perhaps the most dignified person here, with a look of self-possessed humility, is talking to Clara about Amsterdam, which they both know. He seems untroubled by the noise and laughter which surrounds him. His large hands move in a circle as he describes a certain district of the city and asks her, with his usual gravity, how long it is since she was there. 'Doesn't he look a marvellous brute,' murmurs Alice as we go by. 'Such a man, compared to the rest of these!' I pretend to be insulted. 'Perhaps I should introduce you?' She gives me a look of mock irritation: 'Oh, don't be silly. Someone like that has no real interest in women. He is either friends with them, or takes them quickly and leaves, or is faithful to his wife, if he has one. That's obvious to me, even at my age!' How many of these observations has she received from her mother?

I am again unsure why Alice should find me attractive. Is it a certain weakness which makes me more easily controlled, or less inclined to go my own way when it suits me? I have no idea. I look around at the crowded salon. How could I have thought that this was normality? We are all crazed. We are all in Hell. I stare at every face. There are only two women here I have not fucked. One of them is Frau Schmetterling herself. The other is Lady Cromach. She and Princess Poliakoff also stand near the door. Lady Cromach chews on an olive. 'Frau Schmetterling tells me that you write, Herr von Bek. Do you work for the Berlin journals?' I shake my head. 'I am a dilettante, Lady Cromach. I do not know enough about life to be able to write with any authority, and I am, moreover, horribly lazy.'

'Is that why you prefer to stay in a place like this when you travel?'

Princess Poliakoff snorts, saying something coarse to Alice who begins to giggle. I continue to speak to the English woman. 'There are few houses as elegant as this and few which have such excellent ladies. I'm sure you know that most whores have a dislike of men and a crude sort of self-involvement which makes them very dull. How can one possibly be aroused very often or very satisfactorily by a dull woman?'

'I find men much duller than most women,' she says.

'I am inclined to agree with you. And the dullest of all men are German, eh?'

'They have their points. What they lack in imagination they make up for in cleanliness. I nearly married one, when I was a girl. And at least they are not as boring as Frenchmen, who seem to believe their attractiveness is in direct proportion to their vanity. I blame their mothers. And Germany is so modern! Though, as you suggest, a little on the tame side. When were you last in Berlin?'

'Several years ago. My family is content for me to travel.'

'An embarrassment of niggers, eh?'

'Quite so.'

Princess Poliakoff, her hands on Alice, tells my girl a story she heard about the de Polignac circle (she had a brief affair with de Polignac which ended with neither woman speaking to the other for over a year) and some female composer in love with the Singer, as she says, not the Salon. She continues on this theme of gossip by suggesting that there are now so many homosexuals of both kinds in Paris the city will be 'quite depopulated in another quarter of a century'. She speaks to Alice as if she, the Princess, has perfectly conventional sexual preferences. Homosexuals are referred to as 'they'. I find her wit without much substance and let her continue to entertain Alice, who is thirsty for scandal.

I chat to Lady Cromach until we are joined by Clara. The women are friendly. This is a relief to me, though I do not know why. The five of us drift towards the dais to listen to the orchestra playing reasonable Chopin. The more athletic dancers have subsided. 'It seemed to me earlier, this evening,' Clara links her arm in mine, 'that we were all dead; that Mirenburg was destroyed and that we were ghosts dancing in the ruins. You're looking tired, Ricky. Would you care to borrow my little box. It might revive you.' I thank her, but refuse. 'I am trying to restore my sense of perspective, Rose, dear.' She finds this funny. 'You have improved your relations with the child.'

'We have found a balance, I think. I was restraining her too much. And please don't call her that, Clara. She is more grown-up than she seems.' Clara draws in her lips for a second. I wonder how I have angered her. 'I apologise,' she says. 'However, my offer remains, if you need a restorative.' She begins to talk to Lady Cromach. She is particularly fascinated by the Derby and whether the Prince of Wales's horses are always allowed to win. These girls. Their soft bodies brush against me; they smell so wonderful. They have all been mine, most of them in the space of a few days. And they have been Alice's. I hesitate in my rapture. My mood alters radically. We are in danger of losing what is individual to us. Alice has the over-animated, slightly guarded look she reserves for people who make her nervous. Princess Poliakoff holds her arm, hugs her shoulders, whispers in her ear and Alice laughs. Lady Cromach and Clara move to one side to continue their conversation. But I am in no mood to rescue Alice yet, so I take Natalia onto the dance floor for a mazurka. We dance well together. It is strange, however, how trapped I feel here sometimes; I felt more secure in Rosenstrasse when I was not a resident. Natalia laughs and lifts in my arms like a happy gibbon.

When I return to my ladies I discover that Diana Cromach has rescued Alice. They are talking seriously. Alice nods a great deal and smiles at the older woman. Lady Cromach is deliberately setting out to charm her. I relish the notion of an amorous liaison between them. Alice catches my eye. We exchange signals. If it happens I shall not mind at all: it is the best route through to Lady Cromach, who excites my imagination and my lust. I pause beside them for a few moments; then, making my own decision, I leave them to it. I chat to Block, who complains it will be 'months before I can visit Vienna again'. At about two o'clock in the morning I am approached by a furious Princess Poliakoff who wants to know if I have seen Diana Cromach and 'that disgusting little cousin of yours'.

They have escaped the salon. I feel a thrill of curious pleasure, deny all knowledge, and pretend to be utterly disconcerted.

I spend the night in Clara's bed, fucking with a lusty carelessness I have not experienced for a year. It is so easy to summon the recollection of that delicious ambience, knowing my Alice and her beautiful English writer were enjoying each other to the full; that Princess Poliakoff fumed alone, while I relaxed in the arms of a tolerant Rose. I fall back on my pillows to smoke a cigarette, to relive the wonderful happiness I knew. How can I possibly relish it so much when I completely failed to anticipate the disaster to follow? Perhaps that night was a kind of apotheosis; my last true moment of happiness. The gladioli which Papadakis brought are already beginning to discolour at the edges; the leaves have streaks of brownish yellow in them, yet they are still beautiful in their pinks and delicate oranges, their blues and mauves and their deep scarlet. The carnations give off the richest scent. I lie here, resting from heady sensations. I have some pain, mostly in my groin but also, strangely, in my nipples, and my back hurts; but this is nothing more than old age. I had once hoped medical science would progress so swiftly I might expect to outlive the twentieth century, which I perceive as an insane intermediary period between one rational age and another; the Great War is over, but they fight in Spain. And Russia must soon begin another conflict; it is almost her certain destiny. One would need money for such medicine, even if it existed, and my capital shrinks; I have even less than Papadakis fears. My will, when I die, shall reveal a pittance and the name of the chief beneficiary will be unknown to anyone. I doubt that she still lives. Mirenburg has succeeded, for the moment, in restoring her balance. Clara and I take an early-morning stroll. I am anxious to demonstrate my approval of Alice and Lady Cromach and have no intention of seeking them out, at least until lunchtime. I can be certain Princess Poliakoff will make some kind of scene and it would be best for me if I were not involved. 'Let the vixen fight it out amongst themselves,' I think. In heavy coats (mine is borrowed) Clara and I stand beside the river. A thin pillar of steam comes from somewhere on the other side. A factory in the Moravia sounds its siren; cans clank as a milkman's wagon turns the corner, its wheels squeaking, the hoofs of its horse plodding softly on the cobbles: the mingled smell of milk and a horse recently out of the stable brings a reminder of childhood safety. Then the milkman, crouched like a white hare on the high seat, gives voice: 'Fresh milk!' and his bell begins to clang. We stop him and buy a cup, which we share. It is warm and soothing. 'There must still be cows somewhere,' says Rose. Neither of us has any desire to return to the brothel. 'Where now, your Lordship?' We go towards the ornamental lake in the Botanical

Gardens. Our breath creates clouds around our heads, like ecto-plasm. The Gardens are as neatly kept as they ever were, with no evidence of damage, although for some reason soldiers guard the great hothouses. They salute us as we pass. We walk along the gravelled main avenue, between marble statues of nameless heroes, until we reach the lake, which is flanked by willows, pop-lars and cypresses. There is a brownish scum on the surface. Waterbirds make trails in it as they swim listlessly about, occa-sionally diving into the purer water beneath. Clara sniffs. 'It's becoming stagnant,' she remarks. 'It looks so foul and smells so good to me. Why should it remind me of being a little girl?' We stroll through the artificial peace. On the other side of the Gar-dens we enter Baudessinstrasse. Rather than mount the Mladota Steps we take winding Uhrmacherstrasse, with its shops and bourgeois houses; the street progresses slowly up the hill, follow-ing the curve of old roads which led to Castle and Cathedral when Mirenburg was young. There is a clapping noise. I mistake it at first for horses; then down the street towards us at a rapid trot come soldiers with shouldered rifles. The troop surrounds a col-lection of civilians wearing either a defeated or a defiant air. Not a few are hatless, as if they have been seized from their beds or cap-tured while attempting flight. 'Who are your prisoners?' I call to the troubled young captain leading the party. 'Looters and profi-teers,' he says curtly. The majority look ordinary enough to me: chiefly working-class and lower middle-class people from many walks of life. 'They are taking this very seriously,' says Clara. She indicates one of the recently issued notices pinned to a tree. It threatens punishments and offers rewards and is signed by Gen-eral von Landoff, 'Military Governor of Mirenburg for the Duration of Hostilities'. Up beyond the Hussite Square we come upon ruins. 'Oh,' says Rose, 'that's where my milliner used to live. I hope she's not hurt.' Scaffolding is already erected around some of the wounded buildings and workmen attempt to make good the damage done by Holzhammer's cannon. 'Do you want to find out?' I ask her. We visit some local shops, learning that Frau Schwartz has already left the city, to stay with relatives in

Tarndoff. We emerge from a little toyshop in time to see an army band go by, all bugles and fifes, pompous in blue and red, in gold and silver braid. The soldiers are closely followed by about forty young men in badly fitting uniforms wobbling on bicycles. I have read about them. They are the newly formed 'bicycle volunteers'. The cycling-clubs of Mirenburg have joined up en masse. Things begin to take on a comfortably comic aspect. I for one am rather happy that all motor vehicles have been requisitioned for military use. The streets are far quieter than usual. In the coffee houses the students display a new patriotism and drink to the death of Franz-Josef, speak of an alliance with the 'Empire of the Slavs' and go off to apply for commissions in the Army. Exiles enjoy a greater sense of freedom since the Austrian secret policemen have been arrested. Schemes for defence, counter-attack and means of involving the Great Powers in the Wäldenstein Question are noisily discussed at length. The Bourse continues to pretend it is trading. Shops have reopened everywhere. Barricades have been removed, shutters thrown back. Fancy foods have been bought by the ton from grocers whose shelves are virtually empty; nothing can be replaced. Warehouses have been stripped. Boats on the river rock in silent moorings; there is stillness in the market places and people bargain, when they bargain, in secretive voices. The railway stations are deserted. Empty trains stand at empty platforms and a few hopeful creatures read notices of cancellations or rap hopelessly on the shutters of ticket offices. Pigeons and starlings are noisy in the great, hollow roofs; the dusty locomotives are covered with bird droppings. Railway workers lean against the trains, smoking and chatting, adjusting useless watches. Mirenburg's turrets and gables have turned pale in the winter light; she is shocked and vague, like a cripple not yet come to terms with the loss of a limb. The Kasimirsky Palace is heavily guarded. Voices of soldiers are loud in the air. Guns are wheeled up. Walls are continuously fortified. People stand in small crowds near the Central Post Office, hoping to learn that the telegraph has been restored. Everywhere officers move groups from place to place, dissipate gatherings, oversee requisitioned carts of food and raw materials, or stop individuals and inspect their new identity cards. Alice is now officially a Danish national. I have already explained to her how useful this will be in disguising our trail to Paris. At times of crisis it is easier to change one's name and background than it is to stroll uninterrupted in a park. Detachments of cavalry move slowly through Little Bohemia to discourage anti-Semitic gangs who have already tried to burn the Great Synagogue. Mirenburg is no Warsaw or Odessa and it would be a smirch on her honour if she tolerated such uncivilised behaviour. This official protection, of course, enables citizens sympathetic to Holzhammer to claim that Prince Badehoff-Krasny supports the interests of the financiers and foreign bankers. 'There will be no scapegoats,' General von Landoff has promised. 'Only those guilty of profiting from the general misery will be punished.' The Army issues orders on every aspect of daily life, from hygiene to the price of fish. 'The poor have never been so protected,' observes Clara. 'Is this Socialism?' We pass the Liverpool. It has been repaired. It might never have been damaged. 'By next spring,' I say, 'Mirenburg will be gayer and lovelier than ever. Look how wonderfully Paris recovered. The Prussians and the Communards between them should be praised. We'll scarcely remember any of this.' I was not born, of course, in '71, but I visited the city in '86, when I was fourteen, and was impressed by its beauty, though I prefer the denser texture of Mirenburg.

Clara insists we visit the Art Museum 'to look at the Fragonards'. But half the museum is closed and the pictures are being crated. We glimpse a few Impressionists before we are asked to leave. I am infected, however, by Clara's enthusiasm. She is familiar with so many of the names. I have never known a whore like her. Few women have a genuine relish for Art. 'You could teach me so much,' I say. 'You are the best governess in the world.' Appreciating the double entendre she laughs heartily as we descend the steps. 'Let's have lunch out.' I am perfectly willing to agree. Half the dishes listed on the Restaurant Prunier's menu are 'unavailable'. Soups and sauces seem thinner than usual. We make the best of it, congratulating ourselves on our good fortune in being fed by Frau Schmetterling and her cook. 'You seem confident today,' Clara declares as we leave the restaurant. 'Even happy. Like a little boy on holiday from school. Aren't you worried about your Alice? Don't you anticipate some sort of awful scene?' I shake my head. 'I have designs on Lady Cromach myself. Alice will be only too willing to share her new pleasure with me. She owes me that.'

'And Lady Cromach? What will she say?'

'Lady Cromach finds me attractive. I suspect Alice is her passport to me.'

Clara shakes her head. 'You people are such predators! I am amazed by you. It must be a habit of mind, and perhaps of money. Do you inherit it, I wonder?'

'I am in love, Clara. There are different expressions of love. You can accept that, can't you? What a whore will do for her pimp, I will do for Alice and Alice for me. It is the noblest kind of self-sacrifice, and brings pleasure to so many!'

'I'm not sure,' she says, 'that your kind of love is within even my experience.' She pats my arm to show she is not condemning me. 'We had better get back.'

As we arrive on the steps of Rosenstrasse there is an old woman there, already ringing the bell. Clara knows her as Frau Czardak. She is withered to the colour of pemmican, yet her long double-jointed fingers are supple and flexible, for they turn cards all day. She is in great demand with the girls who, with so little emotional security in their lives, look to superstition to offer them an interpretation and analysis of the world. The abstract and the metaphysical are frequently preferred by prisoners of almost any kind, since it is usually the fear of ordinary reality which leads them to their condition in the first place. 'And how soon will the Germans come to our relief, Frau Czardak?' asks Clara. 'Have you seen it in the cards?'

'In the wax. In the wax,' says the old woman cryptically as she proceeds ahead of us. She is greeted by Trudi who directs her to Frau Schmetterling's kitchen. Through the open doors of the salon we see porters still clearing up. Maids sweep and dust. Great baskets of used glasses are carried down. 'Mister' supervises it all with the grim eye of a well-trained guard dog. He might even snap at my heels if I try to interfere with the ritual. He looks impassively at an approaching porter. The man drags a reluctant maid, apparently his wife, who has up to that point been dusting. 'She refuses to visit the dentist. Look!' The porter forces her jaws apart to reveal her blackened, broken teeth, while she glares up at him. 'Does any man – any human being – have to live with that? She disgusts me. She has the habits of a wild beast.' Clara and I pause to enjoy this scene. He sees us and appeals to us. 'In bed, when I require my rights, she bites me – with those horrible fangs! She could poison me. I could die. So what's wrong with wanting to leave her if she won't improve herself? Am I to remain chained to a sub-human because in my youth I thought her habits curable? I support her, don't I? I find her good jobs, too, like this one. But I don't have to live in the same house with her!' He turns back to 'Mister' who blinks once. 'Do I?' At this his wife snarls at him and wrenches herself away. He throws up his hands and looks to us again for sympathy. 'You're laughing at me. You don't care! But this is my life! This is my whole life. I don't believe I shall have another. I am desperate. I am married to a beast and therefore I receive no respect. It is not funny. It is a tragedy.' His wife hisses at him and tries to bite his arm. Unable to contain our laughter we move on towards the stairs to find Frau Schmetterling confronting us. 'Ricky, you must do something. Your girl and Lady Diana.' She drops her voice. 'They've locked themselves in your room. Princess Poliakoff has threatened everything from murder to the Law, and now she's in her room, storming about and breaking things. She had Renée with her last night. The poor child's black and blue. I've had to make it plain to Princess Poliakoff what I think. You may stay, Ricky, but if your friend causes trouble, she must go. In any other circumstances you would all be out, immediately.' She looks frantic. 'I hate trouble. The ambience is so important. I expect people to behave like ladies and gentlemen. You've always been so good, Ricky. But this child!' She pauses, blocking our path up the stairs. 'Will you do something?'

'Princess Poliakoff is an hysterical troublemaker, dear madame, as you yourself must know.'

'You're the man. You must sort it out.' She is firm. 'And before this evening, too,' she adds as we pass.

'What am I to do?' I say to Clara. 'Challenge Princess Poliakoff to a duel?'

'If you're to challenge anyone, it should be Lady Cromach.' Clara is weary of this.

I smile. 'Unfortunately, it is not Lady Cromach who apes the male. What a difficult situation, my darling Rose.'

'And one which your darling Rose will have nothing to do with,' she says. 'I am entirely on Frau Schmetterling's side. It is up to you to settle matters quickly and quietly. At times like these, Ricky, the atmosphere of the house is even more important. Your intrigues and squabbles could drive customers away.'

'I'll talk to Princess Poliakoff,' I promise. And I walk directly to the Lesbian's room at the end of the second landing.

Although it is cold, Princess Poliakoff has opened a window. The room is finished in a sort of Louis XIV style, very much at odds with her own taste. She stands shivering by the gilded fireplace wearing a full set of masculine evening dress. The hat is on the mantelpiece near her hand which rests there, holding a cigarette. Her hair has been pinned and flattened. There is an expression of suppressed agony on her aquiline face. She is genuinely distressed. I have never been impressed by her in this way before. She looks older than her forty or so years. She refuses to appeal to me. 'What a strange pair of cuckolds we make, Ricky.' Since I have acquiesced in this adventure, albeit silently, I cannot feel genuine sympathy – that sympathy of echoed self-pity. 'It's very unexpected,' I say. Then, because it will suit me, I try to pretend anger. 'I thought you had your eye on her, but I never guessed…' I cross to the window and look down into Rosenstrasse. It is already growing dark. An old woman with a dog on a lead walks slowly towards the archway on the opposite side of the street. 'Men never notice,' she says. Women will always say that. What they actually observe is that men frequently do not comment. I am relieved, at least, that she has failed to blame me for the business. I take advantage of her need to see me as a fellow sufferer. 'What are we to do about them?' she wants to know. I suggest that perhaps they will see reason. It can all be cleared up in a few minutes if we are careful to reduce the tension. She is horribly distressed. 'I love Diana deeply. But as for reason, I sometimes think the very word is meaningless to her.' This suggests she has already tried to persuade her lover to have nothing to do with Alice. 'She is a cruel and heartless woman. It's up to you – up to you, Ricky – to remove that little wanton from this house.' I tell her I have given the idea consideration, but there is nowhere to go. 'There is Stefanik's balloon,' she says. 'He's already offered to help Diana escape. You could use it instead.'

'It's an offer he makes to every woman he desires. It's neither a possibility nor a danger.'

'You didn't have a nigger at all, did you?' She knocks the hat, spasmodically, with her hand. 'Why were you lying to me?'

'Oh,' I shrug, 'for privacy.'

'Because you thought I'd try to take her away from you? There's an irony.' She fits another cigarette into her holder. Her hands continue to shake.

I frown, pretending to consider the problem.

'Well?' she says.

'I'll see if they'll speak to me. But you must be patient. I'll come back as soon as I can.'

'Please,' she says. 'This is unbearable. I'm suicidal.'

I leave her and go up to our rooms, knocking softly on the door. 'It's me, Alex. Could you let me in? I'd like to change my clothes.' I keep my voice as light as I can. She – or more likely Lady Cromach – will be suspecting a ploy. Anything I say will seem like an excuse to them. Their curiosity or their tension or their high spirits are all that will decide them. There is some movement from within. Eventually Alexandra opens the door and I enter. She is wearing her Japanese kimono. She kisses me quickly and grins to involve me, to placate me. 'Have you been all right?'

She smells of some new perfume. The door to the bedroom is closed. 'Yes, thanks,' I say. 'And you?'

'Wonderful.' She pushes at her messy hair. 'I'd have told you, only we couldn't ruin our chances. We had to act quickly. That witch has been hammering on the door for half the night and most of the morning. What a harpy, eh? Have you seen her?'

'She's calmed down.' I go directly to the bedroom and open the door. Lady Cromach is in bed. She looks offended, then flushes like a travelling salesmen caught with the farmer's daughter. 'Good afternoon, Lady Cromach. I'm sorry to disturb you. I thought, since lunchtime has come and gone...'

She recovers herself. I can almost see her controlling her colour. She drops her head a little and looks up at me, half-smiling. 'Of course. We have been thoughtless.'

'Understandable, in the circumstances.' From the wardrobe I pick out a shirt and underclothes.

'You have been sailing under false colours.' She is not accusatory. 'How unkindly you misled the Princess. You know she loves proof of the most extravagantly unlikely gossip. Is she all right, do you know?'

I seat myself heavily on the bed and stare into her glowing face. 'She says she is suicidal. That she loves you. She seems very distracted.' The bed reeks of their love-making. I feel almost faint.

'She won't kill herself.' Lady Cromach settles back in my pillows. 'She'd be more likely to kill one of us. The Princess can't bear to be thwarted.'

'Neither can I.'

She puts a hand on mine. 'But you have not been. Have you?' The sheet falls away from her shoulders. She is lovely, like a young boy. 'Alice tells me you are a stranger to sexual jealousy.'

'I am becoming more familiar with it.'

She accepts the flattery. Alice enters to stand looking at us, like a melodrama child which has affected a reconciliation between its parents. She is almost smug. I laugh and ask her to light me a cigarette. She obeys with cheerful alacrity, placing an ashtray beside me. Lady Cromach's hand has not left mine. 'Are you trying to mollify me, Lady Cromach? Or do you plan to include me in this seduction?'

'You're straightforward,' she says.

'Perhaps it's the atmosphere of this place. Perhaps it is the fact that we may all soon be blown to bits.' I remove my jacket, then my waistcoat. Alice takes them from me. 'I'll bring some champagne,' she says. Lady Cromach's eyes have narrowed and her breathing has become rapid. A nerve twitches in her neck. 'Champagne,' she says. 'What else did the Princess have to tell you?'

'Very little.'

Alice returns with a tray of champagne and glasses. She puts the tray on the little bedside table and curls up beside Lady Cromach. 'She must have yelled herself hoarse!'

'I've promised to try to reason with you and then report back to her.' I accept the cold glass.

'And are you reasoning now?' Lady Cromach wants to know.

'In my own fashion. Or perhaps I'm bargaining.'

'You wish me to "give Alexandra up"?'

'You know I'm not so rigid. I have told her I will not object to her sleeping with other women, though I draw the line at other men. I'd like it understood, though, that my feelings must take priority with Alexandra.'

'That's surely up to Alexandra.' Lady Cromach raises an eyebrow at my girl.

Alice says in a small voice: 'I'll do what everyone thinks best.' Neither Lady Diana nor myself are even briefly convinced. 'I'm sure you will,' says Lady Cromach, fondling her head. 'Oh, well, I think it can all be arranged satisfactorily, Herr von Bek. This would not be the first time, eh?' We toast one another with our glasses.

Later I remark to Lady Cromach that she has one of the loveliest bodies I have known. It is like fucking a supple youth with a cunt. It is a rare pleasure. 'You are a pretty rare pleasure for me,' she responds sardonically. I get dressed. We have agreed I should pretend to Princess Poliakoff that I am persuading the women the affair is not possible. I will hint at my ability to blackmail one or both of them. But when I get to her rooms Princess Poliakoff has vanished. A maid at work on the stairs says she saw her go out half an hour ago. Downstairs, Trudi says the Princess left with a small handbag, in a cab. She did not say where she was going. Relieved at this, I return to my women. 'It's almost too good to be true.'

'She has her pride,' says Diana thoughtfully. 'But she also has a taste for revenge.'

I know. She is probably scheming vengeance in one of the empty hotels near the station. She is certainly not dead or planning to die. I clamber into bed. Later tonight I will sleep in Clara's room. In the morning we shall go to breakfast with Alice and Diana. There will be a slightly formal atmosphere until Clara produces her cocaine. Outside large flakes of snow will fall over Frau Schmetterling's garden. Alice will clap her hands. 'It's going to be the most marvellous Christmas!'

The next weeks at Rosenstrasse will be the happiest I shall ever experience. The intimacy between Alice, Rose, Diana and myself will grow. The affection will take on the nature of a family's and I shall fall cheerfully into my rôle of charming younger brother, ready for any sport, undemandingly co-operative. Who could fail to love such a man? We will scarcely notice the food growing poorer and sparser, or the brothel beginning to assume a run-down look. Frau Schmetterling, who will have taken charge of our rations and seen to it that doors and windows are properly barricaded, will not be quite so maternally self-possessed as usual. More and more young officers will attend the salon, and fewer civilians. One officer, young Captain Adolf Mencken, is now resident here. The brothel is an official telephone post.

The snow heals the scars on the city, softening the outlines of the fortifications, muting the sounds of distress. Mirenburg is visibly beginning to starve. There is no word from Germany. Holzhammer has strengthened his encirclement. The dribble of water in the river is brackish and filthy and reveals all kinds of horrors. These, too, the snow will cover. Sometimes in my imagination the brothel in Rosenstrasse will seem to be the only building still standing; the only security in a desolate and mutilated world. But then too often I will begin to notice the reality, the threadbare quality of the deception. Frau Schmetterling maintains it by her will alone. She once leaned easily on her cushions, controlling a universe of comfort, maintaining by moral strength and skill an illusion of absolute sanctuary, but now the effort is visibly draining her. 'Mister' has become more solicitous; her chow dogs can scarcely summon the energy to bark at the clients. She still dusts every piece of china in her vast dresser. Mirenburg is hungry. The meals at the brothel remain reasonable. We eat once a day. Nobody asks where 'Mister' finds his supplies. Nobody asks where the flowers come from.

We move, all four of us, in a web of reference where our needs and attitudes are the only ones worth considering. Alice, of course, is trapped in this more thoroughly than the rest, who at least know on one level that what they are doing can ultimately be self-destructive: we have conspired and chosen, she has merely accepted. Our games, our fantasies, our rituals become increasingly elaborate and abstract, yet we congratulate ourselves that they are 'humane'. So they are, I suppose, in this private world, and we would be impatient if we were forced to consider them in any different context. I am a woman amongst women; my perfume is their perfume; we share our clothes, our jewellery, our identities. Memory is floating scarlets and pinks shading into yellow and grey, the taste of sex, the sensation of being forever relaxed, forever in a state of heightened sensuality, forever alive. I can smell this paper: it has an old dusty odour, and the ink is bitter in my nostrils. After the War I spent a few months in Algeria, much of this time in a whorehouse having some of the atmosphere of Frau Schmetterling's, although it was a much rougher place. It was frequented by certain elements of the French Army. One of the girls, a pretty red-headed Russian called Marya, whose parents had been killed by the Bolsheviks and who had come here from Yalta, was dying by the hour. She was consumptive. She had a little cubicle off the main floor, where we sat on cushions and smoked hashish. On a certain night she had announced that it was 'free tonight, gentlemen'.

One by one the customers went to her as she called for champagne – a bottle with every man – standing in her door in a pink chemise which had brownish stains on it, challenging them to come, while the blood flowed down her lovely chin, and her delicate shoulders and beautiful little breasts shook as she coughed. 'This is a farewell performance.' But gradually even the coarsest of the soldiers began to hesitate and look to one another in the hope that someone would put a stop to the matter. The proprietor of the brothel, a half-Arab who wore a fez and a European suit, remained expressionless, watching Marya, watching the customers, perhaps curious himself to see how far it could all go. The soldiers took up their bottles of champagne and went into her cubicle, but none went very willingly or stayed very long. I still do not know why they went: I like to think it was out of respect for a dying and desperate girl. Perhaps she thought their bodies would bring her renewed life, or perhaps she hoped they would kill her. She died two days later, quietly, full of hashish.

Mirenburg huddles under the snow as if in a mixture of fear and pride. Her bells continue to chime; her lovely churches are crowded every day. There are no birds here now. They have all been caught and eaten. The factories are closed and every able-bodied man marches on the walls as part of his militia-duty. Holzhammer's armour squats not a quarter of a mile from our abandoned trenches on the other side of an expanse of almost unbroken snow. We have heard that German and Austrian diplomats quarrel over the Wäldenstein Question but no decision has yet been reached.

We expect the cannon to begin to fire again soon. Van Geest is still wearing his blanket-jacket. He talks to me one afternoon as we sit side by side on a couch in the gloom of the salon. 'I continue to associate this place with the funeral parlour where we took my mother. Isn't that peculiar? Yet the atmosphere seems exactly the same to me. It always has. Even before the Siege began.

It could be the dark drapery and the smell of incense. The potted palms. Is that all? The cause of the association is beyond me.' He sighs and lights his cigar. 'But I am comfortable here.' Over on the other side of the room, in the half-light, Frau Schmetterling sits at the piano, playing some mindless German song. As I get up to leave I hear a commotion in the vestibule and Thérèse comes storming in pointing behind her at the same porter who, a few weeks ago, complained about his wife's teeth. Thérèse is wearing a feather dressing gown and mules. Only since the Siege have the girls been allowed to dress like this in public. She has lost all appearance of refinement. Her harsh gutter-Berlin rings out suddenly across the room. 'He's eaten Tiger! The horrible old bastard's eaten the cat!' Frau Schmetterling hurries from the piano. 'Not so loud, dear. What's the matter?' Thérèse points again. 'The cat. He said it was a rabbit.' She rounds on the man. 'And he offered me some if I'd doodle him. For a rabbit leg! Or a cat's leg, as it turned out. He's disgusting. Old swine! I'd rather eat *his* damned leg. Tiger was my only real friend.' She begins to weep, every so often pausing to glare at the bewildered porter. All he can say is: 'It wasn't Tiger. Somebody else got Tiger.' Frau Schmetterling tells him he is dismissed.

'One should try to draw the line at cats.' Captain Mencken, all shaded eyes, colourless hair and sandy uniform, comes up to us and borrows a light from Van Geest. 'They are eating worse in the Moravia and Little Bohemia, I hear.' He looks down on us through smoked glasses, a sober lemur.

People seem to have become obsessed with what should and what should not be eaten. Yesterday I was in the kitchen while Frau Schmetterling discussed menus with her cook. Herr Ulric has always impressed me. He was a butcher in Steinbrucke twenty years ago, and he still retains something of the smell of the shambles about his coarse and enormously gentle body. His hands, when at rest, lie upon his thighs as if they grip an axe and his eyes contain that familiar sad tenderness of a betrayer of lambs and ewes. His old calling proves useful again. Herr Ulric was amused by Frau Schmetterling's insistence that the food be described simply as 'meat'. He agreed. 'So long as it isn't described as prime. That nag was hardly the finest horse in the cavalry, even when she was young!' Frau Schmetterling had nodded in that dismissive way she has when she does not wish to hear what is being said to her. Van Geest sighs. 'I feel like one of those dark weeds which grows in the deep sea, which never observes the light of the sky, is never exposed to the air. I wave in fathomless currents. I am moved by profound, slow forces; I am never attacked; I give a hiding place to both predator and prey, yet I am scarcely aware of them and never affected by them. Is this power, do you think?' Captain Mencken hands back the box of matches and looks to me for a reply, but I know Van Geest too well by now to bother to answer. Captain Mencken has little to do and frequently seems embarrassed to be here. He is courteous enough, but always distant. He is unhappy, he has confided to us, with a state of affairs in which our soldiers do battle with starving citizens in their own streets. There have been several terrible incidents. 'We should take the offensive,' he has said. 'That's my opinion. But we wait still for the Kaiser. And the Kaiser will not come. The only relief for Mirenburg depends on the actions of her soldiers. One good cavalry charge could take those positions. Or could have.' Now he moves away from us. 'The horses are growing too weak,' he says. 'Well, you know what's happening to them.'

He goes to the boarded-up window as if he hopes he will get some glimpse of the enemy. 'They're starving us rather successfully, aren't they?' He is one of the few Mirenburger soldiers to have seen active service. Frau Schmetterling returns and settles at her piano. Rakanaspya and Count Belozerski enter, speaking in low Russian voices. The Count has grown a thin pointed beard, and both men have become increasingly serious; they spend all their time together and appear to be discussing metaphysics. Count Belozerski's hair has been allowed to grow, too. It now touches his high fur collar, emphasising his Tartar blood and giving him a Mephistophelean appearance completely at odds with his behaviour, which remains amiably courteous. He has been to see Caroline Vacarescu once or twice, though she is determinedly in pursuit of a rather nervous and flattered Captain Mencken, while granting her favours most frequently to Rudolph Stefanik. She is playing several hands at once. We have heard nothing at all of Princess Poliakoff except a vague rumour she has escaped the city and thrown herself on the mercy of her ex-lover Holzhammer. I enquired at every hotel and boarding house I was able to find. I still fear she has guessed my perfidy and might by now have discovered who Alice really is. She would betray me if she could. She would betray us all. In the Town Hall a day or so ago a fire had been especially prepared for an emergency meeting. The business people of Mirenburg were to meet General von Landoff and his staff to discuss the situation. The big mediaeval hall, with its gilded gargoyles and elaborate flags, was full of loud voices and tobacco smoke. A number of old men were in contentious discourse near the fireplace. Everyone still wore their overcoats. No member of the military staff had yet arrived and merchants and bankers continued to represent themselves as experts in the business of War. There were rumours of an emissary from Holzhammer, of new peace terms which General von Landoff had dismissed out of hand as 'quite impossible'. One ironmaster joked that he had it on good authority that all women under twenty were to be given up to the Bulgarians. 'My mistress was in tears when I got there last night. She knew that it was nonsense, of course, but was I suspect enjoying the melodrama. There is so little entertainment, these days. I told her the story was untrue but that I had made a private agreement with General von Landoff to give her up to his uses in return for my own safe conduct.' No-one there knew anything of the Princess Poliakoff. 'You don't believe you're making sense, do you?' says Papadakis, uncorking a bottle of Chambertin. 'You're being foolish. What are you writing about? The girl? Because I won't listen any more, you're writing it down. Is that it?' Mirenburg is still alive. Her battlements have held off the Goth and the Hun and every empire Europe has known. 'She is indestructible.' Papadakis begins to pour the wine. 'Let it breathe!' I tell him. 'Let me breathe. Let us all breathe! God! You stink of disease. You are putrefying before my eyes. I can smell you night and day!' Clara joins me in the salon. She wears a sable coat, borrowed from Diana, and a matching muff and hat. We are going for one of our walks. Captain Mencken removes his smoked glasses and warns us to be cautious. His eyes have that pale, bloody look of dogs whose hair permanently covers their faces. 'The amount of crime in the city is prodigious...'

We laugh at him as we step into the path which has been cleared through the snow. The dismissed porter is close behind us, grumbling that it has become impossible to please anybody these days. He goes towards Rauchgasse while we turn in the opposite direction, to Papensgasse and the Botanical Gardens. The guards have stamped paths all over the Gardens and we follow them. The smell of burning wood comes from near the Tropical Plant House. The white smoke rising over the snow adds to the haze. The sky is the colour of new steel and from the Moravia a score of belfries begin to peal. The people on that side are mostly Catholic. 'They pray four or five times a day now,' says Clara. She wants to investigate the source of the smoke, but I hold her back. 'It would be best not to find out what they are cooking,' I say. 'Have they become cannibals?' She makes to go on. 'There are rumours,' I say. She shivers and her eyes brighten. 'Oh!' She tries to find a remark and fails. 'How terrible,' she says finally, in a small voice. 'I wonder what would happen to me? Would they prefer to eat me or rape me, do you think?' We take the turning for the ornamental lake. 'Probably both,' I say. Most of the trees are down. They have been used for firewood. The unbroken snow covers their stumps, however, so that it is still possible to pretend the Siege does not exist and all is as it was in September. I walk slowly, savouring the sense of peace. I am a little light-headed from hunger. In the distance glass buildings are heavy with snow. Every other outline seems black. There is a strong smell of urine from the lake. Clara holds her nose. 'They must be using it as a cesspit. I suppose they can't empty the sewage into the river any more, though I don't see what difference it makes.' A soup kitchen has been set up in the Lugnerhoff. The line of people, many of them well-dressed, stretches the length of Korkziehiergasse and goes out of sight around the corner. I see an old acquaintance, Herr Prezant the tobacconist, and stop to talk to him. 'What's the soup like?' I ask him. 'It gets thinner every day,' he says, smiling. He is a grey ghost in astrakhan. 'Soon it will be only water, but we shall still go on queuing for it. By that time we shall not have noticed. It's as good a way as any of starving to death.' He seems to be quite serious. 'Relief will soon be here,' I say. He is fatalistic: 'There is nobody who would wish to help us in the current political climate. You must know that as well as I, Herr von Bek.'

'I am optimistic by nature, Herr Prezant. There's little point in being otherwise.' He offers me his hand and I shake it. It is all bone; yellow with the stains of his calling. Then he turns back into the line and stands there, his shoulders straight, his fingers toying with the brim of his homburg hat. 'He is a brave little old fellow,' says Clara. 'But why are people so frequently passive in the face of misery and death? Have they been reconciled to it all their lives? So few of them seem surprised, let alone outraged. Wouldn't you be angry?'

'I would not be in his position,' I tell her. 'But if I were I should probably behave very similarly. One makes choices, until there are no further choices to make. Then one accepts the results. His choices have led him to that queue. As have his circumstances, too, of course. My circumstances will never lead me to make Herr Prezant's choice. Let's count our blessings, Rose, my love.' There are no cabs. We must walk back. Black smoke floats towards the twilight. Fire has broken out in the Koenigstrasse and has spread for several blocks. The hospital has been evacuated: the patients are lying on stretchers in the street until they can be removed to the Convent of the Poor Clares. The fire is said to be the work of incendiaries, of women patterning themselves after the communards of '71 and deciding it would be better to burn Mirenburg to the ground than to let it fall into the hands of the besiegers. The blaze is soon under control and several suspected 'pétroleuses' have been arrested. A crowd visits the burning buildings to warm itself and to loot whatever food might have survived. A few shots are fired in the dusk. A far less passive crowd rushes up Falfnersallee towards the Mirov Palace and is met by a fusillade. In the confusion some field guns are discharged. We reach Rosenstrasse at dark, barely in time for curfew. Captain Mencken peers at us through the pools of his spectacles. 'You are safe, then?' Clara asks him what is happening. He tells us Holzhammer's agents have been creating dissension in the city. Those agents will soon be under arrest. I remark how hot it has become inside the house. Frau Schmetterling flusters through the door which leads down to the basement. 'He intends to burn us all up!' she says despairingly. 'Please help. It is "Mister" and Chagani!' Captain Mencken and I go down to the furnace room. The boiler is roaring so high it threatens to burst. Two men stand in the flickering darkness hurling log after log through its blinding mouth. 'He will not listen!' wails Frau Schmetterling. 'He continues to cram in fuel. You would think he was in Hell already!' 'Mister' stops suddenly. He is panting. He signs for his friend Chagani to continue their work. He looks at us in surprise. He has an enthusiastic, boyish expression on his ruined face. He is sweating. 'Every room in the house is at tropical heat,' says Frau Schmetterling. Captain Mencken steps forward. 'I think this will do. We are supposed to be preserving fuel.' He speaks gently, even hesitantly. 'There is no point now,' says 'Mister'. 'Not now, sir. Why give them our firewood?'

'You think Holzhammer has won?'

'Holzhammer has won.' For the first time Chagani speaks. He does not look at us, but he drops the log he has been carrying. I recognise him. He sometimes entertains the girls with his monkey and his mimicry. Muscular and yet without strength, Chagani was an acrobat who destroyed his own judgement through self-demand and a lack of faith in his partners. This evening he has decided to wear his red, spangled costume. He steps back towards the boiler room's outer door. The firelight shifts to silhouette him, frozen in loneliness, clinging to his pride as someone might cling to the very sword which had killed them. 'Holzhammer has won.

His troops will be here by morning.' In faded red and tarnished gold he stands stretching his calves, reaching back to a memory of his youth, obstinately continuing to identify the impatience he had then possessed with the subtler forms of optimism he has detected in others and yet been unable to comprehend. 'That's rubbish, Chagani,' I say. 'What on earth's your game? Why have you alarmed "Mister"?'

Chagani laughs suddenly and springs into the depleted wood-pile in the corner. He attempts a pirouette and lands on his back. The timber tumbles around him. He is still laughing. He is very drunk. 'Mister' goes to help him, his hands stretched. Frau Schmetterling says sharply: 'You are not to listen to him. He's always leading you into trouble. Why do you let him? Why do you get him the schnapps?' She crosses to the boiler and with a long iron rod taps and turns and slides until the thing is burning at a normal level again. She whirls around with the rod in her hand. 'Mister' has aided Chagani to regain his feet. The ex-acrobat flexes his upper arms. He is not hurt. 'I still know how to fall,' he says. He glares at us. 'Which is more than any of you do. Can't you see it's over for you? Your luck has failed.' Frau Schmetterling threatens him with the black rod. He arches his back like a ballerina and, limping, allows 'Mister' to help him to the outer door. I watch him as he mounts the steps up to the garden. There are several cavalry-horses stabled there now. The cockatoos, the macaws, the parrot, all have gone, and there are no more orchids. Captain Mencken follows behind Chagani as the man is challenged by a guard. 'It's all right, Huyst.' And 'Mister' looks after his departing friend before descending the steps and tugging something out of his shirt. It is a half-empty stone bottle. Frau Schmetterling takes it, shaking her head, and drops the rod with a clang to the dusty flagstones. Mencken and I return upstairs. 'They are all going mad,' he says. 'It is hunger and alcohol, I suppose. Who can blame them?'

The four of us, out of choice, are dining most evenings off morphine, opium and cocaine. It is better than the food we have, and thanks to Clara the drugs are still plentiful. When we require warming, we drink old cognac. Wilke, summoned by a maid, stands at the top of the steps as we come back up. 'I thought we were on fire,' he says. 'And that was shooting earlier, wasn't it? I was asleep.' His big, passive head is drowsy and his voice is furred. He wears a red-and-white dressing gown; his feet are bare. 'What do you want me to do, chicken?' He addressed Frau Schmetterling. 'It is over,' she says. 'I am sorry you were woken up. "Mister" lost control of the furnace.'

'Do you want me to have a look at it?' asks Wilke. 'It is all right now,' she says. 'Go back to bed.' She kisses him on the cheek as he turns obediently about. He is quite as loyal to her, I suspect, as 'Mister'. They are a strange pair of children. 'I thought the Bulgarians had arrived,' he says, almost to himself, 'and had set us on fire.'

'Could Chagani have some word?' I ask Captain Mencken. Behind his smoked glasses he is inscrutable. 'Hardly!' he says. 'A man like that? It would take much more than a day for Holzhammer to break through into the city. It was rubbish. He was drunk as a pig. Drunk as a pig.' I have sweat and grime all over my face. I go up to Clara's room to bathe. A maid fills the tub for me. We are gasping from the heat. 'Don't touch the radiators,' warns Clara. 'I have already burned myself.' She displays a red spot on the back of her hand. On her mirror she has laid out two thick lines of cocaine. 'Have one of those,' she says. 'It will spoil my appetite for dinner,' I tell her. 'Then have both,' she says with a laugh. She is wearing her broderie anglaise négligée. Her white body, with its firm breasts and big nipples, is beaded with perspiration. She sprays at herself with a cologne bottle. 'Ugh! Who could have expected this? That Chagani is mad. I've always said so. He hates the human race. He'll burn us down, yet.'

'Wilke thought the Bulgarians had arrived.'

'He's not the only one. We're all on edge, Ricky, dear.'

After my bath I go to see my other ladies. They usually prefer to be together until mid-afternoon when they like to receive me. This arrangement suits Clara. She has her naps while I am away. Alice and Diana come to embrace me. They could almost be brother and sister. Twins. 'Oh, those guns again,' says Lady Cromach. 'My nerves! Did you hear them?'

'Nothing to worry about.'

'Why do men always say that to women and children?' Diana shakes her head and leads me towards the bedroom. 'And you seem so pleased with yourselves when you do it!'

'Aha. Perhaps we're talking *to* ourselves.'

'Perhaps you are, my dear.' Diana kisses me again. 'There is a child in all of us sometimes, who cries and must be comforted.'

Alice follows behind us. She has her hands together on her stomach. Diana and I stretch ourselves on the bed but Alice continues to stand. 'We've got to leave,' she says. Our Alice is drawing attention to herself. She is looking a little fatter and, as a result, even lovelier than usual. Her skin's lustre reminds me of pink pearls in the deep sea, still enlivened by the movement of the waters. Her hands press against glass. Behind the glass are shutters, nailed with boards on the outside, and only a few bars of yellow light shed by the houses opposite enter through the gaps. Within the brothel we live almost entirely by artificial light. There is no more gas. Oil and candles are in short supply. She wears one of Clara's grey silk dressing gowns and the remains of last night's theatrical make-up – we had turned her into a doll, a Coppélia. 'This is wretched.'

'There is absolutely nothing we can do, dear.' Diana strokes the linen of my arm. 'Where could we go?' She looks at me.

'They were shooting at civilians,' I tell Alice. 'It was a riot near the Mirov Palace. Clara and I were almost caught up in it, but it wasn't really dangerous.'

'What was Clara doing, letting you go out in that?' says Alice. 'Clara is a fool! Clara will get you killed. She looks for danger. She loves to be near death. It's the way she's made. You shouldn't go along with her silly schemes.'

'We were taking our usual stroll,' I say mildly, looking to Diana for an explanation. Diana gets up and goes into the other room to find her playing cards. Alice has pinched her cheeks together and juts her red lips at me. It is the expression she usually employs when she pretends to know somebody else's secret, or disbelieves a statement, or disapproves of an explanation. 'Don't do that,' I say. 'It makes you look ugly.' I will do almost anything to take that particular expression off her face. 'If you're frightened, then admit it. But you shouldn't try to turn your fear onto somebody else. Clara doesn't deserve that.' She is for the first time, however, thoroughly unreachable. She will not respond. The realisation gives me a physical shock. 'It isn't fair,' I add. But I am losing her. I can sense it. She needs me to give something which I do not have. I do not even know exactly what it is she wants. I would give it if I could. I hold back. Perhaps it is simply that she has used me up. Anything I say will be contrary to my interests. Alice is cold. 'You have changed,' she says. It is as if a judge has reached a verdict. 'You used to be so gay.' I am condemned and sentenced and still my crime is unknown to me. Diana returns. 'Shall we all go down to dinner tonight?' she says. She seems innocent. Has she been speaking about me to Alice? Or against Clara? Nobody could do that unless Alice wanted it.

'Why not?' I reply. 'We'll have Horsemeat Surprise. Or perhaps tonight it will be Pouf-Pouf stew.' My joke falls flat. Alice cries: 'Oh, my God!' and begins to cry into her hands. Diana comforts her. Somehow I have compounded my crime.

'I'm very sorry,' I say.

'It isn't your fault.' Diana is grim. 'You'd better bring Clara here. This is getting out of proportion. At all costs we four must stick together.' Alice looks up. Snails seem to have crawled across her caked face. 'The pair of them are already against us. Can't you see that, Diana?' Lady Cromach puts on her dark dressing gown. 'I'll get Clara. You stay here with Ricky.' As soon as she has left Alice sniffs and stops crying. She glares at me. She goes to her dressing table and begins to wipe the cosmetics from her face. She has become much more skilled with her clothes and her make-up. 'We've got to get away from here, Ricky,' she says. 'We haven't been trying properly. We'll be like those Romans – those people in Pompeii – still making love when the volcano went off. Diana and Clara must take their chances. You surely know of some means...' I am again shocked, both by her disloyalty and her volte-face. Why has she suddenly forgiven me? I am disturbed, yet flattered she should choose me as her conspirator against the others. 'We've got to get to Paris, Ricky.' The traces of tears are nearly gone. She begins to work on her hair, brushing rapidly. She leans into the mirror. 'It would be pointless to take Clara with us. She has no breeding. Well, you can't expect it from a whore, I suppose.'

I am angry on Clara's behalf, yet to defend her would be to lose my child. Alice has fired her warning shot.

'What about Diana?' I ask.

'She's too unimaginative. You and I are the only ones with imagination, Ricky. It is our bond. Remember?' She turns with a lovely little smile. 'Twin souls?'

I laugh. I recognise her motives and her techniques but I can't resist them. She is my muse, my alter ego, my creation. 'Let's at least behave decently.' I attempt to save something of my old standards. 'There's no need to condemn either of them just because we're tired of them. Let's just admit we want to get to Paris together.'

She is almost happy. She blows me a kiss from her reflection. 'All right. That's fair enough. What will you do?'

'I'll make enquiries. I know someone... There's a chance...' This is empty reassurance, of course. She must hope. She must pin that hope on me. She has given me an ultimatum. To lose her would be to lose myself.

'I just want to be on our own again,' she says. 'In Paris. Or Vienna. Wherever you think. But we can't stay here, Ricky. There are too many dangers. Too many awful memories. I want to start afresh. I want to be your wife, as you promised.'

I am enormously elated as she embraces me; I have had a last-minute reprieve. But there are conditions. We hear Clara and Diana coming back. She whispers: 'Get us away.' And she continues with her toilet. 'She's much better now,' I say. 'It was the shooting and the heat. We're all relaxing again.' I laugh. I look at the two women I intend to deceive. They seem merely pleased emotions have settled. I see no reason to feel guilt. It will simply be Alice and me again. We shall finish where we began. Nobody will have lost. There have been no bargains made. But I am already lost; I refuse to consider what I will receive in place of love; or what I shall win to replace the pain and the beauty of worshipping a woman rather than a child. I shall become a coward. The future threatens me and I refuse to acknowledge it. The moment is all that matters. I might have ended my days with affectionate memories and all I shall actually have will be a litany of petty revenges and self-pity. I will come to deceive all women as wilfully as I now plan to deceive myself. I will exploit their romance as mine was exploited. I know all this but I am compelled to continue. Alice has begun to sing that old familiar parting song; finding faults, compiling lists of supposed slights so that she might justify her next decision. And what she can turn against these two friends she can as easily turn against me. I am in that state of disbelief which can sometimes last for days or weeks before the fact of disaffection is accepted. I look away. When shall I be struck? In Paris? Before or after we are married? I will suffer that particular indignity. I will listen to lies about what we have done and distortions of the facts of our life together. I will not leave. I will not, as I should, let her sing that song alone. But all this knowledge is swamped by the tiniest hope that she will change: that what I see is not the truth.

Alexandra. You must not leave me. You must not change. From the triumph of eyes freshly adult she will one day mock my misery. She will refuse the rôle which it will have suited her to play, which will no longer be useful to her. She will change her ambitions, but not her nature. I shall be hardly peripheral to her consideration when not long ago I should have been central. From a citadel of lace and velvet she will look down on a wretch. Now she flashes me a private smile. They are getting changed. They are chatting amongst themselves. They prepare themselves for the dinner. Then Clara and Diana leave me alone with Alice again. 'I must have your guarantee,' I tell her. 'I must know you will not betray me.' She hugs me. She kisses me warmly. 'How could I betray you, darling Ricky? You are my master!' I hold her to me, not daring to look at her face for fear I will see the deception too clearly. 'It's wrong to do this to Clara and Diana,' I say. She pulls away from me. 'That's stupid. What do we owe them?' I sit on the chair, my shoulders stooped. She offers me something in her gloved hand, palm outstretched as if to a pet. It is a little pill of opium. Wonderingly, I take it. She turns away. 'You know, Ricky, that I have no conception of your ideas of morality sometimes. We see things so differently. I don't plan to do any harm to either Diana or Clara. Do you think that?'

'No...'

'I love them both. They are wonderful. But you and I have something special. What purpose would be served in blurting everything out? It can only cause trouble – and pain to others.'

'I should have thought that we owed them –'

She comes to kneel beside me. 'We owe them nothing. That is our freedom.'

I listen to her as a disciple might listen to a holy man; striving to perceive the wisdom, the new attitude, the truth of what she says.

'They're not like Poliakoff,' she says. 'They won't hurt us.'

'We ought to tell them.'

'What's the point?'

As I rise to my feet my legs are trembling. I cannot fathom the changes which have taken place in her strange, dreaming, greedy brain. I am as much at a loss for an explanation as if I attempted to analyse the perceptions and nature of a household pet. Like a pet she is able to take on the colour of any master; to be obedient and passive for as long as it suits her, to respond to whatever desires or signals one might display. But now I disguise my desires, for fear of losing her. Have I therefore lost her to someone who offers her clearer signals? To someone who represents what she calls 'freedom'? At dinner I look suspiciously around the table, at the Russians, at Count Stefanik, at Caroline Vacarescu, even at honest Egon Wilke, chewing his food with as much relish as if it were the finest beef. And Alice is merry. Alice is the darling of the company. Everyone dotes on her. 'You cheer us all up, my dear,' says Frau Schmetterling. She has become much more tolerant of late. Will Frau Schmetterling somehow betray me? I am scarcely in control of myself, though I appear to be as relaxed and as good-tempered and as witty as always. And yet, has Clara taken on that peculiar, impressive dignity of an injured woman; that dignity which induces in any reasonably sensitive man a mixture of awe, guilt, respect, and sometimes envious anger? We drink too deeply. In bed together that night we tire easily and fall asleep. A terrible depression has overwhelmed me. The dream is lost. I am desperate to rediscover it. I get up from that tangle of women early and go to Clara's room to sleep. I help myself to her cocaine. I look through her books and her musical scores and I cannot rid myself of the thought that I have resisted as heartily as has Clara the thought that she might love me and I her. This scarcely affects my obsession with Alice. I want it to be as it was. 'In Paris,' I murmur to myself. 'It will come back in Paris.' And then I ask myself: 'What am I?' I am corrupted and I am revelling in my corruption. I am the victim of my imagination, trapped in a terrible fantasy of my own devising. I am still awake when, at dawn, the Holzhammer guns begin to fire on Mirenburg. She trembles. She cries out. The shells blow up the Restaurant Schmidt and flesh scatters into the morning air; the statues of St Varoslav and St Ormond fall in a haze of white dust, crashing onto the shattered slabs of masonry below. The Liberty apartments, the baroque and Romanesque churches, the domes and the steeples, are falling one by one at first and then in their hundreds. Mirenburg, that city of all cities, is being murdered. She is being murdered. And here is Lady Cromach, startled and anxious, asking if I have seen Alice. Clara is behind her. Have I seen Alice? She cannot have left. But she has taken a coat, a hat. I go out to look for her. The shells are relentless. I can see them going past; I hear their wailing and their thunder. I know her family church, near Nussbaumhof. It is still standing, though most of the other buildings are flattened. I am in time to find her coming down the wide steps, dressed inadequately in a silk tea-gown and a summer cloak. The mysterious vulnerability of her face is emphasised by the'stooped set of her shoulders, her nervous eyes, as she recognises me and comes towards me for a few paces before pausing and looking back at others also emerging from the white Gothic arch. 'What were you looking for in there?' I ask. She begins to shiver. I go up to her and put my own coat around her. 'Comfort?' she says. 'Certainty? I don't know.' I try to lead her back to Rosenstrasse but she will not move. 'It's unlike you,' I say. 'What?' she asks. 'To risk so much danger.' She frowns. 'There wasn't any. The guns started later.' I smile, almost in relief. 'I must leave you,' she says. 'I must leave you all. I must be free.' I am sympathetic. 'So you shall be. You can do what you like. But first we must escape Mirenburg. Get to Paris. Come.'

'No.' She stands firm. I act as if I am dealing with a child. 'Very well.' I lift my hat and return down the steps, feeling that I have somehow hurt her and myself at the same time. Her confusion is infectious. I stop and look back. She is staring at me from those blank eyes. She is staring. 'Come along, Alexandra.' I stretch out my hand. 'I can no longer afford to indulge myself in this fantasy of youthful infatuation. Either you come with me or I shall abandon you.'

'I want you to go.'

I return, one by one, up the steps. The shells are like a chorus of harpies all around us. 'But what of me?' I say. I am still hoping to appeal to her. 'What shall I be left with?'

She looks at me almost with contempt. 'Love and affection,' she says.

I cannot recover myself. Mirenburg is being destroyed. All my romance is being taken from me at once and there is no-one I can blame. This desolation is too complete. She shrugs and joins me. Through all the yelling and all the death we walk slowly home to Rosenstrasse. 'You were lying to me,' she says. 'There is no means of getting to Paris.'

'I will find a way,' I promise. If only I can keep her with me, can get her free of all this terror, we can become calm again. She will love me again. She will know me for what I am, a decent, ordinary, kind-hearted man. In Rosenstrasse everyone is relieved to see us. Alice is put to bed. 'It is exhaustion,' says Lady Diana. 'She is only a child. She's in shock.' For twenty-four hours she hardly moves, although she is awake. We take turns sitting with her. 'Don't leave me, Ricky,' she says suddenly, in the depths of the night. I grasp her hand. I have begun to seek out a plan of Rosenstrasse's sewers; it has occurred to me that this could be our best means of escape. Some of the sewers must run outside the walls, or connect with the underground river. She is so weak. She is fading. Her temperature is alarmingly high. Clara assures me there is nothing seriously wrong with her. I am suspicious of Clara. One is always suspicious of those one deceives. I too am dying, I suppose. That must be why Papadakis humours me so readily, no longer refusing me wine or anything else I demand. He can afford to be charitable. There is never any snow here, only relentless blues and yellows and whites occasionally softened by mist or rain. I can see no green trees from my window. How can they give beauty to me so easily and then take it away just as thoughtlessly? Why should she wish to do that? She stands in the snow with shredded flags limp on her remaining turrets, like a captured heroine. Mirenburg is defeated, but Holzhammer, perhaps so there should be no physical monument to his bestiality, is relentless. Hour after hour the shells fall on the city and at night she is livelier than by day, for her fires are now inextinguishable; her broken silhouettes possess a nobility they lack under the light of the sun. Mirenburg is all but dead. She makes sad, fluttering sounds and little whimpers: the steady booming we hear is the triumphant beating of enemy hearts. If they rape her now, they shall have only the satisfaction of violating a creature which has already made its peace with death. She will give them no pleasure; she will put no curse upon them. They have damned themselves.

We are not allowed outside. Captain Mencken sits beside the telephone, waiting for the instrument to give him orders. In the street there is a horse and cart. We can see it through a hole in the boarded window. All the glass is broken. The horse is dead, from shrapnel. 'Mister' was bringing it back, with our provisions.

'Mister' was killed, too. His body was dragged inside. The cart has remained there for hours. At night its silhouette is thrown onto the blinds by any nearby explosion. 'That cart is the Devil's own carriage,' says Rakanaspya. 'It is waiting for one of us.' He laughs and pulls heavily on his brandy bottle. He is wearing an opera hat and cape. He has an ebony stick in his left hand, together with a pair of gloves. Captain Mencken wishes to know why the window is unprotected when all the others are boarded up. 'We needed some air,' says Rakanaspya. Frau Schmetterling has given shelter to a group of musicians. They are playing now. Their music is exotic, but its inspiration escapes me: there is an Oriental quality to it, though it follows the familiar form of a sonata. The musicians themselves have a slightly Asian cast to their features. Count Belozerski assures me they are not Russian. I have enquired the name of the composer, but I did not recognise it. They are still playing in the morning when I look through the blinds. I can smell the dead horse. In the half-light I see a young, naked child, squatting upon the carcass, picking with its claws at the tough, steaming meat, its own pink body seeming to merge into that of the dead beast, its black eyes hard and wary, like the eyes of a guilty crow. I once used to say that I had an ear for music, an eye for women and a strong distaste for death. While that little orchestra played and while I tortured myself over the question of Alexandra I came to doubt both former statements and to feel thoroughly reinforced in the latter. The whores do not bother to dress in their tasteful finery now. They make love in corners of the salon if they feel like it. Frau Schmetterling is hardly ever present. She has disappeared with Wilke. Only once did I hear her put her foot down in her old, firm way. It was when Inez, the Spanish girl, refused point-blank to accompany Van Geest to the rocking-horse room. 'I will not do any of those things,' she had insisted. 'It is quite true,' Frau Schmetterling had said softly, 'that Inez is not required, Herr Van Geest, to visit the rocking-horse room. Perhaps Greta would oblige?' But Van Geest, lost in the depths of his own brain and very drunk, had insisted that he wanted Inez. 'You said nothing of the rocking-horse room when you asked for Inez or I should have told you, Herr Van Geest, that she was not available. There has always been an agreement, after all.' Van Geest offered to pay double. Inez had considered this and then again shaken her head. Van Geest had said angrily: 'In other establishments girls like you are severely punished. There are houses in Amsterdam which specialise in taming stupid, disobedient young women.' Frau Schmetterling had pursed her lips. 'Then I suggest you wait until you can return to Amsterdam, Herr Van Geest.'

Van Geest had glared and then given up, stumbling back to his room. Inez had begun to giggle in relief. Frau Schmetterling had been disapproving. 'You should not have caused a scene,' she had said. But there have been other scenes since and she has not been present to make the peace. Sometimes, when I have been keeping vigil beside Alice's bed, I have had to go out into the corridor to beg people to be quiet. I have managed to get hold of the plans to the sewers. I have found a way of escape. When Alice murmurs to me and pleads for reassurance I tell her we are as good as free. All she has to do is to regain her strength. Soon she is a little better. I show her the plans. I describe the route we are going to take through the mountains to the border where we shall be able to get the train. She frowns. 'Is there no other way?' I shake my head. I begin to tell her how we shall drop into the sewers, what we can take with us, and what we shall tell the others. 'It's tiring.' She sinks again into semi-sleep. 'I'll leave it to you.' I am disturbed by this response. I have managed to do what she wants and she scarcely thanks me. I cannot fathom this sickness. Clara is certain it is a sickness of the spirit. We can only blame the shock of War. The horse is eventually freed from the shafts and what is left of it is butchered for meat. The naked child disappears. Four or five of our girls put on a tableau meant to take our minds off the relentless sound of shelling. Clara and I watch together, comfortable in each other's company. The tableau represents something Arcadian and employs a great many artificial flowers which, of course, the girls have in abundance. Since only three of them speak reasonable German and the others have only the most limited vocabularies the 'play' becomes quickly incomprehensible with the result that the actresses are soon laughing more than the audience. Clara and I applaud. I glance furtively at her to see if she knows anything of my plan. She seems innocent of suspicion tonight. At dawn I slip away to look for the entrance to the sewer. It is not far from here, joining with the underground river which runs beneath Rosenstrasse. The intense light of the winter day threatens my eyes. I should be glad of Captain Mencken's glasses. I manage to open the metal hatch beneath the archway of Papensgasse and I hear water running below, but it stinks. There can be no fresh water, other than melted snow, left in the whole of Mirenburg. I know that one can go from here to the main sewer, or get to it directly from the riverbed. I lower the hatch and walk down Papensgasse to inspect the river entrance to the sewer. Looking over the embankment wall from this side I can just see it, a murky hole rimmed with slime. It seems large enough. When the Siege is lifted, I wonder, will they redirect the river to its old course or will it continue to follow the new one? There is a familiar whistling overhead. A Krupp shell begins to fall towards me. I run for the relative security of Papensgasse. I hear the shell but I have not heard the gun which fired it, either because it was so far away or because I am so used to the sound of cannon.

The shell falls not far from Rosenstrasse. Out of the dusty débris comes galloping a column of flying artillery. It stops in a flurry of hoofs and steel on the embankment. The soldiers rush to position their guns so they point across the river at the Moravia. I slip back to the brothel and return to Clara. She stirs in her sleep. I am not sure she has noticed my absence. Since we all three take turns sitting with Alice Clara has become used to frequent comings and goings. Later that morning we both get dressed and go to see how the child is. To our considerable surprise she is not only up, she is eating cheese and drinking watered wine. Diana is full of joy. 'What a wonderful recovery.' Clara frowns.

I do my best to disguise my pleasure. Alice must be ready to travel. When Clara and Diana go downstairs together I hug my little girl. 'Are you ready for our next adventure?'

'Oh, yes!' she grins at me, a conspiratorial innocent. 'What's the plan?'

I tell her we shall leave separately tonight. I will wait for her at midnight in Papensgasse, round the corner from the archway. 'It might be easier than I thought. They've moved our guns up to the river. That probably means Holzhammer has broken through the defences and is in the Moravia already. We'll come out well behind his main lines. I'll buy horses, then it's a clear ride to the border and a train.' We hear sounds in the corridor. She says gently, with hesitant fingers on my arm: 'You don't think you'd be happier going with Clara?' I am taken aback. My heart sinks. 'Of course not. Why?' She makes a little movement with her lovely shoulders. 'Nothing.' The door opens. 'I'll be there.'

Clara enters. She seems distressed. Has she guessed? 'It's Van Geest,' she says. 'He's shot himself. God knows why. Downstairs is full of police and soldiers. They don't seriously think it's murder. But the building's now officially occupied. Soldiers are being billeted here. Temporarily, they say, because of the "new emergency", whatever that is.' I return to the ground floor with her, so she will not get suspicious. I blow my smiling Alice a kiss as we leave. The vestibule is still hung with its many portraits of the French emperor whom Frau Schmetterling adored and who, some say, was her first lover. The soldiers show distaste for these pictures and seem discomfited by them. The officer in charge, Captain Kolovrat, attempts to order them removed from the walls. This Frau Schmetterling firmly refuses. She is the only one of us with any authority to resist them; my own choice is to pretend respect and to avoid them as much as I can. Unlike Mencken, these men are used to power and know how to gain it. A soldier must be broken in such a way as to make him wholly reliant upon his superiors, otherwise he cannot be controlled in battle. Most officers employ this knowledge in their dealings with women, first destroying their confidence, then supplying it themselves so that those they would command become entirely dependant upon them. I must admit to being nervous. They remind me of well-trained hounds: their natural ferocity, their terror of their own madness, contained and controlled almost entirely by their wills. Such personalities yearn for uniforms, for rituals. They demand them in others, for they must order a world they fear and thus will simplify themselves and those around them as much as they can. Captain Mencken is in conversation with a police inspector wearing a kepi and gold epaulettes on his maroon uniform. Captain Kolovrat, presumably senior to Mencken, struts about the salon inspecting its contents as if he were kicking his heels in a provincial art gallery. He has a Prussian-style helmet decorated in gold and silver, a black-and-white uniform, and a variety of medals. His hand sticks his sword out behind him like the extended tail of a scorpion. His little fat face is embellished by a waxed moustache and a monocle. He wheels around and marches towards me to be introduced by a defeated Frau Schmetterling, whose only victory has been the pictures. He salutes me. I bow my head. He clicks his heels and says: 'You must understand, sir, that every resident is now under military discipline. Your privileges, I regret, are at an end.'

'They were over when "Mister" died,' says Frau Schmetterling softly. And then, to him: 'I hope you don't expect to find supplies here, Captain Kolovrat. We were living hand to mouth as it was.'

'We shall see,' he says. 'I shall want inventories. Anything we use will, of course, receive a receipt and you can claim full payment from the government after the War. Mencken? Inspector Serval?'

'Suicide without doubt,' says Serval. 'He was probably suffering from some form of delirium. Maybe bad meat, maybe drink, maybe a disease. The doctor will let us know. But he shot himself through the temple with his own revolver. A familiar situation at present.'

'Disease,' says Kolovrat, rubbing at his chubby chin. He rolls the word on his tongue and seems about to spit it out. 'Of course. There must be a medical inspection. I shall send to headquarters.'

Frau Schmetterling is offended. 'I assure you that the likelihood...'

'The likelihood is what a soldier must consider, madame.' He is fastidious and condescending. She falls silent, reconciled for the time being to this man's swaggering rudeness. Mencken seems embarrassed and apologetic. Clara, Diana and I go with the others, girls and clients, into the salon. Alice is mentioned and excused because she is unwell. I present her papers. Kolovrat has had a bureau placed in the middle of the floor. He sits at this now, making up a register. One by one we give our names and nationalities, showing him our identification cards. We are allowed to sit or to stand around the walls of the salon. Outside, the shells are constant and from time to time the whole building shakes or more glass crashes to the floor. Kolovrat's inquisition is frequently punctuated by the chiming of the chandelier over his head. One series of shots seems closer: I realise it is our own artillery, firing across the river. Kolovrat knows the sound, too, and looks up. I fail to read his fat little face. Eventually we are dismissed. Young soldiers stand to attention everywhere. Clara, Diana and myself are asked by Frau Schmetterling to accompany her to her kitchen. Whenever a shell lands nearby she jumps and looks at her shivering dresser, at her wonderful, rattling china. So far nothing is damaged. 'I am worried,' she says, 'about my daughter. With "Mister" gone Elvira has no-one but me...' She sits down at her long table. Trudi, smiling in the background, makes us something to drink. Outside, there is a lull in the bombardment and we can hear Herr Ulric the butcher-cook in the courtyard. His loud healthy voice rings and echoes. He is arguing with a young cavalryman: 'The horse is no good to you and no good to itself. It is dying of starvation!' The soldier is passionate. 'We shall die together!' he shouts. The butcher is reasonable: 'Go inside and fuck one of the girls. While you're at it I'll deal with the horse.'

'You are disgusting!'

The butcher drops his voice and so does the cavalryman. We hear no more and soon the shells are landing again. The building is scarcely ever still. It is as if an earthquake perpetually shakes it. Frau Schmetterling says to Lady Cromach: 'You have connections, I presume, in England. Could you get Elvira to school there? If anything happens to me.'

'Nothing will happen to you, Frau Schmetterling, and of course I'll do whatever I can. Do you wish me to recommend some schools, somewhere where Elvira could stay? I have an old nanny who still lives in London.'

'Yes,' says Frau Schmetterling. 'That's the sort of thing.' She produces a notebook. 'Some names and addresses?'

Lady Diana makes an awkward, affectionate gesture. She frowns and then spells in English. When she has finished she says: 'If anything else comes to mind I'll let you know. You wish your daughter to leave soon?'

'Oh, yes, soon.' Frau Schmetterling's large bosom rises and falls. 'I must stay with my girls. Elvira...'

'We'll see that's she's safe,' says Diana. 'I promise.' Her voice is soft and comforting. It has lost most of that inflexion which makes almost every word seem sardonic. She squeezes Frau Schmetterling's shoulder. The madam sighs. 'Thank you, Lady Cromach.'

Our band has begun to play again in the salon. Presumably Captain Kolovrat has decided this will improve morale. The staccato, nervous quality of the tune becomes increasingly intrusive as we sit in silence round Frau Schmetterling's table, drinking spiced grog and getting a little drunk. The steady thumping of the guns, the shrieks and explosions, seem preferable to the music. Eventually, Frau Schmetterling rises and says she must speak to Ulric about lunch. She rings for the cook. He comes striding in, grinning widely. His leather apron is covered in blood. He bows to us. I envy him his insouciance as much as I envy him his sinewy arms, the strong veins standing out from the hard muscle. As we three leave the kitchen and return upstairs Diana remarks that I seem in unusually good spirits. We reach my door. Alice is sitting in the easy chair, reading a magazine. She kisses us, one by one. There is an air of excitement about her which amuses us all, even Clara. 'The shock has worn off as quickly as it came,' says my Rose.

'That, I suppose, is the nature of such complaints. Particularly in the very young.' Lady Diana thoughtfully strokes Alice's hair.

Alice puts lips to her wrist. We decide we shall all lunch together so that Alice can meet the new Captain. 'That's splendid!' exclaims Alice. At lunch Rakanaspya and Count Belozerski eat in silence, perhaps in mourning for Van Geest. Caroline Vacarescu hangs on Count Stefanik's arm but at the same time spares a bright smile for Captain Kolovrat and another for Captain Mencken, both of whom dine with us. Trudi is helped at the table by a young, red-faced military orderly who sweats visibly and whose smell is almost as vile as the meat we are eating. Egon Wilke, at Frau Schmetterling's elbow, has an embarrassed air about him. He is presumably not comfortable sitting down to eat with so much Authority on either side of him. Kolovrat attempts to make a joke across the table, addressing Mencken. 'Well, here we are, the two oldest professions in the world sharing a table. I suppose that is only proper. What would you rather be, Frau Schmetterling, a whore or a soldier?'

'As a matter of fact, monsieur,' she says in French, 'I am neither. But I think I should rather be a whore. I see it as a superior calling.'

Kolovrat pretends to be amused, again seeking to catch Mencken's eye and being baffled by the expressionless smoked glasses. 'What? Why so, madame?'

'I think there is a considerable difference,' she says coolly, 'between those of us who kill for a living and those of us who fuck for a living.'

Frau Schmetterling has never used such a word in public before. But Kolovrat is the only one who does not realise it. Presumably he thinks the proprietress of a brothel capable of any language.

'In the first place,' he says, 'we do not willingly kill for a living. We are protecting the citizens of Mirenburg. And in the second place, what is sold here, surely is not honest fornication. This,' he waves a fork, 'this is death. This is corruption. The destruction of all true feeling. What has it to do with love? All you women have diseases. They kill my men, do they not? And turn them mad first, eh? Madame, I would prefer a bayonet in the stomach. That's a better death than one you purchase at a whorehouse!'

Frau Schmetterling is calm. 'The only death you will find here is the death of sentimental illusion. But even that...'

'There is a corpse still upstairs awaiting collection!' He laughs and chews the butcher's latest prize. 'That's what I call death. And I say again: I'd rather have a bayonet in the stomach.'

Her smile is almost sweet. I have never seen her in this terrible, baiting mood, but Wilke, plainly, knows it well. He is privately amused. 'Monsieur,' she says, 'there is a wide variety of alternatives. One does not necessarily have a disease and one may not go so far as to stab or be stabbed in the stomach. The soldier takes risks with his life. So do we. But we do not set out to kill or to enforce our wills upon others. I believe that our profession is the better of the two and can more easily be justified in moral terms. I do not wish to kill you, monsieur. I would wish, if I were a whore, merely to satisfy your lust in exchange for a crown or two.' She stares directly into his little eyes and he again looks to Mencken, then frowns. Alice snorts behind her hand. Lady Cromach smiles and tries to silence her. The two of them are like older and younger sister today. I suddenly regret that our time together is over. I shall miss Diana almost as much as I shall my Rose. As we are finishing lunch, Albert Jirichek, a journalist for the *Weekly Gazette*, is granted a brief interview with Captain Kolovrat who is reluctant to speak in anything but the vaguest terms. It is true Holzhammer is in the Moravia, but it is not true he is making steady inroads. 'Our armour is keeping him pinned down and there is every chance he will be defeated by tomorrow.' As Kolovrat continues to speak, Jirichek opens his notebook and begins to scribble rapidly in shorthand. This causes Captain Mencken some amusement. 'Are you unaware, Herr Jirichek, that the *Gazette* was blown apart by shell-fire this morning? I doubt very much if we shall see another edition within the next few days.' It is evident he has no liking for the journal, which takes a mildly left-wing bias. Jirichek has not heard the news. He closes his notebook. He lifts his hand to one and all and departs the room in silence. Most of us laugh at this. I am relaxed, unwilling to leave the company too soon. I know I shall never experience this kind of comradeship again. By tomorrow Alice and I will be far away from the main fighting. By the day after we should have crossed the border into Saxony. From there it will be an easy matter to take the train to Paris. In less than three days we should have new wardrobes, a comfortable hotel and (delightful anticipation!) the finest food in the world. Alice and Diana decide to return upstairs because Alice says she feels faint. I am generous enough to want them to spend what time together they can. I tell myself that jealousy would be petty. Clara and I remain at the table, drinking brandy. Captain Kolovrat watches Alice leave. I feel sudden hatred of him. He begins to court me, because he desires her. His eyes follow her as he speaks to us. 'Yesterday was hard work. The Vlodinya prison was shelled. In the confusion half the jailbirds escaped. We did our best to round them up; we herded them like wild cows but a few honest people got mixed in with them. It was a relief to be sent here. I don't know why they wanted to escape. Those bastards were better off where they were!' He is pleased with his joke and repeats it.

Frau Schmetterling, still intent on baiting him, leans towards him. 'Have you ever been to prison, Captain Kolovrat?'

'Of course not, madame.'

'Has anyone else here been to prison?' Wilke alone lowers his eyes. The rest of us shake our heads.

'It destroys your personality,' she says. 'To maintain your morale you have to become a Top Dog. That means accepting all the ruthless conditions of prison life. You pay a high price by becoming inhuman and coarse. But if you do not become a hardened prisoner you go back into the world with no belief in yourself whatsoever. Prisons have little social benefit, Captain Kolovrat, save to lock a criminal away for a while. Their main task is to make us passive and malleable: whereupon they return us to persuasive friends who are usually outside the law and glad to suggest ways to easy wealth... Destroying the human spirit is not merely immoral. It is anti-social!'

I have never heard her speak so passionately. She has captured Rakanaspya's attention. He asks her, with deference, how she is so well-informed about prison. She shrugs. She has known short spells in Berlin and in Odessa. She has talked to many people whose experience of prison was far worse than her own. 'You know me, gentlemen. I am a law-abiding citizen. I believe in peace and quiet; an orderly society. You will not find me taking up the cause of anarchy. However, I can say from the bottom of my heart that the whole conception of prison is disgusting to me.' With that she continues pecking at a tiny piece of stale cheese. She has brought silence to the company. Perhaps that was her intention. The table is shaken by another blast. Count Stefanik has undone his collar and unbuttoned his waistcoat. He is the kind of man who should wear loose, peasant clothes. Even then he would not seem entirely comfortable. He puts his hand under his beard and pushes it up towards his face. He is wary and thoughtful, as if he listens for Holzhammer's footsteps in the vestibule. He is wanted by the Austrians for more than one offence, including the scattering of nationalist leaflets from the skies above Prague. If Holzhammer arrests him he knows that he, himself, faces prison, if not death. He sighs a deep desolate sigh and rises, excusing himself. 'I feel sorry for him,' says Clara. Caroline Vacarescu makes to follow him, then returns to offer Captain Mencken all her attention. She has given up her hopes, it seems, of balloon-escape. A little later he passes the open door of the salon to go out. He clears his throat and puts on his hat and overcoat. 'The man's a fool to walk the streets!' says Kolovrat dispassionately. 'Perhaps he'd rather be killed than captured,' says Rakanaspya. I am overwhelmed by a sudden depression, a fear of betrayal and loss. I excuse myself. I take Clara's hand and we go upstairs to her room where I insist on making slow, gentle love. She is warm. She is tender. She is womanly. I rise in agitation from the bed. I am disgusted with myself. Another shell explodes nearby. She is baffled by my behaviour. I silence her question with a gesture.

She sits up. 'This bombardment is getting on everyone's nerves. I'm almost praying for defeat now, for peace, even the peace of the grave. If the Bulgarians are allowed…' She cannot finish.

'The house must be evacuated before that happens,' I say.

'Every effort must be made to get the girls out and split up. They must not be recognised for what they are. Frau Schmetterling won't keep this place going as a cheap soldier's bordello. It would destroy the point of it. She has always been clear on that.'

Clara frowns. 'True. But it will be up to the girls. They will be frightened. Are you leaving, Ricky?'

I ignore her question. 'You wouldn't stay here, would you? To service those pigs?'

She lowers her head. 'No,' she says, as if keeping her temper, as if I have insulted her. 'No, I would not.'

'That's good. That's good.' I am distracted. It is almost dusk. I look at my watch. My bag is packed and hidden. I assume Alice has also packed. The time is passing slowly. 'Let's have some cocaine,' I say. 'Then I think I'll go downstairs and see what's happening.' She begins to prepare the drug. 'Be careful,' she says, when I go.

In the dirty snow of the quays the soldiers stagger to their guns with shells from boxes stored for safety's sake behind sandbags on the other side of the street. I watch them through the murk. They are ham-fisted, filthy, worn out. Black smoke billows across the southern suburbs. It would appear Holzhammer has fired that entire section of the city. An officer, mounted on a skinny horse, peers through field glasses and sees nothing. The smoke is oily, moving sluggishly. It is snowing fitfully again. Papadakis! The pain is coming back! It is like shrapnel in my belly! Oh, God, I need a woman here. But I have spent too long taking revenge on women. Now there is none to comfort me. When romance dies, cynicism replaces it, unless one is prepared to relinquish all the consolations of religion at a stroke. I could not. I fled into lies, flattery, deceitful conquest. I fled into mistrustful artifice. Even my wholesome lechery became tainted by fear and wary cunning. I lost my capacity to trust. Was I so dishonest and so hypocritically cruel before Mirenburg? Too much romance was destroyed at once, in the space of a few days. Mirenburg crumbles. The twin spires of St-Maria-and-St-Maria are down. The Hotel Liverpool is in fragments. All the care and artistry of centuries, all the worship, the love, the genius, is ground up as if in a mortar and scattered on the wind. The museums and the galleries, the monasteries and the great houses, fall down before Holzhammer's insane ferocity. It is too late to parley. Holzhammer will not accept anything less than the absolute obliteration of the city. He wants no monuments to remind him of his crime. These are the actions of children, of wild beasts. Love and hope drown beneath the exploding iron. Clara is still in bed when I return. She stretches on her cushions, smoking a cigarette, looking at me with an expression I find unreadable, but which I fear is contempt. 'It is terrible out there,' I say. 'The whole southern side is burning. The Radota Bridge is destroyed and all the statues are down. The river is piled with corpses. Presumably they were trying to get away from the Bulgarians.'

Clara nods to herself and offers me a lighted cigarette which I take. 'Are we to expect them tonight, do you think?'

'Not tonight. But possibly tomorrow. At the latest the day after.'

'Then perhaps we should do something.'

'Yes,' I say. 'It would be a good idea. I have plans. I've some business this evening. I won't tell you about it now, not until I'm certain. But in the morning, everything should be clear.'

I detect a smile on her long lips. She stretches and yawns. I want to see Alice, to remind her exactly of the plan, to be certain that she knows what we are to do. But I console myself that it is simple enough. She will meet me in Papensgasse at midnight, slipping out unseen as I shall slip a little earlier.

'Shall we go to Alice and Diana, to see how the child is?' asks Clara. I dart her a look. 'Leave them. They said they wanted to rest.'

She shrugs. 'Just as you like.' Then she says, 'Come here, Ricky. I want to make love to you.'

I am disconcerted. Off duty she is not normally so direct. But I do as she orders. I undress. She is ferocious. She kisses every part of me. She sits astride me, shoving my penis into her cunt. The pleasure is astounding. It seems altogether fresh. I am exhausted. She throws herself off me, laughing. 'That wasn't fair. But I enjoyed it.'

I kiss her. 'What?' she says. 'You seem to be crying.' Of course I am not crying. Where is Papadakis? I need to piss and the pot is full. I am having trouble breathing. The lamp is flickering. There is not enough air in this room. The flowers are wilting.

As soon as Clara is asleep I get up carefully and go to the cupboard where I have hidden my bag. I dress and creep from the room. The house rocks and vibrates constantly. It will not be long, I am sure, before there is a direct hit. Half Rosenstrasse bears the marks of Krupp now. There is noise and music from the salon. No soldiers guard the door. I am out into the cold, into the darkness, shivering and suddenly very cowardly. I think to turn back, but it would be impossible. I move falteringly between the heaps of filthy snow, through the passage and into Papensgasse. There will be no military patrols tonight, I am sure, to enforce the curfew. I look at my watch. It is eleven forty-five. I will not have long to wait. Soon Alice will be mine alone. Married. I shall be secure with her. She would not dare to betray me. But this will not stop us sharing further adventures – and in Paris! The very prospect warms me and makes me forget how cold I am. Firelight dances on the far riverbank. Men are shouting. There is not much terror in their voices now. They are too weary. The guns fire. The guns reply. Love will come back to me. Alice is late. She will be having trouble getting away from Diana. We shall roll again in fresh linen, with great cups of newly made coffee in the mornings, with delicate lunches in the restaurants of the Champs-Élysées, with drives to Versailles, and in the summer we shall go south to Venice, and I will show her North Africa and bring joy to her exotic heart. But it is twelve-thirty. I hear voices whispering in Rosenstrasse. Has she been caught? Eventually I risk peering round into the street; it is too dark to see anything. Then, at last, someone emerges from the archway and I grin to myself, full of the prospect of escape and further adventure. The woman wears a cloak with a cowl covering her head. I know immediately that it is Clara and I am filled with hatred for her. She has guessed! She has interfered. She lifts a hand to silence me. 'They went hours ago,' she says. 'I thought this might be what you were doing. They left before dark, Ricky.' I fall back against the wall, not fully understanding, not wishing to understand. 'What?'

'Diana and our Alice have gone together,' she says quietly. She takes my hand. 'You're very cold. You'd better come back.'

'No!' I think it is a trick. I pull free of her. 'There was an agreement, Clara. You should not be doing this. Where are they?'

'I don't know. You'll freeze to death, if a bullet doesn't kill you.'

'Where are they?'

'They were as secretive with me as with anyone. They could have joined Count Stefanik. It's my only guess.'

'Stefanik? His balloon?'

'A guess.'

'Where is his balloon?'

'I have no idea where he kept it. It's probably destroyed. It was a guess.'

I begin to run up Papensgasse and through the Botanical Gardens. There are fires everywhere. The soldiers ignore me. I get to Pushkinstrasse and I cannot recognise anything. There are no more buildings. I look up into the blazing night sky in the hope of seeing the airship. The Indian Quarter has vanished. The Customs House is a guttering cinder. Within an hour I am standing in the ruins of her church. The Yanokovski Promenade has become a mass of black rubble. I can see St Maria-and-St-Maria on the hill, twin chimneys of light. Flames course through the Cathedral, glowing from every window. She is roaring as if in pain and anger. And the shells continue. Holzhammer must surely have come to relish the destruction for its own sake. We are at his mercy. And he is not merciful. Little Bohemia and the Synagogue are one hellish pyre. I reach down to pick up a piece of masonry. It is a small stone head, part of the motif above the left-hand column framing the central door: the face of a woman. It seems to me that she stares past my shoulder at a memory. The expression on her face is resigned. Has that expression always been there? For the three hundred years of her existence has she always known this would

be her fate? There is no snow. The Theatre is an insubstantial outline of dancing red and orange. Everything is melting in the heat.
Later I will hear that Prince Badehoff-Krasny had ordered the
remains of the city to be fired. ('This is my Moscow.') Nobody will
ever come to understand how Mirenburg fell, any more than they
will really know how Magdeburg was destroyed or what led to the
extinction of Troy. Man's greatest monuments, his architecture,
never outlast his acts of aggression. At dawn I wade through fields
of ash. I cannot find her. Thin sunlight attacks the drifting smoke.
Little groups of people wander here and there, each with a bundle,
none with any hope. They look at me, some of them, as I pass, but
most trudge on with their heads bowed. There are fewer shells,
now. They fall on ruins and pulverise them. As I pass it, the Casino
collapses in on itself. There is hardly anything left for them to destroy. I cannot find her. Periodically, I inspect the sky. There is no
ship there. I would like to think it has borne her up. In my mind's
eye I can see the bright reds and golds of the balloon's canopy in
contrast to the grey, misty luminousness of the morning. Dressed
in his Chinese silk shirt and riding breeches, with a gaily dressed
woman on either side of him, the young Bohemian aviator lifts a
strong arm to his valves. I can see the balloon rising higher and
higher above the flattened wastes of our murdered city, as if Mirenburg's spirit goes free. I can see her smiling carelessly, merely
enjoying the sensation of flight, forgetful of me and of everyone.
She kisses the bearded cheek of Stefanik not from any particular
affection but from simple, passing gratitude to the person who has
given her this, her most recent, pleasure. One should never attempt
to possess a beautiful whore, or hold on to the soul of a child, nor
assault an idea as fragile as Mirenburg. Alice. I shall never fully
understand why you fled from me. I wish you had been able to tell
me the truth. But, if I were ever to confront you, you would reply:
'You must have known.' and dismiss all responsibility for your
deception. 'You must have known.' But when you deny my suspicions that is a deeper lie still. 'You must have known, that I deceived
you. It is your fault for not admitting it.' Yet did I really ever guess?
Was I not always too afraid of the true answer? They will build a

new city along the fresh course of the river. It will be called Sviten-burg as a sop to the nationalists who are soon, of course, to become Austrian subjects in all but name. It is still little more than an indus-trial village. Its most impressive buildings are its warehouses. Did Alexandra live to marry a well-to-do Swiss and give him little babies in Geneva? She could banish all the old shadows, the mem-ories of a 'wicked past', and have forgotten a lifetime in a matter of hours. And Wäldenstein will become Svitavia again, a province of Bohemia, then a department of Czecho-Slovakia; forty years later that is what she remains, looking to Prague, such a poor imitation of Mirenburg, for her directions. Here in the yellow heat and ease I have spent the past eighteen years peering out at the world I came to fear. The Germans rise again and recover their wealth through patriotism, mysticism and a fascination with steel, as they will always do; the French continue to squabble and refer to past glo-ries as solutions for the future; the English see their society collapsing all around them and find a panacea in American jazz; the Russians stir and dream again of Empire, having revived the methods and ambitions of Ivan the Terrible. And the Italians have conquered poverty, although they had to go to Abyssinia to do it. Wäldenstein, settled in the arms of her new Slavic mother, is left, at least, in peace. When I return to Rosenstrasse, Captain Kolovrat has galloped off about some other importance. The brothel is now almost the only whole building in the street. Captain Mencken commands the two or three soldiers left. He has no orders and he is drunk. The smoked glasses fall down on his nose as he looks at me and offers a bottle. I shake my head. Thérèse and Renée, all lace and dark stockings, sit together on a couch singing a little song together. 'Your wife,' he says, 'is upstairs I believe.' He is perfectly grave. 'Do you speak,' he drinks again, 'Bulgarian by any chance?' He laughs. He appears to have fled into that familiar, self-protec-tive dramatisation which is only one step away from hysteria. I am in no hurry to see Clara. I accept the offer of his bottle. 'We can abandon ourselves to War quite as readily as we can abandon our-selves to lust,' says Mencken, making an effort to hand up the bottle to me. 'And War's so much easier and less mystifying than sex, is it not?' He grins at me. 'I'm serious.' I do not doubt it. He lets his eye drift towards the ladies who are as drunk as he is and are giggling together. 'War doesn't whisper. It doesn't have shades of meaning. It demands courage, of course, and decisive action. It offers glory and threatens death. But lust offers pain and threatens us with life, eh?' He is pleased with this turn of phrase.

The sunlight begins to shine through the shattered boards and glass. I put the bottle back into his hands and with a sigh climb up to Clara and a reckoning. Holzhammer will become Governor Regent of Wäldenstein under the Austrians and will be blown to pieces by an anarchist bomb in 1904. Clara is asleep. There is no confrontation. I feel vague disappointment. I leave her and return to my room, hoping to find a clue. My anger with Lady Cromach is growing. She has deceived me treacherously. And yet my actions were no less treacherous. It is different, I tell myself, but I know it is not. I cannot feel the same anger towards Alice. The room is strewn with all her abandoned finery, with half-packed trunks and bags. I pick up a pair of pale blue silk drawers. They still stink of her. There are no notes. But in a cupboard I find some crumpled sheets of violet notepaper with scraps of Alice's handwriting on them and little pictures of the sort a schoolgirl might draw when bored. I spread them on top of the Chinese dresser. There is a quotation from something: *It's a fine day. Let's go fishing said the worm to the man.* And another scrap: *He is not what I imagined him to be.* I am beginning to shake. 'You are a fool!' I say. 'For *you* could have become what I imagined you to be. You have ruined any possibility of that now. What a woman you might have been.' It is my failure. I feel it as a painter might experience a failure of creativity. It is as if half my own flesh has been torn from me, half my mind stolen. The guns batter my past into the dust and my future has run away into the ruins. I am so horribly betrayed. And it is my own doing. My anger comes on me suddenly and I begin to rip at her dresses, her underwear, her aigrettes, stamping on her little shoes, flinging silk and lace and feathers into the air until my tiredness causes me to collapse, sucking at a hand I have somehow cut, in the middle of the débris. I have tried to destroy everything which reminds me of her, which hurts me. I poured so much of myself into that valueless vessel. As I squat there, weeping and shaking, Clara enters the room. She is wearing a patterned tea-gown over her nightclothes. She moves here and there, replacing ornaments, clearing up broken china and glass. 'She's taken every piece of jewellery,' she says. I moan at her to go away. She stands looking down on me. 'Have you hurt yourself badly?'

'No.'

She closes the door behind her.

When, at length, I return to Clara's room she is asleep again with the sheets drawn over her head. I take off my jacket and my waistcoat and go to sit in the armchair near the window. I cannot sleep. Every time I close my eyes I am filled with bitter images, with a yearning for the recent past and all the happiness I have lost. Mirenburg is gone. Papadakis grumbles at me as he brings back the clean chamber pot. 'You've pissed in the bed again,' he says. 'I know it. I can smell it.'

He has made me stand, leaning on the table and trembling, while he gathers up the soiled linen. 'I'm going to bring the doctor in the morning.' Now the bed is clean. Through the open window comes the smell of hyacinths and the sea. Mirenburg no longer lives; she is a grey memory. She has been biding her time, hiding in a neurasthenic slumber while she waited for the best which would be offered to her: a kind of hibernation because she did not want to accept my offer but was afraid to refuse it, afraid to take any action. What had Diana promised? I doubt if it was anything than a more glamorous, if less realistic, plan of escape. Stefanik's balloon? I get out of the chair. My legs are weak. Clara turns, casting off her covering to hold out tolerant arms. Her face is full of controlled sympathy. How can she forgive me? Why do women do this to us? I begin to weep again. 'We are going away this evening,' she says. 'It is all arranged with Frau Schmetterling. We will take Elvira. Wilke will be with us. How did you plan to escape from the city?' Still snivelling, I tell her about the underground river and the sewers. She pats my shoulder. 'Not bad. It could work.' Eventually I go to sleep. I am awakened by an explosion.

From somewhere within the house I hear voices shouting and the crash of falling plaster. It is dark in the room. I lie on the bed and wait for the next shell. Instead the door opens and Clara stands there, an oil lamp raised in her hand. Frau Schmetterling is with her. The madam holds something in her hands. It is a bloody, palpitating chow dog. 'They have killed Pouf-Pouf,' she says flatly. 'And this poor little one is dying, too.'

Clara is already in her outdoor clothes: a black-and-grey tailormade. Over this she draws a plain cloak of the sort peasant women wear. She points to a bundle at her feet. 'Here are some of "Mister's" clothes. They should fit you. You'll have to leave your wardrobe behind, my dear.'

I have become pliable and obedient. The dog begins to groan. Frau Schmetterling whispers something to Clara and then returns downstairs. I receive a strange feeling of satisfaction as I pull on the rough garments; it is almost as if I shall wear sackcloth in mourning for Mirenburg and my slain imagination. 'I want reality so badly,' I tell Clara. 'She was won over by nothing more than a fantastic promise.'

'Very likely.' Clara helps me button the coat. 'Do you still have the map?'

I give it to her. 'We'll put Wilke in charge, I think,' she says. 'At least for the moment. Are you feeling any better?'

'I want reality,' I tell her.

'This is reality enough for anyone.' She is humorous. 'But I'm sure you'll find a way out of it. I trust your instincts for that. Lead the way, your lordship.'

We leave, the four of us, in the night. In Rosenstrasse we have to pass two soldiers who are still alive, though their bodies are dreadfully mutilated. They call out to us for help. 'I'll deal with them,' says Frau Schmetterling, hurrying us forward.

Wilke and I raise the cover of the manhole. He goes first, swinging the lamp we have brought with us. Our shadows slide this way and that on the moist stones of the shaft. The metal ladder leads us down into the old watercourse. Elvira is too small to keep her head above the water, so I raise her on my shoulders.

Throughout this journey I will find a kind of delicate consolation in being allowed to tend to the child's needs and will catch myself occasionally using the same kind of words and gestures used by 'Mister' in his conversation with her. We wade through shit and corpses to some sort of liberty, emerging on the fringes of the Moravian inferno and joining lines of refugees stumbling towards the cleaner air of a countryside stripped of all its wealth. We walk steadily for two more days until we cross the Bohemian border and are able, with the gold Frau Schmetterling has given us, to get a train to Prague where we separate. Wilke will take Elvira to England. I still have no volition and allow Clara to make every decision. We go first by train to Berlin and the hospitality of my brother Wolfgang, who congratulates me on the charm and the breeding of my English fiancée. Within days, of course, we are taken up by Society. Everyone must hear of our experiences. I recover myself sufficiently to present at least an acceptable façade and I speak with authority of the suffering and destruction I have witnessed. I am asked to write the articles which become that silly book *The 100 Day Siege: A Personal Record of the Last Months of Mirenburg*. I mention nothing of any real importance to me, but for a while I become a hero. Holzhammer's villainy is the subject of a thousand editorials. He is called the Butcher of Mirenburg and the perfidy of Austria-Hungary has shocked, we read, the entire civilised world. But Holzhammer rules and Badehoff-Krasny is exiled and the diplomats gradually do their seedy work so that the Peace of Europe is maintained for a few more years. And Mirenburg is gone. I hear many rumours, but there is no news of Alice. I will talk to anyone who has a grain of gossip. It is still hard for me to accept that so much beauty has vanished as a result of trivial political decisions. There will never be a brothel like Frau Schmetterling's in Rosenstrasse, for there will never be another Mirenburg, with its history and its charm. And psycho-analysis has made us too self-conscious. This is an age of great remedies; they seem to believe there is a cure for human greed. There is not. But neither should the greedy be condemned. They should merely be guarded against. Greed is not evil. What is evil is the manipulation of others in order to satisfy it; the quest for power. That is the crime. Do you hear me, Papadakis? He is still shuffling about in the shadows.

Will you read this, Alice, in your Geneva home? Or did you die with the others in Mirenburg? I could not find you. In London and Dublin we thought to discover news of Lady Cromach, but she had not returned. Someone said she had changed her name 'because of certain scandals' and might be living in Paris. But she was not in Paris. And as for Princess Poliakoff, all we heard of her was that she could have gone to India. They said that on Sunday, 19 December, 1897, when Holzhammer's troops arrived at Rosenstrasse, Poliakoff had sat in her old lover's carriage and directed the mercenaries into the brothel. I can imagine with what pleasure the Bulgarians took our ladies ('All they found later was a pile of bloody lace'). Baby is crying, Lady Cromach used to say. Baby is angry. Rakanaspya was killed, probably by the Austrians. Count Belozerski was wounded but managed to return to Kiev where I believe he still lives, writing about factories. Baby is crying. We are lost. Deserted. That which comforts us grows old and dies. We long to recapture it; the security of childhood, the attention of others. Clara was familiar with Lady Cromach's remarks. But she was not so tolerant of Baby. 'Sooner or later,' she said to me, 'that baby's crying becomes an irritant to our adult ears. It is then we have the right to turn upon the weak and with all due ruthlessness squeeze the life from a silly, mindless creature. If we are to survive, Baby must be destroyed.'

I was not to meet Frau Schmetterling for a long time, after Clara had despaired of my sniffing after Alice's non-existent trail and had returned to Germany alone. Clara said, as she waited on the platform for her train: 'I shall always love you, Ricky, for what you are, as well as what you could have become. But I know you are in love with an illusion, and it is a lost illusion at that. What would happen if you found her, if Mirenburg had not been destroyed? What would have happened if she had stayed with you? You have told me yourself. You know, but you refuse to act on your knowledge. And that is madness.' Now my honest Clara is gone and I am alone with an obsession which has taken up my life and drained from me what was not already drained by the treacherous Alice, who refused to be what I needed her to be. She was myself. The city is gone. She would be fifty-seven years old now. Frau Schmetterling was in Dresden, the proprietress of an ordinary boarding house catering to single middle-class gentlemen. I reminded her gently of our ordeal in Mirenburg. 'Yes,' she said, 'it was ghastly. Hardly a saucer remained of all that crockery I had collected over twenty years.'

I asked if she had heard anything of my Alice. 'No,' she said. 'Not unless she was the one who married the Swiss. I think she was killed, wasn't she? I hope those bastards didn't rape her.' Frau Schmetterling had attempted to protect her girls from the troops but she had eventually left Mirenburg with Renée and Trudi and joined Wilke in Brighton. They had gone to America for a little while, but had not been able to stay. Most of her girls had had no means of travelling so the house had rapidly become a common bordello used by the occupying army. The Bulgarians had been brutes. Everything of value had been stolen during the looting. 'I heard,' the old madam told me, 'that at least one of the girls was killed. Remember Dolly? Natalia told me. I met Natalia outside the theatre, one evening, in Cologne. She was selling flowers. She dropped the whole basket to hug me!' Frau Schmetterling had laughed before she became serious again. 'She was the one who told me about Dolly. Those Bulgars destroyed everything that was delicate. They ruined everything beautiful. They didn't understand the rocking-horse room, so they simply ripped it apart. They killed the acrobat. That friend of "Mister's". *Laches!* He insulted an officer, apparently.'

Natalia had stayed on, she had told Frau Schmetterling, in the hope of filling the madam's place when things calmed down. Several of the whores had had the same idea. But Holzhammer had given the order to destroy every building left standing. 'They were lucky, in the end, to escape with the clothes still on their backs. Natalia left with a returning Bulgarian officer. He knocked her about. She got away from him in Buda-Pesht, she told me, while they were changing trains. She was married. She wasn't on hard times. Her husband had a big flower-business in Cologne. They had two little boys. And Caroline Vacarescu escaped. I don't know how. She married an American and went to live in Ohio, though I believe she's now in California. Elvira's at university, you know, in Munich. She still remembers you carrying her through that sewer.' Frau Schmetterling had winked at me with a trace of her old good humour. 'You'd like her. She's just your type.' I was able to laugh and tell her that I had lost interest in females under twenty-five when Mirenburg was destroyed. 'But what about the balloonist, that Czech?' She thought he had probably tried to get his airship up and had been shot down by Holzhammer's artillery. Much later I heard a rumour that, under an assumed name, he had been killed on the Eastern Front in 1915, flying a plane of his own design against the Austrians. Someone else said he had died with the Czech Legion in Siberia.

Frau Schmetterling had made me eat a huge dinner and had introduced me to her new dogs, two pugs. When I had left she had kissed me and said that I should look after my health. 'It is a shame you'll never make a fool of yourself over a woman again. Your mistake was in refusing to believe that another woman could be a worthy rival. Men will do that.' I had shaken my head. 'I respected her insufficiently. And in my efforts to obscure my motives from her I lost her for ever.' But Frau Schmetterling had been impatient with this. 'Interpret it any way you choose, Ricky. The fact was that you seduced a child and you paid the price for it.' She had shrugged. 'And she would always have been a child, probably, with men like you to look after her. She's a child now, if she married that Swiss. Enjoy youth when it's given to you. It's a mistake to try to imprison it, though. It's too greedy, Ricky. And it never works, my boy.' She is still in Dresden, I believe. We exchange postcards every couple of years. Prince Badehoff-Krasny lived not twenty miles from me, up the coast, until his death. Von Landoff replaced Holzhammer as Governor, after the assassination. Captain Mencken was killed in Papensgasse, firing a carbine at the Bulgarians as they swept round from the embankment. Had

Princess Poliakoff died in Mirenburg? Frau Schmetterling wrote that she might have done. She could not remember if Poliakoff had been with Holzhammer when the Bulgarians took over the brothel, but she remembered the rumour. 'Personally, I think she died in the bombardment.'

Alice. My Alexandra. My little schoolgirl. Your soft body is no longer warm. Your perfume is faint. I see you in your red-and-gold balloon as it drifts up towards the silver sunshine. I wish it was my cheek you kiss as you lean over the rim of the gondola and see the spreading ash, the few remaining ruins, saying, 'Look, there's the Radota Bridge! Isn't it terrible! And there's the Cathedral! And there's Rosenstrasse. Wave, Ricky!' It is so hard to write. The light is very dim for midday. I must tell Papadakis to turn on the gas. Clara married. She runs a restaurant in Liège and has done well for herself, though they say her husband is a drunk. She loved me. She told me she would always love me, but she had to look after herself. I understood. She had given me too much, I said. She had shaken her head. 'It would not have been too much if you had wanted it.' I spent so many cynical years in pursuit of my dream, in revenge on those I blamed for destroying it. And I never found her. She is washed away in that grisly tide. It is ash. She is a ghost. The twin spires glitter in the early-afternoon sun. We look down past them towards the white walls. We are having a picnic. Falfnersallee and the Restaurant Schmidt. Waiting for her. I sip absinthe in the sunshine opposite the Radota Bridge. We visit the dress-shops and the jewellers. Deep in the luxury of the brothel. A riding crop rises and falls. A distant, excited scream. Lady Cromach's smile betrays the betrayer. Clara loved me. That last soft kiss. Alexandra. It was a blow to the groin. I can still feel the bruise. My right hand has started to tremble. Papadakis must bring me some more wine. The sea is too loud. The pain is nothing. I can return to Mirenburg whenever I wish.

The Opium General

T HEY HAD LIVED in a kind of besieged darkness for several weeks. At first she had welcomed the sense of solitude after the phone was cut off. They ignored the front door unless friends knew the secret knock. It was almost security, behind the blinds. From his ugly anxiety Charlie had calmed for a while but had soon grown morose and accusatory. There were too many creditors. The basement flat turned into a prison he was afraid to leave. When she had arrived three years ago it had seemed a treasure house; now she saw it merely as a record of his unrealised dreams: his half-read books, his comics, his toys, his synthesisers no longer stimulated him yet he refused to get rid of a single broken model Spitfire. They were tokens of his former substance, of a glorious past. When she suggested they go for a walk he said: 'Too many people know me in Notting Hill.' He meant the customers he had burned, taking money for drugs he never delivered, and the important dealers he had never paid. He tried to form a unity of his many frustrations: a general pattern, a calculated plot against him. A friend was murdered in a quarrel over sulphate at a house in Talbot Road. He decided the knife had been meant for him. 'I've made too many enemies.' This was his self-pitying phase.

She steered him as best she could away from paranoia. She was frightened by overt instability, but had learned to feel relaxed so long as the signs were unadmitted, buried. In response to her nervousness he pulled himself together in the only way he knew: the appropriate image. He said it was time for a stiff upper lip, for holding the thin red line. She was perfectly satisfied, her sympathy for him was restored and she had been able to keep going. He became like Leslie Howard in an old war film. She tried to find somebody who could help him. This awful uncertainty stopped him doing his best. If he got clear, got a bit of money, they could start afresh. He wanted to write a novel: in Inverness, he thought, where he had worked in an hotel. Once away she could calm him down, get him to be his old self. But there remained the suspicion he might still choose madness as his escape. His friends said he habitually got himself into mental hospitals where he need feel no personal responsibility. He said, though, that it was chemical.

'Nobody's after you, Charlie, really.' She had spent hours trying to win round all the big dealers. She went to see some of them on her own. They assured her with dismissive disgust that they had written off his debts and forgotten about him but would never do business with him again. The landlord was trying to serve them with a summons for almost a year's unpaid rent and had been unnecessarily rude the last time she had appealed to him. She blamed herself. She had longed for a return of the euphoria of their first weeks together. There had been plenty of money then, or at least credit. She had deliberately shut out the voice of her own common sense. In her drugged passivity she let him convince her something concrete would come of his elaborate fantasies; she lent her own considerable manipulative powers to his, telling his bank manager of all the record companies who were after his work, of the planned tour, of the ex-agent who owed him a fortune. This lifted him briefly and he became the tall handsome red-headed insouciant she had first met. 'Partners in bullshit,' he said cheerfully. 'You should be on the stage, Ellie. You can be a star in my next roadshow.' It had been his apparent good-humoured carelessness in the face of trouble which made him seem so attractive to her three years ago when she left home to live here. She had not realised nobody in the music business would work with him any more, not even on sessions, because he got so loony. It was nerves, she knew, but he could be so rude to her, to everybody, and make a terrible impression. At the very last guest spot he had done, in Dingwalls, the roadies deliberately sabotaged his sound because he had been so overbearing. As Jimmy had told her gravely later: 'Ye canna afford to get up the roadies' noses,

Ellie. They can make or break a set.' Jimmy had been Charlie's partner in their first psychedelic group, but had split the third time Charlie put himself in the bin. It was a bad sign, Jimmy told her, when Charlie started wearing his 'army suit', as he had done to the Dingwalls gig.

Over the past two weeks Charlie had worn his uniform all the time. It seemed to make him feel better. 'Look out for snipers, Algy,' he warned her when she went shopping. He kept the shutters of the front-room windows closed, lay in bed all day and stayed up at night rolling himself cigarettes and fiddling with his little Casio synthesiser. He needed R&R, he said. When, through tiredness, she had snapped at him not to be so silly, playing at soldiers, he turned away from her sorrowfully: a military martyr, a decent Englishman forced into the dirty business of war. 'This isn't fun for any of us.' His father had been a regular sergeant in the Royal Artillery and had always wanted Charlie to go to Sandhurst. His parents were in Africa now, running a Bulawayo grocery shop. He frequently addressed her as sergeant-major. Creditors became 'the enemy'; he needed more troops, reinforcements, fresh supplies. 'What about a cup of coffee, s'a'rnt-major?' and she would have to get up to make him one. His old friends found the rôle familiar. They didn't help by playing up to it. 'How's the general?' they would ask. He got out his military prints, his badges, his model soldiers, his aircraft charts. They were on every wall and surface now. He read Biggles books and old copies of *The Eagle*.

His last phone call had been to Gordon in Camden. ''Morning to you, field marshal. Spot of bother at this end. Pinned down under fire. Troops needing supplies. What can you get to us?' Gordon, his main coke-supplier, told him to fuck himself. 'The chap's gone over to the enemy.' Charlie was almost crying. 'Turned yellow. Made of the wrong bally stuff.' She pushed her long pale hair away from her little oval face and begged him to talk normally. 'Nobody's going to take you seriously if you put on a funny voice.'

'Can't think what you mean, old thing.' He straightened his

black beret on his cropped head. He had always been vain but now he spent fifty per cent of his waking time in front of the mirror. 'Don't tell me you're crackin', too.' He rode his motorbike to Brixton and came back with cash, claiming he had been cheated on the price. 'We're going to have transport and logistics problems for a bit, s'a'rnt-major. But we'll get by somehow, eh? Darkest before the dawn and so on.' She had just begun to warm to his courage when he gloomily added: 'But I suppose you'll go AWOL next. One simply can't get the quality of front-line chap.' All his other girlfriends had finally been unable to take him. She swore she was not the same. She made him a cup of tea and told him to go to bed and rest: her own universal remedy. It always seemed to work for her. Dimly she recognised his desperate reaching for certainties and order, yet his 'general' was slowly wearing her down. She asked her mother to come to stay with her for a couple of days. 'You should be on your own, love,' said her mother. She was discomfited by Charlie's rôle. 'Get yourself a little place. A job.'

Ellie spread her short fingers on the table and stared at them. She was numb all over. He had made her senses flare like a firework; now she felt spent. She looked dreadful, said her mother. She was too thin, she was wearing too much make-up and perfume. Charlie liked it, she said. 'He's not doing you any good, love. The state of you!' All this in a murmur, while Charlie napped in the next room.

'I can't let him down now.' Ellie polished her nails. 'Everybody owes him money.' But she knew she was both too frightened to leave and felt obscurely that she had given him more than his due, that he owed her for something. There was nobody else to support her; she was worn out. It was up to him. She would get him on his feet again, then he would in turn help her.

'You'd be better off at home,' said her mother doubtfully. 'Dad's a lot calmer than he used to be.' Her father hated Charlie. The peculiar thing was they were very much alike in a lot of ways. Her father looked back with nostalgia to wartime and his Tank Regiment.

She and her mother went up to Tesco's together. The Portobello

Road was crowded as usual, full of black women with prams and shopping bags, Pakistani women in saris, clutching at the hands of two or three kids, old hippies in big miserable coats, Irish drunks, gypsies, a smattering of middle-class women from the other side of Ladbroke Grove. Her mother hated the street; she wanted them to move somewhere more respectable. They pushed the cart round the supermarket. Her mother paid for the groceries. 'At least you've got your basics for a bit,' she said. She was a tiny, harassed woman with a face permanently masked, an ear permanently deaf to anything but the most conventional statements. 'Bring Charlie to Worthing for a couple of weeks. It'll do you both good.' But Charlie knew, as well as anyone, that he and Ellie's dad would be at loggerheads within a day. 'Got to stay at HQ.' he said. 'Position could improve any moment.' He was trying to write new lyrics for Jimmy's band, but they kept coming out the same as those they'd done together ten years before, about war and nuclear bombs and cosmic soldiers. Her mother returned to Worthing with a set, melancholy face; her shoulders rounded from thirty years of dogged timidity. Ellie noticed her own shoulders were becoming hunched, too. She made an effort to straighten them and then heard in her mind Charlie (or was it her dad?) saying 'back straight, stomach in' and she let herself slump again. This self-defeating defiance was the only kind she dared allow herself. Her long hair (which Charlie insisted she keep) dragged her head to the ground.

That night he burned all his lyrics. 'Top Secret documents,' he called them. When she begged him to stop, saying somebody would buy them surely, he rounded on her. 'If you're so into money, why don't you go out and earn some?' She was afraid to leave him to his own devices. He might do anything while she was away. He'd have a new girlfriend in five minutes. He couldn't stand being alone. She had thought him sensitive and vulnerable when he courted her. They met in a pub near the Music Machine. He seemed so interested in her, at once charmingly bold, shy and attentive. He made her laugh. She had mothered him a bit, she supposed. She would have done anything for him. Could that have been a mistake?

'You've got to find out what you want,' said her sluttish friend Joan, who lived with an ex-biker. 'Be independent.' Joan worked at the health-food shop and was into feminism. 'Don't let any fucking feller mess you around. Be your own woman.' But Joan was bisexual and had her eye on Ellie. Her objectivity couldn't be trusted. Joan was having trouble with her old man yet she didn't seem about to split.

'I don't know who I am.' Ellie stared at the Victorian screen Charlie had bought her. It had pictures of Lancers and Guardsmen varnished brownish yellow. 'I was reading. We all define ourselves through other people, don't we?'

'Not as much as you do, dearie,' said Joan. 'What about a holiday? I'm thinking of staying at this cottage in Wales next month. We could both do with a break away from blokes.'

Ellie said she'd think about it. She now spent most of her time in the kitchen looking out at the tiny overgrown yard. She made up lists in her mind: lists of things they could sell, lists of outfits she could buy, lists of places she would like to visit, lists of people who might be able to help Charlie. She had a list of their debts in a drawer somewhere. She considered a list of musicians and A&R men they knew. But these days all Charlie had that people wanted was dope contacts. And nobody would let him have as much as a joint on credit any more. It was disgusting. People kept in touch because you could help them score. The minute you weren't useful, they dropped you. Charlie wouldn't let her say this, though. He said it was her fault. She turned friends against him. 'Why don't you fuck off, too? You've had everything I've got.' But when she began to pack (knowing she could not leave) he told her he needed her. She was all he had left. He was sorry for being a bastard.

'I think I'm bad luck for you.' Really she meant something else which she was too afraid to let into her consciousness. He was weak and selfish. She had stood by him through everything. But possibly he was right to blame her. She had let herself be entranced by his wit, his smiling mouth, his lean, nervous body so graceful in repose, so awkward when he tried to impress. She should have brought him down to earth sooner. She had known it was going wrong, but had believed something must turn up to save them. 'Can't we go away?' she asked him early one afternoon. The room was in semi-darkness. Sun fell on the polished pine of the table between them; a single beam from the crack in the shutters. 'What about that mate of yours in Tangier?' She picked unconsciously at the brocade chair left by his ex-wife. She felt she had retreated behind a wall which was her body, painted, shaved, perfumed: a lie of sexuality and compliance. She had lost all desire.

'And have the enemy seize the flat while we're there? You've got to remember, sergeant-major, that possession is nine tenths of the law.' He lay in his red Windsor rocker. He wore nothing but army gear, with a big belt round his waist, a sure sign of his insecurity. He drew his reproduction Luger from its holster and checked its action with profound authority. She stared at the reddish hair on his thick wrists, at the flaking spots on his fingers which resembled the early stages of a disease. His large, flat cheekbones seemed inflamed; there were huge bags under his eyes. He was almost forty. He was fighting off mortality as ferociously as he fought off what he called 'the mundane world'. She continued in an abstracted way to feel sorry for him. She still thought, occasionally, of Leslie Howard in the trenches. 'Then couldn't we spend a few days on Vince's houseboat?'

'Vince has retreated to Shropshire. A non-pukkah wallah,' he said sardonically. He and Vince had often played Indian army officers. 'His old lady's given him murder. Shouldn't have taken her aboard. Women always let you down in a crunch.' He glanced away.

She was grateful for the flush of anger which pushed her to her feet and carried her into the kitchen. 'You ungrateful bastard. You should have kept your bloody dick in your trousers then, shouldn't you!' She became afraid, but it was not the old immediate terror of a blow, it was a sort of dull expectation of pain. She was seized with contempt for her own dreadful judgement. She sighed, waiting for him to respond in anger. She turned. He looked miserably at his Luger and reholstered it. He stood up, plucking at his khaki creases, patting at his webbing. He straightened his beret in front of the mirror, clearing his throat. He was pale. 'What about organising some tiffin, sergeant-major?'

'I'll go out and get the bread.' She took the Scottish pound note from the tin on the mantelpiece.

'Don't be long. The enemy could attack at any time.' For a second he looked genuinely frightened. He was spitting a little when he spoke. His hair needed washing. He was normally so fussy about his appearance but he hadn't bathed properly in days. She had not dared say anything.

She went up the basement steps. Powys Square was noisy with children playing Cowboys and Indians. They exasperated her. She was twenty-five and felt hundreds of years older than them, than Charlie, than her mum and dad. Perhaps I'm growing up, she thought as she turned into Portobello Road and stopped outside the baker's. She stared at the loaves, pretending to choose. She looked at the golden bread and inhaled the sweet warmth; she looked at her reflection in the glass. She wore her tailored skirt, silk blouse, stockings, lacy bra and panties. He usually liked her to be feminine, but sometimes preferred her as a tomboy. 'It's the poofter in me.' She wasn't sure what she should be wearing now. A uniform like his? But it would be a lie. She looked at herself again. It was all a lie. Then she turned away from the baker's and walked on, past stalls of fruit, past stalls of avocados and Savoys, tomatoes and oranges, to the pawn shop where two weeks ago she had given up her last treasures. She paid individual attention to each electronic watch and every antique ring in the window and saw nothing she wanted. She crossed the road. Finch's pub was still open. Black men lounged in the street drinking from bottles, engaged in conventional badinage; she hoped nobody would recognise her. She went down Elgin Crescent, past the newsagent where she owed money, into the cherry- and apple-blossom of the residential streets. The blossom rose around her high heels like a sudden tide. Its colour, pink and white, almost blinded her. She breathed heavily. The scent came as if through a filter, no longer consoling. Feeling faint she sat on a low wall outside somebody's big house, her shopping bag and purse in her left hand, her right hand stroking mechanically at the rough concrete, desperate for sensation. Ordinary feeling was all she wanted. She could not imagine where it had gone. An ordinary life. She saw her own romanticism as a rotting tooth capped with gold. Her jaw ached. She looked upwards through the blossom at the blue sky in which sharply defined white clouds moved very slowly towards the sun, like cut-outs on a stage. She became afraid, wanting to turn back: she must get the bread before the scene ended and the day became grey again. But she needed this peace so badly. She grew self-conscious as a swarthy youth in a cheap black velvet suit went by whistling to himself. With only a little effort she could have made him attractive, but she no longer had the energy. Panic made her heart beat. Charlie could go over the top any minute. He might stack all the furniture near the doors and windows, as he had done once, or decide to rewire his equipment (he was useless at practical jobs) and be throwing a fit, breaking things, blaming her because a fuse had blown. Or he might be out in the street trying to get a reaction from a neighbour, baiting them, insulting them, trying to charm them. Or he might be at the Princess Alexandra, looking for somebody who would trust him with the money for a gram of coke or half-a-g of smack and stay put until closing time when he promised to return: restoring his ego, as he sometimes did, with a con trick. If so he could be in real trouble. Everyone said he'd been lucky so far. She forgot the bread and hurried back.

The children were still yelling and squealing as she turned into the square in time to see him walking away round the opposite corner of the building. He was dressed in his combat beret, his flying jacket, his army-boots, his sunglasses. He had his toy Luger and his sheath-knife on his belt. She forced herself to control her impulse to run after him. Trembling, she went down the steps of the basement, put her key in his front door, turned it, stepped inside. The whole of the front room was in confusion, as if he had been searching for something. The wicker chair had been turned over. The bamboo table was askew. As she straightened it (for she was automatically neat) she saw a note. He had used a model jeep

as a weight. She screwed the note up. She went into the kitchen
and put the kettle on. Waiting for the kettle to boil she flattened
the paper on the draining board:

> *1400 hrs. Duty calls. Instructions from HQ to proceed at once to*
> *battle-zone. Will contact at duration of hostilities. Trust nobody.*
> *Hold the fort.*
>
> *— BOLTON, C-in-C, Sector Six.*

Her legs shook as she crossed back to the teapot. Within three or
four days he would probably be in a police station or a mental hospital. He would opt to become a voluntary patient. He had
surrendered.

Her whole body shook now, with relief, with a sense of her
own failure. He had won, after all. He could always win. She
returned to the front door and slowly secured the bolts at top and
bottom. She pushed back the shutters. Carefully she made herself
a cup of tea and sat at the table with her chin in her hand staring
through the bars of the basement window. The tea grew cold, but
she continued to sip at it. She was out of the contest. She awaited
her fate.

London Bone

For Ronnie Scott

Chapter One

MY NAME IS Raymond Gold and I'm a well-known dealer. I was born too many years ago in Upper Street, Islington. Everybody reckons me in the London markets and I have a good reputation in Manchester and the provinces. I have bought and sold, been the middleman, an agent, an art representative, a professional mentor, a tour guide, a spiritual bridge-builder. These days I call myself a cultural speculator.

But, you won't like it, the more familiar word for my profession, as I practised it until recently, is *scalper*. This kind of language is just another way of isolating the small businessman and making what he does seem sleazy while the stockbroker dealing in millions is supposed to be legitimate. But I don't need to convince anyone today that there's no sodding justice.

'Scalping' is risky. What you do is invest in tickets on spec and hope to make a timely sale when the market for them hits zenith. Any kind of ticket, really, but mostly shows. I've never seen anything offensive about getting the maximum possible profit out of an American matron with more money than sense who's anxious to report home with the right items ticked off the *been-to* list. We've all seen them rushing about in their overpriced limos and minibuses, pretending to be individuals: **Thursday: Changing-of-the-Guard, Harrods, Planet Hollywood, Royal Academy, Tea-at-the-Ritz,** *Cats*. It's a sort of tribal dance they are compelled to perform. If they don't perform it, they feel inadequate. **Saturday: Tower of London, Bucket of Blood, Jack-the-Ripper talk,**

Sherlock Holmes Pub, Sherlock Holmes tour, Madame Tussaud's, Covent Garden Cream Tea, *Dogs*. These are people so traumatised by contact with strangers that their only security lies in these rituals, these well-blazed trails and familiar chants. It's my job to smooth their paths, to make them exclaim how pretty and wonderful and elegant and *magical* it all is. The street people aren't a problem. They're just so many charming Dick Van Dykes.

Americans need bullshit the way koala bears need eucalyptus leaves. They've become totally addicted to it. They get so much of it back home that they can't survive without it. It's your duty to help them get their regular fixes while they travel. And when they make it back after three weeks on alien shores, their friends, of course, are always glad of some foreign bullshit for a change.

Even if you sell a show ticket to a real enthusiast, who has already been forty-nine times and is so familiar to the cast they see him in the street and think he's a relative, who are you hurting? Andros Loud Website, Lady Hatchet's loyal laureate, who achieved rank and wealth by celebrating the lighter side of the moral vacuum? He would surely applaud my enterprise in the buccaneering spirit of the free market. Venture capitalism at its bravest. Well, he'd applaud me if he had time these days from his railings against fate, his horrible understanding of the true nature of his coming obscurity. But that's partly what my story's about.

I have to say in my own favour that I'm not merely a speculator or, if you like, exploiter. I'm also a patron. For many years, not just recently, a niagara of dosh has flowed out of my pocket and into the real arts faster than a cat up a Frenchman. Whole orchestras and famous soloists have been brought to the Wigmore Hall on the money they get from me. But I couldn't have afforded this if it wasn't for the definitely iffy *Miss Saigon* (a triumph of well-oiled machinery over dodgy morality) or the unbelievably decrepit *Good Rockin' Tonite* (in which the living dead jive in the aisles), nor, of course, that first great theatrical triumph of the new millennium, *Schindler: The Musical*. Make 'em weep, Uncle Walt!

So who is helping most to support the arts? You, me, the lottery?

I had another reputation, of course, which some saw as a second profession. I was one of the last great London characters. I was always on late-night telly, lit from below, and Iain Sinclair couldn't write a paragraph without dropping my name at least once. I'm a quintessential Londoner, I am. I'm a Cockney gentleman.

I read Israel Zangwill and Gerald Kersh and Alexander Barron. I can tell you the best books of Pett Ridge and Arthur Morrison. I know Pratface Charlie, Driff and Martin Stone, Bernie Michaud and the even more legendary Gerry and Pat Goldstein. They're all historians, archaeologists, revenants. There isn't another culture-dealer in London, oldster or child, who doesn't at some time come to me for an opinion. Even now, when I'm as popular as a pig at a Putney wedding and people hold their noses and dive into traffic rather than have to say hello to me, they still need me for that.

I've known all the famous Londoners or known someone else who did. I can tell stories of long-dead gangsters who made the Krays seem like Amnesty International. Bare-knuckle boxing. Fighting the Fascists in the East End. Gun-battles with the police all over Stepney in the 1900s. The terrifying girl gangsters of Whitechapel. Barricading the Old Bill in his own barracks down in Notting Dale.

I can tell you where all the music halls were and what was sung in them. And why. I can tell Marie Lloyd stories and Max Miller stories that are fresh and sharp and bawdy as the day they happened, because their wit and experience came out of the market streets of London. The same streets. The same markets. The same family names. London is markets. Markets are London.

I'm a Londoner through and through. I know Mr Gog personally. I know Ma Gog even more personally. During the day I can walk anywhere from Bow to Bayswater faster than any taxi. I love the markets. Brick Lane. Church Street. Portobello. You won't find me on a bike with my bum in the air on a winter's afternoon. I walk or drive. Nothing in between. I wear a camelhair in winter and a Barraclough's in summer. You know what would happen to a coat like that on a bike.

I love the theatre. I like modern dance, very good movies and ambitious international contemporary music. I like poetry, prose, painting and the decorative arts. I like the lot, the very best that London's got, the whole bloody casserole. I gobble it all up and bang on my bowl for more. Let timid greenbelters creep in at weekends and sink themselves in the West End's familiar deodorised shit if they want to. That's not my city. That's a tourist set. It's what I live off. What all of us show-people live off. It's the old, familiar circus. The big rotate.

We're selling what everybody recognises. What makes them feel safe and certain and sure of every single moment in the city. Nothing to worry about in jolly old London. We sell charm and colour by the yard. Whole word factories turn out new rhyming slang and saucy street characters are trained on council grants. Don't frighten the horses. Licensed pearlies pause for a photo opportunity in the dockside Secure Zones. Without all that cheap scenery, without our myths and magical skills, without our whorish good cheer and instincts for trade – any kind of trade – we probably wouldn't have a living city.

As it is, the real city I live in has more creative energy per square inch at work at any given moment than anywhere else on the planet. But you'd never know it from a stroll up the Strand. It's almost all in those lively little side streets the English-speaking tourists can't help feeling a bit nervous about and that the French adore.

If you use music for comfortable escape you'd probably find more satisfying and cheaper relief in a massage parlour than at the umpteenth revival of *The Sound of Music*. I'd tell that to any hesitant punter who's not too sure. Check out the phone boxes for the ladies, I'd say, or you can go to the half-price ticket booth in Leicester Square and pick up a ticket that'll deliver real value – Ibsen or Shakespeare, Shaw or Churchill. Certainly you can fork out three hundred sheets for a fifty-sheet ticket that in a justly ordered world wouldn't be worth two pee and have your ears salved and your cradle rocked for two hours. Don't worry, I'd tell them, I make no judgements. Some hardworking whore profits, whatever you decide. So who's the cynic?

I went on one of those tours when my friends Dave and Di from Bury came down for the Festival of London in 2001 and it's amazing, the crap they tell people. They put sex, violence and money into every story. They know fuck-all. They soup everything up. It's *Sun*-reader history. Even the Beefeaters at the Tower. Poppinsland. All that old English duff.

It makes you glad to get back to Soho.

Not so long ago you would usually find me in the Princess Louise, Berwick Street, at lunchtime, a few doors down from the Chinese chippy and just across from Mrs White's trim stall in Berwick Market. It's only a narrow door and is fairly easy to miss. It has one bottle-glass window onto the street. This is a public house that has not altered since the 1940s when it was very popular with Dylan Thomas, Mervyn Peake, Ruthven Todd, Henry Treece and a miscellaneous bunch of other Welsh adventurers who threatened for a while to take over English poetry from the Irish.

It's a shit pub, so dark and smoky you can hardly find your glass in front of your face, but the look of it keeps the tourists out. It's used by all the culture pros – from arty types with backpacks, who do specialised walking tours, to famous gallery owners and top museum management – and by the heavy-metal bikers. We all get on a treat. We are mutually dependent in our continuing resistance to invasion or change, to the preservation of the best and most vital aspects of our culture. We leave the bikers alone because they protect us from the tourists, who might recognise us and make us put on our masks in a hurry. They leave us alone because the police won't want to bother a bunch of well-connected middle-class wankers like us. It is a wonderful example of mutuality. In the back rooms, thanks to some freaky acoustics, you can talk easily above the music and hardly know it's there.

Over the years there have been some famous friendships and unions struck between the two groups. My own lady wife was known as Karla the She-Goat in an earlier incarnation and had the most exquisite and elaborate tattoos I ever saw. She was a wonderful wife and would have made a perfect mother. She died on the A1, on the other side of Watford Gap. She had just found out she was pregnant and was making her last sentimental run. It did me in for marriage for a while. And urban romance.

I first heard about London Bone in the Princess Lou when Claire Rood, that elegant old dike from the Barbican, who'd tipped me off about my new tailor, pulled my ear to her mouth and asked me in words of solid gin and garlic to look out for some for her, darling. None of the usual faces seemed to know about it. A couple of top-level museum people knew a bit, but it was soon obvious they were hoping I'd fill them in on the details. I showed them a confident length of cuff. I told them to keep in touch.

I did my Friday walk, starting in the horrible pre-dawn chill of the Portobello Road where some youth tried to sell me a bit of scrimshawed reconstitute as 'the real old Bone'. I warmed myself in the showrooms of elegant Kensington and Chelsea dealers telling outrageous stories of deals, profits and crashes until they grew uncomfortable and wanted to talk about me and I got the message and left.

I wound up that evening in the urinal of the Dragoons in Meard Alley, swapping long-time-no-sees with my boyhood friend Bernie Michaud who begins immediately by telling me he's got a bit of business I might be interested in. And since it's Bernie Michaud telling me about it I listen. Bernie never deliberately spread a rumour in his life but he's always known how to make the best of one. This is kosher, he thinks. It has a bit of a glow. It smells like a winner. A long-distance runner. He is telling me out of friendship, but I'm not really interested. I'm trying to find out about London Bone.

'I'm not talking drugs, Ray, you know that. And it's not bent.' Bernie's little pale face is serious. He takes a thoughtful sip of his whisky. 'It is, admittedly, a commodity.'

I wasn't interested. I hadn't dealt in goods for years. 'Services only, Bernie,' I said. 'Remember. It's my rule. Who wants to get stuck paying rent on a warehouse full of yesterday's faves? I'm still trying to move those *Glenda Sings Michael Jackson* sides Pratface talked me into.'

'What about investment?' he says. 'This is the real business, Ray, believe me.'

So I heard him out. It wouldn't be the first time Bernie had brought me back a nice profit on some deal I'd helped him bankroll and I was all right at the time. I'd just made the better part of a month's turnover on a package of theatreland's most profitable stinkers brokered for a party of filthy-rich New Muscovites who thought Chekhov was something you did with your lottery numbers.

As they absorbed the quintessence of Euro-ersatz, guaranteed to offer, as its high emotional moment, a long, relentless bowel movement, I would be converting their hard roubles back into Beluga.

It's a turning world, the world of the international free market, and everything's wonderful and cute and pretty and *magical* so long as you keep your place on the carousel. It's not good if it stops. And it's worse if you get thrown off altogether. Pray to Mammon that you never have to seek the help of an organisation that calls you a 'client'. That puts you outside the fairground for ever. No more rides. No more fun. No more life.

Bernie only did quality art, so I knew I could trust that side of his judgement, but what was it? A new batch of Raphaels turned up in a Willesden attic? Andy Warhol's lost landscapes found at the Pheasantry?

'There's American collectors frenzied for this stuff,' murmurs Bernie through a haze of Sons of the Wind, Motorchair and Montecristo fumes. 'And if it's decorated they go through the roof. All the big Swiss guys are looking for it. Freddy K. in Cairo has a Saudi buyer who tops any price. Rose Sarkissian in Agadir represents three French collectors. It's never catalogued. It's all word of mouth. And it's already turning over millions. There's one inferior piece in New York and none at all in Paris. The pieces in Zurich are probably all fakes.'

This made me feel that I was losing touch. I still didn't know what he was getting at.

'Listen,' I say, 'before we go any further, let's talk about this London Bone.'

'You're a fly one, Ray,' he says. 'How did you suss it?'

'Tell me what you know,' I say. 'And then I'll fill you in.'

We went out of the pub, bought some fish and chips at the Chinese and then walked up Berwick Street and round to his little club in D'Arblay Street where we sat down in his office and closed the door. The place stank of cat-pee. He doted on his Persians. They were all out in the club at the moment, being petted by the patrons.

'First,' he says, 'I don't have to tell you, Ray, that this is strictly double-schtum and I will kill you if a syllable gets out.'

'Naturally,' I said.

'Have you ever seen any of this Bone?' he asked. He went to his cupboard and found some vinegar and salt. 'Or better still handled it?'

'No,' I said. 'Not unless it's fake scrimshaw.'

'This stuff's got a depth to it you've never dreamed about. A lustre. You can tell it's the real thing as soon as you see it. Not just the shapes or the decoration, but the quality of it. It's like it's got a soul. You could come close, but you could never fake it. Like amber, for instance. That's why the big collectors are after it. It's authentic, it's newly discovered and it's rare.'

'What bone is it?'

'Mastodon. Some people still call it mammoth ivory, but I haven't seen any actual ivory. It could be dinosaur. I don't know. Anyway, this bone is *better* than ivory. It's in weird shapes, probably fragments off some really big animal.'

'And where's it coming from?'

'The heavy clay of good old London,' says Bernie. 'A fortune at our feet, Ray. And my people know where to dig.'

Chapter Two

I HAD TO be straight with Bernie. Until I saw a piece of the stuff in my own hand and got an idea about it for myself, I couldn't do anything. The only time in my life I'd gone for a gold brick I'd bought it out of respect for the genius running the scam. He deserved what I gave him. Which was a bit less than he was hoping for. Rather than be conned, I would rather throw the money away. I'm like that with everything.

I had my instincts, I told Bernie. I had to go with them. He understood completely and we parted on good terms.

If the famous Lloyd Webber meltdown of '03 had happened a few months earlier or later I would never have thought again about going into the Bone business, but I was done in by one of those sudden changes of public taste that made the George M. Cohan crash of '31 seem like a run of *The Mousetrap*.

Sentimental fascism went out the window. Liberal-humanist contemporary relevance, artistic aspiration, intellectual and moral substance and all that stuff was somehow in demand. It was *better* than the '60s. It was one of those splendid moments when the public pulls itself together and tries to grow up. Jones's *Rhyme of the Flying Bomb* song-cycle made a glorious comeback. *American Angels* returned with even more punch.

And Sondheim became a quality brand name. If it wasn't by Sondheim or based on a tune Sondheim used to hum in the shower, the punters didn't want to know. Overnight, the public's product loyalty had changed. And I must admit it had changed for the better. But my investments were in *Cats*, and *Dogs* (Lord Webber's last desperate attempt to squeeze from Thurber what he'd sucked from Eliot), *Duce!* and *Starlight Excess*, all of which were now taking a walk down *Sunset Boulevard*. I couldn't even get a regular-price ticket for myself at *Sunday in the Park*, *Assassins* or

Follies. Into the Woods was solid for eighteen months ahead. I saw *Passion* from the wings and *Sweeney Todd* from the gods. *Five Guys Named Mo* crumbled to dust. *Phantom* closed. Its author claimed sabotage.

'Quality will out, Ray,' says Bernie next time I see him at the Lou. 'You've got to grant the public that. You just have to give it time.'

'Fuck the public,' I said, with some feeling. 'They're just nostalgic for quality at the moment. Next year it'll be something else. Meanwhile I'm bloody ruined. You couldn't drum a couple of oncers on my entire stock. Even my E.N.O. side-bets have died. Covent Garden's a disaster. The weather in Milan didn't help. That's where Cecilia Bartoli caught her cold. I was lucky to be offered half-price for the Rossinis without her. And I know what I'd do if I could get a varda at bloody Simon Rattle.'

'So you won't be able to come in on the Bone deal?' said Bernie, returning to his own main point of interest.

'I said I was ruined,' I told him, 'not wiped out.'

'Well, I got something to show you now, anyway,' says Bernie. We went back to his place.

He put it in my hand as if it were a nugget of plutonium: a knuckle of dark, golden Bone, split off from a larger piece, covered with tiny pictures.

'The engravings are always on that kind of Bone,' he said. 'There are other kinds that don't have drawings, maybe from a later date. It's the work of the first Londoners, I suppose, when it was still a swamp. About the time your Phoenician ancestors started getting into the upriver woad-trade. I don't know the significance, of course.'

The Bone itself was hard to analyse because of the mixture of chemicals that had created it and some of it had fused, suggesting prehistoric upheavals of some kind. The drawings were extremely primitive. Any bored person with a sharp object and minimum talent could have done them at any time in history. The larger, weirder-looking Bones had no engravings.

Stick-people pursued other stick-people endlessly across the fragment. The work was unremarkable. The beauty really was in the tawny ivory colour of the Bone itself. It glowed with a wealth of shades and drew you hypnotically into its depths. I imagined the huge animal of which this fragment had once been an active part. I saw the bellowing trunk, the vast ears, the glinting tusks succumbing suddenly to whatever had engulfed her. I saw her body swaying, her tail lashing as she trumpeted her defiance of her inevitable death. And now men sought her remains as treasure. It was a very romantic image and of course it would become my most sincere sales pitch.

'That's six million dollars you're holding there,' said Bernie. 'Minimum.'

Bernie had caught me at the right time and I had to admit I was convinced. Back in his office he sketched out the agreement. We would go in on a fifty-fifty basis, funding the guys who would do the actual digging, who knew where the Bonefields were and who would tell us as soon as we showed serious interest. We would finance all the work, pay them an upfront earnest and then load by load in agreed increments. Bernie and I would split the net profit fifty-fifty. There were all kinds of clauses and provisions covering the various problems we foresaw and then we had a deal.

The archaeologists came round to my little place in Dolphin Square. They were a scruffy bunch of students from the University of Norbury who had discovered the Bone deposits on a run-of-the-mill field trip in a demolished Southwark housing estate and knew only that there might be a market for them. Recent cuts to their grants had made them desperate. Some lefty had come up with a law out of the Magna Carta or somewhere saying public land couldn't be sold to private developers and so there was a court case disputing the council's right to sell the estate to Livingstone International, which also put a stop to the planned rebuilding. So we had indefinite time to work.

The stoodies were grateful for our expertise, as well as our cash. I was happy enough with the situation. It was one I felt we could easily control. Middle-class burbnerds get greedy the same as anyone else, but they respond well to reason. I told them for a start-off that all the Bone had to come in to us. If any of it leaked onto the market by other means, we'd risk losing our prices and that would mean the scheme was over. 'Terminated,' I said significantly. Since we had reputations as well as investments to protect there would also be recriminations. That was all I had to say. Since those V-serials kids think we're Krays and Mad Frankie Frasers just because we like to look smart and talk properly.

We were fairly sure we weren't doing anything obviously criminal. The stuff wasn't treasure trove. It had to be cleared before proper foundations could be poured. Quite evidently L.I. didn't think it was worth paying security staff to shuft the site. We didn't know if digging shafts and tunnels was even trespass, but we knew we had a few weeks before someone started asking about us and by then we hoped to have the whole bloody mastodon out of the deep clay and nicely earning for us. The selling would take the real skill and that was my job. It was going to have to be played sharper than South African diamonds.

After that neither Bernie nor I had anything to do with the dig. We rented a guarded lock-up in Clapham and paid the kids every time they brought in a substantial load of Bone. It was incredible stuff. Bernie thought that chemical action, some of it relatively recent, had caused the phenomenon. 'Like chalk, you know. You hardly find it anywhere. Just a few places in England, France, China and Texas.' The kids reported that there was more than one kind of animal down there, but that all the Bone had the same rich appearance. They had constructed a new tunnel, with a hidden entrance, so that even if the building site was blocked to them, they could still get at the Bone. It seemed to be a huge field, but most of the Bone was at roughly the same depth. Much of it had fused and had to be chipped out. They had found no end to it so far and they had tunnelled through more than half an acre of the dense, dark clay.

Meanwhile I was in Amsterdam and Rio, Paris and Vienna and New York and Sydney. I was in Tokyo and Seoul and Hong Kong. I was in Riyadh, Cairo and Baghdad. I was in Kampala and New

Benin, everywhere there were major punters. I racked up so many free air-miles in a couple of months that they were automatically jumping me to first class. But I achieved what I wanted. Nobody bought London Bone without checking with me. I was the acknowledged expert. The prime source, the best in the business. If you want Bone, said the art world, you want Gold.

The Serious Fraud Squad became interested in Bone for a while, but they had been assuming we were faking it and gave up when it was obviously not rubbish.

Neither Bernie nor I expected it to last any longer than it did. By the time our first phase of selling was over we were turning over so much dough it was silly and the kids were getting tired and were worrying about exploring some of their wildest dreams. There was almost nothing left, they said. So we closed down the operation, moved our warehouses a couple of times and then let the Bone sit there to make us some money while everyone wondered why it had dried up.

And at that moment, inevitably, and late as ever, the newspapers caught on to the story. There was a brief late-night TV piece. A few supplements talked about it in their arts pages. This led to some news stories and eventually it went to the tabloids and the Bone became anything you liked, from the remains of Martians to a new kind of nuclear waste. Anyone who saw the real stuff was convinced but everyone had a theory about it. The real exclusive market was finished. We kept schtum. We were gearing up for the second phase. We got as far away from our stash as possible.

Of course, a few faces tracked me down, but I denied any knowledge of the Bone. I was a middleman, I said. I just had good contacts. Half a dozen people claimed to know where the Bone came from. Of course they talked to the papers. I sat back in satisfied security, watching the mud swirl over our tracks. Another couple of months and we'd be even safer than the house I'd bought in Hampstead overlooking the Heath. It had a rather forlorn garden the size of Kilburn, which needed a lot of nurturing. That suited me. I was ready to retire to the country and a big indoor swimming pool.

By the time a close version of the true story came out, from one of the stoodies, who'd lost all his share in a lottery syndicate, it was just one of many. It sounded too dull. I told newspaper reporters that while I would love to have been involved in such a lucrative scheme, my money came from theatre tickets. Meanwhile, Bernie and I thought of our warehouse and said nothing.

Now the stuff was getting into the culture. It was chic. *Puncher* used it in their ads. It was called Mammoth Bone by the media. There was a common story about how a herd had wandered into the swampy river and drowned in the mud. Lots of pictures dusted off from the Natural History Museum. Experts explained the colour, the depths, the markings, the beauty. Models sported a Bone motif.

Our second phase was to put a fair number of inferior fragments on the market and see how the public responded. That would help us find our popular price – the most a customer would pay. We were looking for a few good millionaires.

Frankly, as I told my partner, I was more than ready to get rid of the lot. But Bernie counselled me to patience. We had a plan and it made sense to stick to it.

The trade continued to run well for a while. As the sole source of the stuff, we could pretty much control everything. Then one Sunday lunchtime I met Bernie at The Six Jolly Dragoons in Meard Alley, Soho. He had something to show me, he said. He didn't even glance around. He put it on the bar in plain daylight. A small piece of Bone with the remains of decorations still on it.

'What about it?' I said.

'It's not ours,' he said.

My first thought was that the stoodies had opened up the field again. That they had lied to us when they said it had run out.

'No,' said Bernie, 'it's not even the same colour. It's the same stuff – but different shades. Gerry Goldstein lent it to me.'

'Where did he get it?'

'He was offered it,' Bernie said.

We didn't bother to speculate where it had come from. But we did have rather a lot of our Bone to shift quickly. Against my will,

I made another world tour and sold mostly to other dealers this time. It was a standard second-wave operation but run rather faster than was wise. We definitely missed the crest.

However, before deliveries were in and cheques were cashed, Jack Merrywidow, the fighting MP for Brookgate and East Holborn, gets up in the House of Commons on telly one afternoon and asks if Prime Minister Bland or any of his dope-dazed Cabinet understand that human remains, taken from the hallowed burial grounds of London, are being sold by the piece in the international marketplace? Mr Bland makes a plummy joke enjoyed at Mr Merrywidow's expense and sits down. But Jack won't give up. They're suddenly on telly. It's *The Struggle of Parliament* time. Jack's had the Bone examined by experts. It's human. Undoubtedly human. The strange shapes are caused by limbs melting together in soil heavy with lime. Chemical reactions, he says. We have – he raises his eyes to the camera – been mining mass graves.

A shock to all those who still long for the years of common decency. Someone, says Jack, is selling more than our heritage. Hasn't free-market capitalism got a little bit out of touch when we start selling the arms, legs and skulls of our forebears? The torsos and shoulder blades of our honourable dead? What did we used to call people who did that? When was the government going to stop this trade in corpses?

It's denied.

It's proved.

It looks like trade is about to slump.

I think of framing the cheques as a reminder of the vagaries of fate and give up any idea of popping the question to my old muse Little Trudi, who is back on the market, having been dumped by her corporate suit in a fit, he's told her, of self-disgust after seeing *The Tolstoy Investment* with Eddie Izzard. Bernie, I tell my partner, the Bone business is down the drain. We might as well bin the stuff we've stockpiled.

Then, two days later the TV news reports a vast public interest in London Bone. Some lordly old queen with four names comes on the evening news to say how by owning a piece of Bone, you own London's true history. You become a curator of some ancient ancestor. He's clearly got a vested interest in the stuff. It's the hottest tourist item since Jack-the-Ripper razors and O.J. gloves. More people want to buy it than ever.

The only trouble is, I don't deal in dead people. It is, in fact, where I have always drawn the line. Even Pratface Charlie wouldn't sell his great-great-grandmother's elbow to some overweight Jap in a deerstalker and a kilt. I'm faced with a genuine moral dilemma.

I make a decision. I make a promise to myself. I can't go back on that. I go down to the Italian chippy in Fortess Road, stoke up on nourishing ritual grease (cod roe, chips and mushy peas, bread and butter and tea, syrup pudding), then heave my out-of-shape, but mentally prepared, body up onto Parliament Hill to roll myself a big wacky-baccy fag and let my subconscious think the problem through.

When I emerge from my reverie, I have looked out over the whole misty London panorama and considered the city's complex history. I have thought about the number of dead buried there since, say, the time of Boudicca, and what they mean to the soil we build on, the food we still grow here and the air we breathe. We are recycling our ancestors all the time, one way or another. We are sucking them in and shitting them out. We're eating them. We're drinking them. We're coughing them up. The dead don't rest. Bits of them are permanently at work. So what am I doing wrong?

This thought is comforting until my moral sense, sharpening itself up after a long rest, kicks in with – But what's different here is you're flogging the stuff to people who take it home with them. Back to Wisconsin and California and Peking. You take it out of circulation. You're dissipating the deep fabric of the city. You're unravelling something. Like, the real infrastructure, the spiritual and physical bones of an ancient settlement...

On Kite Hill I suddenly realise that those bones are in some way the deep lifestuff of London.

It grows dark over the towers and roofs of the metropolis. I sit on my bench and roll myself a further joint. I watch the silver rising from the river, the deep golden glow of the distant lights, the plush of the foliage, and as I watch it seems to shred before my eyes, like a rotten curtain. Even the traffic noise grows fainter. Is the city sick? Is she expiring? Somehow it seems there's a little less breath in the old girl. I blame myself. And Bernie. And those kids.

There and then, on the spot, I renounce all further interest in the Bone trade. If nobody else will take the relics back, then I will.

There's no resolve purer than the determination you draw from a really good reefer.

Chapter Three

S O NOW THERE isn't a tourist in any London market or antique arcade who isn't searching out Bone. They know it isn't cheap. They know they have to pay. And pay they do. Through the nose. And half of what they buy is crap or fakes. This is a question of status, not authenticity. As long as we say it's good, they can say it's good. We give it a provenance, a story, something to colour the tale to the folks back home. We're honest dealers. We sell only the authentic stuff. Still they get conned. But still they look. Still they buy.

Jealous Mancunians and Brummies long for a history old enough to provide them with Bone. A few of the early settlements, like Chester and York, start turning up something like it, but it's not the same. Jim Morrison's remains disappear from Père-Lachaise. They might be someone else's bones, anyway. Rumour is they were KFC bones. The Revolutionary death-pits fail to deliver the goods. The French are furious. They accuse the British of gross materialism and poor taste. Oscar Wilde disappears. George Eliot. Winston Churchill. You name them. For a few months there is a grotesque trade in the remains of the famous. But the fashion has no intrinsic substance and fizzles out. Anyone could have seen it wouldn't run.

Bone has the image, because Bone really is beautiful.

Too many people are yearning for that Bone. The real stuff. It genuinely hurts me to disappoint them. Circumstances alter cases. Against my better judgement I continue in the business. I bend my principles, just for the duration. We have as much turnover as we had selling to the Swiss gnomes. It's the latest item on the *been-to* list. 'You *have* to bring me back some London Bone, Ethel, or I'll never forgive you!' It starts to appear in the American luxury catalogues.

But by now there are ratsniffers everywhere – from Trade and Industry, from the National Trust, from the Heritage Corp, from half a dozen South London councils, from the Special Branch, from the CID, the Inland Revenue and both the Funny and the Serious Fraud Squads.

Any busybody who ever wanted to put his head under someone else's bed is having a wonderful time. Having failed dramatically with the STOP THIS DISGUSTING TRADE approach, the tabloids switch to offering bits of Bone as prizes in circulation boosters. I sell a newspaper consortium a Tesco's plastic bagful for two and a half mill via a go-between. Bernie and I are getting almost frighteningly rich. I open some bank accounts offshore and I become an important anonymous shareholder in the Queen Elizabeth Hall when it's privatised.

It doesn't take long for the experts to come up with an analysis. Most of the Bone has been down there since the seventeenth century and earlier. They are the sites of the old plague pits where, legend had it, still-living people were thrown in with the dead. For a while it must have seemed like Auschwitz-on-Thames. The chemical action of lime, partial burning, London clay and decaying flesh, together with the broadening spread of the London water table, thanks to various engineering works over the last century, letting untreated sewage into the mix, had created our unique London Bone. As for the decorations, that, it was opined, was the work of the pit guards, working on earlier bones found on the same site.

'Blood, shit and bone,' says Bernie. 'It's what makes the world go round. That and money, of course.'

'And love,' I add. I'm doing all right these days. It's true what they say about a Roller. Little Trudi has enthusiastically rediscovered my attractions. She has her eye on a ring. I raise my glass. 'And love, Bernie.'

'Fuck that,' says Bernie. 'Not in my experience.' He's buying Paul McCartney's old place in Wamering and having it converted for Persians. He has, it is true, also bought his wife her dream house. She doesn't seem to mind it's on the island of Las Cascadas about six miles off the coast of Morocco. She's at last agreed to divorce him. Apart from his mother, she's the only woman he ever had anything to do with and he isn't, he says, planning to try another. The only females he wants in his house in future come with a pedigree a mile long, have all their shots and can be bought at Harrods.

Chapter Four

I EXPECT YOU heard what happened. The private Bonefields, which contractors were discovering all over South and West London, actually contained public bones. They were part of our national inheritance. They had living relatives. And stones, some of them. So it became a political and a moral issue. The Church got involved. The airwaves were crowded with concerned clergy. There was the problem of the self-named bone-miners. Kids, inspired by our leaders' rhetoric and aspiring to imitate those great captains of free enterprise they had been taught to admire, were turning over ordinary graveyards, which they'd already stripped of their saleable masonry, and digging up somewhat fresher stiffs than was seemly.

A bit too fresh. It was pointless. The Bone took centuries to get seasoned and so far nobody had been able to fake the process. A few of the older graveyards had small deposits of Bone in them. Brompton Cemetery had a surprising amount, for instance, and so did Highgate. This attracted prospectors. They used shovels mainly, but sometimes low explosives. The area around Karl Marx's monument looked like they'd refought the Russian Civil War over it. The barbed wire put in after the event hadn't helped. And, as usual, the public paid to clean up after private enterprise. Nobody in their right mind got buried any more. Cremation became very popular. The borough councils and their financial managers were happy because more valuable real estate wasn't being occupied by a non-consumer.

It didn't matter how many security guards were posted or, by one extreme authority, landmines, the teenies left no grave unturned. Bone was still a profitable item, even though the market had settled down since we started. They dug up Bernie's mother. They dug up my cousin Leonard. There wasn't a

Londoner who didn't have some intimate unexpectedly back above ground. Every night you saw it on telly.

It had caught the public imagination. The media had never made much of the desecrated graveyards, the chiselled-off angels' heads and the uprooted headstones on sale in King's Road and the Boulevard Saint-Michel since the 1970s. These had been the targets of first-generation grave-robbers. Then there had seemed nothing left to steal. Even they had baulked at doing the corpses. Besides, there wasn't a market. This second generation was making up for lost time, turning over the soil faster than an earthworm on E.

The news shots became clichés. The heaped earth, the headstone, the smashed coffin, the hint of the contents, the leader of the Opposition coming on to say how all this has happened since his mirror image got elected. The councils argued that they should be given the authority to deal with the problem. They owned the graveyards. And also, they reasoned, the Bonefields. The profits from those fields should rightly go into the public purse. They could help pay for the Health Service. 'Let the dead,' went their favourite slogan, 'pay for the living for a change.'

What the local politicians actually meant was that they hoped to claim the land in the name of the public and then make the usual profits privatising it. There was a principle at stake. They had to ensure their friends and not outsiders got the benefit.

The High Court eventually gave the judgement to the public, which really meant turning it over to some of the most rapacious borough councils in our history. A decade or so earlier, that Charlie Peace of elected bodies, the Westminster City Council, had tried to sell their old graveyards to new developers. This current judgement allowed all councils at last to maximise their assets from what was, after all, dead land, completely unable to pay for itself, and therefore a natural target for privatisation. The feeding frenzy began. It was the closest thing to mass cannibalism I've ever seen.

We had opened a fronter in Old Sweden Street and had a couple of halfway presentable slags from Bernie's club taking the calls and answering enquiries. We were straight up about it. We called it *The City Bone Exchange*. The bloke who decorated it and did the sign specialised in giving offices that long-established look. He'd created most of those old-fashioned West End hotels you'd never heard of until 1999. 'If it's got a Scottish name,' he used to say, 'it's one of mine. Americans love the skirl of the pipes, but they trust a bit of brass and varnish best.'

Our place was almost all brass and varnish. And it worked a treat. The Ritz and the Savoy sent us their best potential buyers. Incredibly exclusive private hotels gave us taxi-loads of bland-faced American boy-men, reeking of health and beauty products, bellowing their credentials to the wind, rich matrons eager for anyone's approval, massive Germans with aggressive cackles, stern Orientals glaring at us, daring us to cheat them. They bought. And they bought. And they bought.

The snoopers kept on snooping but there wasn't really much to find out. Livingstone International took an aggressive interest in us for a while, but what could they do? We weren't up to anything illegal just selling the stuff and nobody could identify what – if anything – had been nicked anyway. I still had my misgivings. They weren't anything but superstitions, really. It did seem some-times that for every layer of false antiquity, for every act of Disneyfication, an inch or two of our real foundations crumbled. You knew what happened when you did that to a house. Sooner or later you got trouble. Sooner or later you had no house.

We had more than our share of private detectives for a while. They always pretended to be customers and they always looked wrong, even to our girls.

Livingstone International had definitely made a connection. I think they'd found our mine and guessed what a windfall they'd lost. They didn't seem at one with themselves over the matter. They even made veiled threats. There was some swagger came in to talk about violence but they were spotties who'd got all their language off old '90s TV shows. So we sweated it out and the girls took most of the heat. Those girls really didn't know anything. They were magnificently ignorant. They had tellies with chips that switch channels as soon as they detect a news or information programme.

I've always had a rule. If you're caught by the same wave twice, get out of the water.

While I didn't blame myself for not anticipating the Great Andrew Lloyd Webber Slump, I think I should have guessed what would happen next. The tolerance of the public for bullshit had become decidedly and aggressively negative. It was like the Bone had set new standards of public aspiration as well as beauty. My dad used to say that about the Blitz. Classical music enjoyed a huge success during the Second World War. Everybody grew up at once. The Bone had made it happen again. It was a bit frightening to those of us who had always relied on a nice, passive, gullible, greedy punter for an income.

The bitter fights that had developed over graveyard and Bone-field rights and boundaries, the eagerness with which some borough councils exploited their new resource, the unseemly trade in what was, after all, human remains, the corporate involvement, the incredible profits, the hypocrisies and politics around the Bone brought us the outspoken disgust of Europe. We were used to that. In fact, we tended to cultivate it. But that wasn't the problem.

The problem was that our *own* public had had enough.

When the elections came round, the voters systematically booted out anyone who had supported the Bone trade. It was like the sudden rise of the anti-slavery vote in Lincoln's America. They demanded an end to the commerce in London Bone. They got the Boneshops closed down. They got work on the Bonefields stopped. They got their graveyards and monuments protected and cleaned up. They got a city that started cultivating peace and security as if it was a cash crop. Which maybe it was. But it hurt me.

It was the end of my easy money, of course. I'll admit I was glad it was stopping. It felt like they were slowing entropy, restoring the past. The quality of life improved. I began to think about letting a few rooms for company.

The mood of the country swung so far into disapproval of the Bone trade that I almost began to fear for my life. Road and anti-abortion activists switched their attention to Bone merchants. Hampstead was full of screaming lefties convinced they owned the moral high ground just because they'd paid off their enormous mortgages. Trudi, after three months, applied for a divorce, arguing that she had not known my business when she married me. She said she was disgusted. She said I'd been living on blood money. The courts awarded her more than half of what I'd made, but it didn't matter any more. My investments were such that I couldn't stop earning. Economically, I was a small oil-producing nation. I had my own international dialling code. It was horrible in a way. Unless I tried very hard, it looked like I could never be ruined again. There was no justice.

I met Bernie in the King Lyar in Old Sweden Street, a few doors down from our burned-out office. I told him what I planned to do and he shrugged.

'We both knew it was dodgy,' he told me. 'It was dodgy all along, even when we thought it was mastodons. What it feels like to me, Ray, is – it feels like a sort of a massive transformation of the zeitgeist – you know, like Virginia Woolf said about the day human nature changed – something happens slowly and you're not aware of it. Everything seems normal. Then you wake up one morning and – bingo! – it's Nazi Germany or Bolshevik Russia or Thatcherite England or the Golden Age – and all the rôles have changed.'

'Maybe it was the Bone that did it,' I said. 'Maybe it was a symbol everyone needed to rally round. You know. A focus.'

'Maybe,' he said. 'Let me know when you're doing it. I'll give you a hand.'

About a week later we got the van backed up to the warehouse loading bay. It was three o'clock in the morning and I was chilled to the marrow. Working in silence we transferred every scrap of Bone to the van. Then we drove back to Hampstead through a freezing rain.

I don't know why we did it the way we did it. There would have been easier solutions, I suppose. But behind the high walls of my big back garden, under the old trees and etiolated rhododendrons, we dug a pit and filled it with the glowing remains of the ancient dead.

The stuff was almost phosphorescent as we chucked the big lumps of clay back onto it. It glowed a rich amber and that faint rosemary smell came off it. I can still smell it to this day when I go in there. My soft fruit is out of this world. The whole garden's doing wonderfully now.

In fact London's doing wonderfully. We seem to be back on form. There's still a bit of a Bone trade, of course, but it's marginal.

Every so often I'm tempted to take a spade and turn over the earth again, to look at the fortune I'm hiding there. To look at the beauty of it. The strange amber glow never fades and sometimes I think the decoration on the Bone is an important message I should perhaps try to decipher.

I'm still a very rich man. Not justly so, but there it is. And, of course, I'm about as popular with the public as Percy the Paedophile. Gold the Bone King? I might as well be Gold the Graverobber. I don't go down to Soho much. When I do make it to a show or something I try to disguise myself a bit. I don't see anything of Bernie any more and I heard two of the stoodies topped themselves.

I do my best to make amends. I'm circulating my profits as fast as I can. Talent's flooding into London from everywhere, making a powerful mix. They say they haven't known a buzz like it since 1967. I'm a reliable investor in great new shows. Every year I back the Iggy Pop Awards, the most prestigious in the business. But not everybody will take my money. I am regularly reviled. That's why some organisations receive anonymous donations. They would refuse them if they knew they were from me.

I've had the extremes of good and bad luck riding this particular switch in the zeitgeist and the only time I'm happy is when I wake up in the morning and I've forgotten who I am. It seems I share a common disgust for myself.

A few dubious customers, however, think I owe them something.

Another bloke, who used to be very rich before he made some frenetic investments after his career went down the drain, called me the other day. He knew of my interest in the theatre, that I had invested in several West End hits. He thought I'd be interested in his idea. He wanted to revive his first success, *Rebecca's Incredibly Far Out Well* or something, which he described as a powerful religious rock opera guaranteed to capture the new nostalgia market. The times, he told me, they were a-changin'. His show, he continued, was full of raw old-fashioned R&B energy. Just the sort of authentic sound to attract the new no-nonsense youngsters. Wasn't it cool that Madonna wanted to do the title rôle? And Bob Geldof would play the Spirit of the Well. *Rock and roll, man! It's all in the staging, man! Remember the boat in* Phantom? *I can make it look better than real. On stage, man, that well is W.E.T. WET! Rock and roll!* I could see that little wizened fist punching the air in a parody of the vitality he craved and whose source had always eluded him.

I had to tell him it was a non-starter. I'd turned over a new leaf, I said. I was taking my ethics seriously.

These days I only deal in living talent.

A Winter Admiral

After lunch she woke up, thinking the rustling from the pantry must be a foraging mouse brought out of hibernation by the unusual warmth. She smiled. She never minded a mouse or two for company and she had secured anything she would not want them to touch.

No, she really didn't mind the mice at all. Their forebears had been in these parts longer than hers and had quite as much right to the territory. More of them, after all, had bled and died for home and hearth. They had earned their tranquillity. Her London cats were perfectly happy to enjoy a life of peaceful coexistence.

'We're a family.' She yawned and stretched. 'We probably smell pretty much the same by now.' She took up the brass poker and opened the firedoor of the stove. 'One big happy family, us and the mice and the spiders.'

After a few moments the noise from the pantry stopped. She was surprised it did not resume. She poked down the burning logs, added two more from her little pile, closed the door and adjusted the vents. That would keep in nicely.

As she leaned back in her chair she heard the sound again. She got up slowly to lift the latch and peer in. Through the outside pantry window, sunlight laced the bars of dust and brightened her shelves. She looked on the floor for droppings. Amongst her cat-litter bags, her indoor gardening tools, her electrical bits and pieces, there was nothing eaten and no sign of a mouse.

Today it was even warm in the pantry. She checked a couple of jars of pickles. It didn't do for them to heat up. They seemed all right. This particular pantry had mostly canned things. She only ever needed to shop once a week.

She closed the door again. She was vaguely ill at ease. She hated anything odd going on in her house. Sometimes she lost perspective. The best way to get rid of the feeling was to take a walk. Since the sun was so bright today, she would put on her coat and stroll up the lane for a bit.

It was one of those pleasant February days which deceives you into believing spring has arrived. A cruel promise, really, she thought. This weather would be gone soon enough. Make the best of it, she said to herself. She would leave the radio playing, put a light on in case it grew dark before she was back, and promise herself *The Charlie Chester Show*, a cup of tea and a scone when she got home. She lifted the heavy iron kettle, another part of her inheritance, and put it on the hob. She set her big, brown teapot on the brass trivet.

The scent of lavender struck her as she opened her coat cupboard. She had just re-lined the shelves and drawers. Lavender reminded her of her first childhood home.

'We're a long way from Mitcham now,' she told the cats as she took her tweed overcoat off the hanger. Her Aunt Becky had lived here until her last months in the nursing home. Becky had inherited Crow Cottage from the famous Great Aunt Begg. As far as Marjorie Begg could tell, the place had been inhabited by generations of retired single ladies, almost in trust, for centuries.

Mrs Begg would leave Crow Cottage to her own niece, Clare, who looked after Jessie, her half-sister. A chronic invalid, Jessie must soon die, she was so full of rancour.

A story in a Cotswold book said this had once been known as Crone's Cottage. She was amused by the idea of ending her days as the local crone. She would have to learn to cackle. The crone was a recognised figure in any English rural community, after all. She wondered if it were merely coincidence that made Rab, the village idiot, her handyman. He worshipped her. She would do anything for him. He was like a bewildered child since his wife had thrown him out: she could make more in benefits than he made in wages. He had seemed reconciled to the injustice: 'I was never much of an earner.' That apologetic grin was his response to most disappointment. It probably hadn't been fitting for a village idiot to be married, any more than a crone. Yet who had washed and embroidered the idiot's smocks in the old days?

She had been told Rab had lost his digs and was living wild in Wilson's abandoned farm buildings on the other side of the wood.

Before she opened her front door she thought she heard the rustling again. The sound was familiar, but not mice. Some folded cellophane unravelling as the cupboard warmed up? The cottage had never been cosier.

She closed the door behind her, walking up the stone path under her brown tangle of honeysuckle and through the gate to the rough farm lane. Between the tall, woven hedges she kept out of the shade as much as she could. She relished the air, the winter scents, the busy finches, sparrows, tits and yellow-hammers. A chattering robin objected to her passing and a couple of wrens fussed at her. She clicked her tongue, imitating their angry little voices. The broad meadows lay across the brow of the hills like shawls, their dark brown furrows laced with melting frost, bright as crystal. Birds flocked everywhere, to celebrate this unexpected ease in the winter's grey.

Her favourites were the crows and magpies. Such old, alien birds. So wise. Closer to the dinosaurs and inheriting an unfathomable memory. Was that why people took against them? She had learned early that intelligence was no better admired in a bird than in a woman. The thought of her father made her shudder, even out here on this wide, unthreatening Cotswold hillside, and she felt suddenly lost, helpless, the cottage no longer her home. Even the steeple on the village church, rising beyond the elms, seemed completely inaccessible. She hated the fear more than she hated the man who had infected her with it – as thoroughly as if he had infected her with a disease. She blamed herself. What good was hatred? He had died wretchedly, of exposure, in Hammersmith, between his pub and his flat, a few hundred yards away.

Crow Cottage, with its slender evergreens and lattice of willow boughs, was as safe and welcoming as always when she turned back into her lane. As the sun fell it was growing colder, but she paused for a moment. The cottage, with its thatch and its chimney, its walls and its hedges, was a picture. She loved it. It welcomed her, even now, with so little colour in the garden.

She returned slowly, enjoying the day, and stepped back over her hearth, into her dream of security, her stove and her cats and her rattling kettle. She was in good time for *Sing Something Simple* and would be eating her scones by the time Charlie Chester came on. She had never felt the need for a television here, though she had been a slave to it in Streatham. Jack had liked his sport.

He had been doing his pools when he died.

When she came back to the flat that night, Jack was in the hall, stretched out with his head on his arm. She knew he was dead, but she gave him what she hoped was the kiss of life, repeatedly blowing her warm breath through his cold lips until she got up to phone for the ambulance. She kept kissing him, kept pouring her breath into him, but was weeping almost uncontrollably when they arrived.

He wouldn't have known anything, love, they consoled her.

No consolation at all to Jack! He had hated not knowing things. She had never anticipated the anguish that came with the loss of him, which had lasted until she moved to Crow Cottage. She had written to Clare. By some miracle, the cottage had cured her of her painful grief and brought unexpected reconciliation.

It was almost dark.

Against the sprawling black branches of the old elms, the starlings curled in ranks towards the horizon, while out of sight in the tall wood the crows began to call, bird to bird, family to family. The setting sun had given the few clouds a powdering of terracotta and the air was suddenly a Mediterranean blue behind them. Everything was so vivid and hurrying so fast, as if to greet the end of the world.

She went to draw the back curtains and saw the sunset over the flooded fields fifteen miles away, spreading its bloody light into the water. She almost gasped at the sudden beauty of it.

Then she heard the rustling again. Before the light failed altogether, she was determined to discover the cause. It would be awful to start getting fancies after dark.

As she unlatched the pantry door something rose from the floor and settled against the window. She shivered, but did not retreat.

She looked carefully. Then, to her surprise: 'Oh, it's a butterfly!'

The butterfly began to beat again upon the window. She reached to cup it in her hands, to calm it. 'Poor thing.'

It was a newborn Red Admiral, its orange, red and black markings vibrant as summer. 'Poor thing.' It had no others of its kind.

For a few seconds the butterfly continued to flutter, and then was still. She widened her hands to look in. She watched its perfect, questing antennae, its extraordinary legs, she could almost smell it. A small miracle, she thought, to make a glorious day complete.

An unexpected sadness filled her as she stared at the butterfly. She carried it to the door, pushed the latch with her cupped hands, and walked into the twilight. When she reached the gate she opened her hands again, gently, to relish the vivacious delicacy of the creature. Mrs Begg sighed, and with a sudden, graceful movement lifted her open palms to let the Admiral taste the air.

In two or three wingbeats the butterfly was up, a spot of busy, brilliant colour streaming towards the east and the cold horizon.

As it gained height, it veered, its wings courageous against the freshening wind.

Shielding her eyes, Mrs Begg watched the Admiral turn and fly over the thatch, to be absorbed in the setting sun.

It was far too cold now to be standing there. She went inside and shut the door. The cats still slept in front of the stove. With the pot holder she picked up the kettle, pouring lively water over the tea. Then she went to close her pantry door.

'I really couldn't bear it,' she said. 'I couldn't bear to watch it die.'

Doves in the Circle

Situated between Church Street and Broadway, several
blocks from Houston Street, just below Canal Street,
Houston Circle is entered via Houston Alley from the North,
and *Lispenard, Walker* and *Franklin* Streets from the West.
The only approach from the South and East is via *Courtland
Alley.* Houston Circle was known as *Indian Circle* or *South
Green* until about 1820. It was populated predominantly by
Irish, English and, later, Jewish people and today has a poor
reputation. The circle itself, forming a green, now an open
market, had some claims to antiquity. Aboriginal
settlements have occupied the spot for about five hundred
years and early travellers report finding non-indigenous
standing stones, remarkably like those erected by the
Ancient Britons. The *Kakatanawas*, whom early explorers
first encountered, spoke a distinctive Iroquois dialect and
were of a high standard of civilisation. Captain Adriaen
Block reported encountering the tribe in 1612. Their village
was built around a stone circle 'whych is their *Kirke*'.
When, under the Dutch, Fort Amsterdam was established
nearby, there was no attempt to move the tribe which
seems to have become so quickly absorbed into the
dominant culture that it took no part in the bloody Indian
War of 1643–5 and had completely disappeared by 1680.
Although of considerable architectural and historical
interest, because of its location and reputation Houston
Circle has not attracted redevelopment and its buildings,
some of which date from the 18th century, are in poor
repair. Today the Circle is best known for 'The Three

Sisters', which comprise the Catholic Church of *St Mary the Widow* (one of Huntingdon Begg's earliest commissions), the Greek Orthodox Church of *St Sophia* and the Orthodox Jewish Synagogue which stand side by side at the East end, close to *Doyle's Ale House*, built in 1780 and still in the same family. Next door to this is *Doyle's Hotel* (1879), whose tariff reflects its standards. Crossed by the Elevated Railway, which destroys the old village atmosphere, and generally neglected now, the Circle should be visited in daylight hours and in the company of other visitors. *Subway:* White Street IRT. *Elevated:* 6th Ave. El. at Church Street, *Streetcar:* B & 7th Ave., B'way & Church.

– R.P. Downes,
New York: A Traveller's Guide,
Charles Kelly, London, 1924

Chapter One

I F THERE IS such a thing as unearned innocence, then America has it, said Barry Quinn mysteriously lifting his straight glass to the flag and downing the last of Corny Doyle's passable porter. Oh, there you go again, says Corny, turning to a less contentious customer and grinning to show he saw several viewpoints. Brown as a tinker, he stood behind his glaring pumps in his white shirt-sleeves, his skin glowing with the bar work, polishing up some silverware with all the habitual concentration of the rosary.

Everyone in the pub had an idea that Corny was out of sorts. They thought, perhaps, he would rather not have seen Father McQueeny there in his regular spot. These days the old priest carried an aura of desolation with him so that even when he joined a toast he seemed to address the dead. He had never been popular and his church had always chilled you but he had once enjoyed a certain authority in the parish. Now the Bishop had sent a new man down and McQueeny was evidently retired but wasn't admitting it. There'd always been more faith and Christian charity in Doyle's, Barry Quinn said, than could ever be found in that damned church. Apart from a few impenetrable writers in the architectural journals, no-one had ever liked it. It was altogether too modern and Spanish-looking.

Sometimes, said Barry Quinn putting down his glass in the copper stand for a refill, there was so much good will in Doyle's Ale House he felt like he was taking his pleasure at the benign heart of the world. And who was to say that Houston Circle, with its profound history, the site of the oldest settlement on Manhattan, was not a centre of conscious grace and mystery like Camelot or Holy Island or Dublin, or possibly London? You could find all the inspiration you needed here. And you got an excellent confessional. Why freeze your bones talking to old McQueeny in the box when you might as well talk to him over in that booth. Should you want to.

The fact was that nobody wanted anything at all to do with the old horror. There were some funny rumours about him. Nobody was exactly sure what Father McQueeny had been caught doing, but it must have been bad enough for the Church to step in. And he'd had some sort of nasty secretive surgery. Mavis Byrne and her friends believed the Bishop made him have it. A popular rumour was that the Church castrated him for diddling little boys. He would not answer if you asked him. He was rarely asked. Most of the time people tended to forget he was there. Sometimes they talked about him in his hearing. He never objected.

She's crossed the road now, look. Corny pointed through the big, green-lettered window of the pub to where his daughter walked purposefully through the wrought-iron gates of what was nowadays called Houston Park on the maps and Houston Green by the realtors.

She's walking up the path. Straight as an arrow. He was proud of her. Her character was so different from his own. She had all her mother's virtues. But he was more afraid of Kate than he had ever been of his absconded spouse.

Will you look at that? Father McQueeny's bloody eyes stared with cold reminiscence over the rim of his glass. She is about to ask Mr Terry a direct question.

He's bending an ear, says Barry Quinn, bothered by the priest's commentary, as if a fly interrupted him. He seems to be almost smiling. Look at her coaxing a bit of warmth out of that grim old mug. And at the same time she's getting the info she needs, like a bee taking pollen.

Father McQueeny runs his odd-coloured tongue around his lips and says, shrouded safe in his inaudibility, his invisibility: What a practical and down-to-earth little creature she is. She was always that. What a proper little madam, eh? She must have the truth, however dull. She will not allow us our speculations. She is going to ruin all our fancies!

His almost formless body undulates to the bar, settles over a stool and seems to coagulate on it. Without much hope of a quick response, he signals for a short and a pint. Unobserved by them, he consoles himself in the possession of some pathetic and unwholesome secret. He marvels at the depths of his own depravity, but now he believes it is his self-loathing which keeps him alive. And while he is alive, he cannot go to Hell.

Chapter Two

'WELL,' SAYS KATE Doyle to Mr Terry McLear, 'I've been sent out and I beg your pardon but I am a kind of deputation from the whole Circle, or at least that part of it represented by my dad's customers, come to ask if what you're putting up is a platform on which you intend to sit, to make, it's supposed, a political statement of some kind? Or is it religious? Like a pole?'

And when she has finished her speech, she takes one step back from him. She folds her dark expectant hands before her on the apron of her uniform. There is a silence, emphasised by the distant, constant noise of the surrounding city. Framed by her bobbed black hair, her little pink oval face has that expression of sardonic good humour, that hint of self-mockery, which attracted his affection many years ago. She is the picture of determined patience, and she makes Mr Terry smile.

'Is that what people are saying these days, is it? And they think I would sit up there in this weather?' He speaks the musical, old-fashioned convent-educated, precisely pronounced English he learned in Dublin. He'd rather die than make a contraction or split an infinitive. He glares up at the grey, Atlantic sky. Laughing helplessly at the image of himself on a pole he stretches hard-worn fingers towards her to show he means no mockery or rudeness to herself. His white hair rises in a halo. His big old head grows redder, his mouth rapidly opening and closing as his mirth engulfs him. He gasps. His pale blue eyes, too weak for such powerful emotions, water joyfully. Kate Doyle suspects a hint of senile dementia. She'll be sorry to see him lose his mind, it is such a good one, and so kind. He never really understood how often his company had saved her from despair.

Mr Terry lifts the long thick dowel onto his sweat-shirted shoulder. 'Would you care to give me a hand, Katey?'

She helps him steady it upright in the special hole he had prepared. The seasoned pine dowel is some four inches in diameter and eight feet tall. The hole is about two feet deep. Yesterday, from the big bar, they had all watched him pour in the concrete.

The shrubbery, trees and grass of the Circle nowadays wind neatly up to a little grass-grown central hillock. On this the City has placed two ornamental benches. Popular legend has it that an Indian chief rests underneath, together with his treasure.

When Mr Terry was first seen measuring up the mound, they thought of the ancient redman. They had been certain, when he had started to dig, that McLear had wind of gold.

All Doyle's regulars had seized enthusiastically on this new topic. Corny Doyle was especially glad of it. Sales rose considerably when there was a bit of speculative stimulus amongst the customers, like a sensational murder or a political scandal or a sporting occasion.

Katey knew they would all be standing looking out now, watching her and waiting. They had promised to rescue her if he became unpleasant. Not that she expected anything like that. She was the only local that Mr Terry would have anything to do with. He never would talk to most people. After his wife died he was barely civil if you wished him 'good morning'. His argument was that he had never enjoyed company much until he met her and now precious little other company satisfied him in comparison. Neither did he have anything to do with the Church. He'd distanced himself a bit from Katey when she started working with the Poor Clares. This was the first time she'd approached him in two years. She's grateful to them for making her come but sorry that it took the insistence of a bunch of feckless boozers to get her here.

'So,' she says, 'I'm glad I've cheered you up. And if that's all I've achieved, that's good enough for today, I'm sure. Can you tell me nothing about your pole?'

'I have a permit for it,' he says. 'All square and official.' He pauses and watches the Sears delivery truck which has been droning round the Circle for the last fifteen minutes, seeking an exit.

Slumped over his wheel, peering about for signs, the driver looks desperate.

'Nothing else?'

'Only that the pole is the start of it.' He's enjoying himself. That heartens her.

'And you won't be doing some sort of black magic with the poor old Indian's bones?'

'Magic, maybe,' he says, 'but not a bit black, Katey. Just the opposite, you will see.'

'Well, then,' she says, 'then I'll go back and tell them you're putting up a radio aerial.'

'Tell them what you like,' he says. 'Whatever you like.'

'If I don't tell them something, they'll be on at me to come out again,' she says.

'You would not be unwelcome,' he says, 'or averse, I am sure, to a cup of tea.' And gravely he tips that big head homeward, towards his brownstone basement on the far side of the Circle.

'Fine,' she says, 'but I'll come on my own when I do and not as a messenger. Good afternoon to you, Mr Terry.'

He lifts an invisible hat. 'It was a great pleasure to talk with you again, Katey.'

She's forgotten how that little smile of his so frequently cheers her up.

Chapter Three

'**O**KAY, KATEY, SO what's the story?' says Father McQueeny wearing his professional cheer like an old shroud, as ill-smelling and threadbare as his clerical black. The only life on him is his sweat, his winking veins. The best the regulars have for him these days is their pity, the occasional drink. He has no standing at all with the Church or the community. But, since Father Walsh died, that secret little smirk of his always chills her. Knowing that he can still frighten her is probably all that keeps the old shit alive. And since that knowledge actually informs the expression which causes her fear, she is directly feeding him what he wants. She has yet to work out a way to break the cycle. Years before, in her fiercest attempt, she almost succeeded.

To the others, the priest remains inaudible, invisible. 'Did he come out with it, Katey?' says Corny Doyle, his black eyes and hair glinting like pitch, his near-fleshless body and head looking as artificially weathered as those shiny, smoked hams in Belladonna's. 'Come on, Kate. There's real money riding on this now.'

'He did not tell me,' she says. She turns her back on Father McQueeny but she cannot control a shudder as she smiles from behind the bar where she has been helping out since Christmas, because of Bridget's pneumonia. She takes hold of the decorated china pump-handle and turns to her patient customer. 'Two pints of Mooney's was it, Mr Gold?'

'You're an angel,' says Mr Gold. 'Well, Corny, the book, now how's it running?' He is such a plump, jolly man. You would never take him for a pawnbroker. And it must be admitted he is not a natural profiteer. Mr Gold carries his pints carefully to the little table in the alcove, where Becky, his secretary, waits for him. Ageless, she is her own work of art. He dotes on her. If it wasn't for her he would be a ruined man. They'll be going out this evening.

You can smell her perm and her Chantilly from here. A little less noise and you could probably hear her mascara flake.

'Radio aerial's still number one, Mr Gold,' says Katey. Her father's attention has gone elsewhere, to some fine moment of sport on the box. He shares his rowdy triumph with his fellow aficionados. He turns back to her, panting. 'That was amazing,' he says.

Kate Doyle calls him over with her finger. He knows better than to hesitate. 'What?' he blusters. 'What? There's nothing wrong with those glasses. I told you it's the dishwasher.'

Her whisper is sharp as a needle in his wincing ear. She asks him why, after all she's spoken perfectly plainly to him, he is still letting that nasty old man into the pub?

'Oh, come on, Katey,' he says, 'where else can the poor devil go? He's a stranger in his own church these days.'

'He deserves nothing less,' she says. 'And I'll remind you, Dad, of my original terms. I'm off for a walk now and you can run the bloody pub yourself.'

'Oh, no!' He is mortified. He casts yearning eyes back towards the television. He looks like some benighted sinner in the picture books who has lost the salvation of Christ. 'Don't do this to me, Kate.'

'I might be back when he's gone,' she says. 'But I'm not making any promises.'

Every so often she has to let him know he is going too far. Getting her father to work was a full-time job for her mother but she's not going to waste her own life on that non-starter. He's already lost the hotel next door to his debts. Most of the money Kate allows him goes in some form of gambling. Those customers who lend him money soon discover how she refuses to honour his IOUs. He's lucky these days to be able to coax an extra dollar or two out of the till, usually by short-changing a stranger.

'We'll lose business if you go, Kate,' he hisses. 'Why cut off your nose to spite your face?'

'I'll cut off *your* nose, you old fool, if you don't set it to that grindstone right now,' she says. She hates sounding like her mother. Furiously, she snatches on her coat and scarf. 'I'll be back when you get him out of here.' She knows Father McQueeny's horrible eyes are still feeding off her through the pub's cultivated gloom.

'See you later, Katey, dear,' her father trills as he places professional fingers on his bar and a smile falls across his face. 'Now, then, Mrs Byrne, a half of Guinness, is it, darling?'

Chapter Four

THE CIRCLE WAS going up. There were all kinds of well-heeled people coming in. You could tell by the brass door-knockers and the window boxes, the dark green paint. With the odd *boutique* and *croissanterie*, these were the traditional signs of gentrification. Taking down the last pylons of the ugly elevated had helped, along with the hippies who in the '60s and '70s had made such a success of the little park, which now had a playground and somewhere for the dogs to go. It was lovely in the summer.

It was quiet, too, since they had put in the one-way system. Now the only strange vehicles were those which thought they could still make a shortcut and wound up whining round until, defeated, they left the way they had entered. You had to go up to Canal Street to get a cab. They wouldn't come any further than that. There were legends of drivers who had never returned.

This recent development had increased the sense of the Circle's uniqueness, a zone of relative tranquillity in one of the noisiest parts of New York City. Up to now they had been protected from a full-scale yuppie invasion by the nearby federal housing. Yet nobody from the projects had ever bothered the Circle. They thought of the place as their own, something they aspired to, something to protect. It was astonishing the affection local people felt for the place, especially the park, which was the best-kept in the city.

She was on her brisk way, of course, to take Mr Terry McLear up on his invitation but she was not going there directly for all to see. Neither was she sure what she'd have to say to him when she saw him. She simply felt it was time they had one of their old chats.

Under a chilly sky, she walked quickly along the central path of the park. Eight paths led to the middle these days, like the arms of a compass, and there had been some talk of putting a sundial on the knoll, where Mr Terry had now laid his discreet foundations. She paused to look at the smooth concrete of his deep, narrow hole. A flag, perhaps? Something that simple? But this was not a man to fly a flag at the best of times. And even the heaviest banner did not need so sturdy a pole. However, she was beginning to get a notion. A bit of a memory from a conversation of theirs a good few years ago now. Ah, she thought, it's about birds, I bet.

Certain some of her customers would still be watching her, she took the northern path and left the park to cross directly over to Houston Alley, where her uncle had his little toy-soldier shop where he painted everything himself and where, next door, the Italian shoe-repairer worked in his window. They would not be there much longer now that the real-estate people had christened the neighbourhood 'Houston Village'. Already the pub had had a sniff from Starbucks. Up at the far end of the alley the street looked busy. She thought about going back, but told herself she was a fool.

The traffic in Canal Street was unusually dense and a crew-cut girl in big boots had to help her when she almost fell into the street, shoved aside by some thrusting Wall Street stockman in a vast raincoat which might have sheltered half the Australian outback. She thought she recognised him as the boy who had moved in to No. 91 a few weeks ago and she had been about to say hello.

She was glad to get back into the quietness of the Circle, going round into Church Street and then through Walker Street which would bring her out only a couple of houses from Mr Terry's place.

She was still a little shaken up but had collected herself by the time she reached the row of brownstones. No. 27 was in the middle and his flat was in the basement. She went carefully down the iron steps to his area. It was as smartly kept up as always, with the flower baskets properly stocked and his miniature greenhouse raising tomatoes in their gro-bags. And he was still neat and clean. No obvious slipping of standards, no signs of senile decay. She took hold of the old black lion knocker and rapped twice against the dented plate. That same vast echo came back, as if she stood at the door to infinity.

He was slow as Christmas unbolting it all and opening up. Then everything happened at once. Pulling back the door he embraced her and kicked it shut at the same time. The apartment was suddenly very silent. 'Well,' he said, 'it has been such a long time. All my fault, too. I have had a chance to pull myself together and here I am.'

'That sounds like a point for God for a change.' She knew all the teachers had been anarchists or pagans or something equally silly in that school of his. She stared around at the familiar things, the copper and the oak and the big ornamental iron stove which once heated the whole building. 'You're still dusting better than a woman. And polishing.'

'She had high standards,' he says. 'I could not rise to them when she was alive, but now it seems only fair to try to live up to them. You would not believe what a slob I used to be.'

'You never told me,' she says.

'That is right. There is quite a bit I have not told you,' he says.

'And us so close once,' she says.

'We were good friends,' he agreed. 'The best of company. I am an idiot, Kate. But I do not think either of us realised I was in a sort of shock for years. I was afraid of our closeness, do you see? In the end.'

'I believe I might have mentioned that.' She went to put the kettle on. Filling it from his deep old-fashioned stone sink with its great brass faucets she carried it with both hands to the stove while he got out the teacakes and the toasting forks. He must have bought them only today from Van Beek's Bakery on Canal, the knowing old devil, and put them in the icebox. They were still almost warm. She fitted one to the fork. 'It doesn't exactly take Sigmund Freud to work that out. But you made your decisions, Mr Terry. And it is my general rule to abide by such decisions until the party involved decides to change. Which in my experience generally happens at the proper time.'

'Oh, so you have had lots of these relationships, have you, Kate?' She laughed.

Chapter Five

'I WAS SIXTEEN when I first saw her. In the Circle there she was, coming out of No. 10, where the dry-cleaners is now. I said to myself, that is whom I am going to marry. And that was what I did. We used to sing quite a bit, duets together. She was a much better and sweeter singer than I, and she was smarter, as well.' Mr Terry looks into the fire and slowly turns his teacake against the glare. 'What a little old snob I was in those days, thinking myself better than anyone, coming back from Dublin with an education. But she liked me anyway and was what I needed to take me down a peg or two. My father thought she was an angel. He spoke often of the grandchildren he would care for. But both he and she died before that event could become any sort of reality. And I grew very sorry for myself, Kate. In those first days, when we were having our chats, I was selfish.'

'Oh, yes,' she says, 'but you were more than that. You couldn't help being more than that. That's one of the things hardest to realise about ourselves sometimes. Even in your morbid moments you often showed me how to get a grip on things. By example, you might say. You cannot help but be a good man, Mr Terry. A protector, I think, rather than a predator.'

'I do not know about that.'

'But I do,' she says.

'Anyway,' he flips a teacake onto the warming plate, 'we had no children and so the McLears have no heirs.'

'It's a shame,' she says, 'but not a tragedy, surely?' For an instant it flashes through her head, Oh, no, he doesn't want me to have his bloody babies, does he?

'Not in any ordinary sense, I quite agree. But you see there is an inheritance that goes along with that. Something which must be remembered accurately and passed down by word of mouth. It is our family tradition and has been so for quite a time.'

'My goodness,' she says. 'You're Brian Boru's rightful successor to the high throne of Erin, is that it?' With deft economy she butters their teacakes.

He takes some jelly from the dish and lays it lightly on top. 'Oh, these are good, eh?'

When they are drinking their last possible cup of Assam he says very soberly: 'Would you let me share this secret, Kate? I have no-one else.'

'Not a crime, is it, or something nasty?' she begs.

'Certainly not!' He falls silent. She can sense him withdrawing and laughs at his response. He sighs.

'Then get on with it,' she says. 'Give me a taste of it, for I'm a busy woman.'

'The story does not involve the Irish much,' he says. 'Most of the Celts involved were from southern England, which was called Britannia in those days, by the Romans.'

'Ancient history!' she cries. 'How long, Mr Terry, is your story?'

'Not very long,' he says.

'Well,' she says, 'I will come back another time to hear it.' She glances at her watch. 'If I don't go now I'll miss my programme.'

As he helps her on with her coat she says: 'I have a very low tolerance for history. It is hard for me to see how most of it relates to the here and now.'

'This will mean something to you, I think, Kate.'

They exchange light kisses upon the cheek. There is a new warmth between them which she welcomes.

'Make it scones tomorrow,' she says. 'Those big juicy ones they do, with the raisins in them, and I will hear your secret. We'll have Darjeeling, too. I'll bring some if you don't have any.'

'I have plenty,' he says.

'Bye, bye for now,' she says.

Chapter Six

'ALL THE GOODNESS is in the marrow!' declares Mrs Byrne, waving her bones at the other customers. 'But these days the young people all turn their noses up at it.'

'That's not the problem at all, Mavis. The plain truth is you're a bloody noisy eater,' says Corny Doyle, backing up the other diners' complaints. 'And you've had one too many now. You had better go home.'

With her toothless mouth she sucks at her mutton.

'They don't know what they're missing, do they Mavis?' says Father McQueeny from where he sits panting in a booth.

'And you can fuck off, you old pervert.' Mavis rises with dignity and sails towards the ladies'. She has her standards.

'Well, Kate, how's the weather out there?' says Father McQueeny.

'Oh, you are here at last, Kate. It seems Father McQueeny's been locked out of his digs.' In other circumstances Corny's expression of pleading anxiety would be funny.

'That doesn't concern me,' she says, coming down the stairs. 'I just popped in for something. I have told you what I want, Dad.' She is carrying her little bag.

He rushes after her, whispering and pleading. 'What can I do?'

'I have told you what you can do.'

She looks back into the shadows. She knows he is staring at her. Often she thinks it is not exactly him that she fears, only what is in him. What sense does that make? Does she fear his memories and secrets? Of course Father Walsh, her confessor, had heard what had happened and what she had done and she had been absolved. What was more, the Church, by some means of its own, had discovered at least part of the truth and taken steps to curb him. They had sent Father Declan down to St Mary's. He was a tough old bugger but wholesome as they come. McQueeny was supposed to assist Declan who had found no use for him. However, since Father Walsh died, McQueeny revelled in their hideous secret, constantly hanging around the pub even before she started working there, haunting her, threatening to tell the world how he had come by his horrid surgery.

She is not particularly desperate about it. Sooner or later she knows her father will knuckle down and ban the old devil. It must be only a matter of time before the priest's liver kills him. She's never wished anyone dead in her life, save him, and her hatred of him is such that she fears for her own soul over it.

This time she goes directly across the park to Mr Terry McLear's. It might look as if she plans to spend the night there but she does not care. Her true intention is to return eventually to her own flat in Delaware Court and wait until her father calls. She gives it twenty-four hours from the moment she stepped out of the pub.

But when she lifts the lion's head and lets it fall there is no reply. She waits. She climbs back up the steps. She looks into the park. She is about to go down again when an old chequer cab pulls up and out of its yellow-and-black depths comes Mr Terry McLear with various bags and bundles. 'Oh what luck!' he declares. 'Just when I needed you, Kate.'

She helps him get the stuff out of the cab and down into his den. He removes his coat. He opens the door into his workshop and switches on a light. 'I was not expecting you back today.'

'Circumstances gave me the opportunity.' She squints at the bags. 'Who is Happy the Hammer?'

'Look on the other side. It is Stadtler's Hardware. Their mascot. Just the last bits I needed.'

'Is it a bird-house of some kind that you are building?' she asks.

'And so you are adding telepathy to your list of extraordinary qualities, are you, Katey?' He grins. 'Did I ever mention this to you?'

'You might have done. Is it pigeons?'

'God bless you, Katey.' He pulls a bunch of small dowels out of a bag and puts it on top of some bits of plywood. 'I must have told you the story.'

'Not much of a secret, then,' she says.

'This is not the secret, though I suppose it has something to do with it. There used to be dovecotes here, Katey, years ago. And that is all I am building. Have you not noticed the little doves about?'

'I can't say I have.'

'Little mourning doves,' he says. 'Brown and cream. Like a kind of delicate pigeon.'

'Well,' she says, 'I suppose for the non-expert they'd be lost in the crowd.'

'Maybe, but I think you would know them when I pointed them out. The City believes me, anyhow, and is anxious to have them back. And it is not costing them a penny. The whole thing is a matter of fifty dollars and a bit of time. An old-fashioned dovecote, Katey. There are lots of accounts of the dovecotes, when this was more or less an independent village.'

'So you're building a little house for the doves,' she says. 'That will be nice for them.'

'A little house, is it? More a bloody great hotel.' Mr Terry erupts with sudden pride. 'Come on, Kate. I will take you back to look.'

Chapter Seven

S HE ADMIRES HIM turning the wood this way and that against the whirling lathe he controls with a foot pedal.

'It is a wonderful smell,' she says, 'the smell of shavings.' She peers with casual curiosity at his small, tightly organised workshop. Tools, timber, electrical bits and pieces, nails, screws and hooks are neatly stowed on racks and narrow shelves. She inspects the white-painted sides of the near-completed bird-house. In the room, it seems massive, almost large enough to hold a child. She runs her fingers over the neatly ridged openings, the perfect joints. Everything has been finished to the highest standard, as if for the most demanding human occupation. 'When did they first put up the dovecotes?'

'Nobody knows. The Indians had them when the first explorers arrived from Holland and France. There are sketches of them in old books. Some accounts call the tribe that lived here "the Dove Keepers". The Iroquois respected them as equals and called them the Ga-geh-ta-o-no, the People of the Circle. But the phrase also means People of the Belt.

'The Talking Belts, the "wampum" records of the Six Nations, are invested with mystical meanings. Perhaps our tribe were the Federation's record keepers. They were a handsome, wealthy, civilised people, apparently, who were happy to meet and trade with the newcomers. The famous Captain Block was their admirer and spoke of a large stone circle surrounding their dovecotes. He believed that these standing stones, which were remarkably like early European examples, enclosed their holy place and that the doves represented the spirit they worshipped.

'Other accounts mention the stones, but there is some suspicion that the writers simply repeated Block's observations. Occasionally modern construction work reveals some of the granite, alien rock driven into the native limestone like a knife, and there is a suspicion the rock was used as part of a later stockade. The only Jesuit records make no mention of the stones but concentrate on the remarkable similarity of Kakatan-awa (as the Europeans called them) myths to early forms of Christianity.'

'I have heard as much myself,' she agrees, more interested than she expected. 'What happened to the Indians?'

'Nothing dramatic. They were simply and painlessly absorbed, mainly through intermarriage and mostly with the Irish. It would not have been difficult for them, since they still had a considerable amount of blood in common. By 1720 this was a thriving little township, built around the green. It still had its dovecotes. The stones were gone, re-used in walls of all kinds. The Kakatanawa were living in ordinary houses and intermarrying. In those days it was not fashionable to claim native ancestry. But you see the Kakatanawa were hardly natives. They resembled many of the more advanced Iroquois peoples and spoke an Iroquois dialect, but their tradition had it that their ancestors came from the other side of the Atlantic.'

'Where did you read all this?' she asks in some bewilderment.

'It is not conventionally recorded,' he says. 'But this is my secret.'

And he told her of Trinovante Celts, part of the Boudicca uprising of AD 69, who had used all their wealth to buy an old Roman trading ship with the intention of escaping the emperor's cruel justice and sailing to Ireland. They were not navigators but good fortune eventually took them to these shores where they built a settlement. They chose Manhattan for the same reason as everyone else, because it commanded a good position on the river, had good harbours and could be easily defended.

They built their village inland and put a stockade around it, pretty much the same as the villages they had left behind. Then they sent the ship back with news and to fetch more settlers and supplies. They never heard of it again. The ship was in fact wrecked off Cornwall, probably somewhere near St Ives, but there were survivors and the story remained alive amongst the Celts, even as they succumbed to Roman civilisation.

When, some hundreds of years later, the Roman legions were withdrawn and the Saxon pirates started bringing their families over, further bands of desperate Celts fled for Ireland and the land beyond, which they had named Hy Braseal. One other galley reached Manhattan and discovered a people more Senecan than Celtic.

This second wave of Celtic immigrants were the educated Christian stone-raisers, Romanised astronomers and mystics, who brought new wisdom to their distant cousins and were doubtless not generally welcomed for it. For whatever reasons, however, they were never attacked by other tribes. Even the stern Iroquois, the Romans of these parts, never threatened them, although they were nominally subject to Hiawatha's Federation. By the time the Dutch arrived, the dominant Iroquois culture had again absorbed the Celts, but they retained certain traditions, stories and a few artefacts. Most of these appear to have been sold amongst the Indians and travelled widely through the north-east. They gave rise to certain rumours of Celtic civilisations (notably the Welsh) established in America.

'But the Kakatanawa spoke with the same eloquence and wore the finery and fashions of the Federation. Their particular origin-legend was not remarkable. Other tribes had far more dramatic conceptions, involving spectacular miracles and wildly original plots. So nobody took much notice of us and so we have survived.'

'Us?' says Kate Doyle. 'We?'

'You,' he says, 'represent the third wave of Celtic settlement of the Circle during the nineteenth and twentieth centuries. And I represent the first and second. I am genuinely, Katey, and it is embarrassing to say so, the Last of the Kakatanawas. That was why my father looked forward to an heir, as did I. I suppose I was not up to the burden, or I would have married again.'

'You'd be a fool to marry just for the sake of some old legend,' she says. 'A woman deserves more respect than that.'

'I agree.' He returns to his work. Now he's putting the fine little touches to the dowels, the decorations. It's a wonder to watch him.

'Do you have a feathered headdress and everything? A peace pipe and a tomahawk?' Her mockery has hardly any scepticism in it.

'Go over to that box just there and take out what is in it,' he says, concentrating on the wood.

She obeys him.

It is a little modern copper box with a Celtic motif in the lid. Inside is an old dull coin. She picks it up between wary fingers and fishes it out, turning it to try to read the faint letters of the inscription. 'It's Constantine,' she says. 'A Roman coin.'

'The first Christian Emperor. That coin has been in New York, in our family, Katey, since the sixth century. It is pure gold. It is what is left of our treasure.'

'It must be worth a fortune,' she says.

'Not much of one. The condition is poor, you see. And I am sworn never to reveal its provenance. But it is certainly worth a bit more than the gold alone. Anyway, that is it. It is yours, together with the secret.'

'I don't want it,' she says, 'can't we bury it?'

'Secrets should not be buried,' he says, 'but kept.'

'Well, speak for yourself,' she says. 'There are some secrets best buried.'

While he worked on, she told him about Father McQueeny. He turned the wood more and more slowly as he listened. The priest's favourite joke that always made him laugh was 'Little girls should be screwed and not heard'. With her father's half-hearted compliance, the old wretch had enjoyed all his pleasures on her until one day when she was seventeen she had taken his penis in her mouth and, as she had planned, bitten down like a terrier. He had torn her hair out and almost broken her arm before he fainted.

'And I did not get all the way through. You would not believe how horrible it feels – like the worst sort of gristle in your mouth and all the blood and nasty crunching, slippery stuff. At first, at least, everything in you makes you want to stop. I was very sick afterwards, as you can imagine, and just able to dial 911 before I left him there. He almost died of losing so much blood. I hadn't expected it to spurt so hard. I almost drowned. I suppose if I had thought about it I should have anticipated that. And had a piece of string ready, or something. Anyway, it stopped his business. I was never reported. And I don't know how confessors get the news out, but the Church isn't taking any chances with him, so all he has now are his memories.'

'Oh, dear,' says Mr Terry gravely. 'Now there is a secret to share.'

'It's the only one I have,' she said. 'It seemed fair to reciprocate.'

Chapter Eight

TWO DAYS LATER, side by side, they stand looking up at his magnificent bird-house, complete at last. He's studied romantic old plans from the turn of the century, so it has a touch or two of the Charles Rennie Mackintosh about it in its white austerity, its sweeping gables. There are seven fretworked entrances and eight beautifully turned perches, black as ebony, following the lines of the park's paths. He's positioned and prepared the cote exactly as instructed in Tiffany's *Modern Gardens* of 1892 and has laid his seed and corn carefully. At her request, and without much reluctance, he's buried the Roman coin in the pole's foundation. Now we must be patient, he says. And wait. As he speaks a whickering comes from above and a small dove, fawn and pale grey, settles for a moment upon the gleaming roof, then takes fright when she sees them.

'What a pretty thing. I will soon have to get back to my flat,' she says. 'My father will be going frantic by now. I put the machine on, but if I know him he'll be too proud to leave a message.'

'Of course.' He stoops to pick up a delicately coloured wing feather. It has a thousand shades of rose, beige, pink and grey. 'I will be glad to come with you if you want anything done.'

'I'll be all right,' she says. But he falls in beside her.

As they turn their backs on the great bird-house three noisy mourning doves land on the perches as if they have been anticipating this moment for a hundred and fifty years. The sense of celebration, of relief, is so tangible it suffuses Kate Doyle and Mr Terry McLear even as they walk away.

'This calls for a cup of coffee,' says Mr Terry McLear. 'Shall we go to Belladonna's?'

They are smiling when Father McQueeny, evicted at last, comes labouring towards them along the path from the pub and pauses, suddenly gasping for his familiar fix, as if she has turned up in the nick of time to save his life.

'Good morning, Katey, dear.' His eyes begin to fill with powerful memories. He speaks lovingly to her. 'And Terry McLear, how are you?'

'Not bad, thank you, Father,' says Mr Terry, looking him over.

'And when shall we be seeing you in church, Terry?' The priest is used to people coming back to the faith as their options begin to disappear.

'Oh, soon enough, Father, I hope. By the way, how is Mary's last supper doing? How is the little hot-dog?' And he points.

It is a direct and fierce attack. Father McQueeny folds before it. 'Oh, you swore!' he says to her.

She tries to speak but she cannot. Instead she finds herself laughing in the old wretch's face, watching him die, his secret, his sustenance lost for ever. He knows at once, of course, that his final power has gone. His cold eyes stare furiously into inevitable reality as his soul goes at last to the Devil. It will be no more than a day or two before they bury him.

'Well,' says Katey, 'we must be getting on.'

'Goodbye, Father,' says Mr Terry McLear, putting his feather in his white hair and grinning like a fool.

When they look back the priest has disappeared, doubtless scuttling after some mirage of salvation. But the dovecote is alive with birds. It must have a dozen on it already, bobbing around in the little doorways, pecking up the seed. They glance around with equanimity. You would think they had always been here. The distant noise of New York's traffic is muffled by their excited voices, as if old friends meeting after years. There is an air of approving recognition about their voices.

'They like the house. Now we must see if, when they have eaten the food, they will stay.' Mr Terry McLear offers a proud arm to his companion. 'I never expected it to happen so quickly. It was as if they were waiting to come home. It is a positive miracle.'

Amused, she looks up at him. 'Come on now, a grown man like you with tears in his eyes!

'After all, Mr Terry.' She takes his arm as they continue down the path towards Houston Alley. 'You must never forget your honour as the Last of the Kakatanawas.'

'You do not believe a word of it, do you, Kate?' he says.

'I do,' she says. 'Every word, in fact. It's just that I cannot fathom why you people went to so much trouble to keep it dark.'

'Oh, you know all right, Kate,' says Mr Terry McLear, pausing to look back at the flocking doves. 'Sometimes secrecy is our only means of holding on to what we value.'

Whistling, she escorts him out of the Circle.

A Slow Saturday Night at the
Surrealist Sporting Club

*Being a Further Account of Engelbrecht the
Boxing Dwarf and His Fellow Members*

(after Maurice Richardson)

I HAPPENED TO be sitting in the snug of the Strangers' Bar at the Surrealist Sporting Club on a rainy Saturday night, enjoying a well mixed Existential Fizz (2 pts Vortex Water to 1 pt Sweet Gin) and desperate to meet a diverting visitor, when Death slipped unostentatiously into the big chair opposite, warming his bones at the fire and remarking on the unseasonable weather. There was sure to be a lot of flu about. It made you hate to get the Tube but the buses were worse and had I seen what cabs were charging, these days? He began to drone on as usual about the ozone layer and the melting pole, how we were poisoning ourselves on GM foods and feeding cows to cows and getting all that pollution and cigarette smoke in our lungs and those other gloomy topics he seems to relish, which I suppose makes you appreciate it when he puts you out of your misery.

I had to choose between nodding off or changing the subject. The evening being what it was, I made the effort and changed the subject. Or at least, had a stab at it.

'So what's new?' It was feeble, I admit. But, as it happened, it stopped him in mid-moan.

'Thanks for reminding me,' he said, and glanced at one of his many watches. 'God's dropping in – oh, in about twelve minutes, twenty-five seconds. He doesn't have a lot of time, but if you've any questions to ask him, I suggest you canvass the other members present and think up some good ones in a hurry. And he's not very fond of jokers, if you know what I mean. So stick to substantial questions or he won't be pleased.'

'I thought he usually sent a seraphim ahead for this sort of visit?' I queried mildly. 'Are you all having to double up or something? Is it overpopulation?' I didn't like this drift, either. It suggested a finite universe, for a start.

Our Ever-Present Friend rose smoothly. He looked around the room with a distressed sigh, as if suspecting the whole structure to be infected with dry rot and carpenter ants. He couldn't as much as produce a grim brotherly smile for the deathwatch beetle which had come out especially to greet him. 'Well, once more into the breach. Have you noticed what it's like out there? Worst on record, they say. Mind you, they don't remember the megalithic. Those were the days, eh? See you later.'

'Be sure of it.' I knew a moment of existential angst.

Sensitively, Death hesitated, seemed about to apologise, then thought better of it. He shrugged. 'See you in a minute,' he said. 'I've got to look out for God in the foyer and sign him in. You know.' He had the air of one who had given up worrying about minor embarrassments and was sticking to the protocol, come hell or high water. He was certainly more laconic than he had been. I wondered if the extra work, and doubling as a seraphim, had changed his character.

With Death gone, the Strangers' was warming up rapidly again and I enjoyed a quiet moment with my fizz before rising to amble through the usual warped and shrieking corridors to the Members' Bar, which appeared empty.

'Are you thinking of dinner?' Lizard Bayliss, looking like an undisinfected dishrag, strolled over from where he had been hanging up his obnoxious cape. Never far behind, out of the WC, bustled Engelbrecht the Dwarf Clock Boxer, who had gone ten rounds with the Greenwich Atom before that over-refined chronometer went down to an iffy punch in the eleventh. His great, mad eyes flashed from under a simian hedge of eyebrow. As usual he wore a three-piece suit a size too small for him, in the belief it made him seem taller. He was effing and blinding about some imagined insult offered by the taxi driver who had brought them back from the not altogether successful Endangered Sea Monsters angling contest in which, I was to learn later, Engelbrecht had caught his hook in a tangle of timeweed and wound up dragging down the *Titanic*, which explained that mystery. Mind you, he still had to come clean about the R101. There was some feeling in the club concerning the airship, since he'd clearly taken bets against himself. Challenged, he'd muttered some conventional nonsense about the Maelstrom and the Inner World, but we'd heard that one too often to be convinced. He also resented our recent rule limiting all aerial angling to firedrakes and larger species of pterodactyls.

Lizard Bayliss had oddly coloured bags under his eyes, giving an even more downcast appearance to his normally dissolute features. He was a little drained from dragging the Dwarf in by his collar. It appeared that, seeing the big rods, the driver had asked Bayliss if that was his bait on the seat beside him. The irony was, of course, that the Dwarf had been known to use himself as bait more than once and there was still some argument over interpretation of the rules in that area, too. The Dwarf had taken the cabby's remark to be specific not because of his diminutive stockiness, but because of his sensitivity over the rules issue. He stood to lose a few months, even years, if they reversed the result.

He was still spitting on about 'nit-picking fascist anoraks with severe anal-retention problems' when I raised my glass and yelled: 'If you've an important question for God, you'd better work out how to phrase it. He's due in any second now. And he's only got a few minutes. At the Strangers' Bar. We could invite him in here, but that would involve a lot of time-consuming ritual and so forth. Any objection to meeting him back there?'

The Dwarf wasn't sure he had anything to say that wouldn't get taken the wrong way. Then, noticing how low the fire was, opined that the Strangers' was bound to offer better hospitality. 'I can face my maker any time,' he pointed out, 'but I'd rather do it with a substantial drink in my hand and a good blaze warming my bum.' He seemed unusually oblivious to any symbolism, given that the air was writhing with it. I think the *Titanic* was still on his mind. He was trying to work out how to get his hook back.

By the time we had collected up Oneway Ballard and Taffy Sinclair from the dining room and returned to the Strangers', God had already arrived. Any plans the Dwarf had instantly went out of the window, because God was standing with his back to the fire, blocking everyone's heat. With a word to Taffy not to overtax the Lord of Creation, Death hurried off on some urgent business and disappeared back through the swing doors.

'I am thy One True God,' said Jehovah, making the glasses and bottles rattle. He cleared his throat and dropped his tone to what must for him have been a whisper. But it was unnatural, almost false, like a TV presenter trying to express concern while keeping full attention on the autoprompt. Still, there was something totally convincing about God as a presence. You knew you were in his aura and you knew you had Grace, even if you weren't too impressed by his stereotypical form. God added: 'I am Jehovah, the Almighty. Ask of me what ye will.'

Lizard knew sudden inspiration. 'Do you plan to send Jesus back to Earth and have you any thoughts about the 2.30 at Aintree tomorrow?'

'He is back,' said God, 'and I wouldn't touch those races, these days. Believe me, they're all bent, one way or another. If you like the horses, do the National… Take a chance. Have a gamble. It's anybody's race, the National.'

'But being omniscient,' said Lizard slowly, 'wouldn't you know the outcome anyway?'

'If I stuck by all the rules of omniscience it wouldn't exactly be sporting, would it?' God was staring over at the bar, checking out the Corona-Coronas and the melting marine chronometer above them.

'You don't think it's hard on the horses?' asked Julia Barnes, the transsexual novelist, who could be relied upon for a touch of compassion. Being almost seven feet tall in her spike heels, she was also useful for getting books down from the higher shelves and sorting out those bottles at the top of the bar which looked so temptingly dangerous.

'Bugger the horses,' said God, 'it's the race that counts. And anyway, the horses love it. They love it.'

I was a little puzzled. 'I thought we had to ask only substantial questions?'

'That's right?' God drew his mighty brows together in enquiry.

I fell into an untypical silence. I was experiencing a mild revelation concerning the head of the Church of England and her own favourite *pasatiempi*, but it seemed inappropriate to run with it at that moment.

'What I'd like to know is,' said Engelbrecht, cutting suddenly to the chase, 'who gets into heaven and why?'

There was a bit of a pause in the air, as if everyone felt perhaps he'd pushed the boat out a little too far, but God was nodding. 'Fair question,' he said. 'Well, it's cats, then dogs, but there's quite a few human beings, really. But mostly it's pets.'

Lizard Bayliss had begun to grin. It wasn't a pretty sight with all those teeth which he swore weren't filed. 'You mean you like animals better than people? Is that what you're saying, Lord?'

'I wouldn't generalise.' God lifted his robe a little to let the fire get at his legs. 'It's mostly cats. Some dogs. Then a few people. All a matter of proportion, of course. I mean, it's millions at least, probably billions, because I'd forgotten about the rats and mice.'

'You like those, too?'

'No. Can't stand their hairless tails. Sorry, but it's just me. They can, I understand, be affectionate little creatures. No, they're for the cats. Cats are perfectly adapted for hanging out in heaven. But they still need a bit of a hunt occasionally. They get bored. Well, you know cats. You can't change their nature.'

'I thought you could,' said Oneway Ballard, limping up to the bar and ringing the bell. He was staying the night because someone had put a Denver Boot on his Granada and he'd torn the wheel off, trying to reverse out of it. He was in poor spirits because he and the car had been due to be married at St James's, Spanish Place, next morning and there was no way he was going to get the wheel back on and the car spruced up in time for the ceremony. He'd already called the vicar. Igor was on tonight and had trouble responding. We watched him struggle to get his hump under the low doorway. 'Coming, Master,' he said. It was too much like *Young Frankenstein* to be very amusing.

'*I* can change nature, yes,' God continued. 'I said *you* couldn't. Am I right?'

'Always,' said Oneway, turning to order a couple of pints of Ackroyd's. He wasn't exactly looking on fate with any favour at that moment. 'But if you can...'

'There are a lot of things I could do,' God pointed out. 'You might have noticed. I could stop babies dying and famines and earthquakes. But I don't, do I?'

'Well, we wouldn't know about the ones you'd stopped,' Engel-brecht pointed out, a bit donnishly for him. 'So when the heavens open on the day of resurrection, it really will rain cats and dogs. And who else? Jews?'

'Some Jews, yes.' In another being, God's attitude might have seemed defensive. 'But listen, I want to get off the race issue. I don't judge people on their race, colour or creed. I never have. Wealth,' he added a little sententiously, 'has no colour. If I've said who I favour and some purse-mouthed prophet decides to put his name in instead of the bloke I chose, then so it goes. It's free will in a free market. And you can't accuse me of not supporting the free market. Economic liberalism combined with conservative bigotry is the finest weapon I ever gave the chosen people. One thing you can't accuse me of being and that's a control freak.'

'See,' said Lizard, then blushed. 'Sorry, God. But you just said it yourself – chosen people.'

'Those are the people I choose,' said God with a tinge of impa-tience. 'Yes.'

'So – the Jews.'

'No. The money-lenders are mostly wasps. The usurers. Oil people. Big players in Threadneedle Street and Wall Street. Or, at least, a good many of them. Very few Jews, as it happens. And most of them, in heaven, are from show business. Look around you and tell me who are the chosen ones. It's simple. They're the people in the limousines with great sex-lives and private jets. Not cats, of course, who don't like travel. Otherwise, the chosen are very popular with the public or aggressively wealthy, the ones who have helped themselves. And those who help themselves God helps.'

'You're a Yank!' Engelbrecht was struck by a revelation. 'There are rules in this club about Yanks.'

'Because Americans happen to have a handle on the realities doesn't mean I'm American.' God was a little offended. Then he softened. 'It's probably an easy mistake to make. I mean, strictly speaking, I'm prehistoric. But, yes, America has come up trumps where religious worship is concerned. No old-fashioned iconography cluttering up their vision. There's scarcely a church in the nation which isn't a sort of glorified business seminar nowadays. God will help you, but you have to prove you're serious about wanting help. He'll at least match everything you make, but you have to make a little for yourself first, to show you can. It's all there. Getting people out of the welfare trap.'

'Aren't they all a bit narrow-minded?' asked Taffy Sinclair, the metatemporal pathologist, who had so successfully dissected the Hess quins. 'They are where I come from, I know.' His stern good looks demanded our attention. 'Baptists!' He took a long introspective pull of his shant. The massive dome of his forehead glared in the firelight.

God was unmoved by Sinclair's point. 'Those Baptists are absolute wizards. They're spot on about me. And all good Old Testament boys. They use the Son of God as a source of authority, not as an example. The economic liberalism they vote for destroys everything of value worth conserving! It drives them nuts, but it makes them more dysfunctional and therefore more aggressive and therefore richer. Deeply unhappy, they turn increasingly to the source of their misery for a comfort that never comes. Compassionate consumption? None of your peace and love religions down there. Scientology has nothing on that little lot. Amateur, that Hubbard. But a bloody good one.' He chuckled affectionately. 'I look with special favour on the Southern Baptist Convention. So there does happen to be a preponderance of Americans in paradise, as it happens. But ironically no Scientologists. Hubbard's as fond of cats as I am, but he won't have Scientologists. I'll admit, too, that not all the chosen are entirely happy with the situation, because of being pretty thoroughly outnumbered, just by the Oriental shorthairs. And they do like to be in control. And many of them are bigots, so they're forever whining about the others being favoured over them.

'Of course, once they get to heaven, I'm in control. It takes a bit of adjustment for some of them. Some of them, in fact, opt for hell, preferring to rule there than serve in heaven, as it were. Milton was on the money, really, if a bit melodramatic and fanciful. Not so much a war in heaven as a renegotiated contract. A pending paradise.'

'I thought you sent Jesus down as the Prince of Peace,' said Lizard a little dimly. The black bombers were wearing off and he was beginning to feel the effects of the past few hours.

'Well, in those days,' said God, 'I have to admit, I had a different agenda. Looking back, of course, it was a bit unrealistic. It could never have worked. But I wouldn't take no for an answer, and you know the rest. New Testament and so on? Even then Paul kept trying to talk to me, and I wouldn't listen. Another temporary fixup as it turned out. He was right. I admitted it. The problem is not in the creating of mankind, say, but in getting the self-reproducing software right. Do that and you have a human race with real potential. But that's always been the hurdle, hasn't it? Now lust and greed are all very well, but they do tend to involve a lot of messy side effects. And, of course, I tried to modify those with my ten commandments. Everyone was very excited about them at the time. A bit of fine tuning I should have tried earlier. But we all know where that led. It's a ramshackle world at best, I have to admit. The least I can do is shore a few things up. I tried some other belief systems. All ended the same way. So the alternative was to bless the world with sudden rationality. Yet once you give people a chance to think about it, they stop reproducing altogether.

Lust is a totally inefficient engine for running a reproductive programme. It means you have to override the rational processes so
that they switch off at certain times. And we all know where that
leads. So, all in all, while the fiercest get to the top, the top isn't
worth getting to and if it wasn't for the cats I'd wind the whole
miserable failure up. In fact I was going to until Jesus talked me
into offering cloning as an alternative. I'd already sent them H.G.
Wells and the Universal Declaration of Human Rights, the United
Nations and all the rest of it. I'm too soft, I know, but Jesus was
always my favourite, and he's never short of a reason for giving
you all another chance. So every time I start to wipe you out,
along he comes with that bloody charm of his and he twists me
round his little finger. Well, you know the rest. One world war
interrupted. Started again. Stopped again. Couple more geno-
cides. Try again. No good. So far, as you've probably noticed,
you haven't exactly taken the best options offered. Even Jesus is
running out of excuses for you. So I'm giving it a few years and
then, no matter what, I'm sending a giant comet. Or I might
send a giant cat. It'll be a giant something anyway. And it'll be
over within an instant. Nothing cruel. No chance to change my
mind.'

Death was hovering about in the shadows, glancing meaning-
fully at his watches.

'That's it, then, is it?' Julia Barnes seemed a bit crestfallen.
'You've come to warn us that the world has every chance of ending. And you offer us no chance to repent, to change, to make our
peace?' She tightened her lips. God could tell how she felt.

'I didn't offer,' God reminded her. 'Somebody asked. Look, I
am not the Prince of Lies. I am the Lord of Truth. Not a very successful God of Love, though I must say I tried. More a God of,
well, profit, I suppose. I mean everyone complains that these great
religious books written in my name are incoherent, so they blame
the writers. Never occurs to them that I might not be entirely
coherent myself. On account of being – well, the supreme being.
If I am existence, parts of existence are incoherent. Or, at least,
apparently incoherent...' He realised he'd lost us.

'So there's no chance for redemption?' said Engelbrecht looking about him. 'For, say, the bohemian sporting fancy?'

'I didn't say that. Who knows what I'll feel like next week? But I'll always get on famously with cats. Can't resist the little beggars. There are some humans who are absolutely satisfied with the status quo in heaven. But all cats get a kick out of the whole thing. The humans, on the quiet, are often only there to look after the cats.'

'And the rest?'

'I don't follow you,' said God. 'Well, of course, being omniscient, I could follow you. What I should have said was "I'm not following you".'

'The rest of the people. What happens to them. The discards. The souls who don't make it through the pearly gates, as it were?' Engelbrecht seemed to be showing unusual concern for others.

'Recycled,' said God. 'You know – thrown back in the pot – what do the Celts call it? – the Mother Sea? After all, they're indistinguishable in life, especially the politicians. They probably hardly notice the change.'

'Is that the only people who get to stay?' asked the Dwarf. 'Rich people?'

'Oh, no,' said God. 'Though the others do tend to be funny. Wits and comics mostly. I love Benny Hill, don't you? He's often seated on my right side, you might say. You need a lot of cheering up in my job.'

Julia Barnes was becoming sympathetic. She loved to mother power. 'I always thought you were a matron. I felt ashamed of you. It's such a relief to find out you're male.' There was a sort of honeyed criticism in her voice, an almost flirtatious quality.

'Not strictly speaking male,' said God, 'being divine, sublime and, ha, ha, all things, including woman, the eternal mime.'

'Well, you sound very masculine,' she said. 'White and privileged.'

'Absolutely!' God reassured her. 'I approve of your method. That's exactly who I am and that's who I like to spend my time with, if I have to spend it with human beings at all.'

Engelbrecht had bared his teeth. He was a terrier. 'So can I get in, is what I suppose I'm asking?'

'Of course you can.'

'Though I'm not Jewish.'

'You don't have to be Jewish. I can't stress this too often. Think about it. I haven't actually favoured the main mass of Jews lately, have I? I mean, take the twentieth century alone. I'm not talking about dress codes and tribal loyalties.'

God spread his legs a little wider and hefted his gown to let the glow get to his divine buttocks. If we had not known it to be a noise from the fire, we might have thought he farted softly. He sighed. 'When I first got into this calling there were all kinds of other deities about, many of them far superior to me in almost every way. More attractive. More eloquent. More easy-going. Elegant powers of creativity. Even the Celts and the Norse gods had a bit of style. But I had ambition. Bit by bit I took over the trade until, bingo, one day there was only me. I am, after all, the living symbol of corporate aggression, tolerating no competition and favouring only my own family and its clients. What do you want me to do? Identify with some bloody oik of an East Timorese who can hardly tell the difference between himself and a tree? Sierra Leone? Listen, you get yourselves into these messes, you get yourselves out.'

'Well it's a good world for overpaid CEOs...' mused Lizard.

'In this world and the next,' confirmed God. 'And it's a good world for overpaid comedians, too, for that matter.'

'So Ben Elton and Woody Allen...'

God raised an omnipotent hand. 'I said comedians.'

'Um.' Engelbrecht was having difficulties phrasing something. 'Um...' He was aware of Death hovering around and ticking like a showcase full of Timexes. 'What about it?'

'What?'

'You know,' murmured Engelbrecht, deeply embarrassed by now, 'the meaning of existence? The point.'

'Point?' God frowned. 'I don't follow.'

'Well you've issued a few predictions in your time ...'

Death was clearing his throat. 'Just to remind you about that policy sub-committee,' he murmured. 'I think we told them half-eight.'

God seemed mystified for a moment. Then he began to straighten up. 'Oh, yes. Important committee. Might be some good news for you. Hush, hush. Can't say any more.'

Lizard was now almost falling over himself to get his questions in. 'Did you have anything to do with global warming?'

Death uttered a cold sigh. He almost put the fire out. We all glared at him, but he was unrepentant. God remained tolerant of a question he might have heard a thousand times at least. He spread his hands. 'Look. I plant a planet with sustainable wealth, okay? Nobody tells you to breed like rabbits and gobble it all up at once.'

'Well, actually, you did encourage us to breed like rabbits,' Julia Barnes murmured reasonably.

'Fair enough,' said God. 'I have to agree corporate expansion depends on a perpetually growing population. We found that out. Demographics are the friend of business, right?'

'Well, up to a point, I should have thought,' said Lizard, aware that God had already as good as told him a line had been drawn under the whole project. 'I mean it's a finite planet and we're getting close to exhausting it.'

'That's right.' God glanced at the soft Dalí watches over the bar, then darted an enquiry at Death. 'So?'

'So how can we stop the world from ending?' asked Engelbrecht.

'Well,' said God, genuinely embarrassed, 'you can't.'

'Can't? The end of the world is inevitable?'

'I thought I'd answered that one already. In fact, it's getting closer all the time.' He began to move towards the cloakroom. God, I understood, couldn't lie. Which didn't mean he always liked telling the truth. And he knew anything he added would probably sound patronising or unnecessarily accusatory. Then the taxi had turned up, and Death was bustling God off into it.

And that was that. As we gathered round the fire, Lizard Bayliss said he thought it was a rum do altogether and God must be pretty desperate to seek out company like ours, especially on a wet Saturday night. What did everyone else make of it?

We decided that nobody present was really qualified to judge, so we'd wait until Monday, when Monsignor Cornelius returned from Las Vegas. The famous Cowboy Jesuit had an unmatched grasp of contemporary doctrine.

But this wasn't good enough for Engelbrecht, who seemed to have taken against our visitor in a big way.

'I could sort this out,' he insisted. If God had a timepiece of any weight he'd like to back, Engelbrecht would cheerfully show it the gloves.

That, admitted Julia Barnes with new admiration, was the true existential hero, forever battling against fate, and forever doomed to lose. Engelbrecht, scenting an opportunity he hadn't previously even considered, became almost egregious, slicking back his hair and offering the great novelist an engaging leer.

When the two had gone off, back to Julia's Tufnell Hill eyrie, Lizard Bayliss offered to buy the drinks, adding that it had been a bloody awful Friday and Saturday so far, and he hoped Sunday cheered up because if it didn't the whole weekend would have been a rotten write-off.

I'm pleased to say it was Taffy Sinclair who proposed we all go down to the Woods of Westermaine for some goblin shooting, so we rang up Count Dracula to tell him we were coming over to *Dunsuckin*, then all jumped onto our large black Fly and headed for fresher fields, agreeing that it had been one of the most depressing Saturdays any of us had enjoyed in centuries and the sooner it was behind us, the better.

THE END (with respectful acknowledgements to Maurice Richardson and The Exploits of Engelbrecht, *published by Savoy Books, Manchester, UK, and Port Sabatini, Texas).*

Acknowledgements

The Brothel in Rosenstrasse was first published by New English Library, 1982.

'The Opium General' first appeared in *The Opium General and Other Stories*, Harrap, 1984.

'London Bone' first appeared in *New Worlds*, edited by David Garnett, White Wolf, 1997.

'A Winter Admiral' first appeared in the DAILY TELEGRAPH, 1994.

'Doves in the Circle' first appeared in *The Time Out Book of New York Short Stories*, edited by Nicholas Royle, Penguin, 1997.

'A Slow Saturday Night at the Surrealist Sporting Club' first appeared in *Redshift*, edited by Al Sarrantonio, Roc, 2001.